# borderline

## sidetracked part 2

### s.k. kelley

Adapted Edition: April 2024

Library of Congress Control Number: 202191422
ISBN: 978-1-955240-04-8
(digital ebook): 978-1-955240-08-6
Published by Bleeding Heart Books
skkelleyauthor.square.site

*~ ∞ ~*

*for everyone who read my drafts*
*during the many years I spent writing*

*and everyone who gave helpful feedback*
*and encouraged me to continue*

*~ ∞ ~*

# Books by S.K. Kelley

**Sidetracked**
(Part 1)

**Borderline**
(Part 2)

**Afterglow**
(Part 3)

## <u>COMING SOON</u>

**Resignation**
(Part 4)

Follow S.K. Kelley on Bluesky or Twitter @skkelleywrites
or visit skkelleyauthor.square.site for updates!

Sidetracked is a four-part new adult
contemporary fantasy psychological drama series
with slice of life, romance, and thriller elements


**A CONTENT WARNING IS AVAILABLE
IN THE BACK OF THE BOOK
ON PAGE 569**

# one

*Tick, tick, tick, tick.*

I sit alone in a small room at Riverview General Hospital. No one has visited since a nurse popped in to disconnect the heart monitor and IV drip over an hour ago. The ticking clock is the only sound.

But I don't look away from the clock.

I don't want to see the bandages.

Eventually, the immortal doctor—Dr. Eric Corel, according to the name tag clipped to his white coat—returns with his sympathies. He seems genuine, with a touch of pity in his lavender eyes, but he can't do anything to help James either.

*How annoying.*

"You said I can leave today, right?" I ask. "Can I go now?"

He shakes his head. "A detective arrived perhaps twenty minutes ago. She was speaking with hospital staff when I last saw her, but I hear she wishes to speak with you before you leave. Of course, human police shouldn't have any involvement in this matter, but Riverview General is an integrated hospital. I don't have the resources to turn them away myself."

My eyes fill with tears again, but I wipe them away with my

good hand. Today has been more than enough already. Easily the worst day of my entire life. How am I supposed to talk with the police on top of it all? *What am I supposed to tell them?*

"Unfortunately, this means we can only offer acetaminophen for the pain until after you speak with her," he continues. When I glare at him, he clears his throat. "However, I can arrange to have you relocated to one of our inpatient recovery rooms. You'll be more comfortable there."

I sigh, and some of the tension leaves my shoulders. "I guess that's fine."

When the nurse stopped by earlier, she said I received a dose of IV morphine about four hours ago, which wasn't long after I was admitted. I feel...*decent* now, but my side is starting to ache, and my left arm pulses with an uncomfortable warmth. *I vaguely recall being slammed against the wall.* How will my body hold up once the medication wears off?

I should get the meeting with the police detective out of the way as soon as possible.

When I say as much, Dr. Corel agrees. He hands me a pair of fuzzy, non-slip hospital socks and waits for me near the door.

I collect my wallet and plastic hospital mug, but my breath catches as I scan the now-empty table. *Where is the River Sapphire?* It's not around my neck. I check my wallet's zippered coin pocket and glance about the floor around the bed, but I don't see it anywhere.

*Oh, no...*

My clothes were trashed—my shirt cut off my body with scissors—but I didn't think about what might have happened to the River Sapphire until now. Neither the soft-spoken immortal nurse nor Dr. Corel mentioned it.

Was it damaged or thrown out by mistake?

Maybe hospital staff gave it to James while I was sedated. Maybe it's safe somewhere, wherever he is now. *Maybe... I hope...* Who knows what Human-Immortal Affairs would do if they found out I lost it.

*Ugh.*

I don't have time to worry about this.

Sucking it up, I join Dr. Corel at the door and follow him to a recovery room clear across the hospital. It's still a hospital room, white and clinical, but it has a window with a view of the parking lot. I set my things on the bedside table and sit on the edge of the bed. To my relief, the sheets are cotton and do not crinkle beneath my weight.

"I can show the detective in whenever you're ready," Dr. Corel says.

"Now is fine," I say, picking at the edge of the bright green medical wrap on my right hand. "I just want to get it over with."

"Of course."

Instead of leaving immediately, he pauses in the doorway and glances over his shoulder. Light from the window reflects off his glasses, obscuring his eyes, but he offers a small smile.

"Be mindful of what you say," he says.

*Yeah. I understand.*

Even if James hadn't begged me not to say anything to the cops before they took him away, I assume the *severely punishable* clause in the Secrecy Agreement extends to revealing the existence of immortals to human police officers. I'm not even meant to discuss immortal-related topics with other humans.

Ice is an immortal, so I can't easily bring him up. Can I say anything about the attack at all? The detective wants to ask about that, right? Is there no way to avoid it?

*What the hell am I supposed to say?*

After several long, boring minutes in the new quiet room with a new ticking clock, Dr. Corel returns with a female detective. He introduces her before once again excusing himself. She's from Riverview Police Department, but I blanked her name immediately. It was something starting with an S? Or a C? Maybe a K?

*I have no idea.*

The uniformed woman drags a plastic, wireframe chair closer to my bed and sits a couple feet away. Her hair is short and brown, and her soft eyes are brown too. She's clearly human. If her artificial smile is supposed to make me feel any better, it fails miserably.

I don't think I've ever felt worse than I do now.

*And the effects of the morphine are wearing off.*

I situate myself in the most comfortable way possible to keep pressure off my side while she prepares a digital tape recorder on the bedside table. As she finishes, our eyes meet again. I cross my arms over my chest, and my shoulder twinges in retaliation.

Biting my tongue to mask the pain, I hope she didn't notice my grimace.

"Good afternoon," she says. "Jayde Palmer, right?"

I nod.

"How are you holding up?"

*Seriously?*

I can't believe she'd bother asking, and I can't bring myself to grace the question with an answer. Can't she tell how I'm holding up just by looking at me? The bruises? The bandages? The puffy eyes? *The blood in my tangled hair?*

I am obviously not doing well.

But her placid smile doesn't waver. "Is it okay if I ask a few questions?"

"Go for it," I say.

She presses a button on the tape recorder, a red light comes on, and the interview begins.

Question one: "Can you help me understand exactly what occurred this morning? Please explain in detail, if you can."

Her dark eyes drill into me, searching for an answer. Searching for any hint of the truth—a truth I can't give her. A truth she can't have because she's human.

I glance away, chewing the inside of my cheek.

Even if I could tell the truth, I doubt human police can touch Ice. Not only is he an immortal, but he's still my sponsor, and I have no idea how the immortal legal system works. For all I know, *I'll* get in trouble if I implicate him in the attack.

"I don't know if I can help." My eyes pass over my bandaged arms as I look to her again. "I was attacked—I mean, obviously —but I don't remember what happened."

The ease with which I lie surprises me considering how stupidly awful I was at it this morning. I almost feel bad, but lying almost feels justified now. The police think James did this, and I'm being forced to stay in the hospital longer because of it.

I could be home right now. I could be fast asleep in my own bed. *Or trying to figure out a way to contact Human-Immortal Affairs for real help.*

"You don't remember anything?" she asks.

"Nope. Wait—" I deepen my frown and feign thoughtfulness. "I remember being in James' car and looking out the window, and then I woke up in the hospital."

I barely remember anything from the drive, but the image of grey buildings streaking by sticks out to me for some reason. It was like…the car was moving in slow motion. Like the whole world was.

"Do you remember who attacked you?" she asks.

"No."

The woman's expression hardens ever so slightly. "If you know who did this, all you have to do is give us his name. You can trust me, okay? You're safe now."

*Safe? From Ice?*

*You're kidding, right?*

I would laugh, but my mouth is too dry. All I can do is set my jaw and look away again.

As tempting as it is—and it is tempting—I can't name Ice as my attacker. I can't risk breaching the Secrecy Agreement. Not here, not now, not to this annoying cop, and certainly not while James is stuck in a jail cell because of me. I don't care what he said. I won't forget how he helped me, and I won't throw him under the bus now. I will protect him from the police and protect myself from the wrath of Human-Immortal Affairs even if it means protecting Ice in the process.

*Ugh… My hand hurts.*

"It's been a long day," I say. "I'd rather not talk about it. And, like I said, I barely remember anything, anyway."

She sighs. "I want to help you, Jayde, but I can't help if you don't tell me what happened. I understand it was traumatic. You're afraid of whoever hurt you—I know—but you're safe here. This person can't hurt you anymore, so why are you still protecting him?"

"I don't know what you mean. I'm not protecting anyone."

*This sucks.* Even if I am upset with the police, I still want to let loose and blab about everything. About immortals. About Ice. About James' innocence and everything I do remember about what went down this morning.

But I can't.

What good would trying to explain the truth to her accomplish, anyway?

She's human, and I'm human too, so I can't prove the existence of immortals. I don't even have the River Sapphire. She would just think I lost my grip on reality after being attacked, and then Human-Immortal Affairs would send a hitman after me for breaking contract.

*Or whatever.*

It doesn't matter what I say. There's nothing this woman can do for me. The human police can't help, and Human-Immortal Affairs is a ghost, so my only option is to trust James that everything will be fine. For now, I have to stay strong, keep my mouth shut, and do what I can to get us out of this mess.

"You were seriously injured," she reasons, irritation leaking into her concern. "Don't you want justice after what this person put you through?"

*Of course I* want *justice, but…*

"It's easy. Just tell me—"

"I can't," I snap, cutting her off mid-sentence. "I don't remember, okay? So, just— Stop asking about it."

A sharp, throbbing pain radiates up my right arm, and I notice the thin hospital blanket balled in my hand. I picture the stitches in my palm popping from the pressure, but I don't ease up.

"Tell me one thing, at least," she says. "Did James Reid do this to you?"

*Ah—*

I stare at my hand and the plastic hospital bracelet with my name printed on it, and I squeeze the blanket even tighter, so I can't tell whether I'm tearing up from the pain or the frustration of putting up with this pointless conversation. *I hate it. It hurts.* I just want it to stop.

Maybe I can fake an anxiety attack. Maybe she'll leave me alone then. Though, if this goes on much longer, I might not have to fake it.

"Jayde," she says.

I glance up to find that her expression softened to better suit her sympathetic voice. She really pities me. She has no idea what happened and pities me anyway.

*Why is that so sad?*

My grip on the blanket relaxes, and pain flares in my palm as blood rushes into my fingers, but I ignore the discomfort. I bite it back, waiting for her to speak.

The female detective clears her throat before continuing, "We have a witness who claims to have watched firsthand as James Reid inflicted these injuries on you."

*What? How?*

"He's willing to testify in court."

I open my mouth to argue, to accuse her of lying—*because she must be lying*—but I freeze. *The police have a witness.* Someone who saw what happened and called them. Someone who knew James was there.

No way.

*There's no way, right?*

"So, is it true that James Reid attacked you this morning?"

"No—" *If there is a witness...* "I need to see James. *Now.*"

Her eyes widen, just enough for me to notice. "It sounds like you remember more than you're letting on. You don't have to be scared to tell me the truth. We can protect you."

I hold my head in my hands, struggling to breathe. This can't be right. I can't deal with this alone. Not after— *The cruel, dark smile that split his face before he first swung the knife. The blood. Everything. I can't...*

"I don't want to talk to you," I gasp. "I can't—"

"Well, can you at least confirm that our witness was at the scene?" she asks. "His name is Ice Monroe. He said he's your friend? He told us you were staying with him?"

*My friend?*

I bite the inside of my cheek, but I can't hold back the choking laugh. My fingers tangle in my hair, and, as I stare at my lap, tears spill from my eyes and leave tiny dark spots on the pale blue hospital gown.

*He called the police?*

Why? Why call the *human police* and pin the attack on James? What could he possibly get out of doing that?

*Well. I guess it doesn't matter.*

There's nothing I can say now. If it's the same for James, he'll be arrested for no reason with Ice playing the part of key witness. There's no way we can win against him.

"Is everything alright?" the woman asks.

I suck in a deep breath and wipe my eyes, ready to speak— to insist I'm fine—but another sob catches in my throat.

*If I can't figure this out, what will happen to me?* Ice is out there, doing whatever he pleases, and this is clear proof he's not done with me yet.

"Jayde?" the detective asks again.

"Maybe Ice was there," I murmur, shaking my head, "but this is all wrong. It was a, um…misunderstanding, maybe."

"What do you mean?"

Finally, I meet her concerned gaze. "I want to talk to James. Please. You have to let me see him. Even if it's just for a minute, I need to talk to him."

Her frown hardens, and she glances away before stopping the digital recorder. She tucks the device into an interior pocket of her dark blazer. When our eyes meet again, she looks rather perplexed.

"I suppose I could arrange for you to meet with him down at the station tomorrow," she says slowly.

*Tomorrow?*

Sniffling as my tears finally ease up, I nod in agreement.

The detective hands me a tissue from a box on the bedside table. "For now, you should try to calm down."

*Calm down?*

I fall back onto the pillow and dab my eyes with the tissue. It comes away damp and tinged pink from the remnants of dried blood on my face. *This is just great.* Looking past the tissue in my bandaged hand, I stare at the tiled ceiling.

*What the hell is Ice thinking?*

The woman, still sitting beside the bed, asks another question.

I wasn't listening. I have no idea what she said, so I don't respond. Instead, I focus on my breathing, desperate to keep from bursting into tears again. But pretending to be catatonic pays off, as the detective eventually apologizes for upsetting me.

"If you're serious about speaking with James, I can pick you up tomorrow morning, and we can swing by the station," she says. "Does that work for you?"

*Ugh...* I was supposed to leave the hospital today, *but knowing that Ice is the one who called the police...* It's probably better if I stay here for now.

I nod, my eyes still trained on the ceiling.

She thanks me for my time before quietly leaving, but there's no way my time was at all useful to her or her bogus case. *Not that I honestly care.*

Rolling onto my uninjured side, I curl up. My right side pulses, tender and warm, but I don't move. For a long time, I don't move.

I wish I had my phone. *Even...* Even if I couldn't say anything, I'd kill to hear Rose's voice right now.

\* \* \* \* \*

Dr. Corel strolls through the door of my hospital room with a covered dinner tray a good two hours after the female detective found her way out. I sit up and brush my hair from my face as he approaches the bed.

"I see you're still here," he says, not that he sounds surprised. When I nod, he sets the tray on the small bedside table. "How did your talk with the detective go?"

He's an immortal, and my doctor, and he seems to know a little of what's happened, so I feel safe talking to him without hiding everything. After I assure him I didn't say anything I shouldn't have, the words keep tumbling out as I describe the conversation in obnoxious detail.

"It sounds like Ice called the police," I say, frustrated by Dr. Corel's continued lack of surprise. "Why would he do that?"

He sighs. "I can't say. I'm terribly sorry this happened to you, but I assure you that Human-Immortal Affairs has been contacted. They understand the situation."

*Oh?*

"Are they doing anything? Is Ice in trouble?"

He glances away, a pensive look in his soft eyes. "It seems I was not the first to call and report the incident, but they didn't care to give me any details."

*Oh. I see.*

I return my attention to the dinner tray and set up the bed's attached lap table. Lifting the domed cover off the entrée, I find a pasta dish with sliced chicken and white sauce. There's also a slice of toast, a bottle of apple juice, and two white pills in a small paper cup.

"You're welcome to stay overnight if you aren't comfortable leaving," he says. "You've had a long day."

I twist the top off the juice. "I think I'll do that. Thanks."

My body feels like it's falling apart, and I don't want to be left alone. Besides, that female detective is supposed to pick me up in the morning.

*I still can't remember her name.*

"This medication should help you sleep," Dr. Corel says. "Now, do try to get a good rest, Miss Palmer."

"I'll try."

He smiles before leaving.

I take the pills with the juice, and, as soon as the cool liquid hits my empty stomach, I realize I am starving. *When was the last time I ate?* The gas station biscuits and gravy James bought for me this morning?

*Hm.*

The pasta itself is rather bland, but I can't be bothered to care. Being stuck here is surely better than whatever James is doing right now—sitting alone in a jail cell, I'm sure.

*Damn it.*

I hope Ice is happy with himself, knowing I'm in the hospital and James was arrested. Is this what he wanted?

He called Human-Immortal Affairs after I left, and it seems he told them the truth. Do they care what he did to me? Or that he involved the human police department? I haven't heard anything from them myself, but Dr. Corel didn't leave me feeling hopeful.

*What is he trying to prove? That I was a fool for trusting him? Because I already know that.*

I move the empty food tray aside, leave the bed to turn off the overhead lights, and return to lie down. I stare at the white ceiling as sinking despair slowly replaces my concern and frustration.

How long will it take for the pain medication to kick in and ease the pulsing in my side and aching in my shoulders? It's still early—it's still light outside—but I am so, so tired. *The rush of adrenaline. The urge to run. The blade of a sharp knife.* Then waking up here and immediately watching the police take James away. I didn't sleep well last night to begin with, but the conversation with the detective… And finding out that Ice set this up…

*It's too much.*

For now, I can only hope Dr. Corel is right. I can only hope that Human-Immortal Affairs will clear things up with Riverview Police Department. If James is released, I might feel better— even if Ice faces no meaningful consequence for what he did.

*Whatever they do, I hope they do it soon.*

# two

The nurse brings a set of disposable scrubs with my breakfast tray. I thank her, and she leaves, and I stare at the papery, green fabric for a long time before I set them aside.

I eat my cafeteria breakfast and take the prescription-strength acetaminophen that came with it. When I'm done, I wash my face in the adjoined bathroom and change into the scrubs with my eyes shut.

Then I wait for the female police detective—whose name I still can't remember—to show up. It sucks, lying in bed or sitting on the edge of the bed or pacing the room. There's not much else to do. I can walk around or watch TV, but the TV doesn't have any decent channels, and I feel the inexplicable urge to climb out the hospital window every time an immortal actor appears on screen.

*This wouldn't be nearly as bad if I had my phone.*

Rose is probably losing her mind. I told her I'd call yesterday, but I was supposed to be at home. Even if I could remember her phone number, I don't think calling from the hospital phone would be a good idea.

*Aaah...*

Finally, someone knocks on the door.

As I stand, I hope it's Dr. Corel with news from Human-Immortal Affairs. But it's not. It's the female detective. She walks in with a small paper bag in one hand and what looks like clothing folded over her other arm with a pair of shoes balanced on top.

She smiles at me like I never freaked out on her yesterday.

I force a smile in return despite not being overjoyed at seeing her again. I'm just relieved she was serious about dropping by.

"Good afternoon, Jayde," she says, her voice unreasonably chipper. "I brought a change of clothes for you, and I persuaded a doctor to prescribe painkillers and a sleep aid."

*Why? Is she trying to butter me up?*

I still can't confide in her, but I appreciate the gesture. After all, the alternative was leaving the hospital barefoot and wearing paper scrubs. Surely, that would draw even more attention than the bandages and bruises already will.

When I thank her, her smile softens into a more appropriate and realistic expression.

"Go ahead and change," she says before passing the bundle of clothing to me and setting the prescription bag on the bedside table. "We can head out whenever you're ready. I'll wait right outside."

"And I can talk to James?"

She nods. "Yes. We can arrange that."

I thank her again, more genuinely this time, and she steps out of the room. Then I grab a hair tie from my wallet and head into the bathroom to change.

The light wash jeans and unisex Riverview Police Department

t-shirt that fits too loosely are in no way flattering, but the clothes are clean and comfortable, and the shirt's collar is high enough to cover the thin wound on my chest. Even if the two visible bandages and recently exposed cut on my right arm leave little of what happened to the imagination, I think I can handle it. At least I have shoes—even if I have to wear them with the thick hospital socks, and they are the cheapest canvas sneakers I've ever seen.

I only have to wear this for a couple hours, anyway. Once the detective drops me off at home, I can change into pajamas and spend the rest of the day crying and eating freezer-burnt ice cream in my own bed.

*Big plans. Ugh.*

I comb my fingers through my hair, separating tangled strands and picking out flakes of blood as I go. But there's more blood than I expected. More than I thought there could possibly be. Eventually, I give up. I work my hair into a tragically messy bun and hope the remaining dark blood will blend into the surrounding chestnut brown.

As I rinse my fingers, careful to keep my bandaged palm dry, the water turns pink. I watch it disappear down the drain before looking up at the blank wall above the sink.

*Why isn't there a mirror in this bathroom?*

I guess it's not a bad thing.

*I probably don't want to know what I look like.*

After steeling myself a moment longer, I leave the bathroom.

The hospital recovery room is still empty. I was hoping to see Dr. Corel one last time before I left, but I don't care to wait around any longer. So I gather my things from the bedside table, drop the scrubs in the trash, and meet the detective just outside the door.

"Ready to go?" she asks, stepping away from the wall.

"Yeah. Let's go."

I'm not sure I am ready, but what else can I say?

I can't hide in the hospital forever, and I need to tell James what I learned yesterday. I can't let Ice get away with this. Even if Human-Immortal Affairs is working on the issue behind the scenes, I should still do everything I can in the meantime.

*Besides, if James had the River Sapphire when he was taken in, I should try to get it back or at least figure out where it went.*

The receptionist at the discharge counter tells me to stop by in a week or so to have the stitches removed. Then she passes a pen and clipboard across the counter. *The bill.* I brace myself for the numbers of an overnight hospital stay, but she continues to explain, and I read for myself, that my medical fees were covered by an insurance company I've never heard of.

*Some kind of...immortal thing?* Honestly, I'm too relieved by the prospect of not owing money to question it.

I sign the paper, struggling to do so with my injured hand, and I'm finally free—well, free from the hospital, anyway. I follow the detective through the waiting room and out of the building.

Squinting in the bright light of day, I look at the blue sky. It's not raining anymore. The air is warm, almost hot. The clouds are sparse and fluffy.

*The storm is over.*

We soon come to a stop beside a dark police cruiser, and the detective opens the passenger door for me. Only after I stare into the vehicle for an awkward length of time does the gravity of my situation come crashing down on me.

*I was attacked, I spent the night in the hospital, and now I'm going to the police station.*

Suddenly, I feel so small and so alone and so *nervous*, standing in the middle of the hospital parking lot. I didn't enjoy my stay, but at least I was safe in my boring recovery room. After I meet with James at the police station, this woman will most likely take me back to my house, where I will be truly alone.

*All while my real attacker is free.*

This sucks.

I can't tell anyone what happened, which means I can't tell anyone I'm not safe on my own—not even this seemingly well-meaning detective. There is not a single person who could understand the situation I'm in. Not a single person I want to risk getting involved.

Taking a deep breath—forcing down the sense of impending doom—I climb into the passenger seat of the police car. I fiddle with my hospital bracelet and stare out the window to my right as the detective drives.

She makes small talk I can barely bring myself to mumble vague comments to in response. I try *so hard* to remember her name, but it doesn't come back to me.

*Detective What's-her-face it is, then.*

# three

Today is a day of new experiences. First, the ride in the police cruiser, and now stepping inside the police station itself. I've never been here before. I knew where it was—on the west side of town, near the courthouse and not far from Riverview High School—but I didn't realize the interior was so big or nearly as complex.

Obviously, I'm not the one in trouble. I'm a guest. *A victim.* But it's intimidating all the same.

Still feeling small and nervous, I follow Detective What's-her-face down a series of corridors to a wing of the station with a few small interrogation rooms. Through a wide window looking into an empty room, I see only a grey space containing a metal table and three metal chairs.

An uncomfortable grimness settles in my gut, and I turn away, speeding up to return to the detective's side. We stop beside the last door—the last attached chamber, just before the viewing window. She knocks on the door. After a moment, two uniformed men exit.

"This is Jayde Palmer," Detective What's-her-face says. Both men seem to understand who I am. "She wants to speak with James Reid."

Their expressions shift in unison, so I do my best to smile and look well-adjusted as they study me. Then I turn to the female detective for some kind of assistance.

"It will only take a few minutes, right?" she asks.

I nod and point to the door. "He's in there?"

"Yes."

"Can I go in alone?"

She hesitates, and one of the male officers steps in.

"You understand why he's here, right?" he asks. "This man was arrested for a violent crime committed against you. We've collected more than enough evidence to convict him."

I avert my gaze, my arms held close to my chest. "I know, but this is all a huge misunderstanding. I just, um… I need a minute to talk to him. Alone."

"She has the right to speak with him," Detective What's-her-face reasons. "He hasn't requested a lawyer, and she claims he's innocent as well."

The male officers don't look convinced, but they eventually concede after some back and forth that left my head spinning. One man steps into the small room for a moment. When he returns, I'm presented with one condition: The door must remain open while I'm inside.

I'm fine with that—I have nothing to be afraid of—so the female detective holds the door for me to enter before propping it open several inches with a rubber doorstop.

I turn away from the door, my attention having lingered on the door handle with an uneasy hesitance, and I find James sitting on the far side of the same type of rectangular metal table

I saw in the other interrogation rooms.

His head is down. He didn't even check to see who entered.

My breath catches, but I steel myself before continuing forward. My footsteps echo in the room. As I stop a few paces from the table, he finally looks up, and his face contorts like someone kicked him—like my unexpected appearance is the last thing he wanted.

And I freeze.

"Jayde—" He stands from the table, revealing his cuffed hands, white t-shirt, and orange pants. "Are you okay?"

His attention lands on my right arm, and his amber eyes grow wide. *Right.* A nasty bruise developed overnight—one suspiciously shaped like a hand wrapped around my wrist. I hadn't noticed it until this morning, when a nurse changed my bandages and left the arm uncovered so the wound could breathe.

Ignoring the tightening of my chest, I slip my hand behind my back to hide it.

"I'm fine," I say.

If only to avoid the pain in his eyes, I look everywhere but at James. There are two cameras with tiny, flashing red lights in opposite corners of the room. The window behind me is a one-way mirror. From this side, I see only our reflections, but I was just out there. I know we're being watched.

*How much can they hear?*

Glancing to James again, I take one of the empty chairs across from him.

With a sigh, he drops back into his seat, suddenly looking very tired. Seeing him up close, he seems to have healed further since

I last saw him. The bruise around his left eye is now mostly obscured by the darker, sleepless bags, leaving the faint, reddish hatching on the right side of his face and the dark scabs across his nose and bottom lip as the final remnants of Ice's beating.

*Suddenly, I don't know what to say.*

"I'm surprised they let you in," he says, staring at the ceiling. "Since they think I did this and all."

"That's why I'm here," I say before lowering my voice and cupping a hand near my mouth. "I need to talk to you. Are there any microphones around?"

He sits up straight, his brows furrowed. "Not that I know of?"

*Do they use tape recorders to capture all of their audio?*

Instead of asking James if he knows, I examine the table more closely. It seems to be made of solid steel, and I don't see any cables or buttons or anything indicating it has electronic elements. Still, there are cameras, so I can't be too careful.

"Are you okay?" I ask.

"Never been better," he says at normal volume without missing a beat. "These guys are dead set on the idea that I hurt you, and I can't say a damn thing besides, *'Man, why the hell would I drive her to the hospital if I'm the one who sliced her up in the first place?'* Then they ask, *'Well, you clearly know who did it, but I don't see you pointing any fingers,'* and, *'There's a helluva lot of evidence stacked against you, kid. Might as well tell the truth and work out a plea deal.'* So I just stopped saying anything."

*Wow. Okay.*

"Ice set you up," I say under my breath.

"Well, no shit." He tips his head and drops his cuffed hands to the table with a metallic clink. "You think I don't know that? They read me his witness statement and everything."

"Please keep your voice down."

He sighs again but does lower his voice. "You haven't said anything about what really happened to anyone, right?"

I shake my head.

"Good. Keep it that way."

"No problem, but I want to help. What should I do?"

A reluctant darkness flashes through his eyes, followed by a firm frown that unsettles me.

"Nothing," he says.

"Nothing? What do you mean, *nothing*?"

"I mean nothing," he says, his expression level. "Don't talk to the cops. Play Ice's stupid game until it's over."

*What? What game?*

As I try to figure out exactly what he's trying to say, my focus drifts from his face to his hands, still resting on the tabletop. I never noticed before, but his left hand is scarred by several thin, pale lines highlighted by the harsh overhead lights—one on his index finger, two on his middle finger, one on the back of his hand between those two fingers, and one on his ring finger. *They look...surgical, but I can't be sure.* Either way, along with the smaller, more irregularly shaped scars on his knuckles, I imagine the hand was seriously messed up at some point.

*Actually, both of his hands have scarred knuckles.*

It's strange. When I last saw Ice, I would have never thought he busted his hand on brick only a week earlier if I hadn't seen his bloody knuckles right after it happened.

*Speaking of—*

"Have you talked to him?" I ask quietly.

"Ice?" He shakes his head, grimacing. "No. Have you?"

"No." I glance at the neon wrap on my hand. The wound beneath aches with a gentle warmth, the result of having clutched too tightly at the paper prescription bag during the ride here. "I've been in the hospital."

He sighs, seemingly relieved, but he says nothing, and I feel my frown grow more severe as I look up again.

"You're serious…about not doing anything?"

"I'm not human," he says under his breath, not meeting my eyes. "They can't keep me here for long, so it doesn't matter if I fight the charges or not."

"Even if you're right, doing nothing doesn't make any sense."

"It doesn't matter what happens to me," he continues passively. "I keep thinking—and I've had plenty of time to think about it since they locked me in here—that maybe if I just do what Ice wants, he'll leave you alone."

"That is the stupidest thing I've ever heard."

"This whole thing is stupid," he says, his voice rising. "They won't listen if I say it's not me. I tried already, but it's Ice's word against mine, and it's not like I can pin it on him."

My heart quickens. "James. You're not thinking—"

"I don't have a choice, do I?" he asks with a hollow laugh. "I have a record with RPD. Ice doesn't. He's rich, white, well-spoken, well-dressed, never been arrested in his life. As far as these guys are concerned, he's a saint."

"Who cares what they think?" I hiss under my breath, ignoring the stinging in my balled-up hand. "I told the detective it wasn't you. They'll never believe me if you—"

He shakes his head, resolve burning in his eyes. "Sorry, but I don't want your help, Jayde. You shouldn't have come here. You should have left me alone. If you had just stayed at Ice's house instead of looking for me, none of this would have happened."

"You can't be serious—"

I stand from the table, the metal chair screeching against the concrete floor as it shifts backward. James looks from me to the one-way mirror behind me. Nervous hesitation flashes across his face, but he quickly sets his jaw.

"I'm sorry," he says again, his voice low.

"Wait—"

I shake my head, silently pleading for him to reconsider, but he stands too. He looks past me, to the cracked door, with his cuffed hands held loosely at his chest.

"I did it," he says, his voice echoing in the empty room. "I attacked her. I'm ready to tell you guys everything. So, just— Get her out of here."

My mind reels, and I turn away from the table as Detective What's-her-face and the two male officers enter the room with haste. I can't bring myself to react or resist as the uniformed woman ushers me out of the room, the hand she placed on my back my only tether to reality.

I don't understand. Why would James decide to confess? Even if he thinks he'll escape the charges in the end—even if he thinks it might help me...

*Why?*

Then, as the detective asks if I'm alright, I realize I wasn't able to mention Human-Immortal Affairs or ask about the River Sapphire before he went rogue. *Damn it.* I hope there isn't a penalty for misplacing their priceless magical gemstone.

I also realize I'm crying. *When did I start crying?*

She asks once again if I'm okay, and I wipe my eyes with my bandaged arm. "I'm fine. I was just…surprised, I guess."

"I'm also surprised," she admits. "He's kept quiet since we brought him in, denying involvement but refusing to say anything else until now. What did you say to him in there?"

"It doesn't matter," I mutter, glancing away. "It doesn't matter what he says either. He didn't do this. James didn't hurt me."

"Well, what did he say to you? You looked upset."

*At least I know they didn't hear it.*

Without answering, I move to stand in front of the observation window. The two male officers now sit across from James, a tape recorder set in the middle of the table. He looks surprisingly calm while speaking, glancing off to the side and gesturing vaguely with his hands, which are no longer handcuffed.

He wasn't kidding. He's seriously confessing to Ice's attack.

"Are you alright?" the detective asks.

Nodding slowly, I press a hand to the cool glass. I wish I could hear whatever they were saying. Not that it matters. Whatever James tells them—that he broke into Ice's house; that he pulled a knife on me; that Ice's statement is the truth—it's all bullshit.

*This is ridiculous.*

I have to get him out of here. I can't let him be arrested for a crime he didn't commit just because he thinks he's *doing the right thing* by taking the blame. Who knows how long Human-Immortal Affairs will wait to clear up this mess. I can't sit around and hope they take care of everything for me when I'm *so close*.

This can't be the only way.

I bite my cheek, wracking my brain for ideas when TV crime dramas come to mind. Night's into those shows, and we watched a handful of episodes during the rainstorm. Though, I have no idea if the legal system portrayed in crime dramas at all reflects reality.

*Seems I'll just have to wing it.*

"He's lying," I say, my voice unexpectedly cold.

"Excuse me?"

I shake my head, at a loss of what else to do. "Like I said, whatever James is saying in there, it's not true. At all."

Detective What's-her-face joins me in front of the glass. I look away from James, who is still speaking with the two men inside.

"What do you mean?" she asks, her confusion genuine.

*Ugh... She totally thinks he did it too, doesn't she?*

"James did not hurt me," I say—for at least the tenth time. "Isn't there any way I can get him out of this?"

She gives me a long, hard look. She's considering it, which is something, but I don't know if she believes me. And why should she? It's not as though I've been transparent with her either.

*Come on...*

"He brought me to the hospital," I reason. "He stayed there until I woke up, and he didn't run when the police came in. He didn't do this. He's innocent. I swear."

"Why would he confess to the assault if he's innocent?" she asks, her skepticism warranted but annoying.

I peer through the window again and groan as James nods fervently after one of the officers asked him a question. *What an idiot.* He's making this way more difficult than it needs to be.

"I guess, um…" *Oh, god.* "Well, I guess he thinks it'll keep me safe—or something like that."

"Safe from what?" she asks. "Or who? If it wasn't James Reid, who attacked you yesterday?"

*Seriously?*

I step away from the glass and meet her probing eyes. "I don't know why James thinks this will help, but I can't let him take the blame. He had absolutely nothing to do with it."

*That's not entirely true, but it still wasn't his fault.*

Detective What's-her-face frowns before leading me away from the observation window, one hand resting on my shoulder.

"He will have to stay overnight," she says, "but, if what you say is true… I would hate to see an innocent man put away for a crime he didn't commit."

*Is that true? Does she actually care who goes down for it?*
Whatever.

"He didn't do it," I say again, pointedly avoiding her gaze as we walk down the hall. "I am not changing my story, and I will not go to court if you put James on trial for this. Can't I drop the charges or something?"

She sighs. "No. James Reid is facing multiple criminal felony offenses. Our DA wants to move forward with the case with or without your cooperation. He's confident that James is guilty."

*Ugh.*

"But I would like to take your statement and look into the matter further," she offers.

I nod and follow her through the building until we come to a small room that looks like an office—her office, maybe.

As I sit in a chair across from her desk, she spends several minutes asking various questions about what happened yesterday and recording my responses. She asks about my relationship with James, to which I honestly don't have much to say, and my "friendship" with Ice, which is both awful and embarrassing to recount in any capacity.

"Is it true you've been staying with Ice at his parent's home?" she asks, speaking with such authority I can only assume he told her that much himself.

"Since the Fourth of July, yes."

She frowns—probably because I couldn't mask my grimace. "And you were with James the morning you were attacked?"

I hesitate.

*What would Ice have told the police? What will happen if I contradict the information he gave them? The truth doesn't reveal too much, does it?*

Taking a deep breath, I nod. "That's right. I was with James, but everything was fine. He dropped me off at Ice's house in the morning. I just wanted to grab my bag, but..."

Her expression shifts as she records my response on paper. A narrowing of her eyes. A slight tip of the head. Curiosity. Interest.

*Did I mess up?*

I reposition myself in the chair and force an apologetic smile. "That's about where my memory cuts out. James dropped me off, but he stayed in his car. He's not the one who attacked me."

She hums softly, tapping her pen against her desk. Something about the sound makes me nervous.

"You say James stayed in the car? But he also drove you to the hospital, right?" When I agree, her eyes flick up from her notepad. "Are you implicating someone else in the attack, then?"

My heart jumps into my throat, but I swallow and shake my head. "I have no idea what happened inside that house."

Her frown grows more pronounced, but she nods and concludes the interview there. I sign a few documents to confirm I told the truth and wasn't coerced while answering any of the questions.

I told as much of the truth as I possibly could, so I don't feel bad for signing anything.

"Are you going to take me home now?" I ask, a more powerful anxiety creeping into my voice as I return her fancy pen.

She smiles, misreading me entirely.

"Of course," she says, crossing the small room to open the door. "Right this way, Jayde."

# four

It feels like it's been ages since I last saw Oakwood Cottages. I stare at the small, brown detached townhouse through the windshield until Detective What's-her-face makes her way around the police cruiser and opens the passenger door.

She walks me halfway, stopping on the bottom step of the concrete landing. I do not stop there, but I do pause in front of the door to hear her out.

"Do you have a phone?" she asks.

I shake my head.

We don't have a landline. When we moved in, Rose and I both thought it would be a waste of money. *What's the point when we have cell phones?* Or whatever.

Unfortunately, I left my phone in James' car. I have no idea where it is now—the car or my phone.

"Oh. Well, here's this, anyway." She hands me a business card. Her name is Sarah Crain. "Feel free to drop by the station if you want updates on the case. I'll do what I can to help your friend in the meantime."

*Is James my friend?*

I banish the thought, thank her, and slip her business card

into my wallet.

"Of course, I can't make any promises," she says. "There is a lot of evidence stacked against James—now including his own confession—but we may be able to drop the charges based on your statement."

"I'll check in tomorrow."

She nods. "When you do, just ask to see me or my partner, Detective Vega."

*Vega. Vega. Vega. Don't forget that.*

"Thanks again," I say.

If she honestly believes me, it means a lot.

My things bundled under one arm, I offer a small wave, and she returns to her police cruiser.

I watch the vehicle pull out of the parking lot, then I turn back to the front door. I check my wallet, find the candy-striped house key Night gave me, and realize my key is still attached to a keychain on the purse I left in James' car.

Growing frustrated, I try the doorknob.

It's locked, so I check the large planter beside the door. It takes a moment, but I find the spare key where Rose hid it months ago—just beneath the topsoil under a painted stone.

*Thank god.*

I unlock the door, taking care to return the key to its hiding place and lock the deadbolt behind me once inside.

The cottage is exactly how I remember it: neat and empty. Though, the air is stuffy, as the air conditioner has been shut off for a couple weeks. I cross the room and fiddle with the thermostat before heading upstairs.

After throwing my bedroom door open, I haphazardly drop everything from my arms onto my dresser. An orange pill bottle rolls out of the paper prescription bag.

I glance up, the mirror in the center of the photo collage catching my eye for an instant. That instant is more than enough. I take a t-shirt from my dresser and cover the mirror, carefully tucking the fabric between the metal frame and the wall to secure it in place.

*This is just sad.*

But all I want now is a shower.

I upend the prescription bag, dumping a second pill bottle, a roll of white gauze, and a thin roll of medical tape onto the dresser. One bottle contains hydrocodone—Vicodin. Fourteen tablets. The instructions read, *Take 1 tablet by mouth every 12 hours as needed for pain management.* The other is prescription-strength melatonin, which is apparently a thing.

After taking one of the pain relievers, I search my room for a set of loose-fitting pajamas. Then I head to the bathroom.

I cut the hospital bracelet off, carefully strip out of the RPD outfit, and free my hair from the messy bun, all while avoiding the full-length mirror on the back of the door. I don't want to know the extent of the damage after staring at my forearms all morning and glimpsing myself in the mirror in my bedroom. But the temptation eats at me.

Eventually, I give in.

The girl in the mirror is a ratty, bruised mess. A disaster. Tired. Shaky. And, worst of all, she's *me*.

I was almost used to the butterfly bandages on my right arm, the bandage on my left, the neon green wrap on my hand, and the bruise on my wrist, but I hadn't seen much of the other two wounds.

The diagonal slice on my chest, thin but long and already scabbing, runs between my breasts from my collarbone to a point just below my sternum. The cut on my side is covered by a thick gauze pad—elements of what happened yesterday might still be a blur, but I know that one was the worst of the bunch.

*I wish I couldn't remember anything.*

Suppressing a shudder, I take a deep breath and remove the bandages one at a time. The medication hasn't had time to kick in yet, so peeling gauze from still-raw wounds stings like dragging fingernails across a sunburn.

The three cuts that were covered are neatly stitched. Pink and raw with little-to-no scabbing after being covered for a day and a half.

But the cuts and stitches aren't what caught me off guard.

*It's the bruises.*

The hand-shaped bruise on my right wrist—the place where the pad of each finger Ice pressed into my skin is now marked in deep purple. The bruising around the jagged wound on my left arm. The bruise on my shoulder where I was slammed into the wall.

*No wonder I've been so sore.*

And I still have blood in my hair. *Ugh.*

Staring in the mirror, I feel strangely numb. Detached. Like the person I'm looking at isn't really me. *Like it can't possibly be me.*

*But... I know...*

I step back and tear my attention from my reflection to start the shower. As I watch the cascading water bounce off the white bathtub floor, fear builds within me. I have enough life experience to know even small paper cuts sting under running water.

*Doesn't matter, Jayde. You have to shower eventually, and you may as well do it now.*

My left hand reaches for the water, just to check. It's not hot. The stream almost feels gentle against the back of my hand.

Still, I grit my teeth before stepping inside.

A sharp sound escapes my throat, and I drop to a crouch beneath the unforgiving torrent of water. I bite the inside of my cheek. Tears prick my eyes. Maybe I do cry; it's hard to tell. In fleeting moments, the pain is white-hot. But I force myself to stay in the tub, and my wide eyes watch the water run pale pink as it slowly rinses the dried blood from my body.

Eventually, the pain lessens. Or I get used to it.

*This is nothing. This is fine.*

I sit on the floor of the tub, hugging my knees to my chest, ignoring the tightness in my side and throbbing in my palm, until the water runs clear. I don't have the will to properly wash my hair, so I drag myself to my feet and step out onto the plush bathmat.

My breathing comes slow and deep. I let the water drip down my legs for a moment before looking to the mirror on the door.

*At least I'm not crying.*

My reflection still bothers me, though. I don't feel like the girl in the mirror. It doesn't feel real, and the unrealness of it all fills me with an urge to cover the wounds despite the nurse's insistence that they'll heal faster if exposed to air.

*I hate it.* The fresh wounds on my skin. The acute awareness of injury and taut discomfort whenever I move.

But I want to heal, so I'll take the nurse's advice.

Looking away, I flex my hand. I count the stitches holding my palm together. *Fifteen.* Fifteen stitches on a cut hardly three inches long.

*I hate it so much. The stitches and bruises and everything.*

With a sigh, I grab my towel off the rack and pat dry, wary of catching a stitch by accident. Then I slip into my pajamas—a loose tank top and cotton sleep shorts. After wrapping my long hair in the towel, I head back to my bedroom.

*A nap sounds good, but…*

I turn away from the bed to face my desk on the opposite wall. I stare at my closed laptop for *a long time.*

What feels like several minutes pass, just standing in the middle of my room before I muster the courage to step closer and open the laptop. Pulling up the internet browser, FaceSpace alerts me to several message notifications. They're all from Rose, sent over the past two days.

> **Rose:** Hey, I texted you earlier, but you didn't answer. How did things go with Ice?
>
> **Rose:** Are you home yet? (´·-·`)?
>
> **Rose:** Is everything ok?
>
> **Rose:** Is your phone dead? It's going straight to voicemail…
>
> **Rose:** Are YOU dead?

> **Rose:** Hello???
>
> **Rose:** seriously, why aren't you answering?
>
> **Rose:** JAYDE NICOLE PALMER
>
> **Rose:** HELLO???????

*Great.*

I sit at my desk, wincing as fabric scratches my injured side. But I ignore the discomfort and address the string of messages.

> **Me:** I AM SO SORRY ROSE
>
> **Me:** I AM FINE

> **Rose:** OMFG (×＿×)
>
> **Rose:** I was about to call Robbie and freak out. What happened to you???

*What am I supposed to say?* How can I explain disappearing off the face of the earth for two days?

I guess I'll…*make something up?*

> **Me:** Sorry, my phone broke.
>
> **Me:** I haven't been online until now.

That is easily the worst excuse I have ever come up with, but it'll have to do for now. After all, while it is true that I don't have my phone, I can't tell the whole truth. She can't learn about immortals, and she most certainly does not need to know what Ice did or that I spent the past day and a half in the hospital.

> **Rose:** You broke your phone? For real?? (◑｡◑);;

**Me:** Yep. It's totally broken. Getting it replaced soon, though. Good thing I bought phone insurance.

**Rose:** lmao. So how'd yesterday go?

**Me:** It was fine. I picked up my bag from Ice's house and went home.

*I hate myself.*

Leaning back in my chair, I fight the tears budding in my eyes.

**Rose:** Everything's fine, then?

**Me:** Yeah. Everything's fine. I'll talk to you once I get my phone back.

I move to close my laptop, but I pause, my aching hand on the lid. Looking at the FaceSpace home page behind the messenger window, I…

*Should I message Night? Does she know what Ice did?*

*No.* I probably shouldn't ask if she knows anything or mention it to her right now. Finding out about *this* over Face-Space messenger seems messed up.

The laptop lid clicks shut. I leave the desk and flop into bed.

*Aah—*

Pain radiates from my right side, and my hands tremble as they hover over the wound. Once it settles, fading to a dull throb, I drop my hands to the bed and go limp. I stare at my closet across the room, my eyes watering as I struggle to catch my breath.

After a while, drowsiness replaces the throbbing in my side.

A fuzzy, unnatural longing for sleep that I lean into. I roll onto my left side. I stare at the dark impression of a hand on my wrist. The stitches peeking out from beneath my loosely curled fingers.

I'm tired... *So, so tired...*

\* \* \* \* \*

I wake up feeling like my head and mouth are stuffed with cotton. I slap my bedside table, looking for my phone, and my hand knocks over something that rattles as it falls to the floor. When I open my eyes, I see the bruise on my arm and the orange bottle on the grey carpet, and I remember.

My phone is gone.

I just got out of the hospital.

James confessed to attacking me.

*Right.*

I groan as I sit up, but nothing really hurts. I'm aware of the injuries and their uncomfortable warmth, but the pain doesn't seem to register. My mouth is dry, and I have a headache.

But the hunger takes precedence. It's annoying enough to get me out of bed and wandering downstairs, toward the kitchen.

The linoleum is cold on my bare feet, and, for some reason, I look around and consider the lack of dust. The whirr of air conditioning. The fresh paint on the walls, and the way the ceiling light floods the room with neutral, white light.

*I'm thinking about the manor house.* Rain falling outside a large window and collecting in muddy puddles far below. A young man passed out in an old recliner.

*Why?*

I fill a mug with tap water and scrounge for something to eat that won't require cooking and isn't expired. I open the snack cabinet, but I hesitate as my eyes land on the bright red package of M&M cookies. Grimacing, I shove the cookies to the back of the cabinet and shut the door again.

After a few minutes spent poking around, I settle at the small dining table with a bowl of dry, sugary cereal. The taste is off somehow. It might be stale or a side effect of the medication. I can't tell, but I feel better with something in my stomach.

I rinse the bowl. I set it aside and rinse my hands. Cool water pools in my injured palm, and I watch as the stitched wound beneath seems to warble before the water spills over into the sink basin. Then I turn the water off and dry my hands.

In the living room, I find myself in front of the window beside the door. It's dark out, and the parking space in front of the cottage is empty. The space where Rose normally parks. The space where Detective Crain parked to drop me off this morning. The space where Ice parked when he came to pick me up.

I lock the window and close the blinds before returning upstairs, where I nearly trip over something left on the bathroom floor—the pale blue outfit Detective Crain gave me as a courtesy. I toss the clothes into the laundry hamper and pointedly ignore both mirrors on my way out.

Back in my bedroom, I go through the assortment of medical supplies on my dresser. Gauze. Tape. The nurse said exposure to air will help my wounds heal, but Detective Crain went out of her way to get these for me.

I don't have any self-adhesive wrap, so I can't easily bandage my hand, but I can cover my left arm. If I look at it too long, it's like I can still see it. *Nails digging into a bleeding wound.* Before I unwrapped it, I couldn't remember clearly. The gritty details. The senselessness of it all.

But the bruises tell the full story. *A hand wrapped around my wrist. Fingers messing a fresh wound, bright blood soaking grey fabric and dripping from my elbow to the cream carpet.*

Ugh.

I find a pair of scissors and bandage my arm.

# five

It's weird, riding the bus without my phone, unable to listen to music or play idle games or scroll down FaceSpace to pass the time. It's even weirder getting off at the stop in front of the police station and looking up at the building. Concrete, metal, and glass. The Roman-style columns near the entrance feel out of place.

I feel out of place myself as I climb the stairs, almost limping because I took ibuprofen this morning instead of the hard-hitting Vicodin. I didn't want to pass out on the bus and miss my stop or anything.

*Ugh.*

My shirt keeps sticking to my side. I should have bandaged it before I left home. It would have been worth using the rest of the gauze.

*Well, it's too late for that now.*

I carefully peel the fabric from my skin for the umpteenth time and step through the large main doors. When I approach the reception desk at the back of the lobby, the officer on the other side frowns and asks if I need help. He must think I look nervous and confused—like I don't want to be here and have no idea why I came.

*He wouldn't be wrong.*

"I'm looking for an update on a case," I say. "Is Detective Crain here? She's assigned to the case—I think."

After some back and forth, I learn that Detective Crain is not here, but her partner is. The officer behind the desk says he'll let Detective Vega know I'm here and asks me to wait.

So I wait in the lobby for several minutes, standing around and growing increasingly uncomfortable, until a stocky man with dark hair and dark eyes approaches me. He knows my name and introduces himself as Detective Marcus Vega.

He asks how I'm doing.

I avert my eyes and say I'm fine. I just want an update on the case—an update on whatever has been going on with James since I stopped by yesterday.

Detective Vega leads me further into the police station, but he doesn't have much to say. He's less warm and sociable than his partner. A man of few words, I guess. That's fine. The main issue is that he doesn't have any meaningful updates to share.

James corroborated the witness statement Ice gave—*the one the police read to him well before he confessed.* He's still under arrest, facing felony trespassing and assault charges, and he's still sitting in a holding cell somewhere in this building, awaiting some kind of pre-trial hearing.

To placate me, as I became rather upset upon receiving the bad news, Detective Vega leads me into his office. It's a small room with a cluttered desk, not unlike the room Detective Crain took my statement in.

I sit in a plastic chair across from his desk, leaned forward with interest and ignoring the throbbing in my side, as he shows me part of the case files, removing items from a folder or cardboard box. Photographs of blood splattered on sage green walls. Red droplets on cream carpet. A broken vase, fragments strewn across the hardwood just inside the stained-glass front door. Drawings that depict the location of my injuries. James' mugshot. Photocopies of the statement I gave yesterday. A clear bag containing the bloodstained clothes I was wearing—expensive and clearly trashed leather boots included.

The most interesting thing he shows me is a clear evidence bag containing a pocketknife.

When he asks if I recognize it, I shrug, but I know for certain it's not the knife Ice used in the attack.

I don't mention it, obviously, but I seem to recall a strange marbling on the blade as it glinted in the light. Yet the knife in the evidence bag is the type of plain, black-handled folding knife you can find at any department store with a sporting goods aisle.

*He didn't even bother giving them the right knife?*

Whatever.

"I'll be the first to admit that certain aspects of this case don't add up," Detective Vega says, "but it's hard to argue with James Reid's confession even considering a few inconsistencies among the evidence and your conflicting statement."

"Won't it be hard to convict without the victim's testimony?" I ask, willing myself not to scratch the scab on my right arm.

"It's difficult to say. The charges are serious, and our DA's case against him is quite strong."

*Everyone has said that.*

I watch the bagged knife as he returns it to the cardboard evidence box. The fact it isn't the same one leaves me with several questions. *Where did the blood come from?* It is mine, isn't it?

*Disgusting.*

"Well, thanks anyway," I say.

"Is that all you needed today?"

"Um…" *Wait.* I sit up straight and point to the box. "Is there a necklace in there? I was wearing a necklace, and I'd like it back. If that's possible."

"A necklace?" He picks up a sheet of paper and runs a finger down one side of the page before shaking his head. "No. A necklace isn't listed among the items we've collected. Sorry."

"It's fine."

With a sigh, I thank Detective Vega for his time. If the River Sapphire isn't here, there's nothing else he can do for me, so I just watch as he tidies his desk for a moment.

When he's done, I follow him out of the office. We walk down a hallway and turn down another that will take me back to the front of the building. As I look up from my feet, I catch sight of the *very last person I wanted to see* heading my way, accompanied by a female police officer I don't recognize.

Ice's gaze flicks in my direction for an instant. Our eyes meet —his too bright and too blue and too calm. My blood runs cold, like I was suddenly caught in a blizzard, and I can't breathe.

He cracks a half-smile and, without missing a beat, glances away to carry on with whatever he was saying to the officer before we noticed each other. They pass by without incident, and

Detective Vega and I continue toward the lobby. But the air feels thick and oppressive, and I still can't seem to draw a full breath.

*I need to leave. Now.*

"I'll have Sarah contact you if anything changes," Detective Vega says as we approach our destination.

I nod, surprised his voice got through to me at all. I meet his gaze and maintain eye contact and try my damnedest to keep a straight face. To listen. To take another step forward. To cross out of the corridor and into the lobby.

"Have a nice day," he says.

"Yeah," I mumble, my mouth dry. "Thanks again."

I watch him return the way we came. The moment he turns a corner, I slink out of the police station and walk down the sidewalk. *Fast.* My side aches, but I don't slow down even as I pass the bus stop sign. The bus won't pick up for another twenty minutes, anyway, and I can't stand out here that long. Not while I know Ice is inside the station.

I don't know why he's there, but he knows I was just there too. He knows James was arrested, so he knows I'm alone, and he knows I rely on public transit to get around. He could come out to look for me at any time, and I'd be easy to find if I stayed here.

I don't want to run into him. Not alone. Not even in public.

*I can't.*

Without much thought, my heart still pounding and my chest still tight, I find myself several blocks away from the police station, standing in front of an empty bus stop shelter.

I step inside and sit on the metal bench. I draw my knees up and hug them to my chest. I ignore the pain in my side and fight back tears and struggle to control my trembling. I focus on the aching in my palm instead. The tightness around the stitches as my nails dig into my leg.

*Why did I have to see him?*

*I didn't want to. Not today. Not like that. Not out of nowhere. Not at all.*

*What am I supposed to do now?*

The bus arrives on time, pulling to a stop outside the small shelter. I drag myself to my feet and board. I show the driver my summer bus pass. I sit in an empty seat in the very back, and I take the bus straight home.

What else can I do?

Once inside, I thoroughly search the house—going so far as to check Rose's bedroom to ensure I'm alone. I am alone, and I intend to keep it that way. I lock the front door, turning the deadbolt. Then I double-check the window locks on the first floor before I finally retreat upstairs.

I plant myself at my desk, my side aching, and I flip open my laptop. I unlock it and launch the internet browser, which opens to FaceSpace.

Rose hasn't sent anything since this morning, but I click on Night's name in the messenger tab.

> **Me:** Hey, I need to talk to you asap
>
> **Me:** It's important.

I wait a few minutes, but she doesn't read the messages or respond. She's not online and hasn't been active on messenger in a few days. I back out to check her profile, but she hasn't posted anything at all since the day I walked out of Westbrooke to find James.

*Does she have any idea what happened?*

*Is she okay?*

After running into Ice, I feel drained. He didn't even say anything, and he didn't really *do* anything besides glance at me, but I wasn't ready to see him again. I wasn't expecting it. It came out of nowhere.

And he just...*smiled*. Like it was nothing.

*I hate the fact he can do that.*

I stare at the stitches on the palm of my hand for a while. Then I peel the fabric of my shirt away from my side again. Lifting the hem just enough to expose the long, stitched wound, I pick a few bits of lint off the stitches.

It's not quite scabbing over yet. It's sore and warm but doesn't look infected or anything, so I think it's fine. *Probably.*

I change into pajamas, force myself to eat a random protein bar I found on my dresser, and hide in bed. The prescription bottles on the bedside table stare at me for a while before I decide to take a dose of Vicodin. It can't be much later than 5PM, but I take a melatonin capsule too.

Then I curl up in bed on my good side. I stare at the bandage on my arm and wonder why I bothered wrapping it up.

I know I left the house and went into public earlier, but why should I care if my injuries are visible while I'm alone? There's no one around to see them. No one here to make me feel awful and stupid for screwing up. Covering them doesn't change the fact they exist.

Only a handful of people know the truth, and everyone else thinks James did it, so what does it matter? What difference does it make if I sleep the rest of the day away?

There's no one here.

No one to see the scabs.

No one to care if I lie in bed the entire afternoon.

Nothing important for me to do, anyway.

*Ugh.*

I wish I had my phone. I want to call Rose—if only to hear her voice. I could call Robbie. Or my dad. *Or even my mom, assuming her phone number hasn't changed.* I wish I could talk to anyone. Just for a minute.

I wish I could tell someone what happened.

I wish I'd gone straight home instead of trying to pick up my duffel bag. I wish I'd decided to run before Ice stepped out of the room. I should have listened to James.

But I didn't, so this is my life now.

# six

Something woke me, rousing me from a dead, dreamless sleep and landing me flat on my back in bed with my head full of cotton balls.

I peel my heavy eyelids open. The room is dark, with no light streaming in through the slatted blinds over the window, but I can't have been asleep very long. My body still feels foreign and heavy, and my hand trembles as I rub my eyes.

Pushing the comforter aside, I sit up.

My head spins, the start of a headache. Past the mild discomfort and a strange, hazy lag in reality, I recognize gnawing hunger. I ate a protein bar before I fell asleep, but my last meal was a light lunch before I went into town.

What did I even eat? Cereal? Or was that yesterday? Maybe I had a couple toaster pastries? Or a sandwich—though I don't think I have bread.

Is the hunger what woke me up?

*Probably.*

Stumbling out of bed, my eyes catch sight of the bandage on my arm. The bruise on my other wrist. The stitches on my palm. I stare at them in the low light for several seconds. When the beat of surprise fades, I remember.

*Our eyes locked for an instant.*

Shaking my injured hand to dispel the imagined discomfort, I reach for the doorknob with my left. As my fingers brush the metallic surface, I pause.

I suddenly feel…*sick.*

Why am I hesitating? A side effect of the medication, maybe? Can Vicodin cause nausea? Is it because I took it with the melatonin? Is it because I haven't eaten enough today?

I shake my head, pull the door open, and glance around.

The light in the study is on, exactly how I left it before shutting myself in the bedroom, and the space is empty, as it should be. The first floor beyond the banister appears empty too, but I still feel a nagging anxiety.

*Weird. It has to be the medication.*

Even so, I hover in the doorway.

"Hello?" I call to my quiet house.

I don't expect an answer. I'm only trying to prove to myself that I'm alone. I only want to calm my nerves, still shot after running into Ice.

But goosebumps prickle on my arms.

A sense of foreboding thickens the air, and my attention locks on the top of the stairs. Some of the mental haze clears as I grow more alert. Some of the cotton balls leave my head, but the house remains silent, save for the hum of the central AC.

Until I make out a soft noise. Footsteps? Careful and slow and making their way upstairs. The top of a head. Blond hair. A flash of bright blue eyes, reflecting green in the low light of the stairwell.

*No.*

Still holding my breath, I step back. I slam the door and turn the privacy lock. Then I slide down to the carpet with my back pressed against the solid surface.

*He's here? How? What does he want?*

*What do I do? What can I—? God, I can't even—*

I hold my head in my hands, fingers tangled in my hair and eyes squeezed shut as I struggle to think clearly.

*There's no way he didn't see me or at least hear me close the door, and he knows I'm alone. What if he gets inside? I'm completely defenseless. He could kill me—!*

*Ah... My hand hurts...*

*What if the stitches burst?*

I need help.

I pop to my feet and, ignoring the dull ache in my side, search for a phone. My hands run over the top of my bedside table, knocking the pill bottles over and rattling to the floor. *Nothing. Nothing on the dresser either.* As I cross the room to my desk, I freeze with my hand on the handle of a drawer.

*Wait. My phone isn't here.*

It's still wherever James' car is.

*Shit.*

I scan the room, my vision tracking slowly.

*Computer.* What good would it do?

*Window.* I open the blinds and stare at the dark grass far below. Unless I feel like jumping from the second floor while already injured, I'm trapped.

The doorknob jiggles behind me.

I jump, my heart skipping a beat as I turn to look. The door is locked, but the knob semi-rotates several times as someone fiddles with it from the other side.

*He really is here.*

*Will the privacy lock hold?*

*Should I hide?*

I open the window, pop the screen out, and drop it onto my desk to serve as a diversion before I turn back to my dimly lit bedroom. Before I get any further with my nonexistent plan, I hear Ice laugh just beyond the door, and I freeze again.

"Do you think I'm an idiot?" he asks, his humored voice low and calm. "I know very well you wouldn't jump out the window."

*Well, it was worth a shot.*

I don't move. Eyes locked on the door, I barely even breathe.

"You must not have your phone," he continues casually. "I called to check up on you this afternoon, but my call went straight to voicemail."

*He called? Why?*

I grit my teeth. "Go away."

"Ah." He laughs again. "You're no fun."

*Fun?* Anger swells in my chest, but my mouth feels dry.

"Why are you here?" I ask.

"Why?" he echoes, unaffected by my raised voice.

I rub my eyes, desperate to curb the tears forming there. My side throbs with each sharp breath. How long was I asleep? Is the medication wearing off faster because I panicked? Is that a thing?

*Ugh. Why is this happening now?*

"I suppose it is rather late in the day, but I thought this was the perfect time to visit after your accident." The dark, mocking undertones in his otherwise casual voice upset me greatly. "Would you rather be left all alone after such a traumatic experience?"

*Why come here? Why say this to me?*

The tears roll down my face, hot and furious. The taste of salt on my lip. I regain control of my body, wipe my eyes, and face the door. The knob hasn't turned since he first spoke.

*I don't get it.*

"Are you here to kill me?" I ask, my voice surprisingly level.

A pause. A moment of silence, broken only by the breeze coming in through the open window behind me.

Then he laughs again, startling me.

"Kill you?" he asks. "Why would I want to kill you, Jayde? You'd be absolutely no good to me dead—seeing as toying with you at James' expense is high entertainment. So, no, I am not here to kill you."

*I can't believe this.*

"That said, it's terribly boring standing outside your room by myself. Would you mind unlocking the door? I'd hate to have to do anything drastic."

*Drastic?*

My eyes widen further, more tears slipping from the corners. The warm liquid drips from my chin. My fingers twitch nervously as I look to the doorknob and the activated privacy lock.

*I hate this.*

He may be my sponsor, but that doesn't give him free rein

over my entire life, does it? It can't possibly give him the right to treat me this way, can it? I never read anything stating he could do anything remotely like this in the paperwork I signed.

Surely, I don't have to listen to him.

What will happen if I give in and open the door?

*What will he do if I refuse?*

I'm not safe either way. The privacy lock isn't strong. It's not designed to keep out a violent intruder. I'm sure he could easily break it.

*Hell, I could probably break it if I tried.*

I don't want to be complacent and do whatever he asks of me, but nothing good will come of fighting him in this situation. I'm weak—injured and heavily medicated. And alone.

I wipe my damp face again. The bandage on my arm soaks up the worst of the tears.

But I still don't know what to do.

The room is quiet until Ice sighs loud enough to hear through the door. "Open this door, Jayde. Or I will open it myself." His voice is a low growl, full of malicious intent. "You do not want to find out what I am capable of."

*Have I not already found out?*

But my body moves on its own, stumbling to the door, which I immediately unlock and pull open with my bad hand. I ignore the jolt of pain up my arm, more concerned about the person opening the door exposed me to.

Ice takes a step back, away from me and the door, his expression softening as our eyes meet. That fleeting, warm smile is something I used to enjoy. I would seek it out. I would relish it whenever I saw it.

Now, it fills me with a cold dread that steals my breath.

"Close the door," he says.

I step out and do as instructed even as I realize doing so leaves me trapped between him and the door. I'm playing right into his hands, *which is exactly what I wanted to avoid.*

"What do you want?" I ask.

My voice trembles, but I force myself to maintain eye contact and keep a close eye on him. He ignores my question and looks me over instead. His crooked smile fades. The bandage on my arm. The bruises. The cuts. The scab poking out from the low neckline of my shirt.

Scowling, I raise an arm to cover it.

"You're a mess, Jayde."

There are a million things I could say to him now, but all I do is grimace, my brows furrowing as I watch him with intentionally marked distrust.

He chuckles, resting his jaw on his knuckles. "You know, you are rather cute when you're angry."

I tear my gaze away, my cheeks on fire.

How did I ever see anything good in this guy? He's *insane.* Even if he was acting decent before, how the hell did I miss it? Was I just that pathetically lovestruck the entire time? It's not right, and James—

*James!*

"How could you set him up like that?" I cry.

"James Reid?" he asks, though his surprise is quickly waved off with an easy smile. "Human police are stupid and gullible—

as humans tend to be—but there's no need to concern yourself with the matter. Human-Immortal Affairs has everything under control."

"He'll be released, then?" I ask, unclenching my throbbing fist.

"Rest assured, he will not go to prison—human or otherwise."

He crosses his heart, drawing a relaxed X over his chest with his index finger. His too-wide smirk and sparkling eyes lead me to believe he's not taking me seriously, but that half-assed promise sort of lines up with what James and Dr. Corel said about Human-Immortal Affairs. Either way, it's all I have to go on right now.

"Now answer my question," I stammer. "Why are you here?"

He regards me thoughtfully, as though even he isn't quite sure why he came, so I have no idea what to expect. I almost hope he'll make another joke at my expense, but he looks too serious now.

Then he nods, a short motion, and his expression darkens further. "Give me your left hand."

*Why?*

The request doesn't make sense, so I don't move, let alone lift my hand. I tip my head to one side, confused and curious through the remaining brain fog.

He looks at me like I'm an idiot and sighs.

"Just give me your hand," he says.

I don't get it, but I raise my left hand anyway.

It's not until *after* he grabs me by the arm that I realize I've made a mistake. I stare at his fingers, wrapped around the bandage covering my forearm, right above the bruise he left there only a couple days ago.

I look up again, my eyes painfully wide.

He flashes a grin and pushes me back, pinning me against the door with an elbow and a knee. I don't have time to recover before a closed switchblade appears in his free hand. Ivory and swirled steel—the same one as before.

*Knife!*

I completely freeze as a shrill voice in my head repeats the word like an alarm.

Then Ice's grip tightens over the bandage, stretching the skin held together by stitches. The tugging pain drags me back to reality, silencing the alarm and clearing the fog further. I pull at his hand, trying to ease the pressure, but it only hurts my injured palm.

"Let go," I gasp.

His expression is firm, though it would feel more appropriate on the face of someone preparing to chastise a young child for misbehavior. *Disappointment.* Bile rises in my throat as it remains unchanging.

"You asked why I came tonight," he says, his voice a troubling mix of admonition and dry sarcasm. "The reason is simple."

I say nothing, my focus torn between his cool eyes and the knife in his hand, too disturbed to think of forming words. *What would I even say if I tried?*

His thumb presses a button on the side of the knife, and the marbled blade pops out with a sharp metallic click.

"I own you, Jayde."

*What?*

I tear my attention from the knife and lock onto his face again.

His expression softens upon making eye contact, but it does nothing to ease my rising panic.

"I am still your sponsor, and I can't let you forget that."

His voice is disturbingly gentle.

*I don't want to know what he has in mind.*

My free hand stops trying to break his grip on my arm. I ignore the hot throbbing in my palm. Reaching down instead, I feel for the doorknob but quickly realize it's on my left.

Ice has my left arm, and I'm pinned. I can't even push the door open and hope for a chance to slip past him and escape.

"I won't let you forget."

His voice is too soft. Too gentle. Almost drowned out by the blood rushing in my ears. But I know. *He is going to cut me, and I can't do anything to stop him.*

*Wait—*

Drawing a deep breath, I lean into the instinct to fight. Even though I know it's a waste of time, I try to force distance between myself and the blade. I try to kick him off, but he's too close. I shove my free hand between his shoulder and collarbone. Pain flares in my palm, but, no matter how hard I push, he regards me with little more than passive indifference. His grip on my aching, bandaged arm remains secure and too tight.

Desperate, I return to prying at his hand.

*This is hopeless.* My struggling isn't even a minor nuisance. I can only watch as he presses the sharp edge of the knife to the inside of my wrist.

With a sigh, he shifts his weight and slams my left arm against the doorjamb, trapping it in the shallow recess between the door and the wall. I cry out again, but the blade only presses harder against my skin, threatening to puncture it.

My breath comes short and fast, and I meet his eyes. I shake my head, silently pleading with my jaw set. But he merely offers a faint smile before returning his attention to my wrist.

The focus in his narrowed eyes. His expression unbothered even as my nails dig into the fleshy part of his thumb. *It's impossible to look away, but—*

"Hey, wait—!"

The instant metal pierces skin, I stop.

I stop fighting. I stop moving. I give up.

*What else can I do?*

He claims he doesn't want to kill me, but he might slip up if I move. If he slips up now, he could nick a vein and kill me on accident. I've helped Rose study for enough nursing exams to know there are several important things beneath the thin skin on the inside of my wrist. *Blood vessels. Tendons. Nerves.*

A tear runs down my cheek.

I force myself to look away, to my right. I refuse to watch, and I can't bear the look on his face anymore, but I can't stop myself from counting. *Three... Four... Five...* Six cuts. They don't seem particularly deep or wide or long, but each one stings and leaves warmth oozing down my arm. I can picture the red blood leaking toward my elbow only to be intercepted by the hand wrapped around my arm.

*And I just let him do this?*

*Why?*

Once finished, Ice releases my arm and eases up on forcing

me back against the door. I press my injured palm over my burning wrist, holding both arms close to my chest.

I don't look at him, but he doesn't move.

Then he props my chin up with his fingers. I meet his gaze and bare my teeth, frustrated by literally everything. *Him. Myself. The medication. The bitter tears spilling from my stupid eyes.* He observes me for a second before dropping his hand and cracking another smile.

"So much for your summer romance," he says. "Now, you will never forget me."

*No. I...guess I won't.*

A deep sense of regret and loss tempers my anger, and I lower my head. I look to the floor. Tears fall from my nose, joining a few drops of bright red on the pale grey carpet. Crying in front of Ice is so humiliating, but I hate myself for feeling this way. I hate myself for caring what he thinks about me after what he did, and I hate myself for not fighting harder to protect myself.

*I almost wish all he wanted was to kill me.*

*I almost wish it was just...over.*

He takes a step back, distancing himself further. I don't raise my head or move from where I stand, but I watch through my bangs as he cleans his knife with a white handkerchief and returns both to his back pocket.

*Why are you still here?*

"Please go," I breathe.

"If that's what you want," he agrees. "But we'll see each other again soon, so...do try to enjoy this time alone."

*Alone...?*

With that, Ice turns to leave.

He walks down the stairs, but I don't budge until I hear the front door close. After a moment of silence, I straighten up and stare at the hand sealed over my wrist. At the blood that trickled down my arm and soaked into the edge of the gauze bandage.

*What did he do?*

I don't want to know. I honestly don't.

*But he cut my wrist.*

I don't think the wound is anything serious. I don't think it needs medical attention. But I'm bleeding. I have to take care of it. Whatever it is, the wound needs to be cleaned and bandaged.

*Only an idiot would leave it like this.*

Careful, I peel my hand away. My attention follows my hand, and the blood smeared on my stitched palm, hesitant to look aside and assess the new damage. But, when I do, my breath catches. My knees buckle, and I fall to the floor.

*What Ice carved there—*

The six small cuts on the inside of my wrist form the rough, angular shape of a heart. The wound oozes slowly, dark blood pooling at the bottom point before breaking away and trickling down my arm in a warm stream.

*What did he say?*

*"So much for your summer romance?"*

It's almost funny. *It's almost...*

But *why?*

My chest heaves, bringing a choked sob with it. I press my palms into my eye sockets, not caring if I smear blood on my face.

*I never did anything to Ice to deserve this.*

Even after everything James told me—even after I saw what he did with my own eyes—I still wanted to believe that Ice was good. I wanted to give him the benefit of the doubt. I wanted to trust him, so…

*How could he do this to me?*

I cry for a while. I'm not sure how long. A few minutes. Ten minutes. It doesn't matter. All I know is that a tired, numb, empty type of feeling I've never felt before stops the tears as my heart slows and I regain control of my breathing.

I take a deep breath. My hands fall to my sides. I lean back against the door. I watch the ceiling and listen to the quiet house for another minute.

Then I wipe my leaking nose with a clean part of my bandaged arm and drag myself off the floor. I walk downstairs, into the kitchen. I stand in front of the sink and nudge the faucet handle with the back of my hand, and I hold the still-oozing wound under the stream of cool water.

It stings, but less than I expected.

After I rinse both hands, I remove the soiled bandage to reveal the mess that is my left arm. The purple and red bruising. The stitches holding together a jagged, five-inch slice. The new, heart-shaped wound that tints the water pink as it swirls down the drain.

I turn the water off. I fold a paper towel into a square and press it against my wrist, hoping to stop the slow bleed completely.

I look around the empty kitchen.

*How the hell did Ice get inside?*

*The door was locked, wasn't it?*

When I peel the paper towel away, it no longer looks to be actively bleeding. I dig an old box of bright red band-aids out of the junk drawer. It takes three to completely cover the wound.

Then I canvas the first floor.

None of the windows appear to have been tampered with. They're all intact and still locked.

Confused, I check the door. It's unlocked, but there's no sign of damage to the lock or doorknob. *He must have come in this way, though.*

I crack the door and scan the parking lot. I don't see Ice or his flashy silver Porsche anywhere, but…

*The potted plant!*

I always felt that hiding a spare key in a potted plant just outside the front door was too obvious.

Stepping outside, I check the large ceramic pot. When I brush the plant's stems aside, the key is sitting on top of Rose's painted rock instead of where it should be hidden beneath it.

*Ugh.*

I bring the key inside, set it on the bookcase, and lock the door again. Then, leaving every light on, I return upstairs. I step into my bedroom, turn the privacy lock for good measure, and collapse in bed as the numbness turns to exhaustion.

# seven

~ ∞ ~

*It's dark.*

*It's cold.*

*I can't make out a single thing around me, but a gentle sound fills the room, echoing off the walls—assuming there are walls. The sound of dripping. A soft, steady drip, like water falling from a leaky faucet into an empty, metal sink basin.*

*Drip.*

*Drip.*

*It sounds close, but I don't see anything.*

*Drip.*

*Drip.*

*Drip.*

*Is it water?*

*Where is it coming from?*

*I glance at my hands. At the unnatural illumination that leaves me unshadowed in the otherwise pitch-black space. I'm on the ground, on my knees. The surface is cold and hard and smooth against my shins, but there's nothing on the ground beyond the same strange darkness.*

*I heft myself to my feet and look around again, but there's still nothing. No light. No meaningful color variation. Just an inky void and the sound of dripping liquid, collecting in a puddle somewhere just out of sight. I can't even tell which direction the sound is coming from. It's soft but pervasive, as though coming from everywhere at once. The cold is uncomfortable too, soaking through my thin clothes and into my bones.*

*I take a single step. My foot contacts the solid, black ground —I feel it, but it doesn't make a sound. I continue walking, and I still hear nothing but dripping.*

*Drip.*

*Drip.*

*For a moment, it seems louder than before.*

*Then it stops.*

*Everything stops.*

*So I stop too.*

*I listen to the silence, standing in the center of the void. With wide eyes, I stare at the impossibly dark shapes swirling in the equally impossible distance.*

*I stare. I listen. I hold my breath.*

*Out of the silence, my head explodes with sound. A deafening blast. Like a firework. Like the skyrockets I watched with Ice on July fifth, standing a bit too close for comfort. But the sound was off in a way I can't explain.*

*What's wrong this time?*

~ ∞ ~

# eight

My eyes fly open, and I stare blankly at the white ceiling. The round ceiling light is on, which is odd, but I remember why I left it on last night.

*When I came back upstairs after—*

My heart races, and my breathing comes fast and uneven, but I don't move. Even as tears dampen the hair framing my face and pool in my ears, I don't lift a hand to stop them or fix my hair. I just lie on my back and stare at the ceiling as fat tears spill from my wide eyes.

*Why am I crying?*

I had a dream, right? I remember, but nothing happened in it. *It was just a dream. Just a sound.* Nothing happened. I'm fine. *Everything is fine.*

Once my breathing calms and the tears slow, I sit up. My side aches, but my mind is clear. Warm light streams in through the window behind my desk. I remembered to shut it, but the screen is still on top of my laptop.

I look away from the window, to my hands. They tremble gently, still upset by some lingering darkness. The blood is gone, but that's about it. I still exist in a twisted reality where I have stitches on my palm and bruises on my arms and bright red band-aids over—

With a sigh, I crawl out of bed. I unlock my bedroom door and slowly make my way downstairs.

The first floor is untouched and quiet and empty. The front door is still locked, not that it makes a difference, but it eases my mind to know. I turn to walk away, but I hesitate as I step by Rose's bedroom door.

I reach for the doorknob. I don't know why. Maybe it's because I haven't checked her bedroom yet this morning. Maybe it's just because I miss her.

Whatever the reason, I step inside and flip the light on.

The room looks the same as the day she left—not a mess but almost haphazard in its organization. A stack of textbooks on her desk. A pile of folded clothes on her half-made bed. A knit sports wristband beside the abandoned laundry catches my eye. It's black with a tiny, white logo embroidered on the front.

I look at the sweatband, at the band-aids on my wrist, and I swipe the band off the bed before I leave the room.

* * * * *

When I hear a solid knock at the front door, I panic. I take a second to calm my racing heart and convince myself it's not Ice. Then I check the peephole—something I have literally never done before now. I'm not sure who I was expecting to see, but Detective Crain was not high on the list.

The smartly dressed woman is standing alone on the concrete

landing. *She never said she'd come back.* I rush to unlock the deadbolt and open the door. She looks more tired than I remember.

"Good morning, Jayde," she says, forcing a smile.

"Good morning."

"How are you holding up?"

"I'm alright."

I glance at the black band on my wrist. It does a decent job of hiding the band-aids, but I worry wearing it only draws attention to the area.

If Detective Crain notices anything off, she doesn't mention it.

"Sorry to drop in unexpectedly, but—"

"Are there any updates on the case?" I ask, not caring that I've cut her off.

"Yes," she says with a sigh.

The line of her mouth thins, and she glances aside, leaving me unsure if I should feel hopeful or afraid. Then she asks if she can come inside to talk. I nod and lead her through the living room to the kitchen. She sits across from me at the dining table while I watch her carefully.

Ice swore James would be okay. Maybe he wasn't bluffing just to lower my guard. Maybe Human-Immortal Affairs stepped in and did something.

I pick at the edge of the sweatband, my mouth growing dry.

Finally, Detective Crain clears her throat. "James Reid will be released today."

*Today?*

My eyes flick up from the smooth tabletop, and she meets my gaze, seeming to understand and mirror my surprise.

"I stopped by yesterday, and there weren't any updates at all," I say, tripping over my words. "What happened?"

"Everything related to the case vanished last night."

"Vanished? What do you mean?"

"Everything was accounted for at the end of my shift," she says with an uncomfortable shrug, "but it went missing overnight. It's all gone—material evidence, photographs, statements. Even the digital files. Everything related to James Reid and the assault case. The station is staffed at night, but no one reported anything out of the ordinary, so I have no idea how this happened."

"Oh."

*Human-Immortal Affairs doesn't screw around.*

*Well...there go my boots, I guess.*

She sighs, a hint of true exhaustion slipping through. "Since then, we've received orders to stop pursuing the case, and the DA dropped all charges. James is being processed for release right now. He should be out in an hour or so."

"Oh... Good..."

I drop my face into my hands, caught off guard by my watering eyes and the sheer weight the news lifted from my chest. Suddenly, it feels like I can breathe easy again.

"I can give you a ride to the station if you'd like," she says.

A ride? To meet up with James at the police station? *I did leave my purse and phone in his car...*

I accept Detective Crain's offer, and she waits downstairs with a glass of water while I head to my room to pack a bag.

*This is good, right?* James doesn't have to sit in a jail cell, stand trial, or face a prison sentence for something he didn't do.

I'm glad, even if I had nothing to do with his release.

*Unless I did.*

How do I know that Ice, acting as my sponsor, can't get James into more serious trouble? Surely, what happened on the Fourth of July could be held against him. Ice could have told RPD when he pinned the attack on James, but no one has mentioned it, so it doesn't seem like he did.

Instead, he promised that James would be released.

As far as I know, even Human-Immortal Affairs doesn't know about the Fourth of July. Surely, James broke *some* immortal law by kidnapping me and threatening me with a gun.

I stare at my forearms. The bruises. The stitches. The sweatband. A deep uneasiness creeps into my chest.

*Did Ice break any immortal laws?*

Human-Immortal Affairs knows he attacked me—Dr. Corel basically confirmed it. Do they care at all?

*How can I know if they never contact me?*

I swipe the prescription bottles off the bedside table and shove them into my bag, taking my frustration out on the inanimate objects. Then I throw my hair up into a low-effort ponytail and dig a thin flannel out of my dresser to wear over my loose t-shirt.

*Enjoy my time alone, Ice said...*

*Yeah, right.*

Literally carving a heart into my wrist is a personal statement—especially considering what he said after. It was nothing like what happened at his house, when he was obviously using me to get to James.

James may be free now, but I don't think Ice is done with

either of us whether I'm *alone* or not. He'll be back to make me pay for whatever betrayal he thinks I committed against him.

*Or to kill James.*

*But I can't let that happen.*

I owe James for what he did. He's kind of an idiot, but he told me the truth. He braved his fear of Ice to get me out of the house and drive me to the hospital. He was even willing to throw his freedom away just because he thought it would protect me.

Sure, he was dead wrong, but that takes a lot of commitment, and I can't ignore the good intentions behind his actions. *Even if it is annoying.* He's in danger because of me now, anyway. Because I asked for his help.

The least I can do is help get him out of it.

*And maybe I won't have to be alone, after all.*

I pop a double dose of ibuprofen and drop the bottle into my bag. Then I zip it up, sling the backpack over my good shoulder, and leave to meet up with Detective Crain.

# nine

"You're positive you want me to leave you with this man?" Detective Crain asks as I follow her into the police station lobby. "You feel safe with him?"

"Mm-hm."

It isn't the first time she's asked, but I certainly hope it'll be the last. Even if she means well, her company is exhausting, and it's not like I can explain my decision to tag along with James, anyway.

*Honestly, I have no idea what I'm doing.*

"Alright," she says, her voice mild. "Well, he should be out in a few minutes. You still have my card, right? Don't hesitate to call if you need anything."

I think I left the card on my desk. But I nod and force a smile and hope it looks convincing enough.

With a tired sigh, she swipes an ID badge over an electronic lock on a door that leads further into the building. "I hope everything works out for you, Jayde."

"Thanks."

Detective Crain leaves the lobby, and I take a moment to look around. There are surprisingly few people here. Two officers talking near another door. An older woman speaking to the uniformed man behind the reception counter. A couple sitting in plastic chairs across the room.

I could sit too—there are several empty chairs available—but nervous energy overpowers the discomfort radiating from my side. I end up pacing, following a line of white grout on the grey tile not far from the wall.

No one stops me, so this continues for several minutes until James finally appears in the hallway. An officer escorts him halfway down before slapping him on the shoulder and heading back the way they came.

James' grimace is obvious as he turns back toward the lobby, and I try once again to not look like a complete nervous wreck.

He's dressed in new clothes—a plain white t-shirt and jeans—wearing his backpack, and carrying a cardboard box. Eyes wide and not focused on anything in particular after having noticed me, he enters the lobby proper. I sling my backpack over the better of my bruised shoulders, and he stops a couple feet away to give me a wary once-over.

"Hi," I say, if only to break the silence.

*Today, he looks better than I do.* His injuries have cleared up or turned into pink scars, save for a few small, dark scabs and the ghost of a black eye.

"Hi…" He grimaces again, and his eyes flick down to the cardboard box in his arms. "I'm sorry about what I said the other day. Are you okay?"

"I'm fine."

He sighs in relief, and I feel a rush of validation regarding my decision to wear a flannel shirt. It's hot and seems out of place during the summer, but I didn't bother bandaging my left arm. He'd think I look as terrible as I feel if he could see the bruises and ugly scabs. *Worse, he might ask about the sweatband.*

I hate lying, but I can't bring myself to break the truth to him while we're still loitering in the police station.

"I wasn't expecting to see you," he admits. "There's usually not anyone waiting for me when I get out."

"You've been here before?"

"Maybe." He laughs, though his fleeting smile doesn't touch his eyes.

*Ah. I shouldn't have asked.*

"One of the detectives gave me a ride." I keep my voice low as we cross the lobby toward the front doors. "She said the evidence for the case disappeared overnight."

"Disappeared, huh? That's new."

I follow James out of the building and into the summer heat. I was more than ready to get the hell out of here, but he pauses on the concrete steps. He turns to look at me, clearly confused —by me existing, I guess.

"Why are you here, anyway?"

"Because I—" I stare back at him, suddenly confused as to the exact reason myself. "Well, um... I mean, you don't mind that I'm here, do you?"

He shakes his head before continuing down the steps. "No. I don't mind. It's just weird."

"Is it?" I ask, skipping a step to catch up with him and regretting it as the skin on my side stretches a bit too far. "Also,

I left my phone in your car, and I need to get it back."

"Oh. Right. Sorry."

We walk behind the building and make our way to the impound lot two blocks over. James shows some type of documentation to the guard posted at the concrete gatehouse, and they eventually hand over his keys and lead us inside.

I hesitate as we approach the off-white Honda. *Crusty brown stains on the car's exterior, just behind the rear passenger door.* I barely remember it—my hand planted on the strip of white while I leaned on the car for support.

*But it was only a few days ago.*

The escorting officer leaves once they finish signing over the vehicle, and James sets his cardboard box on the hood before unlocking the car.

When he opens the passenger door, the pungent scent of rotting blood wafts out, strong enough to very nearly make me gag. Even so, I hold a hand over my nose and peer inside with a morbid curiosity spurred by my spotty memory of the ride to the hospital.

The backseat is a complete mess. Most of the paper and trash that previously littered the floor is absent, but dark, crusty blood stains the pale bucket seat where I sat a few days earlier.

"I have to take care of this," James says, his face pale. "Now."

I nod, unable to speak, as I climb into the much cleaner front passenger seat. With my backpack in my lap, the scent of rot filling the car, and my injured hand desperately turning the manual crank to roll down the window, I find myself reconsidering.

The moment Detective Crain told me James would be released,

I made up my mind to tag along with him. I had no idea what he planned to do—I still don't, and it doesn't seem like he does either—but I didn't care. I do not want to be home right now. I do not want to be alone. *Especially not if that's what Ice wants.*

But the thought of the blood, *my* blood, soaked into the dingy grey fabric bothers me. The memory of staring through the window as my vision blurred and time seemed to pass in unpredictable ways.

*No.* I'd still rather be here than alone at home.

Instead of saying anything, I reach under the passenger seat looking for my purse, but it isn't there. My jacket isn't either. The police must have cleared the vehicle out after James' arrest. I guess that explains why the floor is significantly cleaner than before.

Before I get a chance to complain, James makes his way into the driver's seat and passes the cardboard box to me. It's not large, but it is surprisingly heavy.

"You mentioned your phone, right?" he asks. "This is most of what the cops took. Whatever wasn't trash or important enough to disappear, I guess. Your stuff should be in there too."

He starts the car, and I turn my attention to the box. Sifting through the contents, I find a lot of random junk. Several CDs but no CD cases. A black spiral-bound notebook. A crumpled, half-empty pack of menthol cigarettes. A paperback novel missing its cover. My jacket, purse, and umbrella are here too, so I figure most everything inside was taken from the car before it went into the impound lot.

I stuff the jacket and umbrella into my backpack and take

my phone from my purse. It's still dead. I would charge it now, but the car's stereo doesn't have a USB port.

*Oh, well.*

With a sigh, I look back to the box.

Digging deeper, I eventually catch a sliver of blue in a tiny, plastic zip bag beneath a worn, leather wallet. I snatch the bag and breathe a sigh of relief upon finding the River Sapphire safe inside. I was starting to think I'd never see it again.

*That should be everything.*

I push the cardboard box down the center console and onto the floor in the backseat. It lands upright beside James' backpack, so I assume it's fine. Then I lean closer to the open passenger window and try to breathe in the hot but fresh air.

"Sounds like you know more than me," James says. His thumb taps the steering wheel, betraying some anxiety, as he watches the road. "Do you have any idea why they released me so suddenly? No one told me anything."

"I told you the evidence disappeared," I mutter. "The detective who picked me up said they were told to drop the case this morning. I think Ice had something to do with it."

"He called the cops on me," he says, his voice flat. "He's the whole reason I was there in the first place. Why go through the hassle of setting me up just to have me released a few days later? I was ready to take the fall for what he did, you know?"

I glance away. "I know, but Human-Immortal Affairs took care of it. I'm sure they weren't happy he got human police involved, anyway, even if he is my sponsor."

We both fall quiet.

*The car smells like death.*

I hug my backpack to my chest and stare out the passenger window, at the cars in the other lane and the buildings that pass by. My side aches, and the scab on my chest itches, but I'm careful to ignore it and not let it show.

"Hey, ah… While I was… Did you see him?"

"I—" My voice catches.

Looking up from the black sweatband peeking out from beneath my flannel's cuff, I meet James' fleeting gaze. I can't bring myself to confirm or deny whether I saw Ice, but my silence only seems to unsettle him.

"What happened?" he asks.

The car pulls into an auto shop parking lot at one corner of a shopping mall complex, and I use the fact that we've reached our destination as an excuse to talk about it later. He agrees, but I think it's only because he knows he'll have a hell of a time explaining the blood in the backseat.

I stand in the shade cast by the building while James talks to someone from the auto shop several feet away. I listen passively while he gestures at his car and says there was *an accident* in the backseat. The man he's speaking with seems entirely uninterested in the details and accepts the job once James stops talking, though it sounds like it will take *a while*.

"Do whatever you have to," his distant voice says as he hands over his key. "Just get the smell out."

When their conversation ends, he meets up with me in the shade. He looks rather drained, but it's hard to say what from considering how hectic life has been for both of us recently.

I ask if he's hungry, because I'm hungry, and he shrugs.

"What do you want?" he asks.

"There's a Chinese restaurant a couple blocks from here," I say, pointing down the street, away from the auto shop. Then I look back to him. "If that's okay."

He watches me for a moment before averting his gaze. "Sure."

With that small confirmation, he tucks his thumbs in his belt loops and starts down the parking lot toward the sidewalk. I adjust my backpack to take the pressure off my shoulder before following after him.

We eat our rice-heavy lunch specials while sitting across from each other at a booth table in the small, family-owned Chinese restaurant. A quiet, pervasive awkwardness hovers over us—the uncomfortable weight of what's happened. We don't talk much, and I spend most of the time gazing through the window at nothing in particular. A tree. A car. A couple walking down the sidewalk.

It bothers me, but, honestly, what is there to say?

Unsure what to do after eating, we end up on the curb in the shade of a tree halfway between the restaurant and the auto shop. James watches cars pull in and out of the shopping mall's parking lot. I stare at the paper takeout box in my lap.

"You are okay, right?" he asks.

"I think I will be. Eventually."

"I'm serious. What happened while I was in there?"

I glance up and force a smile. My nails drum against the side of the takeout box to ease my nerves while he watches me with an intense, uneasy patience.

"You won't freak out?" I ask.

He prickles. "You *did* see him."

"Yeah, but—"

"What happened?" he asks again.

My smile falters, and I look away, over the street instead.

"He was at the police station yesterday," I say slowly. "I dropped in to check in on the case. There wasn't any news, but… he was there too. Ice was there. He didn't…say anything to me. Or do anything. We just saw each other in a hallway for a second. I went home. I locked the door, but—"

I roll up the sleeve of my flannel to reveal the black sweatband, bruises, and scabbing wound on my left arm. He resists looking too closely. I don't particularly want to see it either, but I raise my hand and slip the band off.

*Three bright red band-aids.*

"He, um—"

I can't even bring myself to say it. Not with James' eyes locked on my wrist. He looks from the bandages to my face several times. Blank confusion. Then realization. Dismay. Anger.

I get it. I'm a bit pissed myself.

I don't know how James managed to convince himself I'd be fine while he was in police custody. He thought it was what Ice wanted—and I'm sure it was—but he was wrong to think it would help. He pushed me away in the interrogation room and confessed to attacking me for no reason.

I am upset. But I don't blame him. He didn't know. He couldn't have possibly known.

*Ice did this. Not James.*

"That's why you're here?" His voice seems far-off despite him sitting less than a foot away, and he wrings his hands. "Because he hurt you again?"

"I guess," I agree mildly. "But I did, um… I needed to get my phone back too."

"Right…" A moment of silence. Even in the shade, the air is uncomfortably hot. Then he asks, "Can I see?"

I tug my sleeve down and hit him with a pointedly tragic look, but his returning gaze is equally pained.

*He seriously thought he was doing the right thing.*

I don't want to show it off. I don't want to look at it again. But I can't cover it up forever either. It's more likely to get infected if I do, and exposure to air aids in a wound's healing, and— *Ugh.*

I push my sleeve back up, my fingers hesitating over the bandages. They overlap, so I grip the edge of the bottom one and peel all three off in one go. I gasp at the sting of hot air touching the moist wound underneath. My eyes hardly register the shape—only noting the rawness of it, still smeared with dry blood—and I instead focus on the small relief that it doesn't start bleeding again.

Tearing my eyes away, I hold the hand out to show James. I don't watch his reaction, but I still find myself fighting back frustrated tears as he curses under his breath. Then I shake my arm until the sleeve falls to cover the wound.

"I'm okay. It looks worse than it is."

Right now, I don't care how I feel about what happened. James blames himself enough as things are. I don't want him to worry any more than he already does.

"I'm sorry," he says desperately. "If I had known, I—"

I slip the sweatband on again, wincing as the rough knit fabric scratches against the wound. The pain fades quickly, and I button the cuff to keep the sleeve down.

I say it's not his fault, but it doesn't quell the fire burning in his eyes. He looks away, his expression darkening as he stares out at traffic.

"He won't get away with this," he says under his breath.

*We're both alive and more or less free. Isn't that enough?*

"Just let it go. Please."

We sit in silence for a few minutes. I stare at my lap, listening to the cars on the street.

Hoping to change the subject even if I can't lighten the mood, I balance my takeout box on the curb and slip the River Sapphire from my pocket. I shake it out of the small bag and onto my palm. Both the pendant and chain survived the attack, but a small amount of blood is trapped between the thin, diamond-shaped gemstone and the prongs on its silver base. It's gross, but I scrape at the dry blood with my fingernails.

"Dr. Corel gave it to me while you were sedated," James says, his voice low. "I forgot to return it before I— But it's important to you, right?"

"Um…"

Right now, the River Sapphire is little more than a reminder of the mistake I made in trusting Ice. But what he said last night is true. He's still my sponsor, a title that grants him an unknown level of power over me. No matter what I tell James now, I'm afraid I'll never be able to truly escape that connection.

"I was worried," I say. "But it seems fine."

I put the necklace back into the bag, return it to my pocket, and check on James again. He seems to have calmed down, which is a relief. I wasn't sure how he'd react, but—

With a sigh, he glances at me, looking incredibly tired.

"So," he says, "you got the stuff you left with me back. You want a ride home after this?"

"Home?"

My breath catches, and I shake my head. But his question leaves me flustered. He tips his head, and I can't help but tear my eyes away.

"Actually," I stammer, "I was hoping I could stay with you for a while. Just a few days. Or…something."

"With me?" he asks.

*Ah— Why does he sound so surprised?*

Frustrated at myself for assuming he'd be fine with it, I mess with the cuff of my shirt. "I'd rather not be alone right now, so… I'd really appreciate it."

*He's quiet.*

Worried, I look up to find him watching me with a strange, unsettled confusion. A sort of sick sadness. Then his mouth closes, and his brows furrow, and he looks out over traffic again. I hold my breath until he finally clears his throat and nods.

"Yeah, that's fine. You can stay with me."

# ten

"This is crazy," James mutters, pulling the key from the ignition. "You sure you're alright with this?"

We both agreed that the old manor house—Reid Manor, if I recall correctly—is the best place to stay for now. I don't want to go home, and James doesn't *have* a home, so it was the obvious choice. Still, I find myself hesitating in the passenger seat as I stare through the windshield at the looming building. Neither of my previous experiences here were exactly pleasant.

"I honestly don't have a better idea," I say. "I just don't want to be alone."

"Okay."

The car, while it now smells of chemical cleaners rather than decomposition, is still uncomfortably hot, so I finally step out. The dry summer air isn't much better.

I follow James inside and up to the third floor, and we end up in the same slightly less dusty bedroom he was staying in before. He drops the cardboard box full of confiscated belongings on top of the humming mini-fridge. After taking a spiral notebook from the box, he looks around the room.

"It's weird being back here," he says, scratching his arm. "It's like…nothing has changed."

*Like nothing has changed?*

At the very least, it's much hotter in here than before.

I pass my Chinese takeout box to James, still too embarrassed to look inside his fridge with my own eyes. Then I set my backpack on the bed and dig the Vicodin out of the front pocket. I shed my flannel, drop it on top of my bag, and move to stand in front of the large window.

I look out over the gravel lot and forest beyond. The ground is dry and cracked and riddled with potholes that were surely full of water a week ago. But the sky is now a clear and cloudless blue. If it weren't for the dried mud I saw on the wooden steps just outside and in the foyer as we came in, I suppose it would be kind of like the rainstorm never happened.

*To me, though, it feels like everything has changed.*

Still, James is right: It is weird being here.

"How long do you plan to stay?" he asks.

"Um—"

I turn around. He's sat on the edge of the bed with his backpack in his lap, watching me with an overtly nervous expression.

*How long* do *I plan to stay?*

A few days, like I said earlier? Until it's time to get the stitches removed? I'm sure he'd be willing to give me a ride to the hospital before taking me home. Or a couple weeks? Maybe until Rose gets back from Arizona? I can't stick around longer than that since she thinks I'm home right now, and I do have to go back eventually.

"Never mind," James says. He forces a smile, breaking eye contact to shove the notebook into his backpack. "Whatever you need is fine. It's not like I have anywhere better to be."

"There's a bathroom down the hall, right?" I ask.

He nods and recites the same directions he gave me a few days ago. Of course, I remember as he says it. I cross the room to leave, but I pause in the doorway, my fingernails clicking against the side of the orange prescription bottle in my hand.

The ibuprofen I took this morning has worn off, *but...*

I turn back. "Hey, um— When I took this before, it made me super tired. And dizzy. Should I take some, anyway?"

He stares at me for a moment, frowning as he looks me over.

"Painkillers?" he asks. When I nod to confirm, he glances aside with furrowed brows. "Well, I mean, are you in pain?"

*Ah...*

"Sort of," I say slowly.

He doesn't seem convinced. I tug at the fabric clinging to my side, wincing as my tense and bruised shoulder flexes.

"Okay, yes," I relent. "Everything hurts."

He shrugs, seeming uncomfortable after watching me for so long. "Just take the meds. I don't care. It's fine."

"Thanks." I point to the fridge. "You have anything to drink around here?"

He nods, pops open the fridge, and joins me by the door with a can of generic citrus soda in hand. I'd much prefer water, but I take the can when he offers it to me.

"I hope you feel better," he says.

"Thanks."

We stand in the doorway for a quiet moment. Then he tears his eyes away and steps back, and I head down the hall with purpose. I just want to take the medication, wash the blood off my wrist—and the River Sapphire, I guess—and then take a nap. It's too hot to do much else, but I'm sure the Vicodin will knock me out again.

*At least I want it to this time.*

I push the bathroom door open and step inside.

The room is a mess. It's the same as it was a few days ago, of course, but it still catches me by surprise. The plaster chipping off the walls. Broken floor tiles. Dark rings and yellowing residue staining the once-white porcelain bathtub. I sure hope there's a bathroom with an actual shower tucked away somewhere in this building because I am not touching that.

*Oh, shoot.* Now that I think about it, I totally forgot to pack shampoo or anything. Most of my toiletries are still in my duffel bag at Ice's house.

Suppressing a shiver, I turn to the sink.

It isn't in much better condition than the bathtub. The silver faucet handles are badly tarnished, and the white basin is chipped, revealing metal underneath the enamel.

I set the prescription bottle and soda on an empty soap shelf, turn on the hot water, and hold my left hand beneath the stream. The water runs hot initially, almost scalding for an instant, but it quickly cools and never warms again.

*Of course, there's no hot water. Of course.*

I open the soda can and take a drink. Generic or not, I still don't care for Mountain Dew. I pour the neon yellow liquid down the drain and refill the can with water. It tastes…minerally and vaguely of soda but otherwise okay. I'm sure James would have warned me if the tap water wasn't safe to drink.

*Maybe.*

I take a pill and turn the water on again—the *cold* this time, as though it makes any difference. With a sigh, I remove the sweatband. The knit fabric resists, stinging as I peel it away.

*Ugh.*

Tiny balls of black lint cling to the raw, tender cuts beneath. The wound is sort of red and puffy, the angular shape still partially obscured by dried blood, and the area pulses with an uncomfortable warmth.

I shouldn't have put the wristband on after I took the band-aids off earlier. Hopefully, it won't get infected.

*It's fine. I'll deal with it either way.*

I stare at the stream of cold water. Glance at the bloody heart carved into my wrist. The water. The wound. The water.

And I push my wrist under. *It burns.* I suck in a breath and bite my cheek and pluck the lint from the wound. I move fast, and the remaining blood washes down the drain, and it's done.

I retract my hand.

Cool water drips down my arm as I take a moment to breathe. The stinging subsides, and I meet my wide, green eyes in the water-spotted mirror. My cheeks are flushed, but I'm not crying.

*This is fine. Everything is fine. I'll be fine.*

I forgot to grab band-aids from my bag, so I take a brown fast-food napkin from a stack in the windowsill and fold it into a square before pressing it over the wound. Then I slip the sweat-band over top of that. I carefully adjust everything, tucking the edge of the napkin beneath the fabric.

Feeling better, I move onto the River Sapphire. I throw the tiny plastic bag away and hold the necklace by its thin, silver chain to get a good look at it. There's still dark blood caught in several tiny chain links and cracks in the pendant's base that I couldn't reach with my nails, but it's nothing water can't fix.

Hot water would work better, *but it's fine.*

As I rinse the River Sapphire, the tiny flakes of blood dissolve, turn a brownish pink, and swirl down the drain. The water runs clear after a few seconds, so I turn it off and dry the necklace on the hem of my shirt.

With nothing left to do, I study the clear, blue gemstone. I hold it up to the light streaming through the frosted window. Then I put it on, struggling to fasten the chain at the back of my neck with my messed-up hand. The clasp finally catches, and I drop my arms to my sides.

*Nothing happens.*

At this point, though, I never expect anything.

With a sigh, I pull my ponytail over one shoulder and study myself in the mirror. The faint redness beneath my eyes. The scabs on my arms. The bruise on my wrist. The bottom point of the River Sapphire resting hardly an inch above the thin cut on my chest.

I remember what Ice said when he gave the necklace to me. When he looked at me with unveiled disappointment after nothing happened when I put it on.

*Take good care of it.*

Have I done that? Does it say something about me that I still care about it at all after what he did? That I took the time to wash it off? That I still choose to wear it even though it reminds me of him?

*It suits you*, he said.

Did he mean that? Does he really think the necklace suits me?

*Sure—like a collar on a dog, maybe.*

Ugh. Why *do* I still care about the River Sapphire?

Maybe I shouldn't anymore, but I guess... I don't want everything to have been for nothing. Maybe, eventually, the necklace will let me morph if I keep wearing it.

I splash water on my face and return to the bedroom.

James is sitting in the old recliner, an open can of soda in one hand and his phone in the other. He locks his phone and looks up the moment I step through the door.

After putting the pill bottle away, I sit on the edge of the bed, still holding the can full of water. I look up from my hands to find James watching me like he wants to say something but isn't sure if he's allowed to.

*It's kind of annoying.*

I tip my head, and he startles before setting his phone in his lap and adjusting his position in the chair.

"You good?" I ask.

He blinks, and his cheeks turn pink. "Oh, ah— Well, I was just thinking."

"About what?"

"It's stupid," he says with a weak laugh. "And it's hardly worth all this, but... My record with RPD is clean now."

*I almost forgot.*

I eye him suspiciously. "You mentioned having a record the other day too. You haven't done anything bad, right?"

"Bad? Oh. No. Uh—" Averting his gaze, he takes a quick drink of soda. "Just a few petty misdemeanors. Dumb stuff, really. Trespassing. Shoplifting. Traffic...violations? Dunno."

*Uh-huh...*

He looks to me again and immediately pales.

"About the Fourth of July," he stammers, eyes wide as saucers. "I am so, so sorry. I was—"

Groaning, I hold up a hand to stop him. "I do not care as long as that's the worst thing you've ever done."

"It is," he insists, worrying his hands. "It really is."

\* \* \* \* \*

"Damn it!"

James has been rummaging through the dresser drawers repeatedly for the past several minutes. This time, he's pulled everything out. Yellowed linens—sheets or tablecloths or some combination of the two—lay strewn about the floor, but he still hasn't found whatever he's looking for.

I'm not even sure what he's trying to find. If he told me, I've since forgotten.

The Vicodin has had about an hour to kick in. The effects are strong, relieving my pain almost completely but leaving me fuzzy and sleepy and more or less uninterested in James' plight.

Sure, his rising panic bothers me, but I just want to take the nap I promised myself earlier.

With another slow glance at my charging phone, I step away from the large window. I cross the room and sit on the edge of the bed to better watch James. My head spins from the movement, and it takes a few seconds to right myself.

James turns away from the dresser, hands interlaced behind his head, and looks around the room. Sweat beads on his forehead.

"What's wrong, again?" I ask.

He stares at me, seemingly dumbfounded by my question.

"I can't find the gun," he says.

"The gun?"

This obviously isn't the first time he's explained the problem. It's not entirely my fault I forgot—I think—but a missing *gun* does seem like something I should remember. After all, I've been watching him search the room for it this whole time.

"The one from the Fourth of July?" I ask.

I remember the sound the handgun made as it hit the hardwood after it fell from his pocket. The skittering. The blank look on his face, and the dark shape on the floor in the dimly lit parlor as my mind reeled.

"Yeah. That gun." He notices my frown and sighs. "I left it here, right in the top drawer, but it's not there now."

"Are you sure you left it there?"

I haven't seen the gun. Not when I came looking for James at the end of the rainstorm, and certainly not at any point today.

He groans, gesturing toward the mess of linens on the floor. "I went through every single drawer. And the cops never mentioned my *illegally owned handgun* while drilling into me, so it obviously wasn't in my car or backpack when they took me in. Damn it… I wonder if Ice knew where I was staying. Maybe he came by while I wasn't here? *Fuck.* I'm so stupid—"

I look up from the floor. "Ice knows about this place?"

"Uh…" He blinks, tipping his head. "Yeah. Yeah, he does."

*Oh.* I don't know why I assumed he didn't.

*Well, that's not good.*

I don't particularly care for the thought of Ice running around with a loaded handgun. He's dangerous enough with a knife, and I'm not sure he even knows how to use a gun.

"This sucks," is all I can bring myself to say.

James laughs. Then he runs a hand through his short hair and looks back to the ravaged dresser, with its three empty drawers precariously stacked on top.

"Okay, so…" He lets out a breath and turns to me again. "You don't happen to know where another gun might be, do you? Like at your house? Or somewhere else?"

There is *not* a gun at my house, and I tell him as much. He curses under his breath, massages his temples, and starts pacing.

"Sorry," I mumble.

"It's fine. I should've seen this coming."

"What do you need a gun for, anyway?"

He glances at me for an instant, then looks away again without answering. He steps on the linens as he walks around the room. It bothers me, but I resist the urge to say anything.

After a moment, my head lolls forward, my eyes threatening to close. I lift them up again—both my head and my eyelids—but I'm not sure how much longer I can hold out.

"If you really need one, do you think there's another around here somewhere?" I ask mildly. "This place is massive, y'know, so there might be an old shotgun tucked away in one of those, uh…random storage rooms? Or whatever?"

He stops pacing, his expression thoughtful and brooding. His foot is still planted on one of the linens, and I *hate* it.

"There could be one somewhere," he says.

"There could be."

He glances at the door, his attention lingering there for a moment before he looks back to me. Anxiety creeps into his face as he repeats the cycle of looking between me and the door and the dresser a few times.

Then he asks, "Will you be alright if I step out for a minute?"

I shrug.

What difference does it make if he's here or not? I'll still be tired as hell, and his handgun will still be missing, but who knows. Maybe he will find another gun somewhere. *If he's so convinced he needs one.*

Still, he hesitates before nodding. "Alright. If you don't

mind, I think I'll take a look around."

I nod and fall back onto the bed, my arms splayed out and legs dangling over the edge. The rubber tips of my Converse just touch the floor.

"I'll be right back," he says.

"Okay," I agree, my eyes locked on the ceiling.

"Stay here."

I lift my arm to offer a shaky thumbs-up, as I have absolutely no intention of moving from the bed, and he finally leaves, closing the solid door behind himself. His footsteps retreat down the hallway, fading into nothing, and my eyelids grow heavier. The room is warm and quiet, disturbed only by my own breathing and the soft hum of the mini-fridge.

And I am dead tired.

Yesterday was an unbearably long day. Between Ice and the stupid nightmare that woke me at the crack of dawn, I didn't sleep well last night either.

*Surely, it's fine if I nod off for a few minutes...*

# eleven

It feels like I had just closed my eyes when the soft sound of a heavy door opening rouses me from the verge of sleep. The hinges squeak as it clicks shut again. The thick, cottony veil dulling my senses tells me it's nothing to worry about. It's just James, right? I can ignore the sound—I can keep my eyes closed and slip into a deeper sleep.

I almost oblige. I want to. But the steps on the hardwood are a little too soft. A little too cautious. Something feels off, so I open my eyes to check.

My eyes are open, my vision blurry, but what I see—

*Am I seeing things?*

I am medicated, after all. The Vicodin made me dizzy and tired before. How else could it mess with my head? *Hallucinations?* I blink to clear my vision and fight against the mental fog, but nothing about the room changes.

*He's still there.*

Ice, dark leather jacket and all, stands not far from the bed, scanning the floor with raised eyebrows and a faint smile. Even as he looks up, and our eyes meet, I can't bring myself to do anything but stare back at him.

*Am I dreaming?*

"Oh, sorry," he says, his voice cool and dangerously sweet. "Is this sooner than you were expecting?"

*This is not good. I don't think I'm dreaming.*

I try to move—to stand from the bed—but my body refuses to respond. Both my heart and mind race, fear flaring in my chest at my lack of control. I try to shut the thoughts out. I try to slow down. I try to think rationally, but *it's hard.*

*Why is he here now?*

My eyes flick past him, to the closed door. *Where is James? Is he alright?* While looking around, scanning the room, my attention lands on the black gun in Ice's hand.

I *panic*, and my body suddenly decides to function again.

I leave the bed, but my right leg buckles, sending me straight down. I brace myself for the pain of impact, but I hardly feel my knee or shoulder smack against the hardwood as I land in a heap on the floor.

*I have to get out of here.*

My arms respond just enough to push myself up. I glance at the door again, but Ice stands between me and any chance of escape. Despair trickles in, replacing the initial rush of determination, as I crawl along the floor until I reach a wall to prop myself up against.

"You're cute," he says. He steps closer, leering down at me with a mischievous glint in his eyes. "But why are you so scared? I haven't done anything yet."

*Yet?!*

Then he raises his arm and aims the gun at me.

Eyes locked on the dark muzzle, I press my back into the wall, wishing I could phase through it. Or disappear. Or blink and wake up on the bed and realize this moment was nothing more than a horribly vivid nightmare.

But the gun is still aimed at my head, and Ice flicks a switch on the weapon's side with his thumb—*the safety*. His smirk widens. His finger shifts to hover over the trigger without quite touching it.

"Stop." Mouth dry and chest tight, my protest is weak.

He laughs. Then he switches the safety back on and drops his arm—and the gun with it—to his side.

Tears prick my eyes, and my chin falls to my chest. My numb hand clutches my shirt. I gasp to catch my breath. I struggle to calm myself—to focus on breathing—not caring that I took my eyes off Ice or that my fingers scratch the healing cut beneath the thin fabric.

"Relax, Jayde," he says breezily. "Did you honestly believe I'd shoot you? Just like that?"

*This is unreal.*

I stare at the floor near his feet.

One movement, and he could have killed me. One, tiny movement, *and I would be dead. Just like that.*

He sighs. "No. In truth, I don't care to see you like this."

I look up, glossing right over the gun, to take in his expression. Mild. Calm. Inexplicably soft.

*I hate that he can look at me like that.*

"I wasn't expecting you to come back here together," he says, "but I cannot believe James left you alone. You're so pathetic and defenseless on your own. It's depressing."

*Are you serious?*

I want to scream, but I find myself frozen as he kneels in front of me. He tips his head to one side, watching me with sharp eyes and a curious frown. Grimacing, I tear my eyes away.

"Depressing as it may be, I'm in luck. I'd rather see you than James, and I do have a few questions."

*He wants...to talk?*

I avoid meeting his gaze, certain that whatever I might find there will only frighten me more, but our proximity alone is enough to make me tremble.

*He has James' gun.*

*One, tiny movement, and—*

The gun is still off to one side and pointed toward the floor, but I can't seem to banish the image of a handgun aimed at my head with the safety turned off.

"You mind answering them now?"

I open my mouth to speak without any idea of what I should say, but he stops me by touching a finger to my lips. I'm still trying to keep from looking at him, but he's too close. I can't avoid his shrewd smile.

"There's a catch," he says, resting the handgun's muzzle on the wall inches from my ear. "If I don't like your answers, we're both gonna have a bad time."

*A bad time?*

Finally, I look into his eyes, hoping for some idea of what he means, but there's *nothing*. Trying to read his expression is like staring into a bowl of still water.

"Deal?" he asks.

*Do I have a choice?*

His eyes narrow as he taps the barrel of the gun against the wall in a display of exaggerated impatience. Exaggerated or not, I prickle—reminded of my own fragile mortality—and agree with a frantic nod.

"Good." He flashes a lazy grin. "First question: Were you seriously in love with me before all this?"

My eyes water in frustration as I feel my cheeks heat up. Once again, I search his eyes for any indication of what he wants from me, but his face reveals nothing beyond sick excitement.

*What does he want to hear? What will he do if he doesn't like my answer? What is the truth, anyway?*

Was I *in love* with Ice? Seriously? Maybe, for a while, I did think that. Maybe I thought I was in love, but I'm not sure I know what "love" is anymore. *Still...*

I throw caution to the wind, and I nod.

"That's so funny," he says with an easy laugh.

I bite the inside of my cheek, struggling to remain focused.

"What about now?" A peculiar eagerness creeps into his voice. "If you still like me, you can come back, you know? After all, I'm not mad at you."

"Hell no," I say through my teeth.

He laughs harder, seeming to enjoy himself as though we're having a perfectly normal, friendly conversation. The emotional dissonance leaves a pit in my stomach, so I glance aside to assess the *gun situation* instead.

His grip on the gun is relaxed. As his shoulders bounce with laughter, the tip of the muzzle rattles against the wood molding.

"What a relief," he says, his voice thick with humor. When I look, his grin softens. "I've never cared for romance, but I suppose we both know it wouldn't have worked out between us."

*Ugh. Did you come here just to upset me?*

This sucks, but I might get out unscathed if I keep saying what he wants to hear. I just need to pay attention. I just have to keep a level head—*though, that's easier said than done with a gun held beside it.*

"How's your arm?" he asks with a nod to the arm in question —my left.

"It's fine," I say. "*Thanks.*"

He stares at the black sweatband a second too long. I draw my arms closer to my chest, holding a hand over my wrist. He frowns, his attention flicking back to my face, and his expression darkens.

"Tell me," he says, his voice slightly colder than before. "What do you think of James?"

*Um...*

I check again, but his face, placid and serious, still divulges absolutely nothing meaningful.

*How should I answer?* I don't know James at all. I've hardly spent a full twenty-four hours with the guy.

Does he want the truth even if it's bound to piss him off? Can I tell him that James seems to be doing his best, or does he want me to stroke his ego? To confirm James as the worthless, pathetic loser he believes him to be?

*What the hell does he want from me?*

"Well, I assume you followed him willingly," he says, a hint of tension in his otherwise dry voice. "Is he good to you, at least?"

*Is he good to me? What?*

Of course, I'm here willingly—I'm the one who reached out to James—but I've only been here a couple hours. What the hell does he think I've been doing?

"He's…fine," I mumble. "No complaints, I guess."

Ice watches me with critical eyes that flick between both of mine. He says nothing for an uncomfortably long time, and I worry my answer wasn't vague enough as the handgun drifts closer.

It brushes against my hair. My breath catches in my throat.

*Maybe I should have lied.*

He stares through me a moment longer before refocusing.

Without a word, he glances down and reaches out to touch the River Sapphire with his free hand. My eyes remain locked on his face, his expression full of muted interest but seemingly ignorant of or otherwise unconcerned with my rising anxiety. The pendant lifts as he hooks the thin chain with a finger.

"You still wear this?" he asks. The pendant falls against my skin as he retracts his hand, and his eyes flick up to meet mine. "Isn't it useless?"

I say nothing. I don't have a real answer to give.

Still frowning mildly, he glances away for an instant, sighing as he looks to me again.

"Are you afraid of me?" he asks instead.

"Yes." I struggle to maintain eye contact. "I am afraid of you."

His mouth hitches up on one side. "Oh? Is that so? Is that why you're staying with James now? You think that idiot can protect you?"

*I don't know. I just…*

"Are you hoping he might rescue you a second time?"

*What?*

"I just want you to leave us alone," I say, averting my eyes at the frailty of my voice.

"Us? There's an *us* now, is there?"

As my jaw sets, and I bite my tongue, he laughs.

"You didn't answer my question, Jayde."

His laughter cuts off abruptly, and he repeats the question more seriously. *Do I want James to rescue me?* My heart races at the chill in his voice, but I do feel strangely lucky as he continues watching me, waiting until I recover my senses.

*Do I think James can protect me? Do I want him to find me in this position again? Or confront Ice on my behalf?*

What kind of question is that?

*Ice wants to* kill *James.*

I shake my head. "No."

"Oh?" He smirks again, but he seems vaguely surprised, his eyes sharp and brows furrowed.

I meet his gaze solidly, understanding that I didn't give the answer he expected and not caring as much as I probably should. Then he breaks eye contact and leans closer. His breath warms my ear, and I freeze, every muscle tense.

"Why not?" he asks softly. "You're scared, right? Do you not trust James to help you? Or are you not yet in enough danger?"

I stare past the blond hair tickling my cheek, my vision going glassy. *This isn't fair.* He snuck into the room while I was alone. He threatened me and forced me to play this stupid game, all because he wants another chance to get at James?

*I won't throw him under the bus just to satisfy you.*

As he leans back, he brings the gun to my forehead.

The metal is cool and held steady, right between my eyes. My nails dig into the hardwood floor. I squeeze my eyes shut. I can't move. I can't speak. I can't even breathe.

*This can't be happening. He said—*

*Well, he wouldn't shoot me, would he?*

"Call him here." His voice is low and rough, and, when I don't make a sound, he pushes the gun further, knocking the back of my head against the wall. "Call James."

*No. I won't.*

I don't care what Ice wants. Or what he says. I won't give in so easily this time. I don't think he'll actually do it. Even if I piss him off, I don't think he would shoot me.

*I'm no good to him dead.*

*God, I hope I'm right.*

*Please.*

I force my eyes open. With my head pressed against the wall, held by a gun, I can hardly move. Being under Ice's forceful gaze doesn't help. But I bite my tongue and shake my head anyway.

His expression blanks for an instant, eyes wide like he can't believe I'd blatantly disobey him given the stakes he presented. I called his bluff, and it seems I was right, but his eyes narrow, and he bares his teeth, and my confidence wanes.

The tip of the handgun leaves my forehead and slams against the wall several inches away.

I hear the safety switch off, but I can't bring myself to look. Ice's expression mellows, the line of his mouth softening as he stares at the gun. After a moment of silence, his eyes flick back to my face, and I hold my breath.

"Have it your way, Jayde."

He sneers at me before he pulls the trigger.

My vision goes black as the sound of the blast reverberates through my skull. An awful, metallic ringing fills my ears, the gunshot endlessly echoing inside my head. I raise a hand to cover my left ear, genuinely surprised it's not bleeding.

When my vision clears, I realize Ice is *laughing*—though I can't hear him.

He drops the gun and touches his ear, still laughing. I hear none of it, but he looks hysterical. His usual air of control completely abandoned, he presses his hands to the wall—one on either side of my head—as he struggles to collect himself.

"Are your ears ringing too?" His eyes are wide and bright like an excited child's, and his voice is just audible above the ringing. "So loud! Do you think he heard?"

*I can't believe this!*

I lash out, but Ice catches my arm without effort before I ever manage to strike his obnoxious, smug face. He grins and increases pressure on the tender wound beneath his fingers.

Even as I cry out in alarm, I hardly hear my voice.

"You think he's on his way up now?" he asks.

I scream for him to let go of me, to which he merely tips his head and laughs.

"What?" he asks, quite obviously pretending he can't hear me.

"Let go!"

I tug on my arm, trying to pry it from his grasp, but he has no problem keeping me pinned against the wall and doesn't bat an eyelash when James bursts into the room a moment later. I watch the door ricochet off the wall, but I don't hear the impact.

"Wow." Ice frowns before glancing over his shoulder. "It's rude not to knock."

James hesitates, soaking in the scene laid out before him—me on the floor with my back against the wall and Ice hovering over me, my arm still in his hand. Once he recovers, he bares his teeth and growls something like, *"What are you doing?"* with at least one expletive thrown in.

"What?" Ice calls back, cackling as he finally releases my arm.

I shove both hands against his chest, desperate to put any distance between us, but he doesn't budge. Until James grabs him by the back of his jacket and drags him away by force.

Meeting my gaze for a fleeting instant, he flashes an entirely unconcerned and giddy smile. He then morphs into a cat, easily escaping James' grip, and hops onto the bed. He morphs once again on the other side, no longer wearing the leather jacket.

James glances at me before pursuing Ice.

*Aah— Wait—*

I scramble to stand as James catches up to and tackles Ice, who was still facing the room. Ice's back contacts the large window as James holds him by the shirt collar, pressing him against the glass.

Ice laughs, but he doesn't fight back. He doesn't even try.

Though I can't make out the words through the ringing in

my head, the mockery is clear on his face as he speaks to James before falling back into hysterics. For whatever reason, this seems like exactly what he wanted to get out of coming here.

James cries *"fuck you!"* just loud enough to hear from halfway across the room.

"What?" Ice asks, practically yelling with a hand cupped behind one ear. "Dude, I can't hear a word you're saying!"

James' shoulders shake, but Ice continues laughing even as James slams him against the glass a second time. With a sharp crack, the aged window gives way and shatters. Glass fragments fly everywhere, in every direction, and Ice finally stops laughing. James' grip on his shirt and the heels of his boots are the only things between him and a three-story fall, but his smirk doesn't falter for an instant.

He makes deliberate eye contact with me, his eyes glittering and full of a cryptic curiosity, and he says something—not to me, but to James—though the words are far too soft to hear.

James tenses before releasing his grip on Ice's collar, and Ice falls past the window frame and out of sight.

*Oh.*

Stumbling, I make my way around the bed and skid to a stop beside James, who hasn't moved. From a safe distance, we both peer out the new hole in the wall.

Ice, in his white feline form, gazes up at us from the ground, his fluffy tail thrashing side to side. He looks perfectly fine considering he just fell backward at least thirty feet onto packed gravel.

"Sorry, James, but cats always land on their feet!" With that, he races across the lot and disappears into the trees.

"Damn it," James pants.

He says something else, but it's too quiet, so I shake my head and gesture at the space around my left ear.

"He shot the gun off like *right here*. I can't hear a thing."

The realization horrifies him, and he glances back to the spot Ice had me pinned against the wall. Then he meets my eyes again and repeats his question just loud enough for me to hear.

He asked if I was hurt.

I check my right arm where Ice caught me. The area looks slightly irritated, but the scab wasn't disturbed, and it doesn't hurt. I'm not sure he even grabbed me tight enough to leave another bruise.

"I'm okay."

He sighs in relief, and I notice a wound on his arm. Blood beads around a small shard of yellowed glass embedded just above his elbow.

"It got you, though," I say.

He glances at his arm and sighs again. He removes the half-inch shard and flicks it out the gaping hole that was once a window. Blood oozes from the small puncture.

"Aah—" My hands hover uselessly in the air, resisting the urge to wipe the blood away. "Oh, um… There's a box of band-aids in my bag if you want."

"Nah. I'm good."

He says that, but he's still rightfully agitated as he surveys the bedroom, which is now littered with old linens and a million pieces of broken glass.

I mention the gun and follow as he crosses the room to retrieve it. He picks the black handgun up and stares at it for a second. Then he flicks the safety on and steps away. After he grabs his backpack, I glance back to stare at the small, dark hole in the wall.

*That could have easily been my head.*

*I could have died today.*

"I need to grab a broom," James says in exasperation—and loud enough for me to hear. "You wanna wait here, or—?"

I turn away from the wall. "No. I'll go with you."

I'm still tired, even more than I was before, but I walk out of the room with James, and we make our way down the hall, toward the staircase. It's quiet, the ringing in my head louder than our footsteps on the hardwood.

"Hey," I say. "What did Ice say before he fell?"

He looks at me for a moment. He stops walking, and he opens his mouth as though to speak, but he glances away and shakes his head instead. I can't hear the words when he finally speaks, but I can read his lips well enough.

*"It was nothing. Don't worry about it."*

# twelve

I lift a lacy tablecloth off the floor. I haven't seen any glass on this side of the room, but I shake it out for good measure before folding the delicate fabric and returning it to a drawer. It's been a slow process, my head still full of cotton and an incessant, tinny ringing, but I eventually manage to return the final discarded linens to the dresser.

I think James has been done sweeping up the glass for a while now, but I sit on the edge of the bed to take a break anyway.

My eyes wander over the assortment of items piled near the foot of the bed, left there when James dumped the cardboard box of random stuff taken from his car. Sunlight from the gaping hole in the wall reflects off a few naked CDs and scatters white speckles on the ceiling. A handful of coins in a clear evidence bag. A beat-up BIC pen and a crumpled, half-empty pack of cigarettes.

There's something tremendously sad about it all. It reminds me of sitting in his car during the rainstorm. *And the tired emptiness in his eyes.*

After a moment, my attention falls on James. He's standing near the mini-fridge, holding the box that now contains the remnants of the broken window. He looks around the room, alert and clearly uncomfortable, but we're alone. I'm sure Ice is long gone.

"What's the plan?" I ask.

Turning to face me, he says something. When I remind him I can't hear, he repeats himself louder: "Find a new bedroom."

"A'ight."

I drag myself off the bed and sling my backpack over one shoulder. The bag seems heavier than I remember, but I bundle James' blanket and pillow in my arms too—because the first thing I'm doing once I get into a new room is passing out.

*Sleeping? Is that seriously all I can think about right now?*

It still doesn't feel real.

But I turn toward the window and see the large, empty frame, shards of glass still clinging to the edges. And I look to James and the smeared blood drying on his arm as he picks up his backpack.

*And I picture a gun aimed between my eyes. Ice kneeling far too close. His breath on my ear, taunting me. The uncomfortably cool metal on my forehead.*

I hide my face in the blanket. It carries a scent of dingy sadness and doesn't bring me any comfort.

"You okay?"

He's asked several times now.

I nod and mumble, "Just exhausted," into the fabric.

Obviously, I am in no way okay right now. Judging by the uneasy look James offers when I raise my head, he knows, but he doesn't press the matter. Instead, he looks away and frowns as something dark flashes in his eyes.

He knows I don't want to talk about what Ice did while he was out of the room. He's asked, and I deflected both times. I don't want to think about it, let alone rehash the details to someone else. He doesn't need to know exactly what led up to Ice firing a gun inches from my head. He saw the hole in the wall—the charring and black residue left behind on the wood and peeling wallpaper—and he saw where I was sat on the floor moments after the gun was fired. I'm sure he can piece it together well enough himself.

I don't want to talk about it or how I feel about it. I don't know how I feel about anything right now. Maybe I am just exhausted.

*Maybe I do need a nap.*

"Let's go," he says.

He leaves the bedroom, and I follow, trailing slightly behind until we end up on the first floor. James continues through the parlor toward the vestibule to find a place for the box of broken glass while I wander down a nearby hallway to find a new room for us to hunker down in. Having no idea what's down here, I open doors at random.

A small, empty room with dust motes hanging in the air. A bathroom with a questionably installed tub-shower combo. A room full of old furniture covered in white sheets turned grey by the dust settled on them.

*The bathroom was a decent find, but this is kind of creepy.*

I close the door and move onto the next one, which opens into a dusty room that may have once been a bedroom. The room has a mattress on the floor—with no frame, box-spring, or bedding in sight—an antique dressing table, and an armchair that looks terribly uncomfortable.

I check the last two doors, but there's nothing better, so I return to the single...*bedroom* I found and stand in the doorway.

The light turns on when I flip the switch, but the yellow lighting doesn't make the room any less sad or dusty. The dressing table's mirror is covered in permanent marker graffiti, the single window is small and broken and barred by two wooden boards, and there might be a spider living in the huge cobweb in one corner of the ceiling. But the doorknob lock works, which is... something.

*This might be the best option for now.*

I jump as I notice James in my periphery, hardly a foot away. *I couldn't hear his footsteps at all.* He apologizes and stops beside me in front of the open door.

I laugh, certain I still look skittish, and point into the room. "Will this work?"

"I guess," he says through a grimace.

I step inside. It might be as hot in here as it is outside, and the air is stale, but I'm not in the mood to keep searching. I drop the bedding and my backpack onto the mattress, which looks old but *adequate* and unstained, at least. Then I drop to sit in the middle of it. It squeaks loud enough to hear over the ringing in my ears.

*This is fine.*

I look up from my spot very near the floor to find James looking quite uncomfortable as he steps into the room. He apologizes again, though I'm not sure what for, and we argue back and forth for a few minutes until he agrees to leave me here while he grabs the rest of his stuff from the third floor.

It's not like I want to be left alone, but I don't care what he has to say about it. I am not climbing up and down those stairs again.

He kicks his backpack—which I'm pretty sure still has a loaded gun inside—underneath the dressing table before he leaves the room.

A ringing silence and the awareness of being alone overtake my senses. A small, creeping paranoia comes with it, and I turn away from the door to look up at the room's small window.

*Ice was just here.*

*Aah… I hate thinking that.*

I heft my useless body off the ground and move closer to get a better look.

This window is far smaller than the one in the room upstairs. The glass is indeed broken, but the empty frame is blocked off by two solid wood boards, nailed to the wall on each side. I peek through the gap between the boards. I can't see the gravel road leading back to town from this side of the house. Just a gnarled willow tree, the remnants of what might have once been a garden fifty years ago, and an ocean of trees in the distance.

Stepping back, I tug on the lower board with both hands. I'm weak and very tired, but the attachment seems secure enough— the board does not budge. Satisfied as I can be, I pick a splinter out of my fingertip, return to the mattress, and sit cross-legged in the middle of it.

The plan is to wait for James to get back before taking my nap, so I just watch the door. I listen carefully, but the ringing in my left ear is louder than most anything else.

I watch the door.

My eyelids droop, and my head dips forward, snapping up again as I catch myself. The door is blurry. I rub my eyes, and the image clears. I don't really want to fall asleep yet. Falling asleep while alone backfired on me earlier, but *god, I am so tired.*

Another minute passes, and I wonder what the hell is taking James so long, and I give up on waiting.

I toss the pillow, clean side up, to one end of the bed and fall onto my left side. A puff of dust surrounds me. I sneeze, holding both hands over my mouth until the cloud dissipates.

Then I continue watching the door. I stare at the doorknob, hoping my right ear is functional enough to hear if someone approaches the room. I watch. I listen. I squint. My eyes close, but I open them again. I look away from the door and study my hands instead. The stitches on my palm and the crusty scab around them. The sweatband on my wrist, the edge of a brown napkin poking out from underneath.

I should leave it exposed to air, or at least put new band-aids on, but... *Ugh.*

I look back to the door.

*God, this sucks.*

# thirteen

I don't remember falling asleep, but I must have. Because I wake up. The air feels cool on my face, and my head is clear, but I still hear a faint ringing, and my body aches.

I open my eyes.

The room is lit only by a crack of light streaming in from outside. I roll over to find James asleep in the armchair, which he must have moved closer to the door. He's still wearing the clothes he wore when we left the police station, and the black handgun rests in his lap, partially covered by one hand.

*Ugh.* He has a valid reason to be paranoid, but I was hoping I wouldn't have to see the gun again.

*What time is it, anyway?*

I sit up, groaning as my shoulder and hip twinge with a dull pain. My body has had more than enough over the past few days. I am *ready* to rest. I drag my backpack into my lap and unzip the front pocket, but my hand freezes above the pill bottles inside. Two orange and one white.

*Should I take Vicodin or ibuprofen?*

After yesterday, I don't trust the prescription meds. It dulls the pain to near-nothing, but it makes me tired and careless, unable to avoid the call of sleep. Clocking out might be fine at night, but it's not great during the day.

So I grab the white bottle before dragging myself off the low mattress and to my feet.

*Aah...*

Every muscle that hit the ground when I fell yesterday makes itself known at once. The pulsing in my side. The itching of the healing scabs. I check the stitches on my palm, but they seem fine. My left arm seems fine. My side seems fine. Nothing unusual and no sign of infection. I don't see any new bruises either, which is surprising considering how badly my shoulder and hip hurt.

Crossing the room is annoying, but I make it to where the humming mini-fridge is set up beneath the barred window, and I peek outside. It's light, the sky above the trees a pale blue. A cool breeze blows through the cracks.

*How early is it?*

I glance over my shoulder. James is still passed out in the armchair, so I refocus on the mini-fridge and pull the door open.

It's almost empty, the only contents being two unopened sodas, a few slices of American cheese, and one Chinese takeout box. *James must have eaten his leftovers last night.* To my surprise, the open can I filled with water is inside too and still contains some liquid.

I remove the takeout and can of water, and I swallow three ibuprofen tablets before returning to the mattress. I drop the pill bottle into my bag and stand around trying to figure out how to sit down without hurting myself. The only solution is to get it over with, knowing it will be uncomfortable.

*And, of course, it is uncomfortable.*

I sit with my back against the wall for a moment, breathing through the wave of pain. Then I set the takeout aside and slap new band-aids on my wrist.

With absolutely nothing else to do, I *finally* slip my phone from my pocket. I haven't powered it on yet. I know I should. I should message Rose to let her know I'm alright and have my phone back, but I don't know what else I can say to her. She thinks I'm home. Should I maintain the ruse? Tell her I'm staying somewhere else? *Where?* Should I mention James?

*Aah…*

I hold the power button until the screen lights up. It's 7:23AM, and I have more notifications than I expected.

Ice texted last night. I don't open the app, but the message displays on my lock screen, so I can't avoid it:

**Ice Monroe**          Yesterday, 8:38PM
Thanks for the laugh. We should do it again sometime.

I swipe to delete the notification. I also delete the one alerting me to a missed call from a few days ago.

The remaining notifications not from random apps are from Rose. A handful of missed calls going back to the day I found myself in the hospital. The most recent is from the day after, before I told her my phone broke—she must have believed me. I also have a good dozen text messages and a few more recent FaceSpace messenger notifications. Still nothing from Night, though.

*Damn it.*

I check the texts. They start as casual questions that slowly turned to worry and panic the longer I didn't respond, followed by a few along the lines of, *"Do you have your phone back yet?"*

Her concern is strangely comforting, but it also fills me with guilt I know I can't resolve without breaking the one rule I can't bring myself to break right now.

Maybe that's why I don't open FaceSpace.

With a sigh, I set my phone down, pick up the takeout box, and take a bite, hoping the cold pan-fried noodles will settle the pit in my stomach.

* * * * *

James wakes up just after 9AM.

When I apologize for falling asleep, he says it's fine. I deserve the rest after what I've been through. Whatever. I still feel bad—in part because I'm stuck watching him eat two slices of American cheese and a melted granola bar for breakfast.

When he's done, he stashes the handgun in his backpack, and we head upstairs to patch the broken window.

From where I sit on the bed, which I much prefer over the floor mattress in the new bedroom, I watch James work. He uses sheets of cardboard taken from the vestibule he called a *mudroom*, attaching them to each other and the wall using a roll of duct tape and a staple gun from a closet on the second floor.

He seems focused, but I'm not entirely sure why he wants to patch the window now. The weather should stay dry for the foreseeable future, and it's the third floor, so it's not like anyone could use it to break in.

Maybe he's just trying to distract himself, wanting something to do even if it's relatively unimportant.

I guess I understand, considering I've spent most of the morning playing a stupid idle game on my phone. Matching colorful shapes and being rewarded with snappy musical jingles over and over and over is refreshingly mind-numbing.

After working on the window for a good half hour, James stops and turns away with his hands on his hips. The window is not completely covered with cardboard, but he doesn't seem frustrated with his progress.

"How's it going?" I ask.

For a moment, he stares at me like he has absolutely no idea what I'm still doing here. But he laughs, looking more embarrassed than confused.

"It's going fine," he says. "It's just getting hot."

*That's fair.*

"Are you hungry?" I ask. "Does anyone in town deliver all the way out here?"

He laughs more genuinely. "I know a pizza place that does. DoorDash might too, but it gets pricey."

"Maybe we should go shopping."

I suggested it, but I'm suddenly not sure I feel up to wandering around a grocery store for any length of time. Just climbing the stairs to the third floor left me winded.

I don't hear whatever James says in response—if he said anything at all—but he crosses the room and sits a few feet away on the edge of the bed. I watch him carefully, curious again. He seems uncomfortable around me, but he still hasn't asked me to leave.

"Are *you* hungry?" he asks.

"I ate when I woke up."

He nods, pulls his phone from his pocket, and stares at the screen. His expression shifts, somehow making him look even more uncomfortable, and he starts typing. The phone's cracked screen makes it impossible to snoop from this angle, but he might be texting. When he's done, he falls back onto the bed with a groan, his face covered by his arms.

"Hey," I say. His arm shifts to reveal one amber eye, no longer bruised or bloodshot. "I know you got kicked out of your dad's house or whatever, but why come here instead of literally anywhere else? Don't you have friends you could stay with?"

His eye widens. Then he sits up. As he worries the phone in his hands, he smiles, but his expression carries unease.

"Oh, well, I just…didn't want to bother anyone with the stupid problems I've been dealing with lately." His voice is soft, barely loud enough to piece together. He clears his throat before glancing at me. "Why?"

"Ah… I mean, it seems like you hate it here."

"Does it?" He looks around as though seeing the room clearly for the first time. "I came here a lot as a kid—just to goof off when I had nothing better to do, you know? No one lived here back then either, but it wasn't always this trashed. Maybe that's what sucks about it now."

I try to imagine the property in a lesser state of disrepair, with paint not peeling, windows not broken, and the surrounding area less barren, but it's a real challenge.

"Did you board up the windows downstairs too?"

"Some of them, sure." He laughs, scratching the back of his neck. "I may have broken a couple too—before this one, I mean. By accident, mostly, or to get inside when the doors were locked."

"Your family owns the place, right?" He nods, seemingly wary, but I laugh, and he relaxes again. "Do you hope to fix it up and make it livable again someday?"

He stares at me, his expression rather blank. Then, frowning, he glances away.

"Honestly, I've never thought about it. I don't hate this place —it's not like that, really—but some things have happened… Ah…" He laughs uneasily. "I guess what I mean is: I'm not a kid anymore, and, as an adult, I never come here for good reasons."

He only sees Reid Manor as a place to crash when he has nowhere else to go? That does suck, and I'm sure this whole mess with me and Ice has only worsened the negative association.

"Sorry."

He waves a hand. "It's fine. Nothing you should worry about, anyway."

As he stands and walks back to the window, I remember. The look on his face the day before Ice attacked me. The emptiness in his eyes just before he said, "*I think I'm in love with you.*"

*Did he mean that?*

He never gave me a straight answer when I asked before. He didn't want to talk about it, like he thinks his feelings don't matter at all. But, if it was even partially true then, how does he feel now?

# fourteen

James finishes patching the window. It's not perfect, but it'll keep the birds out. After that, he orders pizza—because, obviously, he was hungry.

Since then, we've been sitting in the first-floor parlor, trying not to melt in the heat. It's almost a hundred degrees outside now. Though, Reid Manor has decent insulation considering how old and wrecked it is. It actually feels cooler down here than it did up on the third floor.

I'm busy trying to relax and move as little as possible, just lying on my stomach on the chaise and watching a nature documentary on my phone, when a notification pops up on the screen.

A FaceSpace message. From Rose.

While trying to dismiss the banner, I accidentally tap it and launch the messenger app. I gasp, dismayed, as I've been avoiding this all day.

> **Rose:** Jayyy, I saw you read my texts. You
> have your new phone now?

"You okay?" James asks from his spot in the armchair halfway across the room.

"Yeah, it's just—"

*Aah— She's already typing.*

> **Rose:** JAYDE
>
> **Rose:** I KNOW YOURE THERE
>
> **Rose:** ANSWER ME!! (⩾ᗣ⩽)

I groan, roll onto my back, and draw the phone to my chest.

"You sure you're alright?"

"Yeah..." I drag myself up to sit. "It's just my roommate."

"Roommate? You have a roommate?"

"Well..." I blink. *Haven't I mentioned her already?* "Yeah, I do, but she's been out of town since the first week of June."

He leaves the armchair and crosses the room. When he stops beside the chaise, I scroll up in the conversation to show off the barrage of messages I missed.

"I told her my phone broke—since I left it in your car—but we haven't talked much since." I laugh despite myself and drop my hands into my lap. "Honestly, I have no idea what to say to her."

James frowns. "She's human."

"Yeah. She's human, but she's also my best friend. What am I supposed to do?"

"Talk to her," he says slowly.

*Right.*

Giving up, I look at my phone, and I type.

> **Me:** Yeah, I just got it back. Sorry.

"Your friend doesn't know about any of this, does she?"

I laugh again. "Are you kidding? I can't tell her anything. She thinks I'm perfectly fine—that I'm still at home."

"Right…"

My phone goes off as Rose responds with a call rather than a text. Suppressing a sigh, I offer James a weak smile. He frowns and leaves the room unprompted, disappearing further into the house, before I answer the phone.

"Hey," I say, trying to sound normal.

"Jayde," she whines. "I've missed your voice. You haven't been ignoring me on purpose, have you?"

"I have not been ignoring you. I just suck at checking FaceSpace on my laptop, I guess."

"But you have your phone back now?"

"Obviously."

She laughs. "You're not still with Ice, are you?"

"No. I am not with Ice. He's old news, thanks."

"Old news?" she asks, intrigued. "Does this have anything to do with the other guy? What was his name, again? Um… Don't tell me— Oh! It was James, right?"

*James.*

I cough. "Literally all he did was give me a ride home."

"Mm-hm. Okay. Anyway, how have you been?"

*Um…* "I've been alright. Bored. Hot—now that the storm is over, I mean. Nothing exciting, you know?"

"You haven't done anything?" she asks.

"Without my phone? Or you?"

She laughs. "That's fair."

"Anyway, I should go."

"Are you busy?"

"Busy?" My teeth click together, and I glance at the empty double door frame James left through. "Not really, but I was just about to go grocery shopping."

*I think it's partially true, anyway.*

She sighs, "Oh, alright. Just so you know, I shouldn't be gone much longer. Like two or three weeks, tops."

"That's great. I can't wait for you to get back."

*Do I even mean that at this point?* It's not as though her return will restore any sense of normalcy. If anything, it'll only cause a whole new mess of problems.

Though, it's not a lie to say I miss her.

I do miss Rose—her and that sense of normalcy. Terribly.

"You'll have to introduce me to your new friend when I get back," she says, her voice playful.

"Which friend? Oh— James?"

"How many other friends do you have?"

*Ha. Ha.*

"Well, um…" I look around the room. I'm not sure exactly where James went or if he can hear me, but I don't want to seem suspicious, so I continue at a normal volume. "I wouldn't say we're friends, exactly."

But Rose laughs, her voice light and casual. "You never did send me a picture of Ice, you know? Think I can snag one of this James character instead? Just as confirmation that this one exists."

"They both exist," I say, not bothering to mask my disappointment. "But, if I happen to see James again, I'll see what I can do."

"Awesome." She sounds genuinely pleased, which is a bit frustrating. "Well, I'm glad to hear you're doing alright. I was starting to think you were in trouble."

*Trouble?*

"Yeah," I agree slowly. "Sorry about that."

"But you said you gotta get going, right? Got a bus to catch or whatever—it comes soon, doesn't it? I'll talk to you later, Jay."

"Yeah. Bye."

"Love you!"

I hang up and stare at my phone screen for a long moment before looking toward the door frame again. He's somewhere back there, but I can't imagine he'd go far.

*Rose will be home in a few weeks.*

Do I want to stay at Reid Manor that long? It seems like me being here is nothing but trouble for James, and Ice knows we're here now, so it's not even safe. James is tolerable, and I still hate the idea of being alone, but I don't know what to think about any of this.

*James. Ice. The manor house.*

I drag myself out of the chaise, wishing I'd thought to bring the ibuprofen with me when I left the bedroom. Shaking off my discomfort and trying to ignore the faint ringing in my ear, I venture further into the house.

I find James quickly, sitting against the wall in the hallway. He's wearing his over-the-ear headphones, staring at his phone, and finishing off a slice of leftover pizza. He doesn't look up as I approach, so I guess he wasn't eavesdropping after all.

*Hm.*

Stopping a foot away, I carefully slide down the wall until I'm sat beside him on the floor. Only then does he offer me a glance and shift one side of the headphones off his ear.

"So, how'd it go?"

I sigh, my shoulders falling—and twinging painfully. "She bought my story, I guess, but she's coming back sometime in the next few weeks. I have no idea what I'll do then."

"I'm sure you'll figure something out."

I frown. Severely.

He watches me for a moment. Then he drops the headphones to hang around his neck. "Does your friend know about me?"

"Sort of." I glance at the band-aids on my wrist. "She thinks I'm home alone right now, but I did mention you before—I told her you gave me a ride after I picked up my stuff from Ice's house."

*The stuff I still don't have.*

"You seriously haven't told her anything?" he asks.

"I already told you—" I sigh again. "She's human. How can I tell her? It's bad enough she knows I was with Ice for so long."

He glances away. "Never mind. I get it."

I'm sure he does.

After all, he's only here because he doesn't want to bother anyone with whatever personal problems he's dealing with. I'm doing the same by not telling Rose what happened. It's so much easier if she thinks I broke up with Ice and it's no more complicated than that. *Isn't that awful?*

"You still want to stay after what happened yesterday?"

The question surprises me. After yesterday, I never seriously considered there was another option, but would it be better if we split up? If I went home and left him to do...whatever he needs to do?

It's weird thinking about our situation like that, but it doesn't matter. Ice has easy access to the cottage too. He could...break a window and climb right in. I wouldn't be any better off there—and certainly not better off alone.

When I look again, James is watching me, wary and frowning. His eyes search my face, but I don't know what he's looking for.

"If you don't mind," I say. He doesn't respond, which makes me nervous, so I keep talking, "I don't feel safe at home, and I don't know anyone who can help me with this right now, or anywhere else I can go, so..."

"Hey, no. Of course I want to help you," he says before freezing and glancing away, his ears red. "To be honest, I don't wanna be alone right now either—what with Ice having it out for me and all, you know?"

*Ah...* "You do care about me."

He stares at the floor, his jaw set, lips pursed, and brows furrowed. Saying nothing, he scratches the small scab on his arm where the window glass pricked him yesterday.

"You didn't say that just to get my attention, did you?"

Finally, he looks up. His expression is uneasy—pained and tired and made worse when he flashes a tight smile.

"Not exactly," he agrees.

"Oh. I thought—" *What did I think?* I pause, and he looks to me again, as though afraid of what I'll say. As though I put any actual thought into it. "Well, I guess I kinda thought you didn't want me around."

"Ah—" His phone slips from his hand and clatters onto the hardwood. "That's not…"

His entire face now flushed red, he averts his gaze, picks up his phone, and stares pointedly at the screen.

*Yikes.*

I look at my phone too. I sift through my email inbox, deleting the spam I received while the phone was dead, and imagine that the ringing in my left ear is the sound of dust motes floating in the air.

"Hey," he says, breaking the long, awkward silence. "What do you think of me, anyway?"

*What do you think of James?*

Slowly, I look up from my phone. His eyes are guarded, but I get the feeling he'd believe just about anything. I could say he doesn't stand a chance—I'm only here because I don't want to be alone. But, at this point, I don't know if that's true. Even if, maybe, I am taking advantage of his generosity, I do feel bad for him.

When I don't say anything, his eyes grow wide, and frustration creeps into them.

"Don't you blame me for what Ice did?" he asks.

"No."

"No?"

*What?* He's surprised I don't think Ice pulling a knife on me out of literally nowhere was his fault?

"No," I say more firmly.

He leans back against the wall. "Huh."

"You didn't do anything wrong," I mutter. "You tried to talk me into going straight home, and I didn't listen. So, no, I don't blame you for what happened."

If anything, it's my fault for not putting my foot down and going home immediately after Ice rejected me. Or for not thinking critically about any of the numerous red flags before that. *God... I can't believe I was such an idiot the past couple months.*

"You're not mad?" he asks.

"At you? No." I pause. "Well, maybe I was upset that you told the police you attacked me, but I understand why you did it."

He sighs. "I'm sorry. I...shouldn't have yelled at you."

"It's fine. I'm over it. Besides, we have more important things to worry about now, right?"

For a moment, he doesn't say anything. Then the ghost of a smile crosses his face before he glances away and scratches his arm again.

"Honestly," he says, "seeing you when I got out was...a relief. I dunno. I wasn't expecting it, I guess. I thought you'd hate me for what I said. Or for letting you go into Ice's house alone. Or for the shit I pulled on the Fourth of July. Or something. Anything."

"I don't hate you."

"Maybe you should," he says under his breath.

I frown. "Are you sure you don't mind me being here? I can go if you want. I'd probably be fine at home. I moved the spare key inside before I left, so..."

"No." He sets his phone down and holds his head in his hands. "Don't leave. You can stay. I don't mind. Seriously. It's just— I keep thinking it might have gone differently if I went in with you. Even if it pissed Ice off. Even if he—"

*If he what? Attacked you instead? Because that definitely wouldn't have helped me.*

"It's fine," I groan. "You were doing exactly what I asked you to do, and there's nothing we can do about it now. You can't change what happened. I'm just glad we're both okay."

He lowers his hands, but he doesn't look at me. He just stares at the floor with a tense frown and glassy eyes.

"You're weird, alright?" I say. "I don't understand you at all. But, after everything I've seen this week, I don't think you're a bad guy. I don't think you're what Ice says you are—or what you say you are. I want to trust you, and I think you deserve a second chance."

"A second chance?" he breathes before looking up.

I glance aside. "Yeah. So…get over yourself. Or whatever."

He almost laughs. Almost.

# fifteen

James recovers from his melancholy, I take a double dose of ibuprofen, and we eat the rest of the leftover pizza. Then it's time for grocery shopping.

We don't even go to Bargain Shop, but I still have flashbacks as we walk down the brightly colored snack aisle. I'm itchy as hell, and it feels like everyone is staring at me, somehow able to see the wounds beneath my flannel, but I try to focus on helping James pick out food.

He lists off several cheap items we've already collected: sandwich ingredients, sugary breakfast cereal, a half-gallon of milk, granola bars, Nacho Cheese Doritos, whatever. Nothing especially nutritious, but I threw in a few apples and a carton of raspberries because I haven't eaten fresh fruit since I left the Monroe house.

"Does that seem like enough for a few days?" he asks.

"It's better than what you had before—which was basically nothing."

He ignores me. "What do you drink? Soda? Juice? Water?"

"Water is fine."

He drops a gallon of filtered spring water into the shopping cart, stirring up renewed concern that the manor's tap water may not be safe to drink. The building is at least a hundred years old. Maybe it has lead pipes or something. I could ask, but I'm not sure I want to know.

"How long do you plan to stay at Reid Manor, anyway?" I ask instead.

"You realize I don't want to be stuck there any more than you do, right?" He frowns, setting a case of Mountain Breeze and a six-pack of store-brand energy drinks into the cart. "But I can't think of a better option. Can you?"

"No."

I hug my arm, wincing as fabric rubs against the stitches on my side. James notices, flashing a look of concern, but I wave it off—grimacing again as my shoulder twinges—and assure him I'm fine.

This is nothing I can't handle.

"We can worry about where you're staying once you're feeling better," he says, glancing around as we enter the next aisle. "For now, try to take it easy. Deal?"

"Sure."

*Oh. Right.*

"Hey, um—" I hesitate as James turns, seemingly surprised at being addressed directly. "I forgot to pack shampoo or anything, so I was hoping to pick some up while we're here."

He blinks. "Oh. Yeah. Of course."

We grab a few more groceries on our way to the health and beauty aisle. I look over the shelving. There aren't a lot of options, so I opt for a 3-in-1 shampoo, conditioner, body wash in *Original*

*Scent*—whatever that means. I'm sure it'll be fine.

I look up from the vague blurb on the back of the bottle and notice James browsing the small selection of deodorant further down the aisle. He drops something into the cart as I approach with my shampoo. Our eyes meet before I drop the bottle in.

Then I glance down—out of curiosity more than anything.

*AXE Gold, Dark Vanilla*

My eyes flick up again, but James pointedly avoids meeting my gaze, his ears a bit pink. As though he thinks I care he's finally decided to invest in deodorant.

"Is that everything?" he asks.

"I think so."

We make our way to the front of the store, check out, and head back to the car, where I immediately peel my flannel off and roll the window down. He apologizes for the broken AC as we pull out of the parking lot.

After that, the ride is quiet.

I look over my arms, at the scabs and yellowing bruises. At the stitches on my palm, and the band-aids on my wrist. I really should take them off, but I hate thinking about it.

The car turns down the long, winding road toward Reid Manor. The pavement gives way to gravel.

It's still quiet, so I glance at James. His eyes are locked on the road. Sweat beads on his forehead. Even while driving, he looks unreasonably tense.

He seems like a decent person—I meant what I said earlier—but neither of us have any idea what we're doing. The situation is complicated. Ice's motives beyond making James pay for whatever perceived injustice he committed remain a mystery, I'm injured, and we're not doing *anything*. It almost feels like we're sitting around and playing house, just waiting for him to show up again.

I hate it.

*And it's still quiet now that we're back.*

Once out of the car, I break the silence by asking James if he wants help carrying everything inside. He looks at me for half a second before shaking his head and taking his backpack and all four brand-new reusable grocery bags himself.

*Whatever.*

I don't argue, and I trail after him, carrying only my purse and flannel shirt.

"I'm curious about the mini-fridge," I say. "Why don't you just use the kitchen? The house has one, right?"

"I mean, yeah—it has a kitchen—but it's pretty bare-bones, and the stove doesn't work right anymore. That might be my bad, in part—did you know dust is extremely flammable?" He laughs. "Anyway, I picked up the mini-fridge a few weeks ago and haven't bothered with the kitchen since."

"Ah."

"Why?" he asks, his voice dry. "You not excited to live off a diet of sandwiches and Lucky Charms?"

"Not particularly."

Expression mellowing, he glances away. "Hey, I'll, um... I'll think about what you said about finding another place."

"It has nothing to do with the kitchen," I assure him with a laugh, holding one of the heavy doors open so he can step inside. "I'm just giving you a hard time. I'm a college student, so I'm used to eating cheap."

"Oh, right," he says, suddenly flustered.

*We don't know anything about each other, do we?*

"Do you go to school?" I ask.

"No." He flashes a trite smile. "I'm the designated family disappointment. Why bother furthering my education when no one expects anything of me in the first place?"

*Oof.*

"Well, what do *you* want to do?"

He says nothing. I open the bedroom door and step inside, watching carefully as he enters behind me, but his expression is surprisingly neutral.

I frown. "Any goals? Plans? Aspirations?"

"I wasn't planning on doing much of anything," he says, his voice mild. He drops his backpack, crosses the room, and sets the grocery bags beside the mini-fridge before turning to cast a cryptic look my way. "This is gonna sound weird, but this is a nice change of pace. Even if Ice lost his damn mind, I got arrested, and you still think I'm a creep."

"I don't think you're a creep."

I toss my things onto the mattress and cross my arms, but he laughs—his tone a little uneasy—before kneeling in front of the fridge to put the groceries away.

"I'm messing with you," he says. "But you did call me weird earlier."

"That is true. You are pretty weird."

Not wanting to drop my broken body all the way to the mattress on the floor, I take the armchair. It is…as uncomfortable as it looks. The old foam padding is thin and firm, and the fabric sheds small, silvery particles onto everything that touches it—including my skin.

*Ew.*

"How long do you plan on sleeping in a chair?" I ask. "It can't be good for your back." *Or your neck, considering the way you sleep in them.*

"Where else would I sleep?" he asks, his soft voice just audible over the faint ringing in my ear.

"I don't know, but I feel bad for you. When's the last time you even slept in a real bed?"

"The bed in my jail cell wasn't the worst."

*Why would you even joke about that?*

My eyes flick down. At my lap. At my hand. At the band-aids.

He has a point, though. Unless he sleeps in a different room, drags a mattress downstairs by himself, or I offer to switch places with him, he's more or less limited to sleeping in the chair or on the floor.

*Hm...*

I shared a bed with Ice for a while, but he was always in feline form. James is defective. He can't just turn into a cat to make it less awkward. The mattress looks to be a full—or a queen, maybe—so it's not like it's small, but I'm not keen on sharing it with an actual person, let alone someone I hardly know who admitted to having repressed feelings for me.

*That's a bit much right now.*

But it's not like I can offer to sleep in the chair for a night. If I tried, I'm sure I'd wake up with aches and pains I didn't know were possible.

Still, he's being *too* nice. Staying in the same room solely for peace of mind despite the uncomfortable sleeping arrangements? I haven't done much of anything besides complain, but he doesn't seem to mind. It's so frustrating. I have to do something to make it up to him.

"If you want, I'll share the mattress with you."

"Whaaat?"

He laughs and stands, having finished sorting the groceries. When he turns to face me, he's holding the bottle of shampoo I bought. I stare back at him, more nervous to hear his answer than I should be.

"Nah," he says slowly, his frown growing more muted. "That'd be weird, right?"

*Figured he'd say that.* Well, at least I offered. He turned me down, so I have no reason to feel bad about it anymore. He can sleep wherever he wants. It's not my problem.

He tips his head, seemingly puzzled. "You know you don't owe me anything, right?"

*What is that supposed to mean?*

"Never mind," I say with a sigh. "But, for what it's worth, I feel like I do."

"You don't. Trust me."

He looks away, tapping his knuckles against the side of the shampoo bottle and oozing a suspicious, vague energy like the vibe he gave off when I sought him out during the rainstorm.

"Why not?" I ask.

He stares me down for a moment before bursting into nervous

laughter and tossing the bottle onto the mattress. "It's nothing," he says, running a hand over his messy hair. "Jeez. Don't look at me like that."

"I just don't get you at all," I groan, leaning further back into the chair.

"Don't worry about me."

I stare at the ceiling. The cobweb in the corner, a large cellar spider clearly visible inside.

*Don't worry, huh?*

When I straighten up again, James is peering through the crack between the boards over the window, his back to me and one hand with faintly scarred knuckles pressed to the wood. He jiggles the lower board—the same thing I did when I first looked over the room—but it doesn't budge for him either. Then he steps back, and my eyes dart down.

I carefully peel the band-aids off my wrist and stare at the heart underneath. It's scabbing over now. The jagged line on my forearm is healing too, the row of stitches where Ice's fingernails dug in and worsened the wound.

*He wants to kill James?*

Did he mean that, or was it another thing he said to upset me? If Ice made a serious attempt on James' life—more than the screwing around he's done so far—could anyone stop him? I'm human. I'm weak, and, even if I weren't recovering from my own injuries, I sure as hell wouldn't be able to help.

*And James is…*

I look up from my arm. He's turned away from the window and watching me with an unsettled wariness, chewing the tiny scab on his bottom lip.

*Give me one good reason why I shouldn't worry about you.*

I stop myself from asking just as my mouth opens. Instead, I ask why he's so concerned about me in the first place. I'm not special—just some random human girl, right?—so it's another thing I don't understand.

He walks closer, stopping only a couple feet away from the chair, and tips his head with his arms folded over his chest.

"What do you mean?" he asks.

*Oh, how should I word this?*

"Why risk getting hurt or going to prison? You didn't even care when the police showed up at the hospital. You didn't think about yourself at all—just what might help me. And I don't get it. I don't get *you*."

He stares at me. Pensive, a little uncomfortable. He scratches the pink hatching on his cheek. Then he sighs.

"I know it sounds crazy," he says, "but I— At this point, I'd probably die for you, Jayde."

*What?*

"Why? You hardly know me."

"If you somehow haven't figured it out by now, I don't have a lot going for me." He smiles, but his eyes are downcast, and he glances away. "You might think I saved your life, but, nah… To me, it feels more like you saved mine."

I frown.

Ice said he doesn't want to kill me. *I'm no good to him dead.* He just wants to hurt James because I talked to him—because he told me what Ice said, and I listened, or whatever the problem is in his mind. He's only hurting me to get to James.

Surely, he realizes that?

"What do you mean?" I ask, itching my hand. "You know, I told Ice I ran into you at the mall. You said he harassed you over that, right? I've done nothing but cause trouble for you."

"Trouble?" Another laugh, hollow and bitter.

My fingers freeze over my injured palm as James steps closer. When I look up, his eyes burn with an emotion I can't quite recognize. Deep and murky, and honestly a little upsetting, but carrying a strange warmth his laugh didn't.

"Listen," he says, his hands balling into loose fists at his sides. "I've spent my whole life getting into trouble. I'm used to trouble. Nothing ever goes right for me. I screw up everything I try to do, and I don't get along with most people, but you're one of the first to actually listen to me—and I mean *really* listen. You don't pity me because I'm different. You don't treat me like I'm less than everyone else. Or try to compensate just to make me feel better. I mean, you're human. You obviously don't care if I'm defective."

I frown more severely.

His eyes flick away, as though something he said startled him. Then he steps back from the chair, putting more distance between us again.

"Anyway," he mumbles, "I feel like maybe there's something to look forward to now. Helping you out. Or getting rid of Ice. I dunno. I just feel like there's a bit of hope, I guess, and it's been a while since I felt anything like that—since I felt anything... *good*. You know?"

"James..."

Nothing about this makes him any easier to understand, and I don't know how to respond. I can't tell whether he's being serious or melodramatic even as his cheeks flush, and he avoids catching my eye directly.

Confused, and inexplicably frustrated, I return to messing with the stitches on my hand.

"It's like I said earlier: The more time I spend with you, the worse these stupid feelings get." He scratches his cheek before looking at me again. "I was hoping it would go away—I thought it would be easier to hate you like I did before—but I don't actually *want* to hate you."

"I guess that's good for me," I mutter.

He smiles. "It's fine if you don't feel the same way. You don't have to like me. You don't have to trust me. I'm serious; it's fine. I won't be upset, and I'll help you anyway. And…what I said at the station the other day… I'm sorry. I didn't mean it. Any of it. You will never understand how grateful I am that you came out here looking for me. After that, I would do anything for you."

*It all comes back to that, doesn't it? To the rainstorm? The driver's license he left behind? And the empty look in his eyes?*

Looking at the heart on my wrist again, my mouth feels dry. "Okay, but… You don't even know me."

"But I want to," he says quickly. "I want to know you."

I stop scratching my hand and meet his eyes again. They're wide, surprised. Then, averting them, he laughs nervously.

"Oh— Sorry. That was weird."

*He's serious?* He's serious about liking me. Seriously grateful that I walked out here to talk? Even considering what Ice did?

"It's okay," I say.

He blinks, still watching me. His amber eyes are bright, almost, but he still looks worried and terribly embarrassed, and I just…*don't get it.*

For me, the day I walked out to Reid Manor in the rain was the day everything fell apart, but maybe it was different for him. I remember the deadened look in his eyes clearly. The emptiness. The exhaustion. He wasn't in good shape. I still don't understand, and I'm not sure I want to, but…

"I guess I wouldn't mind getting to know you better either," I say. "Since we're stuck with each other for now and everything."

*And I have a lot of questions.*

Relief floods his features, relaxing his posture, and he grins. "Thanks—for this second chance, I mean."

I feel the heat on my cheeks, somehow warmer than the surrounding air, and he notices. He breaks into nervous laughter that manages to make me laugh too.

For a moment, I laugh about nothing and watch James laugh about nothing, and I wonder what goes through his head when he looks at me. I don't ask, but, as he turns away, I think I see tears forming in the corner of his eyes.

Though, it could have been my imagination.

# sixteen

I wake up dying on the floor.

*Okay, dying is an exaggeration.*

I feel better than I did yesterday. The ringing in my left ear is almost gone, but the room is hot. Shifting even slightly elicits an unavoidable groan, and the orange prescription bottle looks more tempting than usual when I sit up and unzip my backpack. I take ibuprofen anyway, not caring that my water bottle topples over when I drop it on the floor.

"You alright?" a voice asks.

*Oh.*

James is awake.

I look up to find him in the armchair, eating a sandwich. He watches me with a hint of concern.

I check my phone. It's almost 10AM.

"Just sore," I say, setting my phone down. I find the brush I shoved into my backpack and work it through my hair. My shoulder protests each time I raise my arm, but I ignore it. "Any plans for today?"

"Actually, I was thinking about what you said yesterday—about fixing the place up. I wanna clear out the first floor, or at least pick up some of the scrap wood in the parlor."

*Ah, yes. The parlor.*

Exactly what happened on the Fourth of July is still a bit of a blur, but I seem to remember tripping over a board in there. I'm still not sure why I thought running into the building was a good idea.

"I'll help."

He frowns. "You're hurt. You don't have to help."

"I want to help," I say dryly.

I move, preparing to stand, and James scrambles out of the chair, offering to assist. I stare at his outstretched hand, overcome by a sense of déjà vu. The sight of a tired man with short orange hair and wide amber eyes lined by dark circles in a brightly lit mall. But I take his hand, and he helps me off the floor. I imagine it took some of the stress off my side and bruised hip.

Then he drops my hand and looks away, discomfort creeping into his expression. "I'll meet you out there. Eat something first."

Not wanting to argue, I nod. He leaves with a gun tucked in his back pocket, and I turn toward the window. I cross the room and lean over the mini-fridge to peek through the gap between the boards.

Thankfully, there's not much to see.

* * * * *

I drop a two-by-four onto the pile of wood we've been amassing just beyond the parlor room and pause to hover a hand over my aching side. Maybe James had a point when he said I shouldn't be doing this. Maybe it isn't conducive to the healing process. But I don't want to feel like I'm only taking up space.

Glancing back through the empty door frame and into the parlor, I watch James for a moment. He's knelt on the floor, collecting small bits of garbage into a cardboard box. He pauses to wipe his forehead with the back of his hand.

Then I turn away. This room is small and doesn't seem to have been used for much, but it leads to the hallway with the bedroom, and there's a second, larger door at the back. James mentioned a kitchen and dining room, but I haven't looked for myself yet.

"Hey, Jayde," he calls.

"Yeah?"

I step back into the parlor. He's standing now, assessing the dusty but slightly less trashed room with his hands on his hips.

"Can you grab a broom?" he asks, glancing over. "You don't have to walk up the stairs or anything. There should be one in the utility room out back—past the kitchen, in the conservatory."

"Conservatory?"

He shrugs. "It's like a Victorian sunroom or whatever. Anyway, watch out for broken glass back there; it's wrecked."

"Alright."

*Finally, I get to check out the kitchen.*

I pass through the door leading further into the house and find myself in a dining room. The air is hot and stuffy, worse than in the parlor. The walls are decorated with ornate wood paneling, and a long table sits in the middle of the room, missing all but a few matching chairs. I run a finger over the table as I walk by, leaving a dark stripe clear of the thick dust coating everything else.

There's a box on an otherwise empty display table at the far end of the room, and I look inside, finding what I assume to be glassware wrapped in newspaper. There's a loose page on top. It's also covered in dust, and the edges are yellowed with age. I flip it over to find a date: September 1989.

*Jeez.*

I leave the newspaper and move on to the poorly lit kitchen. Flipping the light switch does nothing, but I continue inside. There isn't a fridge at all, only an empty space where one should be, and it seems like there was recently a small fire—judging by the blackened patch on the old electric stovetop and the oblong hole burnt through the wallpaper behind it, the peeling edges charred.

I snoop a moment longer, but I understand why James decided the kitchen was a lost cause. Fire hazard aside, it's cluttered and dirty, and a family of birds may have set themselves up in one of the overhead cabinets.

At the far end, I find a white exterior door with a decorative stained-glass panel gone cloudy with age. I move the wooden chair blocking the door aside, turn the lock, and step out into intense humid heat.

The conservatory itself is small. One of three large panes of glass on the ceiling is broken and covered by a plywood board. Most of the glass still litters the floor—it crunches, brittle beneath my shoes. A few wall panels are broken too, but they're covered by thick, yellowing plastic. I glance over the old wicker chairs and ceramic pots long missing plants. There's a tall, metal cabinet in the back of the room, where the wall is brick, beside an old, rusted washing machine.

*Calling this a utility room is a stretch.*

I tug the cabinet open and find the broom and dustpan James must have been referring to. Grabbing them, I waste no time in returning to the main house, appreciating what little insulation the building does provide.

James is waiting for me in the kitchen.

I pass the broom to him before washing my hands. The luke-warm water is no longer unbearable. I stare at the stitches on my palm through the clear liquid as it runs off my skin and patters against the metal sink basin below.

"I don't blame you for not using the kitchen," I say mildly.

"It's bad, right?" He laughs. "I was eating ramen until I caught the stove on fire."

I shut the water off and carefully dry my hands on my shirt. "Aren't you worried you'll get in trouble for being here?"

"Nah." He turns to leave, and I trail after him, heading toward the parlor. "I think it's owned by a great aunt—on my dad's side —or it was years ago, anyway. But she doesn't live in Riverview anymore and hasn't since I was real young. No one cares about this place. Seriously no one."

"All the more reason to fix it up, right?"

"Look around," he says, his voice dry. "I can sweep as much as I want, and I can board up all the windows, but it's too late. Reid Manor is over a hundred years old, and no one has done anything with it in decades. It'll be condemned and demolished one day. Just an empty lot and a pile of rubble in a landfill."

"Will you miss it?"

He shrugs. "I don't know. Maybe it wouldn't be so bad if it's gone. I can't keep running away if there's nowhere to run to."

"What are you running from?"

"I don't know."

"Do you want to stay in Riverview?"

"Dunno," he mutters as he begins to sweep. "I've lived here my whole life. Where else would I go?"

The parlor looks better already—brighter, less dusty, and less cluttered—but I feel like all we did was move most of the mess into the next room. At least I won't trip over anything again, I guess. But I get the impression that James' mission to clean it was yet another distraction.

"You have a car." I push the now dust-free chaise back against the wall with my foot. "You could go anywhere, so what's keeping you here?"

"Right now? You."

I groan and drop to sit on the chaise. "Okay, fine, but what kept you here so long before? You're an adult, right? You've had years to leave."

"I guess I have a couple friends in town."

"Oh, so you do have friends? I thought no one liked you."

He stops sweeping and glances over with a hint of frustration and his jaw set. I smile, feigning innocence, and he rolls his eyes.

"Go shower or something," he says, impressively exasperated. "You should be taking it easy, not doing manual labor."

He's probably right.

"Is there hot water?" I ask—*just to be sure.*

He shakes his head. "The water heater is gas, and the gas is shut off. Sorry."

*Knew it.*

"It's fine," I say, dragging myself out of the chair again. "A cold shower might be nice in this heat, anyway."

"I'll be here when you're done."

I pause in the doorway, and, after a moment of hesitation, I glance back at him. "Maybe you should take it easy too."

"I already told you," he says without looking over. "Don't worry about me."

* * * * *

I take a dose of Vicodin with our cheap sandwich dinner after James assures me it's okay to do so. If I'm in pain, I should take the meds. If I fall asleep, it's fine. He'll keep an eye out for me.

*Or whatever.*

By the time the sun sets, I'm more than a little drowsy. Instead of heading to bed, though, we're still hanging out in the parlor, which is now almost presentable. No glass on the floor. No scrap wood. No cobwebs. No thick, settled dust. It's still hot, but, once we finished with it, the parlor became the most livable room in the entire building.

The documentary I was watching on my phone ended a few minutes ago. Since then, I've been lying on the chaise—easily the most comfortable piece of furniture in the room—sprawled on my back and staring up at the dark ceiling. My eyes threaten to close, but I don't want to move, even if it is just to walk down the hall.

James is halfway across the room, sitting in a large armchair. I have no idea what he's doing, but he's been quiet for a long while.

"Hey," I say, breaking the silence.

"What's up?"

My vision tracks slowly as I redirect my attention from the ceiling to the armchair. He's on his phone—not typing, but still focused on the device's dimly lit screen. It softly illuminates his face, deepening the shadows beneath his eyes.

"You gonna sleep in that chair again?" my voice asks.

"Mm-hm."

"You sure you don't want to share the mattress?"

"Yes, I'm sure," he says, not bothering to look up. "The chair is fine. Besides, I'm pretty sure that's just the Vicodin talking."

"Is it?"

He doesn't answer, so I roll onto my side to watch him more comfortably. I don't think he's texting or playing a game. He's just watching the screen, his eyes flicking left to right. After a moment, he swipes up on the screen with his thumb, and the process repeats.

*Is he reading?*

What is he reading? The news? A book?

*What kind of books do you like?*

I run through a series of basic personal questions I could ask to break the tension, but I can't seem to make any materialize. They remain stuck, swirling vaguely in my head, as another wave of sleepiness washes over me.

I almost nod off, but my head snaps up at the sensation of my chin slipping past the heel of my hand. Eyes open wide, my curiosity over whatever he's doing on his phone returns.

"You still like me?" I ask.

I bite my tongue. I meant to ask about the phone—not about his feelings for me *again*—but my mouth clearly had other plans.

He looks up, frowning as our eyes meet.

"Sure," he says, his voice soft. "More than I should, I think."

"Why?" I ask through a yawn.

"Dunno. Sorry."

*Why are you sorry?*

My eyes close before I manage to respond.

# seventeen

Still half-asleep, I shift beneath the thin blanket. The mattress creaks softly and smells faintly of mildew, but the warmth isn't unpleasant, and something about it seems marginally more comfortable than before. Maybe I'm just used to it.

*But how did I get here?*

The last thing I remember is lying on the chaise in the parlor.

I stretch my arm, pleased by the lack of sharp discomfort, but I freeze as my hand brushes against something solid. Fabric. Skin. It startles me until I remember the stupid offer I made last night.

*He must have changed his mind.*

I roll over and find James on the other side of the bed with his back to me. He's lying on the bare mattress without a blanket or pillow, wearing a t-shirt and gym shorts. His breathing is soft and steady, the ringing in my ears having faded enough I can hear it. Seeing him doesn't bother me as much as I imagined it might when I first made the offer.

"Did you sleep okay?" I whisper.

He doesn't move. He's fast asleep.

"Hey… What's your deal, huh? Why are you helping me?"

He doesn't react, but I'm glad he isn't awake to hear. If he ever wants to explain his history with Ice or the real reason why he begged for my forgiveness in the middle of the night during a rainstorm, I'll listen. I want to know. *Desperately.* But, if it's painful, it has to happen on his own time.

*I understand that more than ever now.*

I watch a moment longer. His shoulders rise and fall with each breath. Even from behind, he looks more comfortable than he ever did while sleeping in the chair.

Reaching out, I brush the dark fabric of his shirt with my fingertips. Slow, hesitant, and careful, I rest my palm between his shoulder blades. He's warm. I feel his heart beating.

*Did he carry me here after I fell asleep? I probably would have been fine on the chaise, but...*

My phone's text tone goes off somewhere behind me. The sudden loudness startles me, and my hand presses roughly into James' back before I could retract it.

*Oops.*

My face flushes hot as he shifts, waking up. I pull the blanket up over my nose, unsure what to do and desperately hoping he doesn't realize exactly what woke him.

Then he rolls over and blinks the sleep from his eyes.

"Good morning," I squeak.

His face turns red the instant he registers my face hardly a foot away from his. He sits up in a hurry and drags his hands down his face.

"Oh, god," he groans. "Sorry. I didn't mean to fall asleep."

"It's fine. It's really not that weird."

*Aah...* If anything, the idea of him lying next to me *without* the express intention of falling asleep is far stranger than the thought of him sharing the bed just to get a decent night's sleep, but I am *not* going there right now.

I sit up and push the throw blanket aside to assess my injuries. I'm sore, but my side, hand, and shoulder are the only things that actively hurt. Most of the cut-related pain has been replaced by a pervasive itch. It's a normal part of the healing process, according to the internet, but it's still annoying.

"Was that your phone?" James asks blankly.

*Oh. Right.*

He says it's on top of the mini-fridge, so I leave the floor to grab it, and a second text arrives right as I pick it up. The message on my lock screen…

**Ice Monroe**                     now
It's not a trap. I'm genuinely curious.

"What?" I ask aloud.

I unlock my phone to read the first text.

**Ice:** Have you been home recently?

*No, I've been avoiding it, actually.*

"Something wrong?" James asks.

"It's Ice, but…" *Ugh.* "Never mind, it's stupid."

I stare at the screen. The texts are vague and petty—not exactly threatening—but I'm not sure what to do. Should I respond? Ask what he means? Ignore him?

"He messaged you?"

James steps past me and peeks out the window. He must not

have seen anything suspicious because he looks only mildly concerned when he turns to me again.

"What did he say?"

I shake my head, hesitating before passing my phone to him. James stares at the screen for a moment, thankfully not scrolling up through the conversation at all, and then sighs heavily.

He taps on the screen. "Can I tell him to fuck off?" he asks, his thumb hovering over the on-screen keyboard.

I stifle a laugh. "Please don't."

"I'm not kidding."

He glares at my phone once more before returning it. I hold it in both hands, watching as James kneels to open the mini-fridge. *Oh?* He has a tattoo on the back of his left leg, just below the knee. It's a...*twenty-sided die*, I think?

I'm curious, but...*not now.*

"Should I go home and check?" I ask instead.

"Dunno about that," he says dryly. "Explicitly stating it's not a trap makes it sound an awful lot like a trap."

"That seems a little indirect for Ice, doesn't it?"

I look up from my phone in time to catch him rolling his eyes.

"Seriously? You are way too trusting." He stuffs half a slice of bread into his mouth. "You should work on that."

I start to protest, but a third text distracts me. The new message is also from Ice. It's an image—a screenshot of a map application with a small, blue circle in the center. I recognize the location, a series of winding, interconnected suburban streets, as Westbrooke. The GPS marker is situated directly over the Monroe house. The time at the top of the screenshot reveals it was taken only a minute ago.

"Ice is home right now," I say. James stands, and I point to the time to show him. "See? It's not a trap. We should be fine to stop by the cottage real fast."

"Did you just call it a *cottage?*"

When I look up from my phone to explain the logistics of a cottage cluster, he meets my gaze, absolutely dumbfounded. I end up not saying anything, and he shakes his head.

"Forget it," he says, his voice taut. "I can't believe this. You seriously want to go, at Ice's request, after what happened the other day?"

*A small, black circle—the tip of a gun aimed between my eyes. Cool metal pressed against my forehead. A cold sneer before my vision goes black at the sound of a gunshot.*

I shake my head too, crossing my arms over my chest.

"Nothing happened the other day," I insist. "Besides, my house has hot water and a functioning kitchen. Don't you want a hot shower? Real food? When was the last time you had either? And don't tell me it was in jail."

He stares at me for a moment, a hint of tension in his jaw. Then, with a sigh, he glances away and throws a hand up. "Fine. We can swing by for a minute, but we are not staying long."

* * * * *

The front door is unlocked.

I know I locked it before I left with Detective Crain, so *someone else* has definitely been here since then. It's obvious who, even if I have no idea how he got inside.

I'd rather say nothing, but I opt to give James fair warning.

He insists on going in ahead to check it out and passes me the pillow and throw blanket he was carrying. I let him inside despite him not knowing the first thing about how the house is laid out.

*Whatever. Just let him do his thing.*

I lock the front door behind us and check Rose's bedroom as James heads upstairs, but it seems fine. The entire first floor looks to be untouched. The window locks are intact. Nothing is broken or seems off in any way.

*If Ice came here, why? What did he do?*

James returns from his survey of the house to tell me with a look of mild confusion and more obvious relief that it's empty— as I expected. I thank him before leading the way upstairs.

My bedroom door is cracked.

There are a few spots of dark blood on the pale carpet just outside. My eyes land on the sweatband I'm wearing before I look up at the door again.

Being here, standing outside my bedroom… It's uncomfortable, and I hate that feeling more than anything. It shouldn't be like this. I shouldn't feel afraid in my own house. This is messed up.

"Is this your room?"

Snapped back to the present, I nod and push the door the rest of the way open.

"This is a nice place," James says.

"Thanks."

I flip the light on. My bedroom is quiet. Void of life. Only one thing is out of place—the duffel bag I left at Ice's house is here, sitting on the bed.

*You're kidding.*

I cross the room, drop James' bedding, shed my backpack, and unzip the duffel. I spend a moment shuffling through the contents, but everything is accounted for. Even if none of this stuff is irreplaceable, I was still worried I'd never see it again.

But Ice returned it all.

My clothes—including several newer pieces I bought using the money he gave me. My Converse and flip-flops. The phone charger I left in the den. The toiletry bag I left in the bathroom. Everything.

*I can't believe it.*

As I turn away from the bed, I notice something else that wasn't here before: A folded piece of paper on my bedside table. James is preoccupied, studying the partially covered photo collage above my dresser, so I pick up the paper without saying anything.

It's a short note, written in Ice's neat handwriting on cream stationery.

*I seem to recall you meant to leave with your bag when you stopped by last week. Seeing as I have no use for your belongings. I took it upon myself to return them and save you the trouble.*

*You're welcome.*

*But I have a surprise for you, so we'll see each other again soon. While I'm confident you will hate it, I look forward to our next meeting. Last time was a blast.*

*— Ice Monroe*

Okay…but *why*?

Why return my stuff and leave a stupid note and send vague text messages to make sure I see it?

*How annoying.*

"This is the bag you left at his place, right? The one you wanted to pick up before—"

I jump at the sound of James' voice and look up from the note. He's glancing over the half-unpacked duffel bag and random items strewn across the bed.

"Yeah, um, and it's all there. I didn't notice anything missing."

He points to the paper in my hand. "What's that?"

"Oh, it's…"

My eyes pass over the words again. *There is a threat here, so...* With the soft inside of my cheek pinched between my teeth, I resist the urge to crumple the note into a ball and instead offer it to James.

He meets my gaze, concern flickering in his eyes, and takes the note. He reads it at least twice before looking up again. Then he frowns.

"He thinks this is funny?" he asks blankly. "He seriously gets off on tormenting you, doesn't he?"

*Tormenting me? Me?*

"Don't know; don't care."

I take the note back, ball it up, and toss it at the wastebasket beside my desk. It bounces off the rim and lands on the carpet, but I don't care enough to pick it up.

"I call the shower first," I say, collecting an outfit from the pile of clean clothes on my bed. "You can watch TV downstairs if you want. It should still be logged into Netflix."

He turns away from the bed. "Sure. You locked the door, right?"

"Yes. But feel free to check for yourself."

He follows me out of the bedroom and hesitates just outside the door. I pat him on the arm, and he glances over, surprised by my touch.

"I'll be quick," I assure him. "Try to relax a little."

His frown softens before he heads downstairs, leaving me alone on the second floor. I watch over the banister as he checks the deadbolt.

Suppressing a sigh, I step into the bathroom.

The shower sucks, but it's better than the previous two. The hot water is lovely on my sore muscles, and none of my wounds are raw, so the pain isn't as sharp. Still, my right hand is only semi-functional, and I struggle to wash my hair with only my left. The suds sting the scabbing heart on my wrist, but I manage.

When it's over, I dry my hair and get dressed, happy to wear some of my favorite clothes again even if the expensive, sweet-smelling fabric softener reminds me of Ice's house. Back in my bedroom, I work on putting the rest of the clean clothes away and filling my laundry basket with everything I need to wash.

I hang up the last dress and turn back to my room, feeling a small sense of accomplishment for the first time in weeks.

Until I spot the small, slate grey business card on my desk. Seeing it again leaves a pit in my stomach, but I move closer and pick up the card.

Detective Sarah Crain
Riverview Police Department

She told me to call if I need anything.

I need help, sure, but not from her. Even if she seemed like a decent person, this is way above her pay grade. And I don't want to be questioned like that ever again.

*Sorry.*

I drop the card into the wastebasket, along with the crumpled note from the floor. Then I grab the laundry hamper with James' bedding on top. My side complains, but I make it downstairs in one piece.

James is watching TV. He doesn't look too invested, though. He's on his phone at the same time, texting by the looks of it.

*Who are you texting now? Hm...*

I drop the hamper beside the couch.

"What do you want for lunch?" I ask.

He shrugs but joins me in the kitchen without bothering to pause whatever he was pretending to watch before I interrupted him. The moment I open the first cabinet, I regret offering to cook. I may have functioning appliances, but I totally forgot I'm just about out of food.

He opens the fridge, pulls out a jug of milk, and grimaces. "This expired three weeks ago. When's the last time you were home?"

"Technically, it was just a few days ago…" But I haven't done any grocery shopping since the end of June.

He gives me a look, and I can't help but avert my eyes.

"Don't worry about it," I stammer, shooing him out of the kitchen. "Just, um, go take a shower. I'll figure something out."

I settle on making pancakes with just-add-water baking mix. James returns from his shower as I finish cooking, and we eat the pancakes with butter, syrup, and slightly frostbitten strawberries Rose bought months ago for smoothies and never used.

After promising a legitimate meal, I feel like I cheated him somehow, but he doesn't seem to mind. Probably because he's been living off fast food and junk for months now.

*He almost looks comfortable.*

We talk about nothing in particular, changing the subject whenever something new comes to mind. Unimportant, casual topics. Having breakfast for lunch. The weather since the end of the rainstorm. The gift that is air conditioning. He mentions he knows how to make pancakes from scratch but would need milk and eggs.

"You should cook next time," I say, resting my elbows on the table.

He laughs. "Maybe…"

*It's strange.*

He says he doesn't hate Reid Manor. He has good memories of playing there as a kid. But the property casts a dark shadow over him. A creeping discomfort the moment he steps through the front doors. A preoccupation with some thought. He's like a different person there.

I suggest we stay here instead—it's probably more secure than the manor—but he declines immediately.

*Fine.* But there's no reason to go back right away, is there?

"Hey," I say. He looks up from his phone, his expression curious and mild. "Can we go to the park after the laundry is done?"

Glancing away again, he smiles. "Sure."

# eighteen

I stand atop the curb, rocking on my heels.

Riverside Park is packed.

The crowd—swathes of people milling about on the footpaths and beneath the pavilion and in the grass—twists my stomach into knots. It's not even Wednesday. As far as I know, there isn't an event today. But there are a lot of people. I didn't wear a flannel, and I don't want anyone to look directly at me, *and that's the tree I sat under with Ice in June, and I suddenly don't want to be here anymore.*

I point elsewhere, across the street from the main park, at the bike path winding off into the much less-populated distance toward Riverview Community Center.

"Let's head that way," I say.

"Sure."

James walks in that direction, and I stumble after him, surprised he didn't pause to ask why I don't actually want to go to the park when it was my idea to come in the first place. Maybe he doesn't like crowds either. He seems like the type who wouldn't like crowds.

We walk down the bike path for a few minutes in silence,

until he asks if I want to sit somewhere. I kind of shrug, and he points out a bench in the shade of a maple tree off to the side.

I sit at one end. He sits at the other.

Looking up, the sky is a cloudless blue through the tree's broad leaves. The height of summer has always been my favorite time of year, but, between the rainstorm and the mess with James and Ice, it's been…difficult to appreciate the weather or the outdoors. This feels like the first time I've really been out since *the day I went to Music@ThePark at the end of June.*

It's nice being outside now. The shade keeps the sun off my skin, and there's a slight breeze coming from the direction of the river. If it weren't for the cuts on my arms—and the guy sitting so far away it's awkward—this would feel normal.

But, right now, it's almost as uncomfortable as hovering around Oakwood Cottages' on-site laundromat for two hours.

I glance at James, who continues to avoid looking directly at me, and frown. "Are you scared of me?"

"What? No."

He meets my gaze for an instant before shaking his head and looking out over the grass beyond the shade. As he scratches his arm, his frown softens, and I find myself increasingly unconvinced.

"So, what's your problem, then?"

"Problem? I just—" He laughs once, a soft noise. "I just feel bad. That this happened, and that you're stuck with me, I guess." He looks to me again, forcing a smile. "Sorry. It's stupid, isn't it?"

I shrug. "There are worse people I could be stuck with."

*Like Ice.*

He watches my face, still careful but somewhat less nervous

than before. Then his eyes track over the rest of me, and his expression darkens.

"Are you in pain?" he asks.

"Am I—?"

Glancing over the black sweatband, I pick at a crusty scab beside one of the stitches further up my arm. The bruises are fading, and I feel better than I did this morning. The warm shower helped.

"My side and hand still hurt," I say slowly. "My shoulder is a little rough too, but everything else just itches now."

He thinks about it for a moment. "Humans heal slow, huh?"

"Well, sorry," I mutter, turning my hand over to look at my palm. "Maybe healing is slow-going, but I am supposed to get the stitches taken out soon."

"Let me guess, you want a ride to the hospital too?"

I roll my eyes. "That would be nice."

Smothering a smile, he lifts his arm and checks the spot where glass cut him a few days ago. All that remains is a small, pink scar with a thin scab in the center—more healing than my wounds have achieved in almost a week. As for his face, there is still some shiny, pink hatching on his cheek, a pink mark across the bridge of his nose, and a dark scab on his lip *because he keeps picking at it*, but I'd never believe those injuries occurred hardly two weeks ago if I didn't know better.

Apparently, even a defective immortal heals faster than me.

"I broke my arm when I was eight," he says, massaging the pale scars on his left hand. "The fracture wasn't great—it was a, uh, nasty dirt bike accident, bone sticking out and everything—

but I felt good as new in a month. Fights in middle school. High school. Whatever. Injury is never something I've had to worry about, you know? If I cut my hand like that, it'd be closed up in a week—no stitches required. It still hurts, you know, but it wouldn't last long. And I think I heal slower than most."

"Are you bragging?"

"Ah—" He laughs nervously, so I have a feeling he missed the sarcasm. "No. I'm not trying to brag. It sucks—that you have to deal with it for so long, I mean."

*Yeah. It does.*

I think about Ice's knuckles again. How the wounds closed after a day and fully healed by the time I left his house—not a week after he injured them. Just…faint marks on his skin.

As I run a finger over the stitches on my palm, I try to imagine what it would be like to heal at the same rate. If the stitches were already gone or were never necessary. If I had thin, pink scars instead of ugly, scabbed wounds.

"I guess that's why they prescribed those meds," I say. "Kind of hard to think about the pain when you're passed out."

It was another joke, but his frown deepens.

"It's weird to think how different we are," he says.

"Are we really that different?"

He stares at me for a long few seconds before averting his eyes. "Immortals and humans are nothing alike."

I look away too. I watch the bike path. A woman walking her dog. Her eye color eludes me as she passes by, but she might be an immortal. Someone biking in the opposite direction. Are they human?

*Does it matter?*

Beyond the shapeshifting, a few enhanced physical traits, proclivity for being obscenely attractive, and random supernatural powers, the differences seem superficial. Talking to an immortal feels the same as talking to a human. They make friends the same, and they have the same mess of interpersonal problems. Ice played up the differences and Night acknowledged them, but even she said we were similar—exactly the same, emotionally speaking.

"We probably shouldn't talk about it in public, anyway," I decide aloud. "I still don't know what will happen if I accidentally spill the secret to anyone else."

"You weren't kidding when you said there was a contract?"

I glance up, to the clear, blue sky. "No. I had to sign a lot of paperwork, but it was vague on the details. I can't say anything about *cats* or *related topics* to anyone who doesn't already know."

"We can talk about something else."

"Thanks."

I lean forward, ignore the stitch in my side, and watch James for a moment. He's staring off into the middle distance, clearly processing something that makes him uneasy.

"What do you like to do in your spare time?" I ask.

"Me?" He turns to me, blinking. "I don't know... I guess I like to read. And game."

"What kind of games?"

I scoot closer, cleaving the distance between us in half. I didn't mean to intimidate him, but he shies away without taking his wide eyes off me. When I offer a smile, his expression softens, and he takes a breath.

"Video games," he says. "And tabletop, sometimes. But I haven't played anything in a while."

"Why not?"

He frowns. "Dunno. I haven't felt like it, I guess. But I sold my GameStation a few weeks back, and I don't have a TV anymore, so I can't play even if I wanted to."

"Well, why'd you sell it?"

"To buy the mini-fridge," he says, glancing away.

*That's rough.*

"What about your tattoo?" I ask.

"Tattoo?" He looks to me again, confused for a second before his expression shifts, and he sucks in a breath. "Oh, you mean the D20 on my leg?"

I nod. "I noticed it this morning."

He pauses to think. Then he shifts his leg and tugs up the hem of his jeans to look. The tattoo is roughly two and a half inches in diameter and centered on the back of his upper calf. The clean, bold linework forms a twenty-sided die with *20* on its center face.

"I got it done a couple years ago, but I always forget I have it."

"What's so special about the D20?"

"It's kind of an inside joke—about a game." He sighs as he straightens up and leans back against the bench. "But having a nat-twenty tattooed on my body clearly hasn't done me any good."

"Was it supposed to?"

He laughs. "That's the joke. In this game, rolling a natural twenty means critical success, but I have notoriously bad luck, both in the game and out of it. I thought I should get a nat-one —critical failure. But my friend convinced me to get the nat-twenty instead. For good luck."

"Wow. You really do have friends?"

His eyes narrow dangerously, but he smiles. "You're one to talk, Miss *my only friend isn't even in the same state*."

"She's on vacation," I protest with a laugh.

His expression softens. "Anyway, what do you like to do?"

"Me?" I ask as I come to understand his look of surprise upon being asked a personal question he wasn't prepared to answer. "Oh. Well, I like spending time outside—going for walks and stuff—and cooking, and, um…studying?"

"You like school?"

"Sure." A wholly unintentional defensive tone creeps into my voice. "I'm good at it, anyway. I was a paid tutor during winter term, and it was kinda fun."

"Nah, it's cool," he says with a hesitant smile. "I wasn't… bad at school or anything, to be honest. I just didn't care for the environment. The…people and everything."

It seems like no matter what I try to talk about, it ends up like this—a slow, downward spiral into sadness. Our situation sucks, and I guess James' entire life has sucked, but I'm tired of it overshadowing everything.

*Is it so hard to relax for a few minutes?*

I slip my phone from my pocket and reread my conversation with Rose. She asked what I was doing earlier, and I relented a crumb of honesty and admitted to hanging out with James. She still wants a picture of him—to confirm he's not a creep or whatever.

*I haven't mentioned it to him yet, but…*

Maybe it's something to do.

"So…" I clear my throat. "Rose—that one friend you made fun of me for—is convinced you're a figment of my imagination. She wants a picture to prove you exist."

"What?" he asks in humored disbelief. "You told her you're still talking to me?"

"Mm-hm. I told her I helped you do laundry because you got kicked out of your dad's house. That's all, but she's convinced we're friends or something."

"Are we friends?" he asks, his full attention on me.

I honestly think she's more convinced James is a rebound than a friend, but I'm not about to tell *him* that.

"Are you okay to be friends with me?" I ask instead.

He doesn't answer immediately, but he doesn't turn away either. Then he sighs and says, "I just want to help you. How you feel about me or how I feel about you hardly matters right now."

*Uh-huh. That doesn't answer my question at all.*

"But you can take a picture of me if you want," he says. "I don't want your friend to worry about you. Plus, I think I look okay right now—after the shower and laundry and everything."

"Really?" I ask, caught off guard. "Right now?"

"Yeah. As thanks for getting me out to do something today."

*As thanks?*

I smile, open the camera app, and hold up my phone. "Alright.

Whenever you're ready."

He glances away and slightly upward to watch the sky.

Through my phone's screen, he doesn't look uneasy at all. His expression holds a reflective, serene quality, and he's not directly facing the camera, but it somehow makes for a better image. I take a few pictures, but the one I settle on is almost reminiscent of a fashion shot, like something I might see from an influencer on SnapGram, and I stare at it for a long time.

I already knew, obviously, but James is…quite good-looking. Defective hot mess or not, he's still an immortal. Smooth features, strong jaw, and eyes the color of warm honey. His nose is a touch crooked, and the sunlight accentuates both his healing injuries and the old, white scar that cuts through his left eyebrow, but the angle of the light hides the dark circles beneath his eyes, and his messy, orange hair almost looks like it's on fire.

*Ah… Does he have sun freckles?*

"This is a good one," I admit lamely.

I turn my phone to show him, and he grins.

"Wow. I barely recognize myself." He laughs. "Nah, it's good. Your friend might actually think you're with someone cool."

"With you?" I ask, sending the photo before I have a chance to change my mind. "I thought you didn't even want to be friends."

"Whatever. You're the one who kept asking if I wanted to share the bed with you," he says, but his voice falters, and he glances away as his face turns red.

I laugh. "I was just trying to be nice. I feel bad for your neck."

"My neck is fine."

He laughs again, closing his eyes and hiding his face in his hands. It's an unforced, natural laugh. The kind I've only heard from him a couple times. He seems comfortable, and it takes the edge off, clearing a little of the darkness.

I wouldn't mind seeing him laugh more.

*Oh.*

My phone dings. I hesitate to look, but I force myself to.

> **Rose:** WHAT??? Σ(°ロ°)
>
> **Rose:** That's the new guy? A redhead? Jay, what the hell?? He's cute!

*Oh, god.*

It's embarrassing, but I turn my phone to show him Rose's response. He cracks another smile, and his eyes brighten as they flick up from the screen to meet my gaze.

"The new guy?" he asks, his voice dry. "Am I cute?"

*Now it's my turn to hide my face.*

"You're not unattractive," I mumble.

He laughs again. "I guess I'll take that as a compliment."

"Oh, shut up!"

I uncover my one eye so I can jab his arm with my good hand, and his smile radiates warmth as our eyes meet. *James seems happy right now.* In this moment, there's no sign of exhaustion—no touch of hollow in his eyes. In this moment, we managed to cheer each other up and mess around like we're both fine.

After everything with Ice, this is…a nice change.

\* \* \* \* \*

James doesn't mention wanting to pick up dinner until we have already been on the road for several minutes. It's after 6PM, though, and McDonald's sounds better than another cheap sandwich, so I agree. When I offer to pay as we wait in the drive-thru, he blinks at me and shakes his head.

Honestly, it's kind of annoying.

I didn't really think about it until now—I had bigger things on my mind, I guess—but he's paid for everything since *before* I asked to stay with him at Reid Manor. He clearly doesn't have a job, so where is this money coming from? He went so far as to claim he had to sell a game console to afford the mini-fridge, but I haven't seen him act concerned about money in any other instance.

But he still looks like he's in a good mood, and he thanks the person behind the drive-thru window with a smile as they hand over our order, so I don't ask.

*I don't know anything about his background, anyway.*

We make it back to Reid Manor, and James doesn't linger in the car. He just drags everything out of the backseat and steps out after offering to carry my duffel bag if I take his backpack.

*This is because I complained when I carried it out to the car earlier, isn't it?*

Suppressing a sigh, I leave the car with the food in one arm and his backpack slung over my shoulder. I then follow James around the house and toward the front doors, though I run a few steps ahead to get there before him. I open one heavy door with my free hand, ignoring the scratch against the stitches on my palm.

James hesitates, but he takes a deep breath—visibly steeling himself by adjusting his grip on the bedding bundled in his arms—before walking through ahead of me.

"Should we shake things up and eat in the dining room?" I ask.

He catches my smile and laughs. "Tempting suggestion, but no thanks. I'll just grab another chair and move it into the bedroom for you."

"Have it your way."

Once in the bedroom, most everything we brought in—except for the food and my drink—is unceremoniously dumped onto the floor beside the mattress. Then James grabs the handgun from his backpack and leaves the room to find a chair.

*And case the joint, I assume.*

The door closes.

I carefully lower myself to the floor and unzip my duffel bag. The pillow and sheet set stuffed inside attempt to escape on their own. I help all three out of the bag, toss the flat sheet and pillow aside, and spend what feels like several minutes wrangling the full-sized mattress into the fitted queen sheet.

I collapse onto the covered but somewhat wrinkly mattress and take a moment to recover. My side burns and sweat seems to have broken out on my forehead, but it's done. And James didn't have a chance to insist he should do it for me before I finished.

*Success.*

I roll onto my side and drag my duffel onto the mattress. It only takes a moment to find the pill bottles. White or orange? *Ibuprofen or Vicodin?* Do I want to take the edge off or sleep for ten hours?

*Ugh.*

I sit up, put the prescription bottle away, and take ibuprofen with my sweet tea.

James returns while I'm shuffling through the McDonald's bag. He's carrying a small wicker chair I recognize from the vestibule at the front of the house. I heft myself off the floor, bringing our food with me.

"Where do you want this?" he asks.

*The chair? Um...*

I gesture vaguely toward the armchair he's been sleeping in, and he sets it a couple feet away from the larger chair. I take the seat and get back to digging through the paper bag to divvy out our food. He took so long doing *whatever*, the fries are no longer hot.

But it's fine.

"I assume we're alone," I say mildly.

He stares at his paper-wrapped burger with furrowed brows. "You think I'm paranoid, don't you?"

"No. You have every reason to be worried."

Stopping by the cottage was a risk. Ice snuck into Reid Manor while the building was empty before, so it only makes sense to think he might try something like that again.

"Honestly, I might be a little paranoid," he admits, finally getting around to unwrapping his burger.

"Don't be so hard on yourself."

Eating another french fry, I take my phone from my pocket. I check FaceSpace, but my messages to Night have gone unread. She was active daily before, even during the rainstorm—posting selfies and book quotes and photos of teacups—but she hasn't posted anything in a week.

*I hope she's okay.*

To distract myself, I back out of FaceSpace and check my text messages.

Rose managed to wring more information about James out of me before we left Riverside. His age and a few details that don't make any difference. How we met in the mall in June. How he seems a bit skittish. *Her last text, though…*

> **Rose:** This is the guy Ice beat up, right? Isn't that kind of fucked? (o_o);;

I didn't know how to answer.

I don't condone Ice's actions. I never did, but I let him and Night justify them to me. I tried to justify them to myself. I tried to pretend it never happened. And I feel bad for convincing myself it was fine just because James shouldn't have been there.

Even worse, I feel bad that I wasn't the one to run outside and stop it from happening. I turned away from the window *because I was too scared.*

But I can't let Rose know how bad it was.

> **Me:** Maybe I exaggerated what happened.

> **Rose:** Right… But Ice doesn't like him? Does he know you guys are hanging out?

> **Me:** We are not hanging out. He bought me
> lunch in exchange for using our laundry
> room. That's all.

I glance at James, who I am definitely *hanging out* with at this exact moment. Though, we're both on our phones and mutually ignoring each other while we eat.

> **Rose:** Almost sounds like a date. lol

> **Me:** What a sad date that would be.

I sigh, catching James' attention by accident. When he looks over with a hint of curiosity, I force a smile.

"I think Rose is in love with you," I say. He nearly chokes, and I laugh. "I'm kidding, obviously. But she keeps asking questions. All because I made the mistake of mentioning that Ice may or may not have beaten you up a couple weeks ago."

"Oops."

"Yeah. I told her while I was here during the rainstorm. So she knew about it before he decided to make things infinitely more complicated by…attacking me too. Ugh."

"She still thinks you're at home?" he asks, eyes averted.

"I don't know what else to say. She would freak if she knew I was staying somewhere like this."

He meets my gaze again, his expression unreadable. "Are you going home once she comes back from wherever?"

"She's in Arizona," I say slowly, unsure of the answer myself. "But, um… Probably? I mean, I obviously can't stay here forever. If things haven't calmed down enough for me to go home before then, I'll have to go once she gets back into town."

"Okay."

*Okay? Just okay?*

I want to ask what he plans to do after I leave—whether that's in a few days or not until Rose returns. I almost do, but the question turns itself into, "Do you think things will calm down soon?" before it left my mouth.

His eyes darken in a way they didn't before, when his expression shifted so slightly it seemed unimportant.

"No idea. With Ice involved, it's impossible. He's impossible."

*Impossible? Right...*

# nineteen

I wake up, feeling like I slept straight on the hardwood. Sore, aching, and itchy, with my entire right arm numb and tingling. How did I even manage to sleep so badly? Lying on the wrong side, maybe?

*Ugh.*

I sit up, rub the sleep from my eyes, and look around.

It's still dark outside and dark within the room, but I quickly spot James in the old armchair. His face is faintly illuminated by his dimmed phone screen, and he has his feet propped up on the smaller wicker chair.

Glancing up from the phone, his eyes scan the room. His expression shifts as his focus lands on me.

"You're awake," he says.

"Did you get any sleep?"

"No. I'm— Ugh… I guess I'm worried Ice will show up."

I frown. "What time is it?"

"Like…three?"

I purposely deepen my frown. "You should get some sleep."

He stares at me for a moment, thoughtful and concerned. I look away and blindly feel around in the duffel beside the bed until I find the ibuprofen.

"I doubt he'll show up at three in the morning," I say before popping a few tablets in my mouth.

"Why not?"

"He sleeps at night. Like we should."

He fakes a laugh. I drop my water bottle on top of my bag and look up to find him still watching me.

"Go back to sleep," he says.

I shake my head and scoot back, closer to the edge of the mattress. Then I pat the now-empty side.

"Come on. You need sleep too."

"Over there?" he asks sharply.

When I nod, he hesitates. But he eventually jams his pillow and blanket under one arm and drags himself out of the chair. With another pause, and another glance in my direction, he crosses the room and drops to sit beside me on the mattress.

"You're sure you're alright with this?" he asks, anxiety creeping into his voice as he holds his blanket in a ball in his lap.

"It's only weird if you make a big deal out of it," I mutter.

I return my head to my pillow, and James follows suit with his own pillow. As we face each other, both lying on our sides, he stares at me with a nervous frown and huge eyes that glint green in the low light.

"You're seriously okay with this?"

With a grimace, I pull the sheet up to my chin and roll onto my other side so he can't see my face flushing red. "You're making it weird."

"Sorry." He laughs once, then the mattress creaks as he rolls over. "Goodnight."

"Goodnight."

I want to get back to sleep too, but... *He's worried Ice will show up in the middle of the night?* Ice has been awake at some odd hours before, and he tends to wake up earlier than either of us. Should I worry more about him showing up at an odd hour too?

My fingers brush over the angular heart on my wrist. The six cuts are scabbed over and itchy like the others. More visually unnerving than painful, but...

I think of the note he left in my bedroom.

*We'll see each other soon?*

When did he write that note? How soon is *soon*?

\* \* \* \* \*

The room is hot and stuffy, and my injured side pulses beneath me. I'm lying on the wrong side again. *Aah...* My body creaks as I roll onto my back and open my eyes to stare at the ceiling.

It's daytime. It's hot. James is asleep with his back to me and his blanket discarded on the floor.

I sit up and hold my head until the fresh wave of pain passes. I may have overdone it the past couple days with all the carrying things and walking around and everything. And then to spend the night lying on my right side?

*Today's gonna suck.*

James doesn't shift even as I reach over him to grab the

ibuprofen and water bottle. I take a double dose, check my phone —it's almost 11:30AM—and prod James' arm to wake him.

After eating, we move into the parlor, where the air is less stuffy and the temperature more tolerable. I settle into the chaise again. James and his gun take the oversized armchair halfway across the room. I don't mention the gun. I try to ignore the gun. I don't want to think about the—

*Ugh.*

I hide my face in my phone. I send Night another vague message before texting Rose. Thankfully, she goes off on a tangent about her cousin—one of the family members she's been spending the most time with. She doesn't ask about James or Ice or anything. No updates on when she's planning to drive back up, though.

An hour passes, during which absolutely nothing happens, but James is somehow even more antsy than before.

He's reading on his phone, but his leg bounces, his shoe tapping the hardwood, and he looks around the room every so often like he expects something to have changed. It's starting to make me seriously uncomfortable, and I can't deal with it anymore.

I pause the video I'm watching.

"Have you heard from Ice or something?" I ask, breaking the relative silence in the room.

He looks over from his spot in the armchair. "No."

"Then why are you so nervous right now? And this morning? You seemed fine yesterday. What happened?"

He glances away, setting his phone down to fiddle with the

gun in his lap instead. I hate it, but it reminds me of Ice's note.

*Is that what he's worried about?*

The skin on my arm prickles. I scratch it, trying to beat back the rising sense of discomfort—a strange sense that something is wrong. But, of course something is wrong. My situation isn't at all normal or okay.

"Wanna get out and do something again?"

He shakes his head. "I'd rather stay here."

I ask why, but he doesn't answer. He just stares at the gun in his hand. *This is so annoying.*

"You realize Ice doesn't want to kill me, right?" I ask. "He said so himself. He's doing all of this to get to you—to hurt *you* —and it's obviously working."

Our eyes meet, his shadowed. "Even if he did say that, why would you believe him?"

Scratching the scab on my wrist, I tear my eyes from the gun. I can't look at it and talk about Ice at the same time.

"He's had three perfect opportunities to kill me," I say, speaking carefully to keep my voice level. "He even had your gun last time. I pissed him off—I wouldn't do what he wanted —and he still didn't use it except to scare me and lure you up there."

His eyes widen.

Until now, I haven't mentioned anything specific about what happened when Ice had me alone in that bedroom. I still can't bring myself to explain fully... *The muzzle of the gun pressed against my skin.* I can't. But I'd say almost anything to calm James down, so maybe I can stop thinking about it so much.

"Did he do anything to you?" he asks warily. "Hurt you? Say anything?"

I shake my head. His expression shifts, a more obvious hint of nervous tension in his jaw—eyes narrowed, like he doesn't quite believe me—but he shakes his head too.

"I guess it doesn't matter," he says. "Even if he doesn't want you dead, he still has it out for me, and he clearly has no problem hurting you."

I bite the inside of my cheek.

A part of me still wants to argue, but he's right. Ice may not want me dead, but pulling a knife on me, carving a heart into my wrist, and holding a loaded gun to my head is totally fine. It didn't even phase him. *He thought it was funny.*

A shiver runs down my spine. I shake it off and look to James again.

"I feel like I'm suffocating," I admit. "This sucks, I get that. Everything sucks. It's hot, and I'm sore, and I'm tired. I'm worried about whatever Ice is planning too, but your attitude isn't helping. It's just stressing us out even more."

"I—" His shoulders fall, and he sighs before glancing away. "There's a TV up on the second floor. It's old and only plays a few local channels, but we can check it out if you want."

*An old TV?*

"I can find something for us to watch on my phone if you can bring yourself to sit closer than three feet away from me for a couple hours."

He averts his eyes. "Or...we can go upstairs."

"Whatever. If you really want to watch the local news on a

TV from the eighties… Fine. Have it your way."

After a second of hesitation, he nods and leaves the armchair. He looks at the gun in his hand and then back to me, his expression uneasy and vaguely upset.

"I'll meet you there," he says, none of that emotion carried in his mild voice.

Turning away, he heads up the stairwell and out of sight. His footsteps continue, steady and unhurried, and I let out my breath.

*Ah…* How long does he plan to carry that gun around? I hate looking at it. And my side is killing me. It wasn't nearly as bad this morning—

Standing from the chaise, I lift the hem of my shirt. I brush my fingers over the wound, but it appears to be healing normally. The stitches are doing their job. It's closed and scabbed over and doesn't seem inflamed or especially red. *Is the pain just from sleeping in the wrong position?*

I drop my shirt and check my right hand, which also looks fine. I flex my fingers, wincing at the discomfort of my hand closing all the way. It's an improvement, though, and I'm supposed to visit the hospital to have the stitches removed in the next few days.

I glance at the staircase across the room. Then to the right, at the empty double doorway leading toward the hallway. Then at the stairs again. But I walk back to the bedroom and stand over my duffel bag for a moment.

I took ibuprofen earlier. It's been a while, but I don't feel any better. My side still hurts. My shoulder still aches. Even my hip has been complaining.

I know the Vicodin makes me drowsy, but I can't deal with this today. My body hurts and tensions are high. I don't want to worry about it anymore. I don't want to think about the creeping, prickly anxiety. I don't want to look at that stupid handgun.

So I take a dose before I go upstairs.

James left the door to the second-floor room open, so I find it easily. He's inside, fiddling with an old box TV, which is set up on a low table against the far wall with a couch in front of it. There's an empty bookcase and a few cardboard boxes in the room, but it's otherwise empty. And extremely dusty.

The couch is so small I hesitate to consider it a loveseat, and I'm almost surprised he didn't drag another chair in here. But I don't say anything, lest I give him any ideas.

He smacks the side of the TV, and the image clears.

To my relief, it's not the news. Instead, it looks to be some kind of PBS-type nature channel running a program that, judging by the narration and editing style, was probably recorded over a decade ago.

"There we go." He steps back from the TV, glances over his shoulder, and fakes a smile. "It's not much, but it's something, right?"

"I still think we should just watch a movie on my phone."

Groaning, he drops himself onto one end of the couch, his head thrown back to stare at the ceiling. "After this stupid show ends, we can watch whatever you want. I just thought it might hurt your shoulder to hold your phone up for so long."

*Wow.*

"You can always hold the phone for me," I say, crossing the

room to join him on the couch.

My thigh brushes his as I sit, and his leg shifts to give me more space. I glance over to check on him, but he continues staring at the ceiling with narrowed eyes and a hint of discomfort in the tight line of his mouth.

When I ask if he's okay, he sighs. Then he straightens up. Without ever looking at me before his eyes land on the TV, he says not to worry—he's fine.

*Being this close to me seriously bothers him, doesn't it?*

I feel like I should say something. Apologize for what I said earlier, maybe. I was a bit harsh. He's just stressed out, and I can't blame him for that.

*But...*

My eyes pass over the gun on the couch's far arm, and I look to the TV. The audio is crackly, the picture still slightly blurred. But the show, while not the type of educational show I'd normally pick to watch myself, is fine. It's about baby animals in the wild. Wolf pups. An elephant calf. Flamingo chicks.

After a half-hour or so, the show ends, and I hold James to his word. He turns the TV off. I open Netflix on my phone and pick a documentary about outer space.

"Is this fine?" I ask as he sits back down.

He watches for a few seconds before shrugging and taking the phone to hold in front of us. His comfort level seems to have increased somewhat, perhaps thanks in part to me desperately trying to hold a casual conversation during the previous show.

But I feel the medication kicking in. A distant fuzziness that tugs at the back of my mind and makes the phone screen feel further away than it really is and distorts the prickly sense of paranoia I've been ignoring into little more than an afterthought. It's still there, but I easily dismiss it.

I listen to the narrator's soothing voice explain the formation of stars during the early universe. I watch the expertly rendered CG visuals that morph into a blur of black and red and blue and white when I go too long without blinking.

My shoulder brushes against James' arm by accident, and it doesn't hurt, and he doesn't move away.

Another half-hour, and my eyelids grow heavy.

The narrator's words are almost meaningless, but the ethereal music and recurring imagery of a supermassive black hole instill a primal, existential fear deep within me. A fear of the vastness of space. A fear of the unknown. A fear of the dark—the expansive, inky nothingness of the awful place I visited in my sleep.

*A fear of death.*

"You're scared," my voice says. "Aren't you?"

James' hand, still holding my phone, falls to rest on his knee, and I glance up. He looks…sad, somehow, as he watches me with a careful unease.

"Yeah," he says. "Are you?"

"I'm trying not to think about it."

*Yet I brought it up.*

I look past James to the gun again. The documentary narrator's voice rings hollowly in my mind, and I try to imagine what might be on the screen. Stars? That observatory in Hawaii?

"Why do you even have that gun?" I ask. "Does it make you feel any better? Safer? Braver?"

"I—"

He glances aside. After a brief moment during which I worry I might fall asleep, he sets my phone down and picks up the handgun to examine it in his lap.

My breath catches, but he doesn't seem to notice.

"No," he says. "But I've still been carrying it around all week like I know how to use the damn thing."

"You don't know how to use it?"

He shakes his head. Then he raises the gun and aims it at his reflection in the dark TV screen. There's a cool focus in his narrowed eyes, but it doesn't mask his uncertainty, and his arm wavers slightly. The dreamy music still playing on my phone makes it all the more surreal.

"To be honest, I've never fired a gun," he says, his voice low. "Would I even be able to pull the trigger if it came down to it?"

*Would I?*

With a sigh, he returns the gun to the arm of the couch and drags a hand down his face. "Ice is right about me, you know; I am a coward."

"Are you sure?"

"What do you mean, *am I sure?*"

I blink at him.

*What do I mean?*

I don't think James is a coward. I don't think Ice is right about him at all. I think it's normal to be scared, especially in this sort of unreal situation, but I don't think a coward would do half the crazy shit he's done—good or bad—since I met him.

When I go too long without answering, he looks away and

picks my phone up, once again holding it still with his wrist resting just above his knee. My eyes flick to the screen. The image of an impossibly black orb surrounded by a warped, reddish halo. *The supermassive black hole with its nightmarish capacity to bend spacetime and consume all matter—even light.*

"You said you'd die for me. Why?"

He doesn't respond. He doesn't look away from the phone. His expression hardly shifts at all. *I don't like it.*

I look to the screen held in his hand too. The beautiful celestial scene loses focus, but I can't get the imagery out of my head. The narrator's calm voice can't ease my mind now.

*A gun carelessly aimed between my eyes. Fear seizing my lungs, my very being aware of the immediate threat of death. One squeeze of Ice's finger the only thing between life and the unknowable. Just like a black hole.*

*If you get too close, there's no chance of escape.*

*But what if I'm already too close?*

*What if it's only a matter of time before it sucks me in?*

Eyes wide, staring at the scabbing heart on my wrist, I lean on James' shoulder. He tenses, but he relaxes after a few seconds, and I decide against moving away like before. Instead, I concentrate on the way his shoulder shifts as he breathes. The steady rhythm of his breathing and the narrator's low, droning voice make my eyelids heavier.

*But I still...*

"Do you ever wonder," my voice says, distant and soft, "what it might be like to die?"

*Huh? Is that what I meant to ask?*

The breathing beside me stops for an instant.

Then he whispers, "Yes."

There's something profound about it—his discomfort the moment I mentioned death. The hesitation. The careful, quiet tone carried in that single, quiet word. A wariness. He doesn't want to talk about it, and I realize that, but he doesn't ask me to stop. At this point, I'm not sure I could even if he did.

"Would it hurt?" I ask.

"Well, uh... That depends..."

"On what?"

"On how you die. I guess."

"That makes sense."

"Ah... Why are you worrying about that, anyway?" he asks, shifting slightly. "Ice won't kill you. You said you believe that, right? Or were you lying to make me feel better?"

"No," I say.

I don't think Ice wants to kill me, but that doesn't make me any less afraid of him, and it doesn't stop me from seeing the black hole, the tip of the muzzle with Ice standing behind it, and imagining death every time I close my eyes. To be shot and bleed out. How would I feel, knowing my life is ending? Knowing nothing and no one could save me? Would I black out early on, or would I remain conscious until I lost so much blood my brain shut down?

In my nightmare, I remember the sensation of drowning. The salty, metallic blood flooding my mouth as it replaced the air in my lungs and choked me in the dark.

I shudder, and my eyes land on the gun again.

What if Ice shot me as he stood over me with that same gun aimed between my eyes? I would have died instantly, right? Without feeling anything at all? One second, I would be there, alive in that awful moment, and the next I would be gone.

"I don't want to die."

James freezes. He doesn't move. He doesn't breathe.

Then I feel an arm wrap around me. A hand rests near my shoulder and pulls me closer. The top of my head leans against his jaw. I think I feel his heartbeat, just a little fast, but it might be my own.

In any case, he's quite warm and smells faintly of vanilla.

"You won't die," he says.

I stare at the phone screen. The handsome, green-eyed scientist continues talking about the black hole. How we know more about them than ever before, yet most aspects of their existence and operation remain a mystery to science. How they seem to defy the laws of physics that govern our universe, and how we'll probably never know what exists inside one, beyond the event horizon.

"I would die before I let Ice kill you," James says. His voice's dark intensity cuts through the static and fluff filling my head. "I promise you that much, Jayde."

"Don't say that."

I sit up straight, pointedly removing my head from his shoulder. When our eyes meet, mine grow wide again, and his burn with a bitter fear. Until he really looks at me. Then his expression shifts to one of nervous warmth—or muted concern—and understanding.

"You took the Vicodin," he says.

I force a smile. "Sorry. You don't mind me touching you, right? I just— I'm getting tired, and it hurts to lean the other way, so…"

He glances aside. His fingers, resting just below my shirt's sleeve, shift slightly against my arm, and I remember he also touched me, and my face goes quite hot.

But he says, "No."

And I release the breath I was holding.

"Do you…mind if I fall asleep?"

His eyes, watching the phone screen, soften. "Go ahead. You need the rest."

"Thanks," I mumble, leaning into him again. "Keep watching stuff on my phone if you want. I don't mind. But wake me up before it dies, okay?"

"Okay."

I watch the documentary a moment longer, but I can't stand the thought of the supermassive black hole. That inescapable force. The only thing that will remain in the vastness of space as the universe slowly dies and everything else comes to an end. No stars. No planets. No colorful nebulae. Nothing but the black holes, slowly devouring each other in the cold.

*I can't stand it.*

My eyes close, and I focus on James' breathing instead. I can feel it. Every breath. And his heartbeat. Then I focus on my own breathing. And the sweet scent of whatever stupid deodorant he bought the other day.

*He is very warm.*

*This room is…so warm.*

# twenty

"Hey."

*Hmm…?*

"Hey, Jayde, wake up."

*What is it?*

Enveloped in a warm haze, I shift slightly. A soft numbness seems to fill my limbs—not quite pins and needles, but similar… And my head is full of cotton. Lifting it only worsens the feeling.

*I'm so tired.*

A hand jostles my shoulder. Maybe this isn't the first time either. I'm not sure. But a sound of discontent escapes my throat, and my head lolls to the side again, falling against something solid.

"Come on. Ugh." *James.* "Wake up."

His voice bothers me. Something in the tone.

"What time is it?" I ask, the words slurring together as I yawn.

"This is just fantastic…"

"What?"

I force myself to sit up straight. As I rub my eyes, a thin filament scratches my nose. I open my eyes to find a dark scab cutting across my palm. Plastic stitches.

*Oh.*

When I look up from my hand, I see James.

His eyes are wide and afraid, but they're *beautiful*. My breath catches. His expression startled me at first, but I can't bring myself to say anything now. I can't move, and I forgot what he said. But I can't stop thinking about his *eyes*. I've always liked that amber color. And he never gets this close to me. All I can do is stare.

"You have to get out of here," he says. "I need you to hide. Do you understand?"

*Hide? What?*

I shake my head, my heavy eyelids slipping. "I don't wanna go anywhere. I just...wanna sleep... You said..."

"Jayde—"

Firm hands return to my shoulders, and my eyes snap open again. *James' face... Discomfort. Anxiety. Fear.*

*What's going on?*

"I'm sorry," he says without a hint of apology. "I know what I said, but you can't sleep now. I need you to go up to the third floor. There's a crawlspace. I need you to find it and hide out there for a while. Just a few minutes. Think you can do that?"

I try to rub the sleep from my eyes without scratching myself a second time.

"What?" I say.

"Just—" He groans, raking a hand through his short hair. "Go upstairs, please?"

"Crawlspace?" I ask. The word feels foreign, like I've never said it out loud before. Maybe I haven't. I don't know.

"Yes. On the third floor." He flashes a pained smile, but I

don't respond, so he gestures upward and continues. "It's a square door on the ceiling—like an attic. It can't be that hard to find. Just, um, pull the cord, and it'll open for you. There's a ladder inside."

*A door? A cord? A ladder?*

"Fuck. Can you even climb a ladder in this state?"

I blink at him, and I try to think through what he's said, but nothing connects. Something about a door on the ceiling and hiding and climbing?

*Aah... My head hurts.*

I really do want to go back to sleep, but James stands from the small couch and pulls me up with him. My stomach twists as the world seems to spin, but I shake my hand out of his hold on it once I'm sure I won't fall over.

"Please hurry," he begs, his voice low.

"Whatever. Fine."

"Okay. Thank you. Go."

When my vision clears, I look at him again, and I hesitate. His eyes wide, his face pale. My phone, the screen dark, held in one hand. The black handgun in the other.

*The gun.*

A sickness settles in my stomach, but I shake it off. I ignore the look on his face, and I take my phone from him. I shove it into my pocket before turning toward the door.

"I'm going," I say. "Happy?"

I cross the room and open the door, but my legs wobble as I look out on the hallway. I rest against the doorjamb for a moment to regain my balance. Then James is at the door too. When I glance over, he offers another smile—weak and tired.

He's still holding the gun.

I want to ask if he's okay. Or what's wrong, but—

"Take the other staircase," he says, pointing down the hallway.

*The other...* My eyes follow the invisible line his finger drew to the end of the hall.

I forgot there was a second staircase in Reid Manor. It's in one of the back rooms, and less convenient than the main stairwell that connects all three floors. I've never used it. James said it wasn't safe. Some of the boards are broken—or something.

*So, why should I use it now?*

I feel a gentle push on my back. A hand. I leave the doorway, but I glance over my shoulder. James' eyes are shadowed in the low light of the hallway.

"Once you're up there, don't leave the crawlspace until I come for you," he says. "No matter what you hear. Now, please, go."

He walks toward the main staircase, his footfalls echoing in the stuffy air. He still has the gun, and I, now standing alone in the middle of the hallway, suddenly feel very unsure about this whole thing.

"Wait," I call, my dry voice cracking. "Where are you going?"

He doesn't look back or stop walking. "Don't worry about it. Just go upstairs, Jayde."

*What the heck is going on?*

I turn away and head down the hall, in the opposite direction. I peek into the small, empty room and look up the old, narrow staircase. The light switch doesn't work—or the light bulb is burnt out. So I just take a deep breath and start up the stairs in the dark.

I move slowly and carefully to avoid stepping on any damaged boards, but I still trip a few times on the way.

*My coordination is off. My feet lag behind my intention to move them. The haze over my mind. The slow tracking of my eyes. It's all working against me.*

The task strains my concentration to the max, but I manage to reach the third floor in one piece.

I open the door and step out. I stare down the dark hallway for a moment before running a hand along the wall to find a light switch. *Finally.* The light clicks on with a soft electric buzz, illuminating the hall.

*What am I doing here, again?*

I drift down the hallway, trying to remember why James sent me up to the third floor. I'm not looking for anything in particular, I don't think.

*The look in James' eyes. Impatience mixed with fear. He told me...something...*

I open a door. I peer into the room, at the cardboard stapled and taped over what used to be a large window. There's no glass on the floor now, but I remember... *James pinned Ice against the window. A gun to my head. The sharp shattering of glass, the sound deadened by a ringing in my ear.*

The ringing is gone now too—just like the thin, yellowed glass.

I close the door and move to cross the hallway. When I look up, though, I notice something different. A square panel cutting into the lengthwise boards on the ceiling—a small door with a length of knotted cord dangling from one edge.

*A door. A cord.*

I reach for it, but I'm too short. I jump, but a sharp dizziness overtakes me, and I nearly fall over.

Frustrated, I glance around the hallway for anything that might help and spot a folding footstool leaned against the wall a few feet away, beside another door.

*Of course. James used it while patching the window.*

I set the stool beneath the door in the ceiling and climb on top. Still, no luck. The cord is caught on one corner of the door, so only the very end brushes my fingertips when I stand on my tiptoes and reach as high as physically possible.

*I really am too short.*

Glancing at the floor, I bite my lip.

The only way to grab the cord is to jump while standing on the stool and hope I can catch the loop and pull it free. I might fall, but *this is something I need to do, isn't it?*

So, I grit my teeth. And I jump.

My hand closes around the rough cord, and the small door pops open on my way back down. My feet connect the flat top of the stool. Then something falls from the ceiling, my heart catches in my throat, and I lose my balance. The cord slips from my fingers. I topple backward, and the footstool shoots out from underneath and slides away as I hit the floor.

The impact isn't particularly painful, but I rub the hip that slammed against the hardwood. Then I look up to figure out what spooked me. Slats of aged wood held together with thick rope lead up into the hole the door revealed when it opened.

*A...rope ladder?*

There's a room up there, I think—

*Wait—*

*A door. A cord. A ladder.*

*The crawlspace.*

*What James said—!*

I glance over my shoulder, eyes wide as I stare at the landing at the far end of the hall, where the main stairwell lets out. *I don't hear anything, but—* I scramble to my feet, heart pounding and mind racing. I look up, into the dark crawlspace. At the ladder.

James said I couldn't go back to sleep. He asked me to come up here and hide in the crawlspace. He went downstairs. He took the gun with him.

*Because Ice is here?*

Why didn't he just tell me?

What is he thinking?

My first instinct is to dart down the stairs. To find James. I don't want to hide if hiding means he'll be alone to deal with Ice—the person who wants him dead—but… He has the gun, and Ice only has a knife, so… He should be fine, right?

*He doesn't even know how to use a gun.*

*Ugh.*

I hold my aching head in my hands.

I could never stand up to Ice in this condition—not that I stood a chance against him before. But if I tried now, I'd only get in the way. Only be a hindrance. A liability.

Maybe I should just do what James said. Maybe I *should* hide.

*Yeah, okay.*

I face the ladder again. I climb up. One hand after the other.

One foot after the other. Ignoring the tightness in my chest. The fear of falling. The fear of hearing a gunshot and my blood running cold. *The fear of the black hole.*

I make it up the ladder and heft myself into the crawlspace.

The room is surprisingly large, spanning the full length of the hallway, but the ceiling is low. I can sit comfortably, but I can barely stand on my knees without the top of my head brushing the cobwebs in the rafters. Several old boxes, covered in thick dust surround me on both sides.

When I lift my hand, it leaves a dark impression on the floor, the dust having transferred to my injured palm. I try brushing it off, only to realize the front of my shirt is covered in dust too.

*Gross.*

I carefully turn around and assess the hallway again, but it's still empty and quiet.

*James... Please be careful.*

I take a deep breath before pulling the rope ladder up and dragging it off to one side. Then I close the door using the small knob on the inside. The door clicks shut, held in place by a powerful magnet.

With the door closed, the crawlspace is miserable. Dark and hot and stuffy, it feels more cramped than before. More claustrophobic. The only reprieve is the light filtering in through cracks between the boards in the floor, though it hardly illuminates the space and does nothing to combat the hot, stale air as it threatens to suffocate me.

*But I can't leave.*

Even as I sit before the door, staring at my shadowed hands, and think the inescapable thoughts. That Ice is down there somewhere. That James is in serious danger.

*But I'm too weak. I would only make the situation worse if I left now. I wouldn't be able to help anyone.* My eyes fill with hot tears. *Why couldn't I just deal with the discomfort? Why did I take that stupid pill?*

Then I hear something.

A sound from elsewhere in the house breaks me out of my worrying. The sound of running—someone coming up the stairs, maybe?

I drop low and press my face to one of the narrow cracks in the crawlspace door. I can make out only a sliver of hallway below.

*James.*

He runs through the hall, glancing up at the crawlspace as he passes by, his expression tight and anxious. He looks fine. He doesn't seem hurt at all. But he doesn't have the gun with him —not in his hand, at least.

*What does that mean?*

"What are you trying to prove?" a cool voice asks from the direction of the main stairwell.

*It's him—*

Struggling to adjust my position without making noise, I look through a few different cracks and eventually find a better view despite the strange angle. And I see Ice walking down the hallway at a leisurely pace with his switchblade open and held in one hand.

James ran straight down the hall without stopping. He must

have gone down the broken staircase, back to the second floor. *So, he should be safe for now.*

"This is a waste of time," Ice hisses, speaking to himself.

I hold a hand over my mouth to silence my breathing as he nears the crawlspace door. *Of course, he pauses directly beneath it anyway.* My heart pounds, but I hold my breath, desperate to evade detection.

Then he cocks his head as though something caught his attention, and I shift slightly to follow his line of sight.

*Oh. The footstool.*

He laughs. A breezy sound. And my eyes water.

"Seriously? That was almost too easy."

He looks up with a lazy grin. Bright blue eyes stare through the crawlspace door like it doesn't exist—like he's already looking directly at me.

I pull away from the crack between the boards as panic seizes my chest, worsened by the room's hot mustiness. *Forget breathing quietly, I can barely breathe at all.*

"You're up there, aren't you?" he asks. "Jayde Palmer."

*Ugh.*

The sound of my name spoken so casually in his voice twists my stomach into knots. I wish he'd shut his mouth and keep walking, but he doesn't.

"What will it take to get you down, I wonder?"

# twenty-one

I look around the dark crawlspace. The motion hurts my head.

There's a vent at the far end, at the front of the house. The faint light filtering through suggests it leads outside, but the opening is at most ten inches wide and easily thirty feet above ground.

The crawlspace door is the only way out.

Just when I think things can't possibly get worse, my phone goes off in my pocket—the text tone. *Loud.* The hand that was supporting most of my weight shoots up to silence it, and I lose my balance. I topple over and crash into one of the cardboard boxes. The squared corner scrapes my injured side, and I cry out, caught off guard both by the sharp pain and the several magazines that spill from the torn box and land on me.

Ice laughs in the hallway below as I lie awkwardly crumpled on the unforgiving crawlspace floor. Tears welling in my eyes, I take my phone from my pocket. The light makes me squint, but I manage to read the message on my lock screen.

**Ice Monroe**                                             now
Hey, kid. (°ᵕ°)

And another from earlier, less than fifteen minutes ago…

**Ice:** You're still holed up at old Reid Manor,
right? I'm on my way. See you soon.

*James' wide eyes when he woke me up... Face pale, my phone still in his hand.* He saw the message—a banner must have popped up while he was watching Netflix.

That's why he sent me up here?

*That's why...*

I slam my phone against the hardwood before returning it to my pocket. Then I push the magazines away, ignore the throbbing in my side, and drag myself back to a seated position. As I glare at the crawlspace door, my imagining of the look on Ice's face pisses me off.

*I hate him. I really, truly hate him.*

"What on earth are you doing up there?"

He's still laughing.

Frustrated and not sure what else I can do, I push on the small door. It clicks open and swings down on its hinge, illuminating the crawlspace and stirring up a fresh cloud of dust. I cough and blink, hoping to wake from this nightmare, but my vision clears, and Ice stands in the hallway below.

His smug, humored expression is about what I imagined, but, as our eyes meet, it softens in a way I didn't expect.

"There you are," he says.

"What do you want?" I ask, anger bubbling in my words.

He chuckles. "What do you think I want, Jayde?"

*Hell if I know!*

I tell him to leave.

He feigns offense, pursing his lips while his eyes remain sharp. "Aw. You don't wanna hang out like we used to?" Dropping the act, he laughs again. "Stop playing around. Get down here."

"Why?"

"I don't have time for games today, kid. Cut me some slack."

"Go away. Leave us alone. Please."

His lip twitches, his smile faltering as narrowed eyes betray impatience. The slight tension leaves me nervous, and for good reason, but I… *I don't care if he's mad at James or mad at me, this is seriously messed up.*

He frowns. "You're not making this easy."

"Good," I snap. "Why the hell would I want to make anything easier for you?"

Fire ignites in his eyes, and my nails dig into the hardwood —an automatic reaction as he bares his teeth.

"Get the fuck down here."

"No!"

He looks away, physically turning to stare at the wall, his eyes still wide and posture tense.

Panic wells in my chest, but I don't look away. I don't move. *He cycles through moods too quickly.* I never know what to expect, let alone how I should react. I can't let my guard down —not even for a second.

I glance at the ladder, in a pile beside the crawlspace opening. *Should I do what he wants? Should I—?*

Then I hear a sigh, and I look down as Ice finishes combing a hand through his elegantly disheveled hair. *Ugh.*

"Fine," he says. "You can't possibly stay up there forever."

He walks out of view, further down the hall, but soon returns with the footstool tucked under one arm. He drops it upright and sits upon it. With the open switchblade in his lap and his hands casually interlaced behind his head, he looks up at me again.

"Well?" He flashes a lazy grin. "I'm waiting."

I'm sick of it. Sick of Ice. Sick of his attitude. The sarcasm. Having to put up with it. It's annoying. *I am done with him.* Teeth grit, I reach out. My fingers close around the small knob on the crawlspace door, and I pull it shut.

The powerful magnet engages with a solid click, and a moment of silence follows. A long, tense moment. I stare at the door, slowly realizing.

*I probably shouldn't have done that.*

Ice curses. I hear him stand and kick something—or throw something—and I wince at a second crash as the object hits the wall and falls to the floor.

Another beat of silence. Then a single footstep.

My eyes water furiously. Sweat beads on my forehead. I hold a hand over my mouth, fighting to keep from hyperventilating in the stuffy space.

"Open the door."

His voice is laced with a coldness I've never heard before. But I don't move. I'm not sure I can face whatever I unleashed down there. *What will he do if I leave the crawlspace while he's like this?*

"Open the door. Now."

*And if I don't? What will he do then?*

"Jayde, I swear to god—"

But I can't. Even if I wanted to comply, I can't convince my hand to move. All I can do is stare at the crawlspace door in mute horror.

The hallway is quiet. So quiet. Too quiet.

For a moment, the only sound is my own muffled breathing. Then a small click reaches my good ear, and my breathing pauses.

*BANG—!*

*BANG—!*

*BANG—!*

I scream.

Nothing hit me, but I scream all the same, and several seconds of horrible silence pass before I convince myself to peel my eyes open again.

There, in the boards of the crawlspace door, are three small, circular holes punched clean through the wood. The closest is mere inches from my fingertips. Thin, yellow rays of light shine through them.

*Ice has a gun.*

My hands shake violently, but I force myself to push the door open a second time. I lean out over the opening. My eyes are so wide they hurt as I peer down, and they fill with fat tears when I register the silver handgun.

*It's not even the same gun. It's totally different. But once again aimed at me. The small, dark hole at the tip. If it fired now, surely I would—*

I apologize, my wavering voice hardly a whisper. Tears roll down my face. And the gun lowers, falling to his side.

He sighs. "Just drop the ladder and come down, will you?"

My trembling hand is on the ladder, ready to push it over the edge, when a new voice stops me.

*James.*

Ice groans. "What now?"

I lean further over the opening, my fingers numb from gripping the door frame so tight. James stands at the far end of the hallway, just outside the room leading to the wrecked staircase. As he jogs in our direction, he still doesn't seem to have his handgun on him, and he looks about as frightened as I feel.

He stops a few yards away from Ice, who is still directly beneath the hole I'm watching through.

"James," I breathe.

*Worst timing ever.*

He tears his gaze away from me to look at Ice, and he freezes when he catches sight of the silver gun.

*Did James not know he had one?*

Ice must be thinking the same thing as his attention flicks from the gun in his hand and back to James, and a sinister sneer replaces his prior frustration.

"Ah. This is fine too."

He raises the gun again, this time to aim at James, who is apparently too stunned by the unexpected appearance of a second gun to react. Instead of running, ducking, or doing *literally anything else for the sake of self-preservation*, he glances up at me. His jaw slack. Wide eyes glazed over in confusion.

Ice's smirk doesn't falter. His eyes sparkle dangerously, and his finger hovers over the trigger, and I get the feeling he isn't messing around today. This isn't a game anymore—if it ever was.

He wants James dead, and he's seizing an opportunity.

*No.*

"Wait!" I lean further out over the edge. "Ice—"

*Please, don't shoot—*

*—Oh.*

I thought my grip was secure. I was sure it was before I moved. But my left hand slips, and my injured hand can't compensate. It's not strong enough to support my full weight on its own.

I lose my balance.

*Shit.*

Once both hands drop beyond the edge of the crawlspace opening, it's over. They fall below my knees and into the hallway, and I can't stop the rest of me from following.

Ice looks up, time still moving too slowly. The gun is still in his hand, his finger still on the trigger.

He reacts quickly, but I'm free-falling. He can't avoid me. My hand hits his shoulder. His arm buckles—the arm with a gun at the end of it—and he collapses beneath my weight.

Our eyes meet for an instant, his as wide as mine. Blank shock reflected in vibrantly blue eyes. *And cold fear that isn't entirely my own.*

The gun fires, a deafening blast, and a searing line of heat tears through my shoulder. Then the half of my body that didn't land on Ice contacts the floor—*hard*—and a sharp jolt of pain radiates up my other arm.

I know I screamed when I landed, but I couldn't hear myself. I can't hear *anything*. My vision fades, going black, but Ice jostles me back to consciousness as his hand presses into my back, and he scrambles out from underneath my broken body.

I don't know where he goes. I'm too busy dying to keep track.

James yells something. I recognize his voice, but the screaming pain and ringing in my ears all but erase the words. I don't know what he said or who it was directed toward, and I can't bring myself to care. My shoulder is bleeding—a wet warmth leaking down my arm—and I think I broke my wrist.

*I want to curl up and cry until I pass out.*

Someone drops to their knees beside me. I felt the vibration more than I heard it, but I open my eyes anyway, vaguely relieved to find James looking stricken but otherwise alive and unharmed. I grab him by the shirt with my right hand—the more functional of the two for the first time in several days.

"I'm dying," I choke.

"N–no. You're not dying."

His vacant tone and the blood slicking my right arm lead me to believe otherwise, but I manage to control myself enough to reassess my surroundings. James is on his knees beside me, while Ice stands much further away with his back against the wall. His eyes are shadowed over, and he holds the gun at his side, but he seems to be breathing normally.

*I fell on him. And he shot me!*

*Doesn't that bother him at all?*

"Damn…"

Ice looks up from the floor, and I stare past James, who is frantically trying to keep from completely losing it, to watch him. His still-wide eyes and taut smile betray discontent.

"I shot the wrong person," he says with a hint of surprise in his otherwise even voice.

*That's seriously all you have to say? Bastard.*

James shakes me gently, and I return to ignoring Ice since he no longer seems to be in the mood for murder. Once I force myself into a sort-of-sitting position, I cup a hand over the wound on my upper arm.

Somehow, it hurts less than my wrist, *but the blood—*

I don't think it's coming from my actual shoulder. *No.* My fingers brush the side of my arm, stinging the raw wound beneath. From what I can feel, the bullet just grazed me, but it must have done some damage.

There is blood *everywhere.*

I look to James again. His hands are planted on my shoulders, holding me steady, but he's not looking at me anymore. He's glaring at Ice, who hasn't moved, and he is *pissed.*

*I am too, but is now really the time?*

"James—" My voice comes out as a sob. "It's bleeding."

His attention falls on me again, the fire fading from his eyes as he presses a hand against the one I have cupped over my bleeding arm. I gasp, both at the increased pressure and the stab of pain from the angle of my wrist shifting.

"This looks bad," he murmurs. "Where were you hit?"

"Tch—"

We both glance at Ice.

He *still* hasn't moved from the wall, but he watches us carefully. No longer smiling, his expression is dark and serious. The intensity of it dulls my pain.

"James," he says, his voice cold. "Make yourself useful and get the girl to a hospital before she bleeds out in this godforsaken place."

Without waiting for a response, he turns and walks off at a leisurely pace. I watch as he disappears down the stairwell, unable to understand why his words and manner of departure upset me so much.

Then James removes our hands from my arm, and the flare of pain leaves Ice as little more than an afterthought. He lifts my shirt sleeve and *very uncomfortably* wipes blood away to clear the area. My vision blurs—perhaps from pain, though more likely from the tears flooding my eyes—but it seems I was right.

While blood quickly covers the area again, it looks like the meaty part of my upper arm was grazed rather than anything being shot clean through.

It's a relief, but I'm still concerned.

*Ice* shot *me.*

The blood is overwhelming. Hot liquid, running down my arm and dripping onto the hardwood in thin, red ribbons. *Should I bleed this much if the bullet only grazed me?*

"You need a hospital," James says, his voice tense, surely having come to the same conclusion. "Come on. I'll help you up."

I press my hand over the wound while he slips an arm around my waist to drag me to my feet. My legs feel like jelly. I'm not sure what's wrong, but I can't bear my own weight.

He quickly gives up and leaves me sitting on the floor.

"I'll call an ambulance," he decides aloud, pacing in front of me with one hand at the back of his head. "Shit— I don't have my phone. Where's yours?"

I take my phone from my back pocket and unlock it with shaky hands, leaving bloody fingerprints everywhere I touch.

I apologize for the blood as I hold it up. He grimaces, but he takes the phone and wipes the screen on his shirt before dialing. *Dark stains on faded brown fabric.*

"Hang in there," he says.

He props the phone against his ear as he kneels to pick me up. I sling my bleeding arm behind his neck and stare into his wide eyes, but I can only bear it for a moment before I have to look away.

*He's really scared.*

I feel so pathetic. I can't even walk on my own. He has to carry me downstairs. The most I can do to help is maintain pressure on the wound. *Sort of.*

"I'm sorry."

It's all I could think to say.

He's halfway through a word when the phone distracts him. He speaks urgently to the person on the other end of the line, but the fresh ringing in my ear overtakes his trembling voice, and I find myself thinking about Ice.

*Does he feel guilty?*

Does it matter? He was about to shoot James. I think he really would have done it too, so... *Did I stop him by falling out of the crawlspace when I did?*

My arm grows tired of holding my hand up and against the gunshot wound. My hand is slicked with crimson blood, slipping through my fingers like something from a dream. It dribbles down the back of my shirt, wetting the fabric. But the pain is more of a dull throb now.

I close my eyes.

"Jayde?" James asks.

"It doesn't hurt anymore."

I zone out as he makes his way downstairs. He walks slowly, but we're already at the bottom when my eyes open again. He seems short of breath, but he continues cradling me as he drops to sit on the second-to-last step.

My vision is blurrier than before, though, so I can't quite make out his expression. Only wide eyes.

*Am I crying? I don't...feel like I'm crying.*

"The ambulance will be here soon," he says. "Everything will be fine."

"It's fine?" My voice sounds distant.

"Yeah, it's fine."

My hand falls from my shoulder as I close my eyes again. James presses his free hand to the wound instead, but it doesn't hurt at all. Even the throbbing in my wrist seems to have faded.

"I'd feel better if you didn't do that."

"Do what?"

If he answers, I don't hear him.

I have no idea how much time has passed, but I must have fallen asleep—or something—because the nearby sound of sirens jars me awake. My eyes flutter open, heavy and damp.

After bracing himself, James stands, picking me up again.

A door opens somewhere. A violent, rough sound—one of the front doors, maybe. I hear a couple men speaking to each other, but I can't make out anything they say over the ringing.

"We're over here!" James calls.

*Everything is fine, isn't it?*

I close my eyes again.

If I am bleeding to death, it's not nearly as awful as I imagined. Nothing hurts, really. I just wanna fall asleep. *Though, that might be the medication? Maybe that's why it doesn't hurt either.* Well, whatever. James is holding me, and I feel warm. I don't feel cold at all. And I'm not scared.

*This isn't so bad.*

"Jayde, please don't go to—"

# twenty-two

~ ∞ ~

*It's dark.*

*I can't see.*

*My eyes are open, but there's nothing. No light. No shadow. No noise. I can't see my hands. I can't hear my breathing or feel my heartbeat. There's just...nothing. This place has nothing. Contains nothing. Is nothing.*

*Nothing but an endless, inky void.*

*Like deep space.*

*Like the inside of a black hole.*

*As you near the event horizon—the point of no return—and the black hole draws you in, even light can't escape its deadly pull. You, and the light, are torn apart atom by atom, photon by photon until there's nothing left but the impossibly dense, impossibly dark black hole itself.*

*And, somehow, I've found myself trapped inside the suffocating darkness.*

*But, somehow, the black hole didn't kill me.*

*Somehow, I'm still alive.*

*I move blindly through space for what feels like hours, but I never come across anything solid. No walls. No borders. I can't even feel a floor beneath my feet. There's nothing, and I never spot the faintest hint of light or a glimpse of the end no matter how far I go.*

*Is there an end?*

*Am I alone?*

*I scream for help—for anyone—but no sound escapes my lips. Even if someone else were around, trapped with me somewhere in the vast vacuum of space, they wouldn't be able to hear me.*

*It's hopeless.*

*I give up.*

*I surrender myself to the void. The darkness so tangible I can feel and taste it as it envelops me. Thick and dangerous. Metallic and inky. And, slowly but surely, the darkness—the black hole—sucks me in. It drags me down through the floor like quicksand, and I don't fight it, so I sink.*

*Forever.*

~ ∞ ~

# twenty-three

I wake with a gasp that finally reaches my ringing ears. A dim, white ceiling my eyes finally see. A body I can finally feel. *Finally, I have control.*

Sitting up, slow and careful, I assess my situation.

I'm in the hospital—that much is obvious. A small recovery room with the overhead lights dimmed and a window on one wall. The curtains are drawn, but very little light shines through the cracks. A door on the opposite wall. A rectangular window in the door looks out on a brightly lit hallway. There's some furniture… A short, square dresser. A metal table. A wireframe chair. Overall, the room is similar to the recovery room I stayed in a week ago.

Here, though, an IV bag full of clear fluid hangs from a rack attached to the hospital bed. A thin tube connects it to a catheter taped to the back of my right hand, above the plastic bracelet with my name printed on it.

No electronic beeping. No doctors. No nurses. No James.

So, I'm alone, but that's fine. I didn't bleed to death. I wasn't swallowed by the black hole. I'm alive. *I'm okay.*

I assess myself next.

I'm wearing a pale, blue hospital gown, but the River Sapphire still hangs around my neck. My left wrist is in a brace—not a cast. It seems I didn't break it after all. I run my fingers over the bruises forming in the crook of my elbow. Moving up my arm, I push the sleeve of the hospital gown up to find a thick gauze bandage securely taped to my upper arm, near the shoulder.

But nothing was broken. I didn't bleed out back at Reid Manor. I'm in a hospital room, and I feel fine, and—

*I was shot.*

My eyes grow wide, and I look back to the door. To the clock above it. To the hands on the clock. Now that I see them, I can imagine the ticking of the second hand I can't hear over the ringing in my head. The clock reads just after two. *2AM?*

Where is James?

\* \* \* \* \*

I could have pressed the nurse call button, but I'm too nervous. So I've just been sitting in bed for the past half hour, twiddling my thumbs because I have no idea where James is or where my phone is or what happened after I left the third floor of Reid Manor.

I glance at the clock again. It's almost 8AM. *Ugh.*

Just when I'm about to give in and reach for the red button, there's a knock on the door. It opens a second later. The light from the hallway hurts my eyes.

"Oh, she's awake," a bright voice says—a female nurse carrying a plastic meal tray.

"Ah. Good."

I didn't recognize his distant voice over the tinny ringing, but the doctor who steps through the door after the nurse is Dr. Corel. I wasn't expecting to see him again, but the familiar face is a relief.

"Good morning," I squeak.

He flips the switch by the door, and the bright overhead lights flood the room, beating back all lingering darkness. I blink again to clear my vision. The nurse leaves the meal tray on the bedside table and goes about checking my IV while Dr. Corel approaches my bedside with more leisure, preoccupied with reading something on his clipboard.

There are a lot of things I want to say, but I wait.

"Miss Palmer." He looks up from his clipboard with a muted smile. "It's wonderful to see you awake. How are you feeling this morning?"

"I feel okay." *It's an honest enough answer.*

"Do you know why you're here?"

I hesitate before nodding. "I was shot—by accident, I guess—after I fell out of a crawlspace."

He considers me for a long moment as the nurse removes the IV catheter from my hand. When she's done, she swivels the lap table for me. I move the meal tray myself, and the nurse leaves the room when Dr. Corel asks.

"Yes, you were shot," he says, "and you were lucky. The bullet grazed your deltoid. The injury to your muscle was minimal, and it missed the bone completely, but a small branch off your axillary was nicked. Thankfully, the bleeding was easy to control once you arrived."

While I stare rather blankly, he explains that I did, in fact, sprain my wrist. They had to give me blood products during the minor surgery performed to stop the bleeding, but I'm expected to make a full recovery within a couple weeks.

There is no bad news, only good.

I lift the dome off the meal tray to reveal the ham scramble, toast, and sliced fruit underneath. For some reason, I don't feel like eating.

"I thought I might die," I admit, my eyes focused on the tray, "but I guess it wasn't that bad."

"Yes, it's something of a miracle. If the wound were two or three millimeters deeper—if the main axillary artery were damaged—the outcome could have been far different." He clears his throat, seeming to stifle a sigh. "In any case, James brought up drowsiness as a recurring issue, so I'm taking you off the Vicodin and switching you to another pain medication. You should not have been prescribed an opioid for such minor injuries in the first place, but the new one shouldn't cause any loss of function."

"Thanks—" *Wait.* I look up from the food. "Where is James? Are the police involved again?"

He shakes his head. "No. RPD is not involved. James is fine, and Human-Immortal Affairs was made aware of the situation after your admission last night."

*Human-Immortal Affairs...*

"Do they care about me at all?"

He meets my gaze, his kind smile strained as though he doesn't quite know what to say. And that tells me everything I had already assumed before.

Human-Immortal Affairs does not care about me—the human,

Jayde Palmer—at all.

It doesn't matter if I'm part of their exclusive Human Immortal Program. To them, I still hold less intrinsic value than Ice does. I'm less important. I have fewer rights. Less agency. Simply because he's an immortal, and my sponsor, while I'm only human.

"They claim to have agents closely monitoring your situation," he says. "All I can do is share my input with them as a third party."

*Monitoring... Right.*

"Can I talk to them?"

"Unfortunately, the way Human-Immortal Affair's advocacy program works—" He pauses to sigh and adjust his glasses. "You would have to go through your sponsor to speak directly with a representative."

"Oh." *Of course, that's how it works.*

"I apologize. But I can have someone run out and find James for you. I think I know where he might be."

"Thank you."

I glance at my breakfast tray. I know I should be hungry, but I feel even less like eating than I did before.

"All things considered, you're healing well," Dr. Corel says. "A nurse will stop by to remove your stitches soon. Try to stick around until then, at least."

"No problem there."

"Good luck, Miss Palmer."

Before he leaves, I ask him to call me Jayde. Then I force myself to eat, set the meal tray aside, and wait with my eyes glued to the door.

# twenty-four

Standing near the foot of the hospital bed—just close enough to catch myself if I lose my balance—I test my joints. Whatever painkiller was in the IV is starting to wear off, but the discomfort from my sprained wrist is still strangely minor. I roll my shoulders and wince at a twinge of pain. My hip feels about the same.

I hear a click to my left and pause.

The door opens. When James pokes his head inside, my eyes fill with tears. *What is that about?*

He steps in alone with his head down and closes the door behind himself, still angled away from the room. Then he turns and looks up. He freezes when he sees me. Worry and a desperate hesitance play about his face.

*Why…?*

My inexplicably watering eyes linger on his disposable, green scrub top as he approaches before stopping hardly a foot away. His trembling hands are balled into fists, and the shadows beneath his puffy eyes look darker than ever under the harsh lighting.

"You're okay?" His voice rings hollow in the quiet room.

"Yeah. I'm okay."

He lets out a breath. His lip quivers, but his shoulders and hands relax slightly. Then his expression softens, more tired than afraid. He closes the distance between us and pulls me into a hug.

*Arms wrapped around me, hands firm on my back.*

My cheek still pressed to the papery fabric over his chest, my breath catches. The air-conditioned room is quite cold. But James is *warm. His heart is racing.*

I wasn't expecting him to *hug* me, and I can't bring myself to move whether I want to return the hug or not, but there's something nice about it. *Maybe I needed a hug after everything…*

As he steps back, he apologizes.

For what? *The hug?*

"Are *you* okay?" I ask.

"Yeah."

I don't believe him for a second, but I return to the raised hospital bed, and he drags the room's single plastic chair closer before sitting. Then he reaches into his pocket and pulls out my phone.

"Ah… I thought you might want this back. Again."

I take the phone, but I don't look at it—not even to see if it's still turned on. I just set it face-down on the bedside table. I don't care about my phone.

"Are you sure you're okay?" I ask.

He stares at me for a second. Then he sighs and averts his eyes. "No. After you were admitted, uh… I waited until they moved you here—when Dr. Corel said you were stable—and then I spent the night sitting out in my car. I…couldn't sleep."

"You just sat in your car? Aren't you tired?"

He frowns. "You're seriously worried about me right now? Ice shot you, you know?"

"I know. I know I was shot, but—"

*But what, Jayde? But* what*? Talk about something else.*

"How much do you know about Human-Immortal Affairs?" I ask—it was the first thing that came to mind.

"What?" I'm ready to elaborate when a flicker of under-standing crosses his face, and he scratches his jaw. "Oh, uh, Human-Immortal Affairs... It's just a government agency, right? They deal with interactions between humans and immortals and make sure the secret doesn't get out. That's the whole reason they got me off the hook with RPD before, right?"

I sigh. It seems like he doesn't know much either, but, being an immortal himself, he surely knows more than I do.

"They run the Human Immortal Program," I say mildly. "They made the River Sapphire, and Ice filed my sponsorship paperwork through them. It sounds like, since I know about immortals now—*aware*, I think, is what they call it—they basically own me."

His brows furrow. "*Own* you?"

"It feels like Human-Immortal Affairs doesn't care about the safety or freedom of humans at all, whether they know about immortals or not. Do you have any idea why?"

He averts his eyes and rests his elbows on the edge of the tall bed. Chin propped in his hands, his frown deepens. After a moment spent glancing around with that uneasy and murky expression, he meets my gaze again, but he doesn't look any more confident than before.

"I'm sure you've already figured out that immortals sit above humans on the social ladder," he says. "It goes humans, immortals, and the government—in that order."

The air quotes used to emphasize the word *government* at the top of James' gestural ladder make me a little uncomfortable, but I don't interrupt. It turns out I don't understand a lot about immortals and the society I now share with them. And I would like to know as much as I can.

James scratches the back of his neck. "The government is— Well, the human government—everything you see on TV and the news or whatever—is part of it, but there are a bunch of ultra-rich, power-hungry immortal men with god complexes the size of the sun pulling the strings behind the scenes. A lot of assholes who do whatever they want just because they can. It's not much different than the human part, really, but immortals have more control."

I already knew the vice president was an immortal, but this is the first I've heard of an immortal shadow government. *Honestly, it sounds like a conspiracy theory...* I don't know how much to believe, but I never thought to ask Ice or Night how any of this works, so I don't have much else to go on.

"And Human-Immortal Affairs is like that too?" I ask. "I mean, obviously they're part of the government, but Ice made it sound like they were just a bunch of bureaucrats."

He blinks at me like he isn't quite sure what I'm trying to get at—or maybe he wasn't expecting me to mention Ice so casually.

"I mean, I guess he's right," he says. "Human-Immortal

Affairs has power, but they're a small piece of the pie. They're not in control of everything, and I don't think they actually *do* much beyond keeping immortals a secret and managing people like…you."

I sigh. "Dr. Corel said I can't contact them without going through Ice. Plus, it sounds like, by their standards, he hasn't even done anything illegal."

James averts his eyes again, and his leg begins to bounce.

"Why do you think I told you not to talk to the police?" he asks, his voice low. "I may not know much about the mess you're in with Ice, but I do know that saying anything against him would only get you in more trouble. No matter what he does to you. Or to me."

"To you?"

"I—" He looks up, flustered, and shakes his head. "Well, it's just… I mean, you said Ice is your sponsor, right? But I'm literally nobody—just a defective…delinquent—so I'm sure they don't care about me." A beat of silence, and he clears his throat. "Anyway, as far as stupid legal perks go, I can barely get out of paying parking tickets, but I'm sure Ice could get away with killing either of us with a slap on the wrist."

"What is Human-Immortal Affairs for, then? Do you guys even have your own police?"

"Oh, yeah. RSP—Riverview Special Police. They exist."

He looks away, scowling. *Yikes.*

I guess it only makes sense he'd be acquainted with immortal police too. *"Special Police", though? Ugh.* I pick at the edge of the brace on my arm. It hides the heart completely, which would be nice if the scab underneath didn't itch so much.

"Now that you mention it," he says with less vitriol, "I'm surprised no one talked to me before I left the police station last week. RSP usually show up like, *'We'll let you off with a warning this time, Reid, but you gotta stop letting these normie cops pick you up.'* But they've also never wiped my record clean after bailing me out, so maybe Human-Immortal Affairs works differently?"

How many times has RPD picked James up?

*Never mind. Maybe I don't want to know.*

I stare at my hands. "I honestly can't say I'm surprised. They haven't said anything to me about what's going on either."

"Sorry. The system is stacked against humans and always has been. That's probably why neither of us have heard from the cops—or Human-Immortal Affairs, I guess."

This is so unfair. If they don't care about what he's doing, how am I supposed to stop him?

James sighs. "I still can't believe he shot you."

"It was an accident," I mutter. "I landed right on top of him."

"Yeah, but—"

I shake my head. "He aimed the gun at you. I didn't mean to fall, obviously, but I had to do something, right?"

"He wouldn't have shot me."

"How do you know?" I snap. "You literally just said he could get away with killing you, and it sure didn't look like he was screwing around. What if I had stayed up in the crawlspace? What if he shot you, and you died? Huh? What then, James?"

His eyes are wide, cheeks pale, and I realize I have ahold of his shirt. The papery green material balled in my fist. *Oh.* With a sigh, I let go. I lean back. I focus on my breathing and the faint, throbbing pain in my hand.

James clears his throat and glances away, still uncomfortable. Then he makes a sound, almost like a short laugh.

"If I died?" he echoes. "Have you considered that Ice might leave you alone if I weren't around?"

"What?"

"He only hurt you to get to me, right? Well, it worked."

"James—"

He drops his head into his hands. "If it weren't for me getting involved, you'd be fine. Safe at home, probably. I shouldn't have gone to see you before I— Ugh. None of this had to happen, you know? I should have just— Damn it…"

*This again?*

I want to comfort him, but I don't know how. I don't know what to do. Or what I could say. He's clearly hurting, but how am I supposed to help? I can't go back in time and change things or heal my wounds or magically get rid of Ice. I can't make him believe me when I say I don't blame him.

"He's only doing this because of me," he continues, his voice wavering. "He hurt you because you talked to me or because he knows I care about you or some other bullshit. It doesn't matter. Whatever the reason, I pissed him off, and now he's taking it out on you. It's my fault you're in the hospital now, and it's my fault he'll try something like that again."

"It was an accident!"

He freezes.

"Ice was about to shoot *you*, and I was only hurt because I got in the way. How many times do I have to tell you? None of this is your fault."

He looks up from his hands with watery eyes. And I take a deep breath. *I have to say something.*

"Back in June, when Ice first told me about immortals, he gave me a choice. He didn't force me to sign the Secrecy Agreement. He didn't force me to accept the River Sapphire or stay with him. I could have walked away at any time—and, yeah, obviously in hindsight, I should have. But I didn't. Dumb or not, I made those decisions myself. I got myself into this mess. Not you."

*Even if he doesn't believe me, I—*

"I told Ice you bumped into me at the mall. I got you involved, and I made the choice to go looking for you after you came to apologize for what you did. I didn't have to believe anything you said. I didn't have to stay the night and wait until morning to go back. You didn't force me to stay with you either. I could have walked back myself—I know you wouldn't have stopped me—but I chose to listen. I wanted to hear you out. I—"

*Where am I going with this?*

I sigh, folding my arms over my chest. "Anyway, I don't regret giving you a second chance. If it weren't for you, I'd probably still be stuck in Westbrooke, wasting my time pining over someone who doesn't care about me, so… Yeah. Don't feel bad. At least not for anything Ice has done."

James seems to have calmed down, as though listening to me rant sapped what little energy he had left. He wipes his eyes and glances away again.

"It's hard not to blame myself, you know?" His voice is quiet, full of weariness. "I get what you're trying to say. I really do, but… It's hard to even look at you sometimes. Every time I do, I remember how stupid and careless I've been the past few weeks."

*Trust me, you're not the only one who feels that way.*

"Just so you know, if Ice was planning to shoot you back there, I don't regret taking the bullet myself."

"Jayde, I—"

I look away. "You should get some rest. I'm not sure how much longer they plan to keep me here, but I'll be fine."

\* \* \* \* \*

*Rest is best, rest is best.*

The young immortal nurse preaches it so many times as she changes my bandage, gives me my first dose of naproxen, and removes my old stitches that the mantra sticks in my head. I'm not sure if she knows the finer details of my situation, but she doesn't ask, and I don't explain more than I have to.

Though, she does say I can take the brace off to shower as long as I tape plastic over the dressing on my shoulder. James is fast asleep on the padded bench seat underneath the window, so I take advantage of that the moment the nurse leaves.

My hair is *blood-free.*

As I step back into the room, I check on James again. He hasn't moved from where he passed out a few hours ago, his body a bit curled with his back facing the room.

*I wonder… Was he being honest with himself when he said he didn't think Ice would shoot him? Why would he feel so strongly about it?*

Some time later, there's a knock on the door, and Dr. Corel lets himself in. He notices James still passed out across the room before looking to me with a pleasant smile.

"How are you feeling, Jayde?"

"I'm alright." *Frustrated, but alright.*

"How is James?"

"Tired. But I think he's okay too."

Dr. Corel asks a few routine questions while checking my vitals and the closed wounds now free of stitches:

*Have you experienced any unusual aches or pains?*

Not really; just the usual ones.

*Have you been out of bed at all today?*

Yes. A few times.

*Can you move around well on your own?*

Well enough, anyway, considering I managed to take a shower.

"Everything looks great," he says—finally. "You're cleared for discharge. Do you have somewhere safe to go from here?"

*Somewhere...safe?*

I didn't think to ask James if he had any idea where we should go after this before I forced him to lie down. We can't just go back to Reid Manor. The building is huge and old and impossible to secure. It was never safe to begin with. *And now there's a ton of blood up on the third floor.*

"I'll talk to James when he wakes up," I say. "I'm sure we can figure something out."

His attention passes over me and lands on the sleeping man. He frowns, the expression mild and thoughtful but somewhat uncomfortable to look at for some reason. And I think about what James said earlier.

"Hey, um— Is it true that Ice won't get in trouble for anything he's done? Is there really nothing I can do?"

"Human-Immortal Affairs assured me they're looking into your case." *He said the same thing before, but his voice seems even more distant now.*

"What about the police?" I ask.

"Police?" His eyes flick to the clipboard in his hand. "Unfortunately, your specific situation doesn't fall under police jurisdiction—immortal or human."

My *specific situation* seems like exactly the type that should fall under some kind of police jurisdiction. *Immortal society really is the worst.* Or are humans not protected by immortal police at all? Maybe I fall into some grey area only Human-Immortal Affairs can address?

*Not that they're doing a satisfactory job either…*

Dr. Corel clears his throat, and I look up from my lap.

"If you don't mind me asking, how did it come to this—a squabble between James and your sponsor?"

*A squabble, huh? That's certainly one way to put it.*

I frown. "If you don't mind *me* asking, how did you know who I was the first time I came in?"

"I have some experience with the Human Immortal Program myself," he says, offering an apologetic smile, "but rumors have been circulating since late June that Ice Monroe, a member of a prominent local family, sponsored a young human woman. James simply confirmed the details when he brought you in."

*Rumors, huh?* I stifle a groan, but he answered my question, so I feel obligated to answer his.

"James got involved by chance, and Ice wasn't too happy I met him, even if it was by accident. Anyway, I guess there's some history there, but some other…stupid…things happened. I mean… It's obviously more complicated than that, and I don't know how it came to *this*, exactly, but—"

"You don't want to discuss it, and that's perfectly fine."

But I shake my head, my hands balled around the fabric of my hospital gown. "What happened yesterday… I don't know what James told you, but Ice aimed the gun at him. If I hadn't tumbled out of the crawlspace when I did, he'd be the one in the hospital right now. Or he'd be dead."

"I see." His expression darkens for an instant before he smiles a soft and surprisingly warm smile. "Well, Jayde, considering the circumstances, it sounds like James is lucky to have you looking out for him."

*Lucky? Yeah, right.*

I sigh. "I know I'm cleared for discharge, but is it okay if I stay a while longer so he can sleep?"

"Of course."

# twenty-five

"I'm sorry for being such a pain in the ass earlier."

"You're fine." I sigh, still trying to stuff the bottom half of the hospital gown into the waistline of my slightly bloodstained shorts.

It's not a good look, but at least no one will think I'm wearing nothing but a hospital gown. Once everything is situated, I turn away from the bed and find James staring out the window. He glances from the parking lot outside to the phone in his hand.

"Have you thought about where we should go after this?" I ask.

"Where we should—?" He turns to face me, his brows furrowed. "You still want to stay with me after that?"

"Was that not the plan?"

I stare at him, as dressed and ready to leave the hospital as I possibly can be, and he stares back with the blankest look on his face. For a long moment, the only sound is the faint, tinny ringing in my ears—and the ticking clock, I assume.

Then he sighs, glances away, and scratches the back of his neck. "Yeah, okay," he mumbles. "I can probably afford a couple nights in a motel."

*That works for me.*

"Cool. Let's go," I say, taking the first step toward the door.

I stop at the discharge counter to sign a document that once again says my stay was covered by my new mystery insurance. The informational handout the medical clerk hands me says I can take the wrist brace off in two or three weeks. She also tells me which pharmacy to pick up my new prescription from.

Then James and I leave the hospital together.

It's hot, and the air is even hotter in the car. It's parked in the sun, doesn't have AC, and rolling the windows down only does so much, but at least the car is clean. The interior still smells vaguely of chemical cleaner.

"Where to first?" he asks, leaning against the steering wheel.

"The pharmacy," I say, "and then, um… I guess we have to stop by Reid Manor to grab our stuff."

He leans back, groaning as he rubs his eyes. "Yeah, I guess we have to. Let's get it over with, then."

We park outside the pharmacy, and James lets me borrow his jacket and five dollars while he waits in the car. I feel like I might spontaneously combust on the short walk through the parking lot, but I'd rather not walk around in public while obviously wearing a hospital gown tucked into bloodstained denim shorts.

Keeping my head low, I grab a water bottle and box of gauze squares on my way to the pharmacy counter. The pharmacist rings up my items and fills my prescription—which is also covered by my new insurance.

Then I return to the car, where I shed the jacket immediately. James tosses it into the back seat before pulling out of the parking lot.

The drive to Reid Manor is quiet. I don't know what to say. He doesn't know what to say. And, as I watch the trees at the edge of the gravel road, I develop a nagging suspicion that he doesn't want me to tag along with him anymore for some reason.

*For some reason? Yeah, it's almost certainly because of Ice.*

He parks the car off to the side of the front landing, but neither of us exit the car right away. He drops his head to the steering wheel. I stare through the windshield, at a busted window boarded over with plywood.

*It is weird being back here.*

But it's very hot in the car, and I'm ready to change into a real shirt, so I pop the door open and step out.

"Give me a minute," he says, his voice tired.

When I glance over my shoulder, at James with his head still down and arms crossed on top of the steering wheel, I realize I don't remember what happened very clearly.

I remember falling asleep with my head on his shoulder and the general events that led up to Ice shooting holes in the crawl-space door. After that, all I can really remember is the image of a silver gun aimed at James, who didn't move. My hand slipped. I remember that, and I remember a lot of blood, but I don't remember the ambulance or getting to the hospital or anything.

I was still medicated, so I must have fallen asleep once the immediate danger had passed. But James didn't have that luxury. He didn't manage to sleep at all.

*How awful...*

"Are you coming?" I ask.

"Yeah."

One of his hands leave the steering wheel to open the door, and he drags himself out of the car.

"We'll be quick," I assure him as we meet up at the bottom of the steps. "I don't want to be here either, you know? But at least our stuff is all on the first floor."

He nods, his expression uneasy, then pulls one of the front doors open and steps inside. I follow. The mudroom and parlor beyond seem unaffected by the incident that occurred upstairs, and I don't glance at the staircase on our way through.

The bedroom looks exactly how we left it, which is to say it looks like a sparsely furnished room in an abandoned building a couple of squatters were hiding out in.

James leaves the room carrying his backpack and an armful of stuff—whatever food we still have, I presume—and I take the opportunity to change into a normal outfit. My entire body complains, but I'm fully dressed and on the floor trying to wrangle my fitted sheet off the mattress by the time he returns.

"Is your bag packed?" he asks.

"Just this left," I groan, finally unhooking the fabric that was caught on an exposed bedspring.

I stuff the sheet set and my pillow into my duffel bag. When I stand, a shock of pain shoots up my left leg. I grab my hip, jarring my wrist in the process.

"Are you okay?"

"Mm-hm... I guess I just need to be more careful." I clear my throat. "You think you can carry my bag out, though?"

He averts his eyes and picks up the duffel. "Grab my blanket, and let's get the hell outta here."

I bundle his blanket and pillow in my arms and follow him through the house and outside. I walk down the steps, and the realization I might never come back is like…a weight off my chest. As I watch James stuff my duffel bag into the trunk, I wonder if he feels the same.

Does he also hope he never has to stay here again?

*Did I only add to the bad memories of this place?*

Once in the passenger seat, I push the bedding into the back before I buckle my seatbelt.

Then the driver-side door slams shut. The sharp sound makes me nervous to glance over, but, when I do, his hands are relaxed on the steering wheel. He takes a deep breath before turning the key in the ignition.

The car sputters to life and backs up, wheels spinning in loose gravel until it turns, leaving Reid Manor behind. I watch the building in the side mirror until we round a bend in the road. And, just like that, it's gone.

I'm leaving. *And I'm still with James.*

I watch out of the corner of my eye as he drives. Now, he looks slightly annoyed, or perhaps anxious, with his focus on the road and nothing but the road.

Sticking with him isn't a bad idea, is it?

The alternative is going home alone since I can't afford to put myself up in a motel or hotel or whatever. Even if there were someone else I could ask to stay with, I can't risk it. Almost everyone I know from high school or RCC is friends with Rose and would definitely tell her how wrecked I am the moment they saw me.

*Ugh. Speaking of Rose—*

I still haven't turned my phone on.

*No, no, no.* That is not something I want to deal with right now.

"Hey, um—" I hesitate, as I hadn't thought of what to say before opening my mouth. "What motel were you thinking of?"

"Mm... There's a decent one on the east side of town—called Windmill something, I think? I've stayed there a couple times before, and it's not too expensive."

"Never heard of it, but I'm sure it's fine."

"How long do you want to stay there?" he asks, taking his eyes off the road for a second to glance at me.

*Aah—* "You're leaving it up to me? Shouldn't you decide since you're the one paying for it?"

"Dunno."

*You don't know?!*

"Well, how many days can you afford?" I ask.

"Two or three, probably."

"Without it being trouble?"

His eyes narrow. "Two or three."

I frown. "And then what?"

"I'll figure something out," he says with a sigh. "But you don't need to worry about my money. I have it under control, so just accept the help."

I give up and look away.

At this point, I don't care if he's telling the truth or lying just to make me feel better. There's some comfort in the idea he can at least pretend he has *something* under control either way. Because I certainly don't feel like I'm in control of anything right now.

I tap my nails on my phone's screen as I watch buildings pass by through the rolled-down window. We drive through downtown for a while before turning right—to the east.

Eventually, we pull into a half-empty parking lot.

Windmill Valley Motel is a modest, U-shaped complex. The building itself is two stories tall, with a terracotta roof and warm grey exterior dotted with red doors. It's not fancy—not that I expected much—but the neon vacancy sign is lit. Rooms start at sixty-five dollars a night.

"This way."

I follow James across the parking lot toward the motel's main office. Or is it a lobby? I haven't stayed at a motel like this in at least ten years, so I have very little idea how it works.

Maybe I'll just stand behind him the entire time.

The office is quite small, containing only a reception counter, a complimentary breakfast table with nothing on it, and a half-empty water cooler. The man behind the counter looks exceptionally bored, though I detect a hint of distaste in his emerald green eyes as we approach. *Because I'm obviously human or because I look like I just got out of the hospital?*

"Checking in?" he asks. When James nods, the man's eyes flick to me again. "You want a room with one bed or two?"

James looks to me, and I shrug.

"If it's cheaper, one is fine," I say.

He averts his eyes, swallowing and paling slightly. Then he

looks back to the motel clerk and says, "Two beds, please."

"A'ight. You guys'll be in room 19."

I fold my arms over my chest, irrationally incensed as he pays eighty-five dollars for a room with two beds. Is he seriously so opposed to sharing a bed that he'd rather pay an extra twenty bucks a night just to avoid it? *I thought money was an issue.*

Whatever.

*I don't want to share a bed with him, anyway.*

The clerk hands over the key for room 19—an actual key attached to a plastic placard, rather than a keycard—and James sends me to find the room while he goes back to the car for our bags. So I'm alone when I unlock the door and step inside.

It's a motel room. It's fine. Two full-size beds on tall frames with a double-width end table between them. A desk/dresser combo. An old flat-screen TV mounted on the wall across from the beds. There's also a kitchenette at the back—just a microwave atop a mini-fridge set up beside a counter and sink.

The air is hot and stagnant, but I find the thermostat just outside the bathroom and get the AC running. Cool air pours from a vent high on the wall.

*Oh, thank god.*

Then I climb onto the bed furthest from the door leading outside and sit in the middle of it. It's the most comfortable bed I've been in since leaving home.

I drop my head to the pillow and stare at the white ceiling.

*I can't believe I'm here right now.*

# twenty-six

It's not late. I'm not even tired, really. I'm just lying around, pretending to watch the cheesy sitcom playing on TV.

I plugged my phone in a while ago, but I'm still too scared to turn it on and face Rose…or anyone else. And James is being awkward and quiet as usual, reading on his phone on the other bed.

We should probably talk, though.

About this. About whatever the hell we're doing.

I turn the TV off and drag myself up to sit. An achy pain radiates through my back as I return the TV remote to the bedside table, and I realize it's about time to take another dose of naproxen.

This sucks, but at least I'm not stuck on the floor anymore.

"Hey, James." I hesitate as he looks up from his phone, but I have to know. "You don't mind helping me out like this, do you?"

He frowns. "Not really. Why?"

"It just seems like you're mad at me or something."

"Mad at you? No, it's more like—"

He cuts himself off and clears his throat before turning to face me properly. He looks flustered and uncertain. I'm not sure what I was expecting, but that's not quite it.

"I'm not mad," he says. "I just worry sometimes that if I, uh, look away for too long, I'll look back, and you won't be there—like it was all a dream. But looking at you makes me nervous too. I've got this weird feeling you might…look in my eyes and figure out everything I'm thinking, and—" He laughs, scratching the back of his head as his ears turn red. "Well, if you knew, I'm sure you'd think I'm even more pathetic and disgusting than you already do."

*Why does this feel familiar?*

I sigh. "Well, lucky for you, I do not think you're pathetic or disgusting at all, so…"

He stares at me like he doesn't believe me, but I'm serious.

James has been incredibly accommodating, while I contribute next to nothing. Considering the mess we're in, I wouldn't blame him if he wanted nothing to do with me.

"Actually," I say, "I really appreciate you doing this for me. I know it's a lot of trouble. Letting me stay with you and waiting at the hospital and paying for this motel and everything? You didn't have to do any of that."

"Don't worry about it. I said it's fine."

He glances away, frowning. I watch him carefully, but I still don't get it. Why does he look so guilty all the time? Why is he still so convinced I hate him?

"I don't think you're a bad person, James. Honestly. You're way too hard on yourself."

"You think so?" he asks, his voice low as he stares at nothing in particular. "Have you considered that, maybe, you're just not a very good judge of character?"

I force a smile. "It almost feels like you don't want me to like you."

He tenses and turns to face me with wide eyes. "That's, uh—Fuck." He hides his face in his hands. "I'm sorry. I didn't mean that. I just— Ugh."

"Do you want to leave?" I ask, even more confused. "Do you have somewhere else to be?"

"No." His voice is so soft, the faint ringing drowns it out.

"Then what's your problem?"

"My problem?" He laughs and looks at the ceiling, his strained smile more of a grimace. "You mean, besides the obvious? Besides the fact I've landed you in the hospital twice now? Besides the guy who literally wants to kill me just for talking to you?"

"Um—" I avert my eyes. "Yes? Besides all that."

A moment of silence.

Just me sitting still and James staring at the ceiling and the sound of cool air rushing through the vent on the wall between the beds. The anger slowly drains from his expression. Then he sighs and looks over again.

"Hey, uh—" Unease tugs the corners of his mouth down, but he sighs a second time and meets my eyes. "What do you really think about me? After the past few days? After what you've seen?"

*What do I—?*

I tip my head, genuinely confused. "I don't know. I mean, I like you more than I did before I actually talked to you. Before,

I thought you were crazy, but now I think you're just…having a hard time? You're kinda weird and sad, I guess, but you've done a lot for me, so… Yeah. I don't know."

"Weird and sad, huh?" He groans, falling back onto the bed. "Well, I guess that's not the worst thing someone's said about me, but it still sucks."

I don't know why I laugh. "Did you expect something else?"

"Not really," he says, though he sounds strangely placated.

I crawl to the foot of the bed and unzip my duffel bag. The new prescription is right on top. The bottle says to take one tablet three times a day for pain management. A glance at the clock confirms it has been at least eight hours since the painkiller I took with lunch at the hospital.

Maybe that's why I feel like garbage.

I take one.

"What are you gonna do after this?" he asks.

*After what?*

When I glance over, he's sitting on the edge of his bed, staring at the ground with a soft frown, hooded eyes, and his hands interlaced in his lap.

"What will you do?" I ask.

He flashes a muted half-smile. "No clue."

"Me either."

Finally, he looks at me again, his shaky smile having faded. "You don't have any family you can stay with?"

"No."

"No one?"

I shake my head. "Not in town, anyway. My dad lives in

Santa Cruz with his new girlfriend, and my brother is in LA for school. I…honestly don't know where my mom is right now. I haven't talked to her in a while. But I can't stay with any of them looking like this."

"I can only afford a few nights here," he says, his frustration mild but building. "I can't stand the thought of you sleeping in the back of my car, but I can give you a ride anywhere you need to go. Anywhere. I mean it. You'd be safer staying with literally anyone else."

"Safer?" I ask dryly. "Maybe until I reveal the stupid immortals secret by accident and get assassinated by Human-Immortal Affairs or whatever."

His eyes dart away. "Any friends?"

"You already know I don't." As he sighs and massages his temples, I fold my arms over my chest. "But you're okay with sleeping in your car, huh?"

"It wouldn't be the first time," he says under his breath.

I feel my expression harden. "That was your plan if I told you I had somewhere else to go? You'd just…hide out in your shitty car in a parking lot somewhere?"

"I— Ugh." He stands from the bed, runs his hands through his hair, and grabs his backpack as he crosses the room toward the door. "Never mind. Forget it. I'll figure something else out. Just— I need some air, okay?"

"Oh, um…"

"Don't worry," he says, his voice so low I can barely piece the words together. "I'm just gonna go out and pick up something to eat. I'll be back in twenty minutes."

My hand falls into my lap, and my eyes follow it. "Okay."

"I'm sorry—again," he says before leaving.

I stare at the door, my anger ebbing in the room's cool silence. Then I crawl out of bed and cross to the door myself, where I stand unmoving for a moment.

James is a mystery, almost as much as Ice was.

I slide the chain lock into place and turn back to the room.

And I still can't believe he spent an extra twenty dollars for a room with two beds if he can seriously only afford a few nights. But then he leaves to pick up food when we already have some?

I guess it was just an excuse to get away. Maybe, to him, that time alone is worth the ten dollars.

My eyes wander over the room and land on my phone, on the bedside table. I have to turn it on eventually. I can only hope Rose hasn't tried to get ahold of me since last night before I passed out.

There's only one way to find out, though.

I pull my hair over one shoulder and sit on the edge of the bed. My hand trembles as I reach for the phone, but I hold the power button until the backlight turns on.

There are fewer notifications than expected. The usual from idle games and news apps. A casual text from Rose about a shady restaurant she went to last night—it doesn't seem like she was worried when I didn't respond. And one from Ice.

> **Ice:** Well! That wasn't a fun surprise. Are you still alive?

The text is from this morning. If I'd turned my phone on

right after James gave it to me, it would have interrupted the conversation we had before he fell asleep.

I can't believe he'd text me at all, and I stare at the screen for so long it dims and goes black. Then I unlock it again and open the conversation. My thumb hovers over the screen for a long time.

*What should I say? Should I say anything?*

He doesn't deserve a response, but I can't help myself.

> **Me:** Would you care if I weren't?

I'm upset. I'm angry. *I...*

My hand finds its way to the River Sapphire.

Even if it's stupid to indulge him by responding, it's not like he can find me here—at this random motel clear across town from Westbrooke.

I back out to check FaceSpace instead. None of the other app notifications are important, and I still don't have any messages from Night. She hasn't read the ones I sent or been online at all.

Honestly, I'm worried. But Ice wouldn't hurt her, right?

*I could always...ask him...*

My text tone goes off, scaring me. Another text from Ice. I click the banner.

> **Ice:** Of course. I'm offended you feel the need to ask.

*Of course*, he says.

As pissed as I am—and as meaningless as his feelings are after what he did—I know he didn't *mean* to shoot me. It was an accident, but the gun in his hand with the safety switched off wasn't. Aiming it at James wasn't.

My thumb hesitates over send, but *I need to know.*

> **Me:** Were you going to shoot James?

I stare at the screen. At the read indicator beneath my text. At the icon that tells me Ice is typing something in response. My heart races, but I hold my breath.

> **Ice:** Perhaps I considered it. Would you be upset if I had?

*How can he even ask that? It's sick.*
I can't talk about this anymore.

> **Me:** Is Night okay?

The message is marked as read immediately.

I wait for several minutes, focused on my last message or the photo above his name—the selfie we took on the Fourth of July. I tap the screen each time the backlight dims, but he doesn't respond. He doesn't type anything at all.

*What does that mean?*
I don't ask, but I do remove the photo from his contact card.

\* \* \* \* \*

For a while, I worry James won't come back.

I sit on the edge of the bed and glance between my phone and the locked door and hope he hasn't decided to abandon me at this motel because pawning me off on some other random person in my life didn't pan out.

Maybe turning the conversation on him was a little harsh. But he said he would be back in twenty minutes, and it's been at least thirty. *I know it was an estimate, but—*

I jump at a series of knocks on the door.

Obviously, I *know* it's James, but I'm still a little on edge.

I unlock and open the door, and I'm almost surprised to find him holding a brown paper Taco Bell sack and what looks to be the new watermelon freeze I've seen advertised online a few times over the past month. He hands it to me. I take it and step aside for him to come in.

"I'm sorry," I say.

His attention lands on me more directly, and he frowns. "What are you apologizing for? You didn't do anything."

"But I—"

"I upset you first." He walks past me and sits on the edge of his bed while I remain near the door. "Don't apologize to me."

After latching the chain lock again, I move to stand near the foot of the bed. James looks a bit bummed, and I imagine he spent the whole time he was out feeling bad about himself.

I sigh and point to the bag in his lap. "What'd you pick up, anyway?"

"Just value menu stuff. You don't mind Taco Bell, do you?"

"Everyone likes Taco Bell every once in a while, right?" I hold up the pink freeze. "To be honest, I have been curious about this, so…thanks."

His expression shifts slightly. "Yeah. No problem."

*Ugh... We're just having a normal conversation now.*
*Shouldn't I tell him that Ice texted me?*

I want to mention it—kind of. I want to trust James, *but I...*

No matter what he says to the contrary, I get the feeling he doesn't want me around anymore. He wants me to stay somewhere else, even if it means he ends up sleeping in his car. And I don't understand. I didn't get that vibe from him at all until this morning.

He hands me a paper-wrapped burrito, and I sigh again as my eyes land on the plastic hospital band on my wrist.

"Do you have scissors? I can't seem to pull this thing off."

"Yeah. In my bag. Very front pocket."

He shrugs his backpack off, and I sit beside him to look while juggling my drink and burrito in one arm. Sure enough, there is a small, beat-up Swiss Army knife in the front pocket. The attached scissors are tiny and terribly dull, but they do the job. I am free from the hospital bracelet. I toss it across the room and return the knife to James' bag before focusing on the food.

I feel like it's been ages since I last had Taco Bell. Rose and I don't eat fast food often. It's more expensive than eating in, and I usually felt up to cooking something in the evening.

*I kind of miss cooking.*

As James avoids my gaze, I wonder if I can convince him to...*stay somewhere else?* Is my house safe? Ice managed to get in even after I moved the spare key, but it might be our best option if James really can't afford more than a few nights here. It's more defensible—and more comfortable—than Reid Manor, anyway.

*I want to trust him, but I still feel the need to keep him where I can see him. The Fourth of July proved he can be unpredictable too. Maybe I shouldn't forget that...*

His eyes flick in my direction. I nearly choke on my burrito.

"Are you still mad at me?" he asks.

"No?" *Do I look mad? Oops.* "I was just wondering what we should do in two or three days when we can't afford a motel room anymore."

He frowns. "I mean, I can swing longer if I have to, but—"

"I don't need you to take care of everything for me. It makes me feel useless. I don't have a lot of money, but I can pull my own weight. I do have a house, you know?"

His frown becomes a grimace. "That's not—"

Not what? *Safe?*

He thinks sticking together isn't safe at all? *Maybe he's right, but...* He's not really safe anywhere, is he? And there's no reason I should believe Ice would leave me alone if I went home by myself.

"Never mind," I mutter. "I'm sure we'll figure something out."

# twenty-seven

~ ∞ ~

*I open my eyes to nothing, and a pit settles in my stomach. The deep, dark, inky void—a place I've been before. But I take another breath, and my heartbeat slows, because...it feels different.*

*As I look around, the darkness seems brighter than before, and the usual dangerous, foreboding atmosphere is gone. It's not a total void either. Small lights fade in and out all around, flickering like stars or fairy lights in the distance. They're pretty and strangely comforting, moving like lazy fireflies.*

*I glance at my hands, which are lit by an impossible light, and I realize I've only come here in dreams.*

*I'm asleep.*

This is a dream.

"Jayde—"

The voice seems distant, fuzzy and soft, like it came from an old TV, but I recognize it. *How?* I spin around and find her standing only a few feet away. A young woman with feathery black hair and bright blue eyes.

"Night," I gasp.

She forces a smile. Her short hair and pale nightdress flutter in a gentle breeze I can't feel, and her form is unnaturally illuminated against the surrounding darkness.

*The same as me.*

I check my hands again, surprised when I notice something missing. *My injuries.* I look myself over, but they're all gone. My skin is smooth and unblemished. No itchy scabs. No wrist brace. No physical discomfort.

My fingers brush over the inside of my wrist. *Even this…*

"It's been a while," Night says, her voice now crystal clear.

*No kidding.*

My first impulse is anger. She ghosted me. I've been trying to get ahold of her for days. But she sounds tired, and her obvious malcontent makes the skin on my arms prickle.

She clears her throat. "I apologize for that."

"This is a dream," I say slowly, glancing around the seemingly endless space. *But…* "Is it really you?"

"Yes. This may be a dream, but it is real, and I am really here talking to you."

"What is this place?"

"You've been here before?" When I nod, her eyes widen ever so slightly, and she looks around too—as though she hadn't before. "Well, in that case, I suppose this is your dreamscape. It's a place you go when you need time to think."

*My dreamscape…*

"I never expected a human to have such a highly developed dreamscape," she continues mildly, holding her chin. "It seems you don't have much control over it, but I'm still impressed."

I stare at the lights floating in the distance.

"You're...inside my dream?"

"Yes. As part of my psychic ability, I can sometimes visit the dreamscapes of others—it's a rare skill." When I look to her again, her soft frown grows more pronounced. Strained. *Why?* "I'm sorry it took so long to find you. To be honest, I've never tried to meet with a human in dreams before."

I shake my head. "You never answered my messages. I was worried something happened, so I'm glad to see you, but... Why are you here now?"

The chill in my voice catches me off guard, and I don't think it was lost on her because her expression shifts, darkening. Then she averts her gaze.

"No, I'm fine, but—" She sighs and refocuses on me. "Well, I suppose you understand why I'm here now? If it makes any difference, I swear I had no idea anything was wrong until last night."

*Last night?*

*Three small circles in old wooden boards. Ice aiming a gun at the crawlspace door. Staring down the barrel, at the tiny black hole. And James—*

*Stop.*

I'm not at Reid Manor. Everything is fine.

"What happened last night?" I ask.

"Ice came home with blood on his shirt. A gun in his hand. He was...agitated." She pauses, eyes scanning the dark floor, and then takes a deep breath. "Once I calmed him down, he told me he shot someone—you. He said it was an accident. But he also said you're with James? I had no idea. Before, he claimed he only broke up with you before you left, but now I—"

"He told you he *broke up with me*?" I ask sharply, caught off guard by the casual wording. "Do you have any idea what he did?"

"No." Shaking her head, she searches my face desperately. "He said he overreacted, but I—"

*Overreacted?*

She looks away, flustered. "He wouldn't explain, and he made me promise I wouldn't speak with you, but he's not acting like himself lately. It's…not good. Even if it means betraying his confidence this way, I had to do something. I can't sit by and pretend he's fine anymore. I didn't know what else to do."

I watch her carefully, but I don't know what to say.

How am I supposed to explain what happened—what Ice did to me? How can I tell her? *She's his sister.* It's one thing if he lied and convinced her I left under normal conditions, but she still ghosted me at his command.

*If only she read my messages… Ugh.*

"Jayde, I need to know," she says, her voice wavering. "What happened between you and Ice the day you left?"

"He attacked me."

"He—?"

I glance at my arms, *and there they are.* Every wound, fresh and dripping blood like the day it was first inflicted. The cuts aren't painful, but the metallic scent and the sight of blood and purple bruising turns my stomach. The thick liquid soaks my shirt and slicks my arms. I can't even make out the shape of a heart on my wrist through the deep red as it drips from my fingers and pools on the dark floor.

*There's no way I bled this much in real life.*

"With a knife," I say.

"No."

A sharp crackle cuts the air like a lightning strike, and I look up. Night fell to her knees. She stares at the black floor, shaking her head. Her eyes are wide, both hands held over her mouth.

"This is impossible," she mumbles, shaking her head. "The blood... No. There's no way Ice did this to you. Is there?"

"He did." Somehow, my voice is level, and I don't feel sorry for her at all. "He found out I talked to James and didn't like it, I guess. Because James told me all the awful things he said about me—the day he caught him sneaking around in the backyard. After that, I just wanted to go home. I came back to pick up my bag. But he attacked me—to get back at me or James for... whatever he thinks we did wrong. Who knows? Anyway, James took me to the hospital. I spent the night there, and I just got the stitches taken out this morning."

My injuries stop bleeding, having closed and scabbed over, and the bruises fade, but the blood remains—slicking my skin, dripping from my fingers, and soaking the loose t-shirt as it clings to me in a most unpleasant way.

"Why?" As she gasps to catch her breath, her hands ball in her hair and tears fill her eyes. "How could I let this happen?"

"Hey, it's— I mean, it's not *your* fault."

"No. You don't understand. That morning, I— I knew he was

upset, but… I swear I didn't know James was involved. My dream was… But I never expected *this* might happen." She fumbles over her words, still shaking her head. "I shouldn't have agreed to leave him alone. I knew Ice was upset after you left without saying anything. Why did I listen to him? I knew you wanted to go home. Why didn't I wait for you to come back?"

"What?"

She freezes and looks up with huge eyes, streaming tears. She blinks, her lips thinning. Then, in an instant, she's standing several feet further away. Her cheeks are wet. She hugs her arms close to her chest, and her expression is more guarded.

"I'm sorry, Jayde."

*Wait—*

"You knew Ice wanted to be alone with me?"

She glances aside. "Well… I assumed that was the main reason he wanted us out of the house for so long, but I swear I *never—*"

Taking a deep breath and avoiding my gaze, she worries her trembling hands. She's obviously trying to collect herself, so I wait.

*This is my dream. I have all night.*

Finally, she clears her throat. "I went grocery shopping with Smoke—per Ice's request. The storm was essentially over, and we needed to go anyway, so I didn't think much of it. It felt…routine. Then he called an hour or so later and asked me to drive all the way down to his apartment in Palo Alto to grab something and swing by a specialty shop in San Jose to buy…"

She hesitates and drops her hands to her sides.

"Well, I suppose the details hardly matter. But we made the trip to the Bay Area like he asked, so we weren't back in Riverview until evening. When we finally got home, Ice was clearly unhappy, and I admit that something felt off. There was a... strange smell in the house... Like chemicals or paint... I asked about it, but he wouldn't explain exactly what happened. He told me he broke up with you—that you wouldn't be coming back, and I shouldn't speak with you again."

*Broke up with me?*

I feel worse every time she says it.

"That's why you didn't answer my messages?" My mouth is dry. "You didn't even read them. You haven't been online in days. He told you not to talk to me anymore, and you just listened to him? Why?"

The color drains from her cheeks. "Jayde, I— You have to understand the relationship I have with Ice. He needs to trust me —he has to trust *someone*—but please believe me when I say I never thought it was this bad. I never once imagined he might have hurt you, and I had no idea James was involved, so, when he asked me to stop talking to you, I just—"

"You should have helped me. I thought we were friends."

"I loved being your friend," she cries, turning away with her hands over her eyes. "After hearing what he did, I honestly... I feel so sick. I wish I hadn't listened to him this time."

*This time?*

"Why did you talk to James, anyway?" Her voice is low but rings in my dreamscape as though she were standing beside me. "If you left for any other reason—*literally anything else*—I'm sure he would have let you go home without a fight. I told you before that they have history, but there is not one person on this planet Ice is convinced he cares less for. Perhaps it's childish. I don't know. But it explains why he was so upset that you left him after speaking with James."

"Left him?" My bare foot splashes in the still-warm blood as I step forward. "You're wrong, Night. I didn't *leave* Ice. I didn't even believe what James told me about him, and he still attacked me. He told James himself that he doesn't care about me at all."

"Ice? Doesn't care about you?" She laughs and turns to face me with a bitter, uneasy smile and sparkling tears streaming down her face. "Trust me, Jayde, I know that stupid man better than anyone. You were right to say that about me. And I can tell you right now that he has never shown so much interest in another person until he met you. He played himself up more than I've seen in years. He took you out on public dates and told you about us and involved Human-Immortal Affairs. He is *obsessed*, and he doesn't even realize it. I don't think he knows what to think of his messy feelings for you."

"Then why? Why would he do this?"

She hesitates, leaving a moment of heavy silence that chills the air. I wipe the blood from my wrist until it clears enough to reveal the scarred heart underneath. Then both hands ball into fists at my sides.

"I don't know," she admits. "He's never done anything… quite like this before, but for it to cause him so much pain—for him to want the three of you to suffer so badly—I can only imagine…"

She pauses again to sigh.

"Are you still with James?" she asks.

"I don't know if I should tell you. I think Ice wants him dead."

Her eyes flick to the side. "I know. He said you were only shot because you...*got in the way.* You must have been in the same place the other day, at least."

*Damn it...*

Even after everything she's said—or perhaps because of it—I want to believe her, but I don't want to put myself at risk. I don't know what to say.

"Is he safe?" she asks.

I blink. "James? Yeah. We're both safe."

"Oh, good." She forces a smile. "He must care about you—if he risked coming back to our house for you."

*How much can I say?*

"He, um..." My hands relax as, surprisingly, thinking about James calms me down a little. "Yeah, I guess he must. I can't tell you where we are, obviously, but he's letting me stay with him in the meantime. He's not...so bad."

"No, he's not." Her smile fades. "It's like I said, I...haven't spoken with James in years, but he was always kind to me when we were kids."

"Were you friends?"

"He was friends with Ice. Once upon a time."

"What happened?"

She shakes her head. "I don't know. Honestly. They've never told me."

*There's something weird about this conversation...*

"You're not afraid of him, are you?"

"Of Ice?" Her expression blanks for an instant, but she shakes her head again. "He terrifies me, sure—I can never tell what he's thinking, and I know the self-destruction he's capable of—but I'm not afraid of him."

"Even after what he did to me?"

She steps back. "Please don't misunderstand me, Jayde. I am disgusted by what he did to you, and I can't believe he seriously tried to shoot James. Even if I know he's angry with James for existing and angry with himself for losing you this way, taking his frustration out on you is absolutely inexcusable."

"So, you agree he's only doing this to get at James?" I ask through my teeth.

"You surprised him—you and James both, I imagine." Her tone is tense and oddly hesitant. "He wasn't expecting you to meet, let alone that you might seek him out, but this is… He took it too far. There's something wrong with him. I know that, but I…"

She turns away again, shaking her head.

"I'm sorry. I've said too much already. I should go."

"Um…"

A vibration shakes the ground. I glance aside as the small lights floating in the void take on a reddish hue and dart around more erratically.

Looking back to Night, her shoulders shake. Her hands tangle in her short hair, and the gentle breeze affecting her becomes a gale, pulling at the light fabric of her nightdress. As she drops to the ground in a tight kneel, I hear another crack like breaking glass. A second tremor nearly throws me off balance.

She's breaking down. And so is my dreamscape.

*Is this part of her ability?*

"I'm not mad at you," I say lamely. "I just want to understand how this happened. It seriously feels like it came out of nowhere."

"Ugh! Of course, you don't understand, Jayde. There's nothing for you to understand. I messed up. I encouraged you. But Ice did this anyway. And James… And now I—"

I take another step forward. "Please, calm down."

"Do not tell him we spoke," she begs, her voice hanging too loud in the air. "Please. It would only make things so much worse."

*Who? Don't let* who *know?*

I reach out to touch her shoulder, but I'm too late.

With the shattering of glass like the shattering of the window in the third-floor bedroom at Reid Manor, the dark ground fractures beneath my feet, and I fall, leaving Night behind. My stomach ends up in my throat, and the blood that followed me down splatters my face. I wipe it away, but, when I open my eyes again, I can't see a thing.

I'm falling through the thick, inky void. The sensation is familiar and uncomfortable and annoying, but I'm not afraid of the black hole tonight. I'm not afraid I'll never wake up.

This is a dream.

In reality, I'm safe in bed in a motel.

But my baffled mind wanders.

The first time I woke up here only to find myself still sleeping. The dread the suffocating darkness planted within me. Drowning in blood. *The dreamscape is where you go when you need time to think?* Ice and James were both in that dream. It was the first time I saw that cruel smirk. A flash of silvery metal.

*Is that what I needed to see?*

*Is that what my subconscious wanted to tell me?*

Why didn't I realize sooner? Why did I just...ignore every one of Ice's red flags? If I'd only looked past my own childish feelings, maybe I could have stopped this from happening.

*Unless fate is real, and I am cursed.*

~ ∞ ~

# twenty-eight

I wake with a start when my dream-self hits the bottom.

My eyes are dry, and I'm safe in the motel bed, kept warm in the air-conditioned room by the lumpy comforter. I take a moment to catch my breath before reaching for my phone.

It's just after 3AM. No new notifications.

*Thank god.*

I check on James. The room is dark, the only light filtering in from the parking lot through gaps between the slatted blinds, but he looks to be fast asleep. Unmoving, eyes closed.

*I…kind of want to wake him up.*

He should know about the texts I exchanged with Ice yesterday. He should know that I spoke with Night—that she knows what Ice did. Even if she did mean I shouldn't tell James, doesn't he deserve to know? He's probably in more danger than I am, but I…

*Ugh. No. I do not want to tell him.*

I lie down again. I close my eyes and listen to the air conditioner and try to fall asleep. For a long time. But, no matter how hard I try, I can't seem to manage. I make it to the verge of sleep, and then I picture *something. A memory. An image from a nightmare.*

*I can't even tell the difference anymore.* But the sensation of falling snaps me back to wakefulness.

I check my phone—5:28AM.

And I give up on sleeping.

I creep out of bed. I take a dose of naproxen and make a bowl of cereal and sit at the desk while I eat. Then I clean up and return to the bed, where I play Candy Crush for an hour and a half. I switch to another game I rarely play and complete all fifteen daily tasks for the first time in over a week. Then I roll onto my side and find a nature docuseries to watch on Netflix.

Two and a half episodes in, I hear movement to my right. The sun has been up for hours, so the room is brighter, and I watch James sit up in bed. He stretches and rubs his eyes, his short hair a mess. After blinking, he turns to look at me.

"Hey," he says, his voice rough with sleep.

"Hey."

"How long have you been up?"

*Eh...* The alarm clock on the bedside table reads 10:26AM, but I stifle a sigh and meet his gaze.

"Not long," I say mildly. "A couple hours, maybe."

He nods. "Whatcha watching?"

"Planet Earth." I've watched it at least once already, but it's peaceful and comforting, and god knows I could use some peace and comfort right now. "Have you seen it?"

"Maybe when I was a kid. You like documentaries, huh?"

"Sure. They're not the most exciting or anything, but I always learn something new, and I don't feel like I miss anything too important if I get distracted for a few minutes."

"Makes sense."

This is the perfect opportunity to say something. *But what's the point?* I can only communicate with Night in dreams, and Ice only messaged me to get under my skin. Would telling James accomplish anything beyond stressing him out more?

*Maybe it's not worth it.*

I don't bring it up, and he grabs something to eat before leaving the room to pay for the second night.

A few hours later, James' mood has improved further—thanks to the full night of sleep and a hot shower, I assume. I haven't heard anything from Ice or Night either, so I try to put yesterday and my dream behind me. Now, I just want to relax and enjoy this time hanging out in a place I know for certain is safe.

As James sits at the desk while eating a sandwich, he seems more comfortable than usual. I still feel like something is bothering him—something he doesn't want to talk about with me, I guess—but it might just be the whole situation. Or my injuries. *Or both.*

Either way, whenever I catch his eye, his expression shifts ever so slightly, and he looks away. This time, however, our eyes meet, and he doesn't avert his. Instead, his gaze flicks down to my neck.

"Why do you still wear that thing?" he asks.

"Hm?" I realize he means the River Sapphire, and my heart quickens. "Oh, um, I figure I'm part of the Human Immortal Program whether I like it or not, right? Besides, it's supposed to let me morph eventually. I might as well keep wearing it in case it decides to start working."

"You sure it's even real?"

I gasp. "Of course, it's real! Human-Immortal Affairs sent a letter about it and everything."

"Oh." His cheeks flush, and he glances at his sandwich. "Well, I just thought it might remind you of Ice or something."

*Oh.*

"Maybe it does, but I think it would be cool to figure it out and turn into a cat, you know?"

"Yeah, I know," he says, his eyes narrowing as his frown grows more pronounced. *Being defective. Right. He can't morph either.*

I apologize, but he sighs and waves it off.

"Do you have any idea how I might get it to work?" I ask, hoping to clear the air. "The letter they sent said it can activate in a ton of different ways, but I've run out of things to try."

He thinks about it for a moment.

"Have you tried kissing it?" he asks. "It works in anime— like magical girl shows? I know your necklace isn't a magic item or whatever, but you never know."

*Why does he look so embarrassed?*

"No, I haven't tried that."

The chain is just long enough I can lift the pendant to my lips without taking it off. I close my eyes and kiss the cool gemstone, but I don't feel like anything happened, and opening my eyes confirms it.

"Still nothing," I say, more disappointed than I should be.

I drop the necklace. As it falls back to my collarbone, I meet James' gaze, and he releases the laugh he'd been so obviously holding back. He even has to set his sandwich down and wipe his eyes as he collects himself.

"What?" I ask. "Did I look stupid?"

"No. It was…actually kinda cute."

I laugh. Because, no matter what he says, there is no way I didn't look absolutely ridiculous kissing my necklace.

* * * * *

It's been a long day.

A long day spent doing absolutely nothing.

I'm bruised and sore and tired, so I've just been relaxing in bed and half-watching the TV between messing around on my phone and exchanging a few sentences with James.

He's done the same. He stepped out for another solo drive earlier, but he spent most of the afternoon sitting at the desk or on the edge of his bed, reading on his phone in between commenting on whatever game show rerun is playing on the TV or asking me some inane question.

It's not unpleasant, exactly.

If it weren't for the constant, nagging discomfort, this would almost feel normal. It's just strange considering our situation, and I remember the reality of it every time I glance at my arm or wince at a sudden tightness in my hip or shoulder.

I open another idle mobile game and get to popping brightly colored bubbles. I complete several stages, successfully wasting more time.

Then James clears his throat. "You sure you don't want me

to drop you off at home or something?"

"What do you mean?"

"You don't have to stay with me, you know?"

"I know I don't *have* to," I say. He blinks a few times but doesn't respond, leaving me even more confused. I lock my phone and set it aside. "If you're worried about money, we can stay at my house instead."

His eyes grow wide. "You'd want me to come too?"

"Um… Yes?"

His face blanks further.

The thought of going home plants a tickle of anxiety in my chest, but I feel bad about the money, and I'm even more worried about James' safety after speaking with Night. I don't want to put either of us in unnecessary danger, but staying in a motel forever is hardly sustainable. We can't just go back to Reid Manor, and *I do not want to be left alone*, so it seems like the most logical option.

I sigh. "Of course, you can come with me. You've let me stay with you this long, so it's the least I can do. Besides, I don't particularly enjoy the thought of you sleeping in the back of your car during the hottest part of summer either."

His face turns red, and he averts his gaze, making it all the more difficult to not feel embarrassed. It shouldn't be embarrassing at all. I'm only trying to find a solution that benefits us both, but… His jaw sets as the surprise fades from his eyes, and a strange, heavy sadness replaces it.

*Why look so conflicted? I'm trying to be nice.*

"It would only be for a week or two, right?" he asks warily.

"Your roommate will be back by the end of July, right?"

"It's almost the end of July already," I say, though that doesn't answer his question.

Maybe I don't want to answer the question. Maybe I don't want to put any sort of strict limitation on the offer. Rose knows about him, so maybe it would be okay for him to stick around a bit longer if he still needed somewhere to stay.

*I don't know.*

"Yeah, I guess it is," he agrees.

I frown. "What do you think, though? Can we stay at my house for now?"

He stares at his lap, at his hands. He looks tired. Frustrated, maybe. He massages his thumb for a moment before he drags his hands down his face and finally meets my gaze again.

"Sure," he says.

"Really?" I'm honestly surprised.

"Yeah." He offers a short nod, though he doesn't look pleased. "We can go to your place tomorrow."

# twenty-nine

"You sure about this?"

"Yes."

"You're sure you don't just want me to drop you off?"

I look up from my lap as James drives with his jaw set and hands firmly planted on the steering wheel. He's been like this all morning, and it's driving me crazy.

"It's not a problem," I say, forcing an even tone. "I don't want to be alone right now, anyway, so I'd actually feel better having you there with me."

His eyes narrow, but he doesn't respond.

"What? Do you *want* to be alone?"

"No," he says. "But I don't wanna cause trouble either."

*Ugh.* "If I can convince you to do even a couple chores around the house while I lay in bed and feel sorry for myself, I'm sure you won't cause any trouble."

His expression softens. "You know that's not what I mean."

"You don't know if splitting up would stop Ice from bothering me," I mutter. "But I do know I wouldn't feel safe at home on my own, and I would…probably worry about you too."

He sighs. "I wish you wouldn't say things like that."

"Why not?"

He ignores me and instead asks how to get back to my place from here. I give up and help direct him from the interstate to Oakwood Cottages.

"It's this one, right?" he asks, pointing to my building.

I nod, and he pulls his car into the empty parking space in front. Then he looks at me and opens his mouth, but I have a feeling I know what he's about to say before he utters a single word.

I shake my head and hold up a hand. "James, I am not letting you leave on your own right now. I am far more afraid of Ice than I am annoyed by you."

"Fine." He forces a smile. "You win. I'll carry the bags inside if you unlock the door."

I squint at him for a few seconds before I finally grab my purse and step out of the car. I half expect him to dump my duffel on the curb and take off without me, but he's carrying both of our bags and a pile of bedding when I glance over my shoulder after unlocking and opening the front door.

The living room is empty. I step inside, so I can hold the door open for James to come through with his heavy load. Of course, he dumps everything on the couch so he can canvas the building as he did the first time.

"We're alone," he says on his way down the stairs.

I lock the deadbolt.

James offers to carry my duffel upstairs. I thank him, and he follows me into my bedroom, where he sets the bag on my bed.

"Need anything else?"

"Not right now, thanks." I'm distracted by the shirt covering the mirror over my dresser, but I glance away to offer him a smile. "Make yourself at home, though."

He mirrors my smile, unease and all, and scratches his cheek. "Yeah, thanks. For now, I'll go…put the food away."

"Okay."

"Okay," he mumbles as he slips out of my room.

The door clicks shut. I listen to James walk down the stairs, and then I reach for the shirt over the mirror.

I avoided the mirror in the motel bathroom. I avoided looking at myself before or after my shower last night. But I don't want to live like this. Seeing the shirt over the mirror is just as depressing. So I catch the fabric with my fingers and carefully remove it from where I wedged the hem behind the frame.

Honestly, my reflection isn't that bad. Staring at myself, wearing a loose-fitting shirt, I look fine. Tired. Concerned. My hair up in a horribly messy bun. The top of the scab on my chest peeking out from the collar of my shirt. But I look alright, and the bruises on my arms have almost faded.

I'm still wearing the River Sapphire, but I keep thinking about what James said—and what Ice said too. The necklace does remind me of him. I wish it didn't, but I meant what I told James. I have to believe it will work eventually.

Maybe, if it does, Human-Immortal Affairs will care. Maybe they'll step in and do something.

I fiddle with the pendant, going through the cycle of things I've already tried. Taking it off, putting it back on, rubbing it, tapping it, anything I can think of, even kissing it again, but nothing happens.

*Damn… Maybe they're right. Maybe it is useless.*

My eyes wander toward my jewelry box—the small, wooden box I use to store the jewelry I never wear. My fingers brush the delicate chain clasp at the back of my neck, but I hesitate.

*No. I have to believe it will work.*

With a sigh, I let my hair down and brush it nicely for the first time in days. I fix my bangs. I slap my cheeks to hype myself up. And I head downstairs to check on James.

He's in the kitchen, peeking through the cabinets. He looks quite unimpressed, and I brace myself as he turns to face me.

"You barely have any food here."

Obviously. There's no more here than there was the last time we stopped by. But I spent the first half of July at Ice's house and the second half with James, *and there wasn't much left the few days I was staying here in between...*

I shake my head. "Well, let's figure out what we need, throw out anything else that's expired, and go shopping while I still feel up to walking around."

"Sounds good." He takes his phone from his pocket and starts typing. "I'll make a list. First thing: milk."

"All of the appliances work, so feel free to put whatever you want on the list."

"Ha ha," he says without looking up.

I smother my smile, drag the trash can closer, and set my phone up to play music on the counter. I don't know what James listens to, and I don't have a favorite genre, so a popular music playlist should be fine? *Right?*

"Also, the WiFi password is on the freezer door."

"Thanks."

*First things first.*

I open the snack cabinet and stand on my tiptoes to reach the back. I pull the M&M cookies out and stare at the red packaging. The best-by date was a week ago, but there are still several inside.

I almost want to eat them. But holding the package brings to mind— *A perfect, pleasant smile. An awkward conversation. A sense of danger I ignored.*

My head fills with static. I want to throw them away.

But my grip on the plastic package tightens, and I turn away from the cabinet. James is standing in front of the fridge, messing around on his phone.

"Do you want these?" I stammer. He glances over his shoulder, and I force a smile. "They technically expired a few days ago, but I'm sure they're still fine."

"Oh. Sure."

He accepts the package, and I watch as he removes the stack of remaining cookies from inside. Then he drops the empty packaging in the trash. And an inexplicable sense of relief washes over me, leaving me feeling lighter.

We spend at least a half-hour sorting through the cabinets and fridge to locate and discard expired food. There's more than I expected, and the kitchen looks terribly barren when we're done. But we laughed and joked with each other while we worked. My shoulder only bothered me a few times, we put together a decent shopping list, and it was actually kinda fun—more fun than doing it myself would have been, anyway.

"Wanna go shopping now or take a break?" I ask as I cross the room to pause the music.

"We should get it out of the way now."

"Okay."

When I look up, James has dipped out of the kitchen. I take a few steps toward the table to peek into the living room. He's digging through the backpack he left on the couch. Then he removes a black notebook and returns with it.

He sets the notebook on the dining table. I watch with

heightened interest as he flips through several pages too quickly for me to read any of the scrawled notes written on them before he stops on a blank page.

"What's your address?" he asks.

"This address?"

I'm a bit confused when he nods, but I tell him. He repeats the address back to me and writes it on the page in pen, underlining my last name after I confirm he recorded everything correctly.

"Why not keep it in your phone?" I ask.

"I'm more likely to remember if I write it out by hand."

"Ah."

He closes the notebook, sets the cheap BIC pen on top, and meets my gaze with the most casual smile I've ever seen— coming from him. It catches me off guard. A fluttering fills my chest for a moment, but I'm not sure he noticed my expression shift.

"Alright," he says, still smiling. "Let's go."

# thirty

It's been two days, and something is starting to feel...*off*.

While grocery shopping, James finally relented under my insistence that he stop paying for literally everything, and we split the cost. It was a relief, honestly, because we bought quite a lot.

Then I cooked dinner. It was the first time I'd cooked anything from scratch in weeks. I read the recipe off my phone, and James sat at the table and talked with me the whole time. The conversation was about nothing, really, but he smiled and did not make fun of me for accidentally overcooking the chicken.

After eating, we double-checked the locks on the first floor. I made sure he didn't need anything, and he stayed downstairs while I went up to my bedroom. I was so worn out, I fell right asleep.

In the morning, James was still passed out on the couch, so I cleaned the blood off the carpet outside my bedroom door using bathroom tile cleaner I found under the sink.

The rest of the day was...fine.

We didn't do much of anything—a load of laundry after James woke up, and then we stayed inside. We were existing.

Resting. Recovering. Washing dishes or watching TV or talking about air conditioning or sitting at the dining table and playing Uno while the casserole baked.

It was less awkward than I expected considering how awkward we are. He's no replacement for Rose, but I don't mind having him around even after last night.

After we ate dinner, I picked out a movie on Netflix, and we watched it together. He kept his distance and sat on the opposite side of the couch. I tried talking to him a few times, but he barely said anything, so I gave up. Then, halfway through the movie, I heard him sigh.

Under his breath, he asked, "Is this really okay?"

When I asked what he meant, he looked at me. The room was dark, but the light from the TV reflected in his eyes. He hadn't looked at me like that in a few days, and the sadness in his expression rubbed off on me.

"Is it okay that I'm here with you like this?"

*Like this?*

*What does that mean?*

I didn't know what to say. I didn't have an answer.

So I shrugged. Then I refocused on the TV and wished I had the guts to say *something* or move a little closer. But I never did either, and I spent the rest of the movie thinking, *What does "like this" mean to him? And what does it mean to me?*

Why do I want him to stay here? Why am I so worried? Is it just because I don't want to see *anyone* get hurt?

When the movie ended, he said it was getting late, and we looked at each other again. It was just after eight-o-clock. It wasn't that late, and I wasn't nearly as tired as I was the previous day. I really wanted to say something then—I don't even know what I would have said—but I didn't. I kept quiet.

He smiled, though, and said, "You should get some sleep."

His tone bothered me, but I agreed.

I walked upstairs by myself, exactly as I had done the night before without thinking. But, unlike the first night, I spent at least an hour unable to sleep, staring at the ceiling and wondering how I really feel about James.

I'm no closer to understanding now than I was last night, and he's yet to say anything this morning to sway my opinion one way or the other.

I rest my arms on the table, wishing they didn't both ache, and glance across the kitchen.

James is cooking breakfast. He mentioned using his mother's recipe for the pancakes. He smiled while he talked about her, but I caught a melancholic haze in his eyes, and he changed the subject quickly.

Glancing back to my hands, I flex the fingers on my right. With the stitches gone, the wound is scarring over, the scabs thinning. There's not much pain anymore, and my fingers move without issue, but a mild discomfort and strange numbness linger in my thumb at times.

"How's your hand?"

"Which one?" I ask.

"Either one, I guess."

I look up from my hands—one healing and one in a brace—to find James turned away from the stove as something sizzles away behind him. His concern is muted, and he doesn't look nearly as stressed as any other time I recall him asking how I feel.

*Good.*

"I'll be alright," I assure him. "My wrist hurts, but my right hand is getting there. It goes numb less than it used to, so… maybe there isn't any nerve damage after all."

"That's great."

*Hopefully.*

He finishes cooking and brings a plate for me before taking a seat across the table. The pancakes are light and fluffy—way better than the just-add-water baking mix ones we had before. Sure, pancakes are easy, but he has the recipe memorized and everything.

*Why was I so surprised to learn he's a decent cook?*

When I ask if he likes cooking, he shrugs.

"I only know how to make a few things," he admits. "My mom loved cooking, but…she didn't have the chance to teach me much, and it was easier to heat up a freezer meal or whatever. I guess."

"Well, what else can you make?"

He blinks. "Spaghetti?"

*I think everyone can make spaghetti.*

"You'll have to make it sometime."

He sort of smiles before glancing away. "Sure, but we'll have to buy tomato sauce—I didn't think about it the other day."

As we eat, I suggest we go for a walk before it gets too hot. Because it has been *too long* since I've been able to get out, and I'm sure the exercise would be good for my joints.

"A walk?" he asks. "To where?"

"There's a park behind the cottages—Windsor Park. There are a few walking trails, and there's a little wildlife pond in the center. With ducks and turtles and everything."

"A duck pond? I had no idea there was anything like that around here." He seems interested, but he falls quiet for a moment before nodding. "If you feel up to walking, I don't see why not."

It's too bad we already threw out the stale bread.

*I always do without thinking.*

As I slip my shoes on, I note the lack of an ache in my right side. My hip is still a bit tender, and I have some weakness in the leg, but I can bend over without sharp pain. And fabric hasn't stuck to the wound on my side since a few days before the stitches were removed.

*I'm healing.*

When I turn back to the room, James looks ready to go too. He swapped his jeans for long athletic shorts and almost looks comfortable with himself.

I flash a smile—*getting out is something small I can do for both of us.* "Okay, follow me."

He nods, and the hint of brightness in his eyes makes me feel more confident that going for a walk isn't a questionable idea in my still-questionable condition.

And we're off.

I glance at the blue, blue sky before leading James behind the cottage. I tell him a bit more about the park—the woods and the trails and my sentimental attachment to the place—as we walk close to the trees until we reach the trailhead signage at the start of the shortest route.

## Windsor Park Wildlife Pond
.4 miles

Surely, sitting around won't make me less sore. Surely, I can walk a mile without dying. Plus, the exercise and fresh air will be good for me. *Right?*

James stares down the path with wide eyes. "It's like…an actual hiking trail in the woods in the middle of town?"

"Yeah. It's mostly flat, though." I peer down the trail, surveying its carefully maintained, packed-earth surface. "Shouldn't be hard to walk, even for me. Come on."

"I've lived in Riverview my whole life, and I've never seen this before."

I laugh, and he follows as I walk past the sign. The trail is wide enough for him to walk alongside me, and, to my surprise, he does. *Good.* I half expected him to make things awkward and trail a few feet behind the whole time.

"You like hiking?" he asks.

I laugh. "If you can call this hiking. I couldn't tell you the last time I went out to a real trail in the mountains or anything."

"Fair enough."

It takes more time for us to make it to the center of the park than it used to take me to walk there alone *before*. I stop at a drinking fountain while James makes his way to the edge of the water. When I meet up with him again, he's watching a family of ducks swim several feet out. Another group of birds is flocked around someone clear across the pond as they scatter food on the ground.

After a moment of quiet, he asks if I want to sit.

I agree, and we find the nearest bench to take a break. The air is hot, but it's not unpleasant in the shade. And James didn't put as much space between us as physically possible for once.

"I seriously had no idea there was anything like this around here," he says, leaning forward with his eyes focused on the water across the trail. "Maybe it's not so surprising since I grew up on the north side of town, but… This seems like a nice place to relax."

I grin. "Right? We're barely a quarter-mile from the road, but it almost feels like we're out in the wilderness. You can't even hear the cars from here."

"Yeah, this is cool." As he meets my gaze, his expression softens. "I think the trees make me a little claustrophobic, though. It kinda makes me miss the coast."

"The coast?"

"I used to go all the time." He looks up thoughtfully, as though trying to remember. "I like the sky. The breeze. I like… the sound of the water—the waves, you know? I don't even mind the seagulls crying. It's never quiet on the coast. There's always something to listen to." Then he sighs. "And it's never this hot."

"We should go sometime."

I said it without thinking, and it caught us both by surprise. His ears turn red as he stares back at me with wide amber eyes, and I laugh to keep from looking too embarrassed.

"I mean, I haven't gone to the coast in years either," I say, passing a strand of my hair through my hands. "You don't have to take me anywhere, obviously, but I should definitely go sometime."

"Maybe you can go with your roommate when she gets back."

*Ugh… Why do I want to go with* you, *though?*

"Maybe you can come with us?" I say, glancing over.

He sort of laughs. "Yeah, I dunno. Maybe."

Unsure what else I could say, my eyes dart to my lap. I pick at the edge of the wrist brace and try to imagine spending the day at the coast—with or without James—but I can't.

*Even so… He didn't say no.*

On our walk back to the cottage, he stops in the middle of the path rather abruptly. He points out a cluster of purple wildflowers blooming off the side of the trail at the base of a tree. I don't move, but he steps off the packed earth to get a closer look. He kneels in front of the flowers.

*For some reason…*

My phone was already in my hand. I can't help but switch away from my conversation with Rose to take a photo while he isn't paying attention.

For what feels like a few minutes, he stares at the flowers like they remind him of something. Then he glances over his shoulder with a strange wistfulness in his soft frown, and I slip my phone into my pocket.

# thirty-one

A notification interrupts a video ad on my mobile game, but it wasn't one I was expecting, and I have to read it again to be sure my mind didn't make it up.

> **FaceSpace** now
> Carmen Choi commented on your photo.

I tap the banner, and FaceSpace opens to the candid photo of James I impulsively uploaded before falling asleep last night. Looking up from my phone to scan the second-floor banister, I can just make out the sound of the shower running over the AC.

I lean back in my chair and scroll down to the comments.

> **Carmen Choi**
> Σ(°口°) Is that James Reid???

I tap to reply. I type out a few different short answers, deleting each one without posting it, but she messages me before I settle on anything safe to share directly on my timeline.

> **Carmen:** Hey, girl!
> **Carmen:** It's been a while. What's up?

"Uh…"

*What should I say?* I doubt she knows what's been going on with me or James or Ice. She is an immortal, so I *can* talk about it if I want, but no one else knows, and she likes to gossip…

> **Me:** Nothing exciting. Just sitting around at home.
>
> **Carmen:** Have you heard anything from Night lately?
>
> **Me:** No, sorry.
>
> **Carmen:** Dang. I haven't heard from her at all in a couple weeks now. tbh, I'm kinda worried. ( ° ^ °;;)

I feel bad for the flicker of relief I feel upon realizing she ghosted *all* of her friends and not only me. I wish I could reassure Carmen, but it's not my place to say anything. Night must have a reason for staying offline right now.

> **Me:** I'm sure she's fine.
>
> **Carmen:** Are you still seeing Ice?
>
> **Me:** No
>
> **Carmen:** No? ( ◑ ₎ ◑);;
>
> **Carmen:** I guess it makes sense if you're hanging around James now, tho. I haven't heard from him in a hot minute either. Kinda thought he was dead. lmao
>
> **Me:** You know James?
>
> **Carmen:** Sure.

*I think Night mentioned that Carmen knew him somehow… I could ask what she knows—*

> **Carmen:** But how'd you guys meet up?
>           Seems like a weird move to be
>           dating Ice and then sharing pics of
>           James on FS out of nowhere.
>
> **Me:** It's a long story. Totally boring.
>
> **Carmen:** Ok ok
>
> **Carmen:** But are you guys dating?? ( ͡° ͜ʖ ͡°)
>
> **Me:** No. We're just hanging out.
>
> **Carmen:** Wild. How is he? No one's seen him
>           since the 4th. A few guys were
>           getting worried. lol

*Were they?* I guess he really does have friends out there.

In that case, maybe it's a good thing I shared the photo. She'll at least tell those who were concerned about him—if not everyone in her friend circle—that he's absolutely not dead.

> **Me:** He seems okay.
>
> **Carmen:** Oh, good!
>
> **Me:** He hasn't talked to anyone since the 4th?
>
> **Carmen:** afaik, no one's heard anything, but
>           it's good to know he's ok.
>
> **Carmen:** Anyway, tell me if you hear from
>           Night. Or if you (and James ig??)
>           wanna get out and do something. I'm
>           usually free Wednesdays and
>           weekends!

**Me:** Alright, thanks.

Her offer to hang out is tempting, but I don't want her to see me like this. I could say I was in a car accident or something—it's not like she could prove otherwise—but I don't want the fact I'm a complete mess to get out before I have my story straight.

Maybe I shouldn't ask more about James right now to avoid her asking more questions.

*Ugh...*

I lock my phone, set it aside, and drop my head to the table. With my eyes closed, and a beam of warm sunlight on my back, I could almost fall asleep, but a stitch of discomfort in my shoulder keeps me tethered to reality.

A few quiet minutes pass. Eyes closed, listening to the air conditioner and thinking about what I should make for lunch.

Then I hear footsteps coming down the stairs. *Blue eyes. A flash of white. Reflective metal. Blood dripping.* My eyes snap open, and I try to play it cool as James joins me in the kitchen.

"You okay?" he asks.

I take a deep breath and sit up before forcing a smile. "I'm fine. Wanna...watch a movie or something?"

"Sure."

We make sandwiches and move into the living room, where I find an indie film that looks interesting while he sits just far enough away to make it a little weird.

A half-hour into the film, my phone dings in my back pocket. A FaceSpace message. I assume it's from Rose, but the red notification bubble appears beside my brother's photo instead.

*Robbie... I haven't heard from him since my birthday.*

Nerves building, I tap his photo.

> **Robbie:** hey, how are u? i havent been online much... but i saw the pics you shared. did u get a boyfriend or smth while i wasnt paying attention? ahaha

*Seriously?* I shared ONE picture, and we're not even together in it. Why does everyone think we're dating?

> **Me:** I've been okay. The guy's just a friend, though.
>
> **Robbie:** that's cool
>
> **Me:** How are you?
>
> **Robbie:** good. tired and working a lot yknow, but good ahaha
>
> **Robbie:** so what have u been up to? besides making new friends

*For better or worse. Um...*

> **Me:** I haven't done much else, tbh. Just taking it easy now.
>
> **Robbie:** Rose still in AZ?
>
> **Me:** Yeah

I watch my screen, a bit puzzled as he types something for an unreasonable length of time.

> **Robbie:** you sure that guys not ur boyfriend? hanging out and u share a pic without tagging him? i mean ive never seen u share pics of guys before lmao

I think James has a FaceSpace account, but I haven't looked. Besides, he doesn't even know I took the picture. I only uploaded it because I thought it was nice and fit with the other nature photos I took during our walk.

> **Me:** Not dating. He's having a hard time, so
> I'm helping him out.

*No need to mention I'm also having a hard time, right?*

> **Robbie:** ok its cool lol
>
> **Me:** Did you ever find out where mom moved
> to?
>
> **Robbie:** yea, shes in texas

*Wow.*

I glance up from my phone. James seems absorbed in the movie, but I missed the past several minutes, so I have no idea what's happening. Not that I care enough to ask. The first part was good, but I'm too distracted—stuck wondering why just about everyone has assumed we're dating.

Rose is one thing, and Carmen's reaction hardly surprised me, but *why Robbie?* He's not the type to care about that kind of thing at all.

*All I did was share a photo…*

I watch James' profile, growing a bit frustrated with myself.

It's not that I don't like him, but he's not the type I'd imagine myself going for—in a different way than how I felt Ice wasn't. He's quiet and generous, but he's even more nervous than I am, and we spend most of our time awkwardly avoiding eye contact.

*But...*

*The tears in my eyes when Dr. Corel said he'd have someone find James. And the look on his face when he first stepped into the room. Fear. Relief. He hugged me, and he was so warm, and—*

His expression shifts slightly, and he glances at me, and I prickle. My face heats up, and he grimaces as I start laughing.

"What?" he asks sharply.

"Nothing," I say, still laughing. "It's just... It's nothing."

\* \* \* \* \*

Thankfully, the photo of James generates no further questions or comments despite Rose and several others having liked the post it's a part of, but I still have a strange urge to delete it. Maybe because James doesn't know about the photo, and I feel a tiny bit guiltier every time I receive a notification related to it.

*Ugh.* There's no point in deleting it now, though.

Everyone who cares has already seen it.

I close FaceSpace and steal another glance at James. He's on his phone—reading, I think. I've wanted to ask what he's reading a few times before, but I never have.

*I guess this is a perfect opportunity.*

"Hey, what are you reading?"

He looks over, his expression an interesting combination of surprise and embarrassment. "It's a, uh... It's a fantasy novella. I follow a lot of indie authors on Twitter and read their books. It's kind of a guilty pleasure, I guess."

"Guilty pleasure? You think it's weird to read?"

He laughs. "No. It's not the reading that's weird. I just don't know many people who go out of their way to read self-published books. They're not always perfect, I guess, but I've found a ton of great books and authors online. A lot of heart."

He clears his throat and glances away. "Anyway, ebooks are affordable, and I can read no matter where I am. I can't carry a ton of real books around all the time, you know?"

*A worn paperback novel missing its cover comes to mind.*

"It's cool," I say. "To be honest, I haven't read much since high school, but I try. I read a book during the rainstorm."

Though, if it's that simple, why is he so embarrassed to talk about it? There's nothing strange about reading for fun, even if your taste in books happens to be self-published fantasy.

*Maybe he's into weird subgenres… Or erotica.*

"I thought about writing a book once," he says idly.

I grin. "You should give it a shot. It seems like you have a lot of free time you could spend writing."

He flashes a trite smile before returning his attention to his phone without responding.

I'm still actively avoiding my phone, and the room is quiet, so I turn the TV on and start the next episode of Planet Earth to act as background noise while we otherwise sit around doing nothing.

After several minutes, my phone goes off in my pocket *again*, and I jump at the sudden vibration and sharp sound. James snickers at my reaction, and I counter with a halfhearted glare.

I check my phone. It's Rose again.

**Rose:** So, are you and James dating yet?
( ͡• ͜ʖ ͡•)

*How many times do I have to say this today?*

**Me:** No. We are not dating.

**Rose:** But you are still hanging out?

I'm not sure how to respond, so I don't, but that doesn't seem to stop her. She's still typing.

**Rose:** Anyway, guess what??

**Me:** What?

After a moment, she sends a photo of a tired woman holding a tiny, pink newborn baby. I recognize her. She's related to Rose. We've met once or twice before. The photo and baby are adorable, but the message that follows damn near stops my heart.

**Rose:** Sara finally had her baby!! 2 weeks overdue lmao, but I can come home soon! \(T▽T)/

Oh… *Shit.*

With everything going on, I totally forgot that's why she stayed in Arizona so long. Her cousin was *pregnant*. She was waiting for her to deliver.

I shake my head, hoping to clear it, but my stomach twists into knots at the deeper implications of Rose's return. I've been trying to ignore it. Being home and feeling okay made pretending to be fine easier. But she's human, and I purposefully left her in the dark about *everything*.

I'm a wreck. My wrist is in a brace. I'm covered in scars and scabs. Hell, I even joined a secret experimental program while she was gone!

She knows I've been spending time with James—obviously, considering I just shared a picture of him—but she has no idea we're practically living together. She thinks I've been at the cottage alone ever since I left Ice's house, but I can't abandon James now just to maintain that illusion. Whatever he says, I am not okay with leaving him alone while Ice still has it out for him.

I take a breath and ask *when* she plans on heading out. Then I look up from my phone and find James watching me. He must have noticed my rising panic.

"Everything alright?" he asks.

"Yeah…" I force a smile. "But Rose is coming back soon."

"Your roommate?"

I nod.

His soft, "Oh?" and mild frown make for an annoyingly underwhelming reaction. He puts his phone away and offers me his full attention, but he somehow looks *less* concerned than before I said anything.

"Just look at me." I hold my scarred arms out. "What am I supposed to tell her? She doesn't know anything about what I've been through these past few weeks."

His frown deepens, and he looks up from my arms to meet my gaze. "You want to hide it? Is that a good idea?"

"What else am I supposed to do?"

My phone goes off again. A quick glance reveals her answer to be *Wednesday*, and I grit my teeth. Wednesday is *three days* away.

"I don't care if it's a good idea or not," I admit. "I don't want Rose involved— No. She can't get involved at all. She's human. I can't break the Secrecy Agreement, and she can't find out about Ice or what he did."

His eyes flick down, but he nods before meeting my gaze more solidly. "Alright. How can I help?"

# thirty-two

Rose's ETA: two days from now.

Last night, James and I argued as to whether or not he should leave. He doesn't want to stay because he doesn't want to cause any more trouble or drama or whatever. But I don't want to be left alone, so he finally agreed to stick around until Rose gets here.

I'm half-surprised I didn't come downstairs in the morning and find him gone. But, to my relief, he was fast asleep on the couch at 8:30AM, and I felt silly for worrying about it half the night.

After breakfast, I decide it's time for some last-minute damage control and convince James to give me a ride so I can do a bit of shopping—though, convincing him doesn't take much effort on my part. I figure I can't do anything about the wrist brace, but there are a few things I need to buy if I'll have any hope of convincing Rose my life has been even slightly normal while she was gone.

We first stop by a drugstore, where I toss a tube of potentially gimmicky scar-reducing cream and a few brands of concealer into a handbasket because I have no idea which is best.

At the cash register, James insists on paying. I argue, but I barely have enough to afford everything I want, so I give up.

Then we go to Century Plaza Mall.

As we walk through the large, glass doors, I falter. *We met here. By sheer coincidence. By accident. Because we bumped into each other, and I dropped my bags on the floor.* The memory is strangely bittersweet, and I wonder if he thought about it too, but it's awkward, so I don't bring it up.

We eat lunch in the food court and wander around for a while before I finally step into one of the more affordable clothing stores with James close behind.

I browse the clearance racks, but long sleeves aren't in season and won't be for a few months. There's a rack of heavily discounted spring stock at the back of the store, but there aren't many tops with sleeves long enough to cover my forearms. I can't afford to be picky—though, I'm not sure I can realistically afford more than one shirt to begin with.

I only own a few long-sleeve shirts as it is. Even in the winter, I tend to wear a t-shirt under a sweatshirt. But Rose might think it's weird if I start wearing a hoodie 24/7 in the middle of summer, so I continue looking and eventually collect two summery cardigans, a flannel shirt, and two lightweight tops with three-quarter length sleeves and relatively high necklines.

As I'm debating whether I should dip into my savings to buy clothes, James clears his throat.

"I can pay for it," he says.

I frown. "Are you sure?"

"Yes. Get whatever you want, and stop worrying about my money. Just consider it payment for crashing at your place.

Seriously. I owe you that much."

*Does he?*

*Didn't I let him stay because I thought* I *owed him?*

His expression is level and unconcerned despite me squinting at him, but the offer bothers me. He's paid for so much already, and, just a few days ago, it seemed like he barely had any money left after paying for the motel.

Still... The clothes will help, so I accept and busy myself with looking around the store a bit more.

I study a display of clunky bangles, now worrying over my wrist. The other injuries can be blamed on an accident in a pinch —perhaps I fell through a window; *ha!*—but the heart is the one scar I can't explain away. Sure, it's hidden for now, but I only need to wear the wrist brace for another week or so.

The last thing I want is for Rose to think I did it to myself, so I need to come up with another way to hide it.

*Will makeup do the trick?* It's still scabbed over, so the texture might show through. Casually wearing bangles would be super out of character for me and would only draw more attention to my wrist, but she'd surely call me out for wearing the sports wristband I took from her bedroom too.

I expect things will be bad enough wearing long sleeves. She *knows* I live in tank tops during the summer.

"Need anything else?" James asks.

"Um..."

I glance at the shirts draped over my arm and around the store again, but I don't feel the allure of spending someone else's money today. I just feel guilty. James isn't like Ice. He doesn't have the same kind of money. I shouldn't take advantage of his generosity—*or his feelings for me.*

"No." I offer a smile. "This should be enough."

"You sure?" he asks, mirroring my smile rather easily.

"I'll be fine. Thanks, though."

James has done more than enough over the past couple weeks. It seems like he's constantly spending money on me since Ice dropped me in his lap, and he hasn't complained once.

*Am I wrong about his money?*

Maybe it was unfair to assume, but everything I've seen and heard about him so far points to James being on the lower end of middle class. The twenty-year-old junk car. Living with his father before getting kicked out. Relying on Reid Manor for shelter. The quality and type of food he bought while staying there. The cheap motel we booked.

I thought he wouldn't have money to spare, and then he offers to spend over a hundred dollars on makeup and clothing without a second thought. And even asks if I need anything else?

*Am I overthinking it?*

I pile the clothes on the counter, and James presents the cashier with the same card he used to buy lunch and the drug-store makeup.

*Yeah, I'm probably overthinking it.*

But I'm done shopping for today.

As we leave the mall, I mention dinner. After some prodding, James agrees to make spaghetti, so we stop by a store on the way home to pick up the last few things he needs.

Now, the smell of browning beef fills the air, and I watch

from the dining table as he drains the cooked beef in the sink using a metal colander as the water runs hot. Then he rinses the meat under the steaming water.

"Are you supposed to rinse meat like that?"

"Dunno." He laughs, but his smile becomes muted as he shuts the water off and shakes out the remaining liquid. "I remember my mom used to cook ground beef like this. It's just this random, vivid memory I have of her from like twelve years ago. And I guess I've just…always done it the same way."

"Oh. Right. This is her recipe?"

"Yeah." He returns the meat to the pan, and it makes a lovely sizzling noise. "Anyway, it's not that weird. Rinsing it makes the sauce less greasy or whatever."

I want to ask about his mom. I don't know much about James' parents beyond her interest in cooking and the fact his dad sucks. But I haven't talked about my parents much either, and I'm not sure I want to invite a conversation about them.

So I just listen and try to imagine what his life might have been like twelve years ago.

\* \* \* \* \*

James sits on the edge of my bed. He glances around my room, looking marginally uncomfortable but otherwise alright, which is an improvement compared to the last time he came in for more than five seconds.

*Why did I call him up here?*

I want to admit to uploading that picture without permission because it's still haunting me. But we could have stayed downstairs to talk about that. I don't know.

"Is everything okay?" he asks.

I force a smile. "Yeah, I'm fine. But there's, um…something I need to tell you." When he doesn't say anything, I sigh. "I kind of took a picture of you the other day and shared it online."

"Online?" he asks in surprise. "Like on FaceSpace?"

"Yeah, I shared it on FaceSpace."

I pull the post up on my phone and show him, explaining how the photo I shared is part of a larger post about our walk to the wildlife pond. As he flicks through the images, he mumbles something before returning my phone, clearing his throat, and glancing away.

"Well, at least it's not a bad photo, I guess."

I flash a smile to hide my nerves. "No. I liked it. That's why I posted it, but I probably should have asked first. Do you want me to take it down or anything?"

"No, it's fine," he says, still frowning as he looks at nothing in particular across the room. After a moment of quiet, he looks to me again. "But, uh… I actually have pictures of you on my phone too. From someone's FaceSpace. I've had them for a while, so I can't even remember who shared it. Sorry. It's kinda messed up, huh?"

*It is weird, but—*

"What pictures?"

He bristles—though, whether he's embarrassed or guilty, it's hard to tell—but he must realize I'm only curious because he sucks in a breath and nods. He slips his phone from his pocket, scrolls through images, and then turns the screen to show me.

Oh. *That* picture.

It's a photo of me sandwiched between Carmen and Night at the Summer Solstice festival at Riverside Park. It was taken the day I met her, and my face is beet red, but I'm smiling. He swipes the screen. The second picture is of me sitting on a bench —during the Music@ThePark event several days later. My hair is up in a neat, braided bun, and the River Sapphire rests near my collarbone.

"Looks like it was Carmen," he says mildly, taking the phone back. "I guess that makes sense."

"You know Carmen?"

He sighs. "Everyone knows Carmen. Even you, apparently."

"And you know Night?"

Our eyes meet, and a guarded chill washes over him. A strange uneasiness. He looks a little confused—or disappointed, maybe. I feel like Night often looked similar when she talked about James.

*Maybe they're the real ones with history.*

"Of course, I know Night," he says, his tone incredulous and frown more pronounced. "She seriously didn't tell you anything?"

"No. She made it sound like you guys barely knew each other."

"Ha…" He glances away with a blank, muted smile. "Figures she'd say that."

*Seems I was right.*

"Were you guys friends as kids or something?"

"I don't know." He sighs again, his frustration ebbing. "They obviously don't wanna admit that we used to be friends, and they ditched you even faster, so…fuck 'em."

*They*, huh?

Another sigh, and he looks at his phone. "Anyway, I'm sorry I saved those pictures. I'll delete them now. Bet you think I'm even creepier, though, huh?"

"It's just a couple pictures." After a beat of silence, I laugh. "Honestly, that's nothing compared to what Ice did."

He grimaces. "Do I even want to know?"

"I don't know. But he, um… He spent a few days stalking me in his feline form—before we met, I mean. One day, he followed me to the store, so he could introduce himself…properly."

"How do you know?"

"I didn't believe him when he first told me about immortals —I mean, why would I?—so he morphed to prove it, and I recognized the cat he turned into as one I saw around the cottage a few times."

Disgust tugs at his lips. "You're kidding."

"I'm not! He owned up to it and everything." My smile falters, and I sigh. "I should have broke things off right there, so maybe you're right. Maybe I am a bad judge of character."

"You and me both," he mutters, glancing away.

I hesitate, picking at the velcro tab on my wrist brace, then take a breath, but my voice is still quiet. "You're starting to grow on me, though, so I hope I'm not wrong about you."

"Yeah… I'd hate to prove myself right again."

He doesn't look at me, but he doesn't move either—his hands tightly interlaced in his lap—and the room falls silent. I glance away again and pick up my phone. But I don't even unlock it. I just watch the dark screen.

*This is awkward, but…*

"Thanks for everything, James. You didn't have to pay for any of that stuff. You didn't have to help me at all. And I don't just mean today, either. But I… I really appreciate it. It means a lot."

He still doesn't look at me, but his expression softens, and he nods. "It's no problem. Honest."

# thirty-three

Rose will be home in a few hours.

She called right after she and Kyle crossed the Arizona-California border. I tried to sound happy while we talked on the phone, but I feel like the entire world is already crashing down around me. Everything will change the moment we see each other. And I have no idea what she'll do.

*What if she realizes I'm hiding more than she thought?*

*What if James accidentally says too much?*

*What if I say too much?*

*What if, what if, what if...?*

I slap my cheeks and head downstairs, ready as I'll ever be, wearing a top that hides every scar except for the one on my palm. My left hand is still in a brace, but I'm not worried about that.

"So... How do I look?"

James studies my appearance for a moment, but he's not taking me seriously. Even if he hasn't admitted it, I know he thinks I'm making a big deal out of nothing.

"You look fine," he says. "You almost look totally normal."

I shove him with my good hand. "That's not funny."

He laughs, but his expression grows earnest. "I know you don't wanna hear this, but I still think you should be honest with her."

"I can't tell her what Ice did."

"Obviously not…" He glances aside, scratching his arm. "But you shouldn't hide everything, right? You guys live together. She'll see your injuries eventually, and the longer you hide them, the worse it'll be when she finds out you lied to her."

I tug my sleeves down. "I know. It's not like I *want* to lie, but I don't know how to explain any of what's happened without mentioning immortals—or Ice."

After a moment of silence, our eyes meet again. He looks disappointed, and I understand more than he probably realizes. I'm not happy about this either.

"She's your friend," he says. "I won't tell you what to do, and I'll keep quiet if that's what you want."

"Yeah. Thanks. For now, I think that's all we can do."

* * * * *

"Jayde!"

Rose dumps her suitcase just inside the door and pulls me into a tight hug. *A bit rough on my shoulder.* Then she steps back and takes another look at me. Her grey eyes zero in on my wrist, and her expression shifts slightly.

"What happened?"

Her concern is mild—more curious than anything.

"Oh, this?" I smile and hold my braced hand up. "It's nothing.

I tripped and sprained my wrist last week, but I'm fine."

She purses her lips. "And you didn't tell me?"

"Yeah, sorry."

At least she got here after the worst of the bruises faded. She would lose her mind if she knew I spent time in the hospital. I'm sure she will find out eventually, like James said, but I still need to work out how to explain everything without bringing up anything I shouldn't.

*Still...* Part of me regrets not mentioning my injuries or the hospital visits before, even if whatever excuses I might have given her at the time were weak. I only have myself to blame, but it feels like pretending nothing was ever wrong is the only thing I can do.

*I'm stuck. And I hate it.*

Whether she buys my story about tripping or not, she abandons the subject. She drops her stuffed duffel bag onto her suitcase and walks past me, further into the living room.

Then, as expected, she turns her attention on James.

He's been hovering by the couch since I first let Rose inside, and he hasn't said a word. I close the door, careful to lock it, and join them, only to find her practically drooling as she scans him head to toe.

*Gross.*

"This must be James." A hint of unnecessary approval slips into her voice. With a devious glance in my direction, she says, "Though, he's not as hot as he looks in photos. I feel like I've been catfished."

*Seriously, Rose? He's right here!*

I glance at James in time to catch his reaction—a terse smile betraying mild offense—and I laugh nervously.

"So, what?" she asks with a wide smile. "Why is he here now, huh? Are you two together or something?"

"Um—" I hesitate. *How should I answer?*

While I wouldn't go that far, our relationship is complicated. James has been repressing his feelings for me, and I'm starting to think I might feel *something* for him. We've been staying together for a couple weeks now, but we're not *together* together, right?

*Unless...*

Wait— Is that what it looks like? *Is that how it is?*

When I glance at James again, at a bit of a loss, he breaks eye contact and looks to Rose. "Yeah," he says, totally throwing me under the bus without any warning. "I guess we are."

"I knew it!"

She laughs and slaps me on the shoulder. I bite my tongue to keep from flinching as her pinky brushes the healing gunshot wound hidden by my shirt's thin sleeve.

*Ow. Damn.*

"I knew something was up," she says, smug as hell, "but, of course, Jay's too much of a scaredy-cat to tell me herself after how it went with the last one. You've been spending more time together than you let on, haven't you?"

*The last one. Ice.*

"You're not wrong," I mutter before James has a chance to say anything else.

She steps away to collect her luggage, and I exchange a wide-eyed glance with James while I rub my aching shoulder. *At least he looks guilty.* I help Rose by opening her bedroom door as he hangs back and returns to sitting on the couch.

"I expect details," she hisses as she steps into her room.

*Details regarding a relationship I wasn't aware I was in five minutes ago? Great...*

I tug on my sleeves, worried she might see *something* if she looks only a tiny bit closer, but she continues into her room and piles her things onto her bed beside the mess of laundry.

"Just shut the door," she says. "I'll be out in a few."

I close the door, and my guard falls as I turn and cross the room to confront James. He frowns, looking entirely concerned and even more apologetic.

"Sorry," he says, glancing away. "Do you want me to leave?"

*Leave?* After you blindsided me by asserting yourself as my boyfriend? Are you joking?

I almost reply with the scathing sarcasm running through my mind, but I quickly realize why he felt the need to ask.

*Rose is here. This is our house.*

He probably thinks I'm mad because we disagreed over how to handle her return or because of what he said to her just now. Or maybe he only asked because of some unspoken understanding that *this*—whatever it is—was only going to last until she got back.

But that's not it.

I'm not mad or upset, and I never planned to kick him out the moment Rose came home. No. Even if I won't be alone now, the thought of him leaving still makes me nervous.

I sit beside him.

"Is leaving safe?" I ask.

"Safe for you or safe for me?"

*That's exactly what has me so nervous.*

"For either of us, I guess."

He offers a half-hearted smile. "Now that your friend's back in town, you really will be better off without me around. Ice probably won't bother you if you're alone with her, but he might if I'm still here. You've at least considered it, haven't you?"

"Of course, I have," I say under my breath, staring at the hands balled in my lap. "But…"

He laughs, soft and uneasy, and I look up as he shakes his head. His smile is uncomfortable and sad, and I frown as our eyes meet, suddenly unsettled myself—because it kind of looks like he already intends to break up with me.

"I cannot believe I'm saying this right now, but… I almost wish you *didn't* care about me. It's so much harder to work up the nerve to leave—"

"You *can't* leave," I argue, struggling to keep my voice low. "You literally just told Rose we're dating."

He drags his hands down his face. "I know. I'm sorry."

"I'm not mad, but, even if I am safe here with her, you won't be safe on your own, right?"

"It's not safe for us to be together, either." After a moment of hesitation, he reaches out to touch my arm. His fingers are warm, even through my sleeve. "I don't care what happens to me, Jayde. I just want to do what's best for you."

*For me?*

My nails dig into the wrist brace, and I bite the inside of my cheek. *This really is a lose-lose situation, isn't it? Is there any way to protect everyone?*

"I don't want you to leave," I say.

His hand falls away from my arm, and I meet his eyes again, not surprised that he looks unhappy and conflicted.

"Are you sure?" he asks.

"Yes. I want you to stay."

He frowns, his brows furrowed.

*This is so frustrating!* He says he doesn't want to leave. Every time I ask, he says the same thing. *But he still...*

Sure, I understand why he thinks leaving might benefit me, but that's exactly why I'm not okay with it. I don't want him to end up sleeping in his car, and I don't want him to put himself in more danger because of me. No matter what we do—whether he leaves or stays—we can't be sure we'll both be safe, but he must realize the danger he'd be in if he were alone.

After a moment spent staring me down, he sighs. "Okay. Fine. I'll stay a while longer if that's what you want."

"Thank you."

I have a feeling he's only willing to drop it because we don't have time to argue. Rose will come out of her room any time, and it would only cause trouble if either of us look upset when she does. But he better not bring it up again later. I don't care what he thinks or how it could theoretically impact my safety. Making himself an easy target is out of the question.

"But you're right," he says, forcing a smile. "It would be pretty weird if I left after what I said."

"Right... I guess we're dating now, huh?"

"I could tell her I was joking," he mumbles, his ears quite red. "I just kinda said it because I thought it might keep her from asking more questions about your hand. I didn't think of what to do after."

"No. It's fine."

He blinks. "You're serious?"

"I don't mind if she thinks we're dating," I say. He opens his mouth, but I shake my head. "I mean, you like me, and it's not like I hate you or anything. Besides, if you're staying here, it makes sense, doesn't it?"

"Does it?" he asks blankly.

I ignore the warmth in my cheeks and roll my eyes. "At the very least, it'll be easier to explain than the truth would be. What do you think? Wanna give it a shot?"

"Oh, uh—" He shakes his head, shedding some of the tension held in his jaw while his eyes remain quite wide. "Yeah, I guess that's alright…if you're okay with it."

"Okay. It's a plan, then."

I hold a hand out toward him. He stares at it for a few seconds before relaxing one of the hands in his lap and moving to accept mine with it. His palm is clammy and warm, but he releases the breath he was holding and flashes a more genuine smile.

"I'll do my best," he says.

I squeeze his hand. "Same."

Rose's bedroom door opens, and I drop James' hand as I turn to look.

"Hey, guys, check it out," she calls, raising a cloth tote bag above her head. "I got your souvenirs right here."

"Souvenirs?" James echoes in confusion.

Rose plops down beside me and reaches into the bag. The first thing she removes, she hands to me. It's a lightweight hoodie—pastel pink with a digitized, vaporwave aesthetic depiction of the Grand Canyon on the front. The second thing is a nondescript cardboard box, but she describes the contents as an upcycled wind chime made using a wine bottle and lightning glass—the result of desert sand being struck by a lightning bolt.

James says it's called *fulgurite*.

Rose calls him a nerd.

I thank her, figuring the wind chime is it, but she takes one last thing from the bag and passes it across me to James. He looks more surprised to have received something than I am surprised she went out of her way to buy a men's shirt.

"It's a large," she says flippantly. "It should fit you."

He holds it up to get a better look. The front of the black t-shirt has a large circle containing a desert-themed horizon line in highly saturated sunset colors. With *ARIZONA* printed in a digital font below, the shirt also has a vaporwave look and *almost* matches the hoodie she gave me.

"Thanks," he says.

*He's still confused.*

"Now, then." She tosses the empty bag across the room. It does not make it all the way to her bedroom door, but she looks away, claps her hands together, and jumps up from the couch without any care. "Movie night. Upstairs."

James moves the TV to the second floor, and the three of us transform what used to be the study into a tiny movie theater.

Once everything is set up, I order pizza while Rose picks out a Netflix-original horror movie that came out while she was in Arizona.

Downstairs, I check the locks. The house is secure, so I head back up, flicking the lights off on my way. Rose is curled up in her large beanbag chair. We only have two beanbags—considering we normally only have two people living here—so James and I share mine. They're decently sized, so I don't find it uncomfortable even if I'm positive it bothers James in some way.

*But we're supposedly dating now, so I guess he's sucking it up.*

Hardly ten minutes into the film, a gory ghost flashes across a mirror on screen. Rose squeaks in alarm and James flinches, caught off guard by the shameless jumpscare, but their reactions spooked me more than the actual movie did, and it's disappointing. Vivid, shocking imagery paired with a jarring, discordant sound effect normally gets me. I've never been particularly good at handling horror movies before.

I lean into James' shoulder. He's so focused on the film, he barely seems to notice.

I watch the screen a while longer. I try to get into it, but my mind keeps wandering. Because I've seen worse than a ghost in a bathroom mirror on a TV screen. Ice isn't a character in a scary movie. He's not fiction or fantasy or an intangible ghost. He's real, and so are the scars he left behind.

*Unfortunately.*

A bitter taste fills my mouth, and I look to my lap.

James thinks it's only a matter of time before Ice stirs up more trouble because we're still together. It's hard to argue. It's hard to guess what Ice might do, but would he really try anything like what he's done before with Rose here? Would he risk her finding out about immortals too?

*I don't know...*

When I return my attention to the movie, the situation seems tense. The main character is making their way through a dark, musty room—an attic or basement. I can barely make out anything. The only light in the shot is the tiny, flickering flame of the character's lighter, and it casts his nervous face in heavy shadow.

The ominous music peaks. The sound of breathing grows more pronounced. And a loud knock startles me.

I jump, my heart racing.

Then James snickers, and I realize the knocking was not part of the movie. It was real; a series of solid knocks on the front door.

*It's the pizza, you ditz.*

I roll my eyes, nail James in the rib with my elbow, and crawl out of the beanbag. He flashes a smile and gives me the pizza money we pooled earlier before returning his attention to the film.

I expected *him* to get the pizza, but *it's fine*. I guess he's more invested in the movie than he expected.

*Men.*

Rose catches my eye and holds up the TV remote in a silent offer to pause the movie. I smile at her but shake my head. With a shrug, she looks back to the screen.

I sigh, adjust my sleeves, and head downstairs.

Rose wouldn't understand, but I don't care if I miss anything. Horror movies aren't as appealing or captivating when you're literally living one. She doesn't know, and James might be under the impression I'm more optimistic about our situation than he is, but there's hardly a moment I'm not thinking about it.

I unlock the front door, almost dazed by how disinterested I am in Rose's *movie night*. I just want to grab the pizza and spend time with my friends. Maybe I can get my mind off the darkness once the movie is over.

That's all I want.

So I open the door.

Upstairs, the TV speakers belt more jarring, discordant music followed by a piercing, distorted scream. Rose squeals in elated surprise. Maybe the ghost appeared again. Maybe the main character discovered his missing girlfriend, dead and mutilated on the floor in the stuffy basement. Maybe it was something else entirely.

I don't know.

Then she laughs. As she says something I can't make out over the TV audio and the screaming in my head, I wonder if whatever happened on screen compares at all to what I'm dealing with.

"Jayde. It's good to see you."

# thirty-four

"How's your arm?"

With a relaxed posture and two large pizza boxes balanced on one arm, Ice Monroe runs his free hand through his hair. He cracks a wicked smile at whatever face I pulled upon recognizing him, and he waits for me to respond.

But I don't respond.

I can't bring myself to say anything.

He sighs and drops the easygoing act, his free hand falling to his hip as he frowns. "I see your roommate finally returned from her vacation. Does she know what's happened here while she was away? Anything at all?"

I shake my head.

Rose may know a few things about the fictionalized version of Ice I described to her before he hurt me, but she knows nothing about what he's done. *I made sure of that.*

"Good." He smiles, the expression thin. "I'd hate to drag her into your mess, but I want to make something very clear."

When he doesn't continue, I steal a look at my hands. They're trembling, so I lace my fingers together to still them.

"What is it?" I breathe.

"Surely, you don't believe I'm so noble I'd let you and James off the hook just to save face in front of some human girl worth less than you?"

I grit my teeth.

*James was right. We're still not safe, and now...*

I look up to meet Ice's sharp gaze.

"What do you want?" I ask, my voice surprisingly cold.

"To see what you're capable of," he says.

*Me?* I glance over my shoulder—at the empty living room for only a second—and he chuckles.

"Is James with you?" he asks.

"Yes," I say through my teeth.

"I see." His eyes flash in the low light as some emotion I don't recognize crosses his face. "I suppose I shouldn't be surprised, but, as long as he's still here, you'll be hearing from me again."

*Why? What did either of us actually do?*

There are so many things I want to say, but I've already spent too long at the door. I don't want to risk Rose or James coming downstairs and seeing him. So I swallow my fear and snatch the pizza boxes off his arm.

"Thanks for the pizza."

His brows furrow. "You're welcome."

He glances down as I reach for the doorknob. His smile fades, but he doesn't say another word or stop me from closing the door.

I lock the deadbolt. It clicks louder than I feel it should.

After adjusting my grip on the pizza boxes, I peek through

the slatted blinds beside the front door. With his hands tucked in his jacket pockets, Ice walks down the concrete path toward the silver Porsche parked in the space beside James' beat-up Honda. He pops the driver-side door open and steps inside. The door shuts, and the car rumbles to life, barely making a sound.

I can't see him through the tinted windshield in the dark, but the vehicle pulls out of the parking space and exits the lot. I'm hardly satisfied even when the red taillights drive out of view, but I close the blinds and take a few calming breaths.

Then I return upstairs, where I announce the arrival of food.

My upbeat tone is horribly fake, and my nails dig into the cardboard to keep myself from jittering, but no one seems to notice.

Rose nods and pauses the movie, still shaken by whatever went down on screen while I was busy making conversation with my real-life antagonist.

"Let's take a break and eat downstairs," she says.

"That's fine."

She stands to stretch before approaching. I pass the pizza boxes to her, and she goes on her merry way past me and toward the stairs. Then I look to James, who slips his phone into his pocket. He hefts himself out of the beanbag, but he lingers beside me rather than walking by.

I feel my expression shift, and I hug my arms tighter.

"You alright?" he asks.

I shake my head. I'm hiding enough from him as it is, but this is one thing I cannot justify keeping to myself.

"You were right," I say, weariness slipping into my voice as

I blink to stop my eyes from watering. "It's not safe here."

"What do you mean?"

I still have the money James handed me, so I offer it back to him. He stares at the bills in my trembling hand before meeting my eyes again, a tense concern in his set jaw.

"I don't think Rose being here will phase Ice at all."

His eyes widen, and he steps away to look out over the banister and into the living room. "You saw him? Is he still here?"

"No. He's gone. Please keep your voice down."

"There's no way he would do anything like—" He pauses and rubs his jaw before looking to me again. "With Rose around?"

"I have no idea, James. It's Ice."

"Right…" With a sigh, he tucks the money away, clearly struggling to maintain a calm exterior. "This is worse than I thought. Maybe I should—"

Loud, upbeat pop music starts playing in the kitchen, and Rose calls for us. I reply with, "One second!" and cross my arms over my chest, still staring James down.

"Don't even finish that thought," I groan. "This is bad, yes. But we don't have time to deal with it right now. I don't want Rose to get suspicious."

His frown deepens. "If you're sure…"

"For now at least, everything is fine. Ice left. I watched him drive off, and the door is locked. Just pretend to have a good time tonight. We can talk about it later, okay?"

"Fine," he agrees, his voice low and gaze averted.

I plaster a smile on my face, but the best he can muster is painfully uneasy. *Ugh.* If anything tips Rose off tonight, it'll be his attitude. Hopefully, he can keep it together for a couple more hours. She spent the whole day driving, so I can't imagine she'll stay up much longer.

With a sigh, I lead him downstairs to join Rose in the kitchen. She's in a *fantastic* mood, and it's contagious as usual. Even in this terrible, uncertain situation, she's a breath of fresh air.

"How'd you guys meet, anyway?" she asks from where she sits on the kitchen counter with her legs crossed over the edge.

"I already told you, didn't I? I tripped over him at the mall."

She cackles, shoulders bouncing with hearty laughter. "Okay, sure, but you literally tripped over him? I mean, that does seem like something you'd do, but seriously?"

"Yeah. I threw my brand-new stuff all over the floor and everything," I say, feeling my forced smile come a little easier. "Since then, I guess…he's just been helping me out a lot."

Her expression shifts curiously, turning rather shrewd. "So, how long has he been staying here?"

"Staying here?" I ask, feigning confusion. When she rolls her eyes, I laugh. "Oh. Um. I guess it has been a few days. That's not a problem, is it?"

She sighs. "Of course not. I don't mind if he's here, but you really didn't need to hide it from me. You're so dramatic."

*Me? I'm being dramatic?*

"Right. Sorry."

"Also, is he always this quiet?"

He sighs. "I'm thinking about the movie. That's all."

"Oh, yeah?" She laughs. "You were pretty into it, huh?"

He looks from her to me with some concern, and I offer him

a smile. Maybe hearing Rose say it's fine for him to stay will make him feel less guilty about it.

But he doesn't reply, instead focusing on his phone.

Rose doesn't seem to mind. She's more interested in catching me up on small details of her trip to Arizona and her long drive back to Riverview with Kyle. Apparently, they spent half the drive up I-5 behind a truck pulling a Gothic-styled tiny house, and she has several decent photos to show for it since they tailed the truck when it stopped for gas in Modesto.

The three of us manage to polish off half the pizza, even with James acting more lethargic than usual. Then we return upstairs to finish the movie. As I sit beside James in the beanbag, I pour my complete focus into watching the TV, hoping it will distract me.

Hoping I can learn something from it.

* * * * *

Of course, I learn nothing.

Because the main character died at the end.

Out of everything in the movie, his death bothers me the most. He lost his girlfriend. His childhood best friend. He fought tooth and nail to find a solution to the malevolent haunting he faced. But, in the end, it was all for nothing. He thought he made it. *I* thought he made it.

Then he died not even thirty seconds before the credits rolled.

Lots of horror movies end with the main character's death. I never thought about it too deeply before, but now it feels senseless and upsetting.

I'm probably overthinking the whole thing. It was just a movie. It doesn't mean anything or have any impact on my reality.

*But it's still a tickle in the back of my mind.*

"Goodnight, guys," Rose says.

She shuts herself in her bedroom, and I stand in the middle of the silent living room for a moment. Then I look back to James. He's nervous. I know it's about Ice and not the movie, but I wonder if the ending bothered him too.

"You still wanna talk about it, don't you?" I ask, my voice low. When he glances away and nods, I sigh. "Alright, come on."

He follows me upstairs and into my bedroom. I flip the light on and close the door before turning to address him. He's visibly upset now, his expression tense and hands balled into loose fists.

*I hate this.*

"I know what you're gonna say, James, but I am not letting you leave on your own. After what Ice said, there is no way you can convince me to let you go."

He forces a laugh. "Do you think you could stop me?"

I bite my tongue. *But he had better not try.*

"What did he say to you?" he asks.

"Nonsense, mostly," I mutter. "It's Ice, you know? Nothing he said actually meant anything."

"He wants me gone, doesn't he?"

I sigh. "So what if he does? You plan to do whatever he says?"

"No."

"Do you *want* to leave?"

His eyes widen, and he glances away. "No."

"Then stay."

A beat of silence. Then he sucks in a sharp breath and looks past me to the closed bedroom door. He takes a step.

"I should go downstairs," he says. "Get some sleep, okay?"

As he walks by, I turn and grab his arm. He freezes. His skin is warm. Neither of us move for a long moment.

"Stay with *me*, James. Please."

His shoulders droop as he lets out a breath. "Jayde—"

I catch sight of his downcast eyes, set jaw, and trembling lip in the mirror. My chest grows tight, and I stop looking, but I don't let go of his arm. *No matter what, I can't let him leave. That's exactly what Ice wants, and I don't want to know why.*

"No," I say. "If I wake up tomorrow, and you're not here, Ice will be the only person I can go to for help. And I really don't want to do that."

"But you would?" he breathes. When I say nothing, he glances over his shoulder, eyes wide and afraid, and he sighs. "Fine. You win. I'll stay."

"Thank you."

"But, uh… I do need to go downstairs and grab my backpack."

I hesitate, but I release his arm and step away from the door. He pulls it open and pauses in the doorway, glancing back at me.

"You know I'm not worth this, right?" His voice is low and soft. "I'm not worth any of this. You should just let me go. Forget about me and move on with your life."

"I can't live with that."

The faintest, saddest smile crosses his lips, and then he turns away and disappears down the stairs. I wait in the doorway for him to come back. Thankfully, he does, and he changes out of his day clothes in the bathroom before joining me in the bedroom.

I turn the privacy lock.

Finally able to relax, I sit on the edge of my bed, while James drops his backpack near my dresser. He stares at his tired reflection in the mirror.

"Honestly, I should thank you," he says.

"For what?"

He shakes his head, flashing a wry smile. "Giving a shit."

"Mm… I'm half surprised you didn't take off without saying anything when I let you go downstairs alone."

"You shouldn't be," he says with another sigh. "It's just more proof that I'm a coward."

I frown. "You think leaving is the right thing?"

"I don't know if there is a right thing, but I don't want to leave if it'll hurt you. Because I do care."

"I know."

*And that's exactly why I can't let you go.*

\* \* \* \* \*

I can't sleep.

I can't stop thinking about the movie. The main character's pointless death. The cruel glint in Ice's bright blue eyes. Everything James said before he finally quieted down. And I can't decide whether convincing him to stay or letting him leave would be more selfish of me. Maybe both options are a little selfish.

*Maybe I'm a selfish person.*

But I don't care.

I refuse to give in to Ice's demands. I won't hand James over. If he wants to hurt us, I won't make it easy for him. I can't. I meant what I said. I wouldn't be able to live with it. *At least, if everything spirals out of control now, I can convince myself I tried.*

Staring at my bedroom door in the dark, I sigh.

Behind me, James' soft voice startles me—not enough to make me flinch, but certainly enough for it to take a moment to register what he said. He asked a question:

*"Can I touch you?"*

*Ah...* A month ago, that would have thrown me into a flustered panic, but it doesn't now. *Why is that?*

I roll over to face him, careful to keep pressure off my injured shoulder. He looks nervous and exhausted, and, as much as I wish I didn't, I can relate.

"I thought you were asleep," I admit.

"I can't sleep."

"Me either."

"I know you're upset," he says. "And I know it's my fault. I just want to help, but… I guess I'm not sure how much of this is real and how much is an act."

*This? Us?*

Now that's surprising.

"An act? For who? Rose?" When he doesn't answer, I laugh. "Sure, you sprung it on me out of nowhere, but I didn't have to accept. Besides, Rose is cool. She'd let you stay even if she didn't think we were dating."

He averts his eyes, frowning as he scratches his cheek. "But…you went along with it anyway?"

"Sure. I mean, how is what we've been doing this past week not the same as dating? Does slapping a title on it so it makes sense to other people really change anything?"

"Well… I…"

"I'm not using you—if that's what you're worried about. I'm not…" I catch myself growing frustrated and sigh. "I'm not hiding behind you just because I'm scared of Ice."

"I wouldn't mind if you were," he mumbles into his hand. "You don't have to lie to me if you are."

*Ouch.*

"I'm serious, James. Believe it or not, I do like you, and I do care about you, and I wouldn't have *gone along with it* if I wasn't already thinking about it."

Finally, his eyes flick up. "Wait, what?"

*Seriously?*

"Maybe you are an idiot," I mutter.

"Yeah," he says slowly. "If you haven't figured it out by now, I need the most basic shit spelled out for me sometimes." When I roll my eyes, he smiles—but only for an instant. "Anyway, you never answered my question. Do you mind if I touch you or not?"

I watch him as wide, amber eyes stare back at me. With a sigh, I tear my gaze away and roll back onto my uninjured side, both for my own comfort and to hide my terribly warm cheeks.

"Go ahead," I say, my voice muffled by my pillow. "Just

don't make it weird."

He chuckles. "Okay."

A few heartbeats later, warm fingers brush my arm. His touch is soft and careful, and I hold my breath for a moment as he touches the band-aid over the wound near my shoulder. His hand lingers there for several seconds.

Then he takes a deep breath and retracts his hand. The bedding shifts behind me, and the room falls quiet.

*Hm…*

I think I misunderstood what he was asking. Maybe it's sad or desperate or embarrassing, but I thought he meant something more like a hug or cuddling or *something*. I definitely wasn't expecting whatever *that* was.

Just…a touch.

*What is he thinking?*

I want to ask why he thought I'd pretend to date him—or why he wouldn't care if I were using him—but… Instead, I close my eyes and let the silence be.

Several minutes pass, though I still can't fall asleep.

Then, a tired murmur behind me, "She's gonna find out about us, you know."

"Us?" My eyes open to the dark outline of my bedroom door.

"Cats. Immortals, I mean. She'll find out eventually. I can't morph, but with me here, and your scars, and Ice threatening to start shit… It's only a matter of time. One of us will slip up, and she'll find out."

*I know, but…* "It doesn't matter. I can't tell her anything. You didn't see the Secrecy Agreement, but telling anyone would get me in a lot of trouble."

"I can tell her. I mean, Ice told you no problem, right?"

"Please don't."

A moment of silence.

"Fine," he murmurs. "I won't. If that's what you want."

Without moving any closer, he drapes an arm over my side and promptly falls asleep, his breath settling into a soft, steady pattern after only a moment.

This is closer to what I expected from his request to touch me. I don't want him to feel like he has to repress his feelings for me anymore, but he's obviously still scared of me—too afraid to risk crossing a line I haven't even drawn.

*Idiot...*

# thirty-five

James makes breakfast, thoroughly impressing Rose with his pancake-flipping skills. After we eat, I ask for help setting up the wind chime. Rose stays in while James steps outside with me.

There's been a hook on one of the roof beams just outside the front door since we moved in, but we've never had anything to hang there. We never could decide whether we wanted a planter or a sun catcher or whatever. I haven't asked, but I assume that's why she thought of me when she saw the wind chime.

I slide the bubble-wrapped glass out of the cardboard box and unwrap the bundle to reveal exactly what Rose had described. The body of the wind chime is made from the bottom half of a clear wine bottle. Strings of colorful glass beads fill the interior, and four interesting, jagged chunks of milky glass—the lightning glass…or fulgurite, I suppose—hang from longer strings.

It's a handmade piece of art, like something I might have seen at the solstice festival. I'm surprised something so plain would catch Rose's attention.

James is tall enough to reach the hook without standing on a chair, so I pass the wind chime to him. It makes a pleasant musical tinkling as the various pieces interact.

He's in a better mood today too. He's obviously tired, but his eyes hold a gentle warmth when he meets my gaze after I thank him for the help.

Once we're back inside, he excuses himself to shower, and Rose flags me down to join her on the couch.

"I'm ready for those details," she says with an easy smile.

*The instant we're alone. Of course.*

But I smile and sit beside her. "What do you wanna know?"

"James helped you get out of Ice's place, right?"

*Oh.* Hearing his name spoken so casually makes me falter. I nod, but the only thing I can bring myself to say is, "Mm-hm."

"Why'd you leave all of a sudden? I know things were weird and only getting weirder, but, back in July, I thought you were really into him."

"I was." *Despite the red flags I ignored.* "But I guess I got tired of waiting for something I knew would never happen."

She smiles, one eyebrow quirked. "I see. So you moved on to someone it could happen with instead?"

"That's not how it is at all."

"No?"

"No." I take a breath and glance away. "I wasn't supposed to like James, and I honestly wasn't expecting to. But…I guess you're right in the sense he's not nearly as frustrating as Ice was. I mean, he is frustrating, but at least I know he cares about me."

"Why'd you need his help to get out, anyway?"

I shrug. "I didn't *need* anyone's help. I wasn't trapped there, and I was already planning to leave after the rainstorm, remember? It was just convenient to have James drive me home. Besides, Ice hates the rain. But I guess all the time I spent bored out of my mind at his house finally put the pointlessness of our relationship into perspective."

*At least that much is true.*

Rose mulls it over for a quiet moment, and then sighs. "I knew it wouldn't work out the second you said he didn't want to sleep with you."

A shiver, visceral and unpleasant, runs down my spine at the mere thought. I shut it away immediately.

"Yeah, well, good riddance," I mutter. She laughs, as what she said was merely a joke that hit too close to home, and I try to relax. "What do you think about James, anyway?"

She purses her lips, her chin cradled in her hand. "He's a total dork—and kinda jumpy—but he's cute, I guess. And he's always watching you when you're not paying attention. That's how you can tell someone really likes you, you know?"

*Is it?*

"Wasn't that necklace a gift from Ice, though? Why keep wearing something your ex gave you? It's weird, especially if he doesn't like the guy you're with now."

I reach for the River Sapphire, having completely forgotten it was there. The gemstone is cool against my scarred palm. I put it on out of habit this morning, the same as every other morning.

*Should I take it off?*

It would be a total disaster if it randomly activated with Rose around, but the idea of not wearing it feels wrong, somehow. I can't stand the thought of giving up and leaving it in a jewelry box on my dresser.

"I don't know. We were never actually dating, so he isn't really my ex, but... Yeah. I don't know. I like the necklace, I guess. Do I have to throw it out just because the guy who gave it to me sucks?"

"Hm..." She scoots closer to get a better look. "It is cute. I've never seen anything like it, so I bet it was hella expensive too. If I were you, I'd sell it just to get back at him, but—"

"Oh, no, I can't do that," I say through nervous laughter.

She squints. "I was gonna say, *but you're not me.* Nah. You are way too nice. You'd probably feel guilty if you got rid of a gift even if you hated it. The five million lame souvenirs scattered all over the house are proof of that."

I laugh for real.

"I like the souvenirs, you know?"

# thirty-six

My eyes open, but the room is still dark. It's quiet. No sunlight peeks through the cracks in the closed blinds. I'm not sure what woke me up, but I hear James' soft breathing behind me, and I feel a bit better.

Though, my conversation about Ice with Rose comes to mind, and I'm suddenly wide awake with an urge to check the front door.

Careful to keep quiet, I sit up and push the comforter aside. James has his back to me, but I whisper his name, and he doesn't respond or shift, so I assume he's fast asleep.

*Good.*

I check my phone—3:47AM.

Then I slip out of bed and step out of the room. The house is quiet, the loudest sound being the hum of the central AC.

I walk downstairs. It's dark and empty, and everything looks to be how we left it, but I wander through the space. The kitchen window? *Locked.* The small window in the half-bath? *Locked.* The front door? *Locked.* Both windows in the living room? *Locked.*

Everything is locked. The house is secure. But my nails itch the scab over the heart on my wrist.

*You're fine, Jayde. Calm down.*

After rubbing my eyes, I return upstairs.

I hesitate in the doorway. James hasn't moved, but a sense of surreality washes over me. An uncomfortable awareness of the strange life I've found myself living since June.

Carefully, so carefully, I close the door. I keep the knob turned, so it shuts without making a sound, while my other hand lingers half on the door's edge and half against the doorjamb. I turn the privacy lock. Then my hands fall from the door, and I move closer to my bed, where I stand for a moment.

*Is he right? Is there a right thing?*

With a sigh, I crawl into bed. I tear my eyes from the door and lie flat on my back. I stare at the dark ceiling for a long time. Then I roll onto my side to face James' back. I watch his shoulder rise and fall for a few minutes before I finally close my eyes.

Somehow, even after how poorly I slept, I still wake up first. It's almost 9AM.

I could probably fall back asleep if I wanted, but I don't care to accidentally sleep until noon, so I sit up. As I rub my eyes, I note the lack of obvious discomfort in my wrist. Testing the joint more thoroughly, there is some tension when I bend my wrist back, but it's tolerable.

*Ah.* I knew this was coming. My wrist was only sprained, and I wasn't meant to wear the brace forever, but the heart will be more difficult to hide than the other scars have been.

*Maybe I'll keep it on for now.*

With a sigh, I leave the bed to cover the scar on my chest

with concealer.

Over breakfast, Rose asks if James and I want to go to the river with her—to go swimming. It's sad. I never realized until now that I probably won't get the chance to swim at all this summer. How could I without revealing my scars?

*Thankfully, today...*

"Sorry, I can't." I flash a smile as I raise my left hand. "I'm supposed to wear this a few more days."

"Oh, duh. I guess it was dumb to ask, but I'm going out with a few friends and thought you might want to tag along."

"Maybe next time," I say, knowing I'll almost certainly find an excuse to turn her down the next time too.

I catch James frowning, but he doesn't say anything. He just continues eating, and Rose carries on to tell me all about her plans to visit a swimming hole just out of town. *How frustrating...* I honestly wouldn't mind swimming. The weather is perfect for it. But I'm not sure my shoulder or wrist would appreciate the physical activity.

Rose heads out after breakfast, leaving me and James alone. A lingering paranoia that Ice might show himself remains, but I'd rather it happen while she isn't around if it has to happen at all.

I lock the door behind her, and I turn back to James.

"She won't be back for hours, so... What do you wanna do? We don't have to stay here if you don't want."

He offers a smile. "I don't mind staying in. 'Cause of the AC, you know."

For once, and out of nowhere, I feel like I'm more concerned about our predicament than James is. He didn't see the intensity in Ice's eyes or hear the threat he made. But it's for the best. I would have had an impossible time convincing him to stay if he knew how seriously Ice wanted him out.

We end up on the couch, watching a weird supernatural drama series on Netflix. A few hours pass. We make sandwiches for lunch.

As we eat, Rose texts to let us know she won't be back until dinnertime. That's fine. It works out better for me, but I make sure to ask her to let me know when she's on her way under the guise of wanting to know when to start cooking.

Then I take my wrist brace and long-sleeve shirt off, set them on the arm of the couch, and plop down at one end of the couch.

I'm far more comfortable wearing a tank top, and I don't mind if James sees the scars. Most of the scabs are healing, thinning or fallen away completely. The bruises are gone, and the cuts don't look awful—considering how they looked a couple weeks ago, anyway.

James returns from the kitchen. He hesitates, his eyes lingering on me a moment longer than usual, and then he continues to the couch. He sits to my right, leaving only a few inches between us.

I unpause the TV.

Several minutes pass. The lights are off, and the blinds are shut, and the air conditioner chills the room. The show we're watching is compelling, but I can feel James' warmth next to me, and I'm suddenly quite sleepy. I didn't do myself any favors by waking up in the middle of the night.

I yawn and lean my head on his shoulder. He stiffens for an instant, sucking in a breath of air, but he quickly relaxes and slings his arm over my shoulder.

*This isn't so bad.*

"Are you tired?" he asks.

"Maybe. I've had a hard time sleeping lately."

"It's okay," he says mildly. "I get it. If you fall asleep, I'll catch you up on the show."

"Okay. Thanks…"

*He really is so warm.*

\* \* \* \* \*

James wakes me up when my phone goes off—Rose is on her way back. I put my long sleeves and brace back on before heading into the kitchen, and he helps cook. Rose pulls up outside just as we finish.

Rose pulls up outside just as we finish.

We eat dinner, during which Rose regales us with the inane gossip she heard while hanging out with the friends she hadn't seen in two months. Thankfully, her friends are human, so absolutely none of it had to do with me.

Then we put on a movie.

After the movie, Rose calls it a night, and James and I move upstairs.

We sit across from each other in the middle of my bed, and we talk. We talk about Rose and my relief that they seem to get along. We talk about the TV show we were watching earlier—I guess it was canceled after the second season, but I still want to finish it.

His smile softens. "I thought it would be weird staying here, but it's not so bad. It feels…kind of normal."

"I thought so too."

"Seriously," he says with a soft wistfulness, glancing away. "I haven't had anything like this in…years, so… Well, I'm glad you asked me to stay."

"Yeah?"

"Yeah."

Our eyes meet again. He raises a hand, both the motion and his expression hesitant, and he touches my face. His palm is warm, and I lean into it. Then he closes the distance between us and presses his lips to my forehead. The gesture—a kiss—is warm and tender, but my breath catches.

*Something.*

*The dark. A distant roll of thunder. Reflected blue light illuminating a shadowed face covered in scabs and bruises. The scent of damp and sweat and tobacco smoke. And the foreign sensation of lips brushing the top of my head.*

*The dark, trashed parlor room at Reid Manor. The muffled sound of rain. Fear and despondent aching and sinking cold.*

Suddenly, I am crying.

Suddenly, fat tears spill from my eyes and stream down my face, and I can't do a damn thing to stop them, and I am extremely confused.

"Hey—" James retracts his hand. "Oh, ah— Are you okay?"

Gasping, I wipe my eyes with my sleeve. "I have no idea what just happened, but I'm fine. It's nothing. Aah... I'm sorry."

"No, I'm sorry," he mumbles, his open hands hovering above my shoulders.

"I, um..."

He searches my face for a moment, concern etched into his soft features, and my breath hitches again, a shuddering inhale as I try to curb the tears with my hands. *I just...can't stop.* I don't even understand why I'm crying, and it's more frustrating than anything else.

"I'm sorry," I say again.

His eyes grow wide, but only for a moment. Then he takes a deep breath and holds out his arms. "Here."

I fall into him, and he holds me. He combs his fingers through my hair while I sob, tears streaming down my hot face. I try to focus on his warmth and his racing heart and controlling my own breathing.

"It's okay," he says.

I nod, my cheek pressed near his shoulder.

*I know. I should be fine. Right now, we're both fine, but—*

"I love you," he says, his voice low. "I don't know how you feel about me, but I... I love you, Jayde. I would do anything for you."

*I know.*

# thirty-seven

Rose doesn't suspect a thing.

Hiding my scars using long sleeves or concealer or some combination of the two is working, and she still hasn't questioned the sleeves, since I keep the air conditioner cranked up and the indoor temperature fairly low.

She likes James too. He's not her type at all, which is probably for the best, but she seems to find his awkwardness endearing. She thinks he suits me—*whatever that means*.

But it doesn't make a difference.

No matter my state of healing, or her belief that I'm perfectly fine, or how well she and James get along, I'm still living a nightmare. I'm afraid to be myself in my own house. Rose is my best friend, but I'm lying to her. I hate it, and the emotional toll has only worsened with each passing day.

Ice's continued silence isn't helping. I haven't heard from him since the pizza incident. He could call or text or, god forbid, show up at the front door at any moment, and I'd be absolutely powerless to stop him.

I can barely even share how I feel with James. He's trying to remain optimistic for my sake, but I know he's struggling too.

My random breakdown last night shook him pretty badly.

He seems fine today, but…

I splash water on my face.

*Is there anything I* don't *have to feel guilty about these days?*

I turn the faucet off and return downstairs.

Rose is out again, this time meeting a friend for lunch. Some guy in her nursing program, I think. Of course, I took full advantage of the opportunity to get comfortable the instant her car pulled out of its parking space.

I look up from the pink Grand Canyon sweatshirt balled up on the coffee table. James is still on the far side of the couch, where I left him, but now he's on his phone. Typing. In the middle of a text conversation, maybe?

I step closer and ask who he's talking to.

"Me?" he asks blankly, glancing up from his phone.

I nod.

He regards me with some level of awe, either thinking my interest in what he's doing is weird or admiring me the way he apparently does when he thinks I'm not paying attention. It's hard to tell.

"Oh, uh— Matt," he says finally.

"A friend? I was starting to think you didn't have any."

"We'll see." He averts his eyes and scratches his jaw. "He's not too happy with me. I skipped out on his Fourth of July party after swearing I'd stay the whole night, and— Well, I ghosted him and everyone I know after that."

*One of the friends who was worried about him, then?*

"I see," I say before sitting beside him.

He flashes a timid smile. "I guess he heard about the picture you shared, but I bet he's just jealous I've been ignoring him to spend so much time with you."

"What? Really?"

"Nah." Humor warms his voice as he laughs. "We have been talking about you, though. He thinks I'm hiding you or whatever. I mean, he's nagging me about the Fourth too, but I think he's just happy I finally responded. Anyway, he wants to meet you."

"Oh."

It's hardly fair that James has a friend he can be open with, but I wonder... *Has he told this friend anything?* He's an immortal too, I'm sure, but does he know about the situation with Ice?

I don't ask.

"Matt's cool," he continues more casually. "He's been my best friend— Well, no... He's been my only real friend since high school. You'd probably like him. He's sort of like Rose— or more like Carmen, I guess."

*Now, that's a surprise.*

I offer him a smile. "You met my best friend, so it only makes sense I meet yours, right? We should go out and do something."

"Yeah. You're right. I'll try to figure something out."

As he glances at his phone and resumes typing, I remember—

"Hey, I don't have your phone number. We're not even friends on FaceSpace or anything."

"Oh. You're right. I guess we should fix that, huh?"

I laugh. "Yeah. Since we're supposed to be dating and all."

He tells me his number, and I send a short text—*Hi!*, along with a string of emotes—to make sure I typed it in correctly. His phone doesn't vibrate or make any sound to indicate the message went through, but he glances up from the screen with a soft smile, so I figure he got it.

*Another thing...*

If he keeps his phone on silent, how much time does he spend texting while I'm not paying attention? He's on his phone quite a lot, but he uses it to read, so I usually assumed he was reading. He *says* Matt is his only friend, and that he ghosted everyone, but is he serious or being dramatic?

*Carmen mentioned a few guys...*

How many friends does he have besides me and Matt? Does he have any family he talks to? His father? Siblings? Cousins? *Does Ice have his phone number?*

For all I know, he could be texting a lot.

Before I can ask, my phone goes off. I shoot a suspicious look at James, who scratches his jaw. Then I check the notification.

**James:** Hi. I love you... ( ^_^;)

My heart flutters as I stare at the text. It's not like it's the first time he's said something like that. He told me he loves me just last night, but *seeing the words written down like this...*

It's the first time they really hit me, and it's been long enough for me to wonder if I might feel the same way. *Or something.*

I care about James; I really do. I want to protect him from Ice, but... I still worry we're only together because neither of us have anyone else we can go to right now.

After all, we are stuck in the same sinking boat.

*Maybe he was right.*

Maybe we're only together out of necessity.

Maybe I am using him.

*Is that true?*

"Everything okay?" he asks, only mildly concerned.

My face flushes hot, and I laugh. "Oh, sorry. It's nothing."

His eyes linger on me a few seconds longer. Then he returns his attention to his phone and leans back into the couch. I itch the scab on my exposed wrist.

*I can leave the brace off if I want, but…*

James sighs. "I— I think I take Matt for granted sometimes."

"Oh?" I look up from my wrist and inch a bit closer. "What do you mean?"

"He's been there for me for years. No matter what. Even when everyone else ignored me or…bullied me for being defective or whatever." He pauses to mess with his phone. "Here. Look."

He opens a FaceSpace photo album, and I watch as he scrolls through countless photos of variable quality that were clearly taken while he was in high school. They all feature James and a slightly shorter, athletic boy with tanned skin, golden eyes, and wavy auburn hair, who is always grinning and flashing peace signs, thumbs-ups, or finger guns.

I'm no detective, but that guy must be Matt.

Judging by the photos, he was a basketball player and part of the popular crowd in school. Even so, it seems he dragged James almost everywhere he went. James looks confused, with a nervous or obviously fake smile plastered on his face, in some of the photos, but he's beaming and looks to be having a genuinely great time in many others.

*It's cute and does remind me of my relationship with Rose.*

"He seems like a good friend."

"He is," he murmurs, staring at his phone screen with a frown. "He's a better friend than I deserve."

He continues flicking the screen until it displays a professional group prom photo. Both Matt and James are dressed in formalwear with their hair slicked back, but they're making silly faces, and one of Matt's hands form bunny ears behind James' head. The photo includes four other guys goofing around in a similar manner. *One looks almost exactly like James.*

"Who is that?" I ask, pointing to the boy.

"Oh, him?" He laughs. "That's my brother, Jesse."

"Brother?"

I snatch the phone from his hand and zoom in to get a better look at him and Matt—*ah...they look so happy*—before scrolling to focus on the one he identified as Jesse. Save for slightly different haircuts and a minor difference in weight, they are identical.

"You have a twin."

"Yeah, sorry." He scratches the back of his head as he glances aside. "We haven't talked in a while, so I guess I never thought to mention it."

I peek over the top of his phone to glower at him with feigned suspicion. "I don't know anything about you, do I? What else are you hiding from me?"

He laughs again, his ears turning pink. "Nothing! Jeez."

I flash an easy smile and take one last look at the picture before returning his phone. "You have FaceSpace, though, right?" I ask. "Can I add you?"

"Oh. Sure. If you want," he mumbles, glancing away.

I unlock my phone, open FaceSpace, and search for him. He's easy to find, as *James Nathaniel Reid*, because we have Carmen as a mutual friend.

His account is private, so there's not much to see other than the generic cover image and the selfie set as his profile picture—though, in the photo, he's wearing a dark jacket with the hood pulled up and part of his face out of frame. *It's...a little telling.* I'm almost surprised there isn't a lit cigarette in his hand.

"I'm not very active," he admits.

He accepts my friend request, and I take a moment to creep his timeline. *He wasn't kidding about being inactive.* The most recent post was made about a week ago, but it's a viral video shared by someone who tagged at least a dozen others in the post. The last thing he shared himself is from July second.

**James Nathaniel Reid**
I hate this fucking place.

*Hm. A vague post? Really?*

"You weren't kidding," I say. "And I thought I was neglecting my account recently."

He offers a half-hearted smile. "Sorry to disappoint you. My life isn't very interesting, so there's not a lot worth sharing."

"That's fine. Mine wasn't interesting either—until recently."

I tag him in my wildlife pond post and put my phone away.

# thirty-eight

We talk for over an hour. Laughing and swapping lighthearted anecdotes about our outgoing best friends and their childish high school antics. He seems happy, and I feel more comfortable than I have in weeks.

Time just…*slipped my mind.*

I forgot when Rose said she planned to get home. I forgot, but she still came back, and I realize too late—right as I hear a key turn in the lock across the room.

I move, but she steps through the door before I have time to grab my sweatshirt. I reached for it, but we make eye contact as my fingers brush the fabric, and I freeze under her gaze. Her eyes scour me, soaking up the scars my camisole leaves exposed. Her expression shifts from confusion to surprise to deep thought.

Until this moment, I never fully appreciated the way James' eyes tend to pass over my scars like they don't exist. They hardly upset him anymore, like they've become an afterthought—like he's accepted them whether he likes them or not—but Rose sees the scars so vividly I'm not sure she sees me at all past them.

I bring the sweatshirt to my lap, but I don't bother pulling it on. I'm too ashamed, honestly.

Her alarm fades, and she pointedly looks away. Then, slowly, *so slowly*, she hangs her purse on a hook beside the door. She stares at it for a long time while I wait for her to say something. *Anything*.

*What is she thinking? She's mad, but—*

"I knew you were hiding something," she says, her voice low and dry.

She looks to me again, her eyes narrow and lips thin. The usual carefree, party-girl Rose is long gone. And, as she shakes her head, I feel like I killed her.

"I *knew* it," she says. "But I don't understand why you'd hide something like this."

*Like this? What does she even think* this *is?*

I want to leave—to run upstairs and get away. I want to avoid the conversation entirely. But I know she wants an explanation. She deserves one. *After all the lies and misdirection...* My mouth is dry, but I set the sweatshirt aside and stand from the couch.

"I— I don't know what to say," I stammer.

Her hands land on her hips. "You can start by explaining what *really* happened while I was in Arizona."

"I—!"

Cutting myself off, I glance back at James. He hasn't moved from his spot on the couch, but he looks terribly uncomfortable. And deeply concerned.

*Damn it...*

I should have settled on an excuse weeks ago when I had time to come up with a good one, but I just...*didn't want to*. I didn't want to think about it. I didn't want to think about her finding out

I was hurt or seeing my injuries or anything. I have nothing *to* say.

Even so, I force myself to meet Rose's sharp gaze. "I wish I could, but I… I can't tell you anything."

"What is that supposed to mean?" she asks before gesturing at James. "Your new *boyfriend* obviously knows all about it. I mean, you're not hiding any of this from him, are you?"

I shake my head and slap a hand over the heart on my wrist, desperately hoping she hadn't noticed it.

"I just…can't talk about it with you," I mumble. "I'm sorry."

"You have a mouth, don't you?"

"Yeah, but—"

"Then *spill*, Jayde."

She steps further inside, and I flinch.

Desperate, I turn to James, who already moved to stand at my side. He glances at me before refocusing on Rose. His posture is defensive, his expression serious, but I'm sure he has no idea how to handle this any better than I do.

*Rose is human. What can either of us say?*

"She's under oath to keep quiet," he says, his tone careful but uncertain. "I know it doesn't make any sense, but there's no telling what might happen if she says something she shouldn't."

Savage grey eyes flick in his direction. "Don't tell me *you* had something to do with this."

"No," I gasp. My nails dig into my wrist. "James didn't do anything. Just drop it, Rose. Please."

She looks between us several times before folding her arms over her chest. I frown, eyes watering as I feel utterly naked under her sharp gaze. It's not her fault, but I can't believe a single look shattered the fragile self-esteem I worked so hard to regain after that first day.

*The injuries aren't even that bad.*

As healed as they are now, they're little more than raised, pink scars or thin, brown scabs. If I hadn't panicked, I probably could have explained them away as an accident. A car crash. Or a fall through glass. They're just cuts. How would she be able to tell the difference?

*But it's too late for that.*

"Who did this to you?" she asks.

My heart races. "Who?"

*I never wanted her to find out like this. Why did I let myself get so comfortable? How could I be so careless?*

James rests a hand on my shoulder. I start at his touch—the warmth against my bare skin—and I can't seem to catch my breath again.

"I can tell her," he says, his voice soft.

"Tell me what?"

"No!"

*What should I do? I don't know what to say.*

I do not want her to find out about immortals. I do not want her to know exactly how I was hurt. I don't want her to know what he did. *I wish she didn't know about him at all!*

"No way," she breathes. "Could it be…? That guy you were seeing before? Ice Monroe, right?"

*Ice Monroe—*

His name is like an electric shock. The warmth drains from my face, and I stare down at the coffee table, my vision blurring as my wide eyes fill with hot tears. My wrist hurts, but I don't dare ease up on holding it.

I should have been more careful. I should have been smarter. Telling her that he was violent toward James was a mistake. I said too much.

*I should have listened to Ice.*

*I should have stopped talking about him.*

Rose isn't stupid. Of course, she would figure it out. She had the puzzle pieces. All she had to do was put them together.

*Ugh. Damn it!*

Hot, angry, bitter tears flood my eyes, and I can't tell whether James rubbing my back is helping or making me feel worse. Either way, I don't have the heart to ask him to stop.

All I can do is jam my face in the crook of my elbow to curb the tears. And I still don't move my hand from my wrist even as it begins to ache.

James says my name, his voice soft and concerned. He whispers again that he can tell her. He can shoulder the responsibility, whatever it is. He doesn't mind, and I won't get in trouble if he's the one who says it.

Through my grit teeth, I tell him to shut up.

*One more mention of Ice, and I'm done.*

He went easy on me when he attacked me before. He never hurt me *too* badly. He wanted me to call James for help. It's like Night says—it's like he actually *cares* about what happens to me in some disgusting, convoluted way.

James is the person he really wants to hurt.

*What if he decides he needs Rose out of the way too?*

"Have you gone to the police?" she asks, concern overtaking her anger. I can't help but laugh, though my stomach churns at the thought. "Jay, if he did this to you—"

"It doesn't matter." My voice is cold and surprisingly level. I drop my arms, and, as I look up at her through the tears I couldn't curb, I feel a twisted smile tug at my lips. "It doesn't matter what happened or who did this. I can't tell you anything, and there is *nothing* you can do to help. You shouldn't even know about it."

She shakes her head, confused. "I can call for you. Just—"

My eyes grow wide, and the tears abruptly stop as she reaches for her pocket. I shriek something like "*no*" mixed with "*you can't*" and lunge forward to slap the phone out of her hand.

We stare at each other as her phone hits the floor.

It bounces across the carpet, falling still and quiet several feet away. My hands move to cover my mouth while her arms fall limply to her sides.

"You can't," James says behind me, his voice remarkably calm. "It sucks—trust me; I know—but calling the cops won't help. It would just make things worse."

"Worse...?" Rose tears her eyes from my face to look at James. "What do you mean?"

He doesn't answer, and she turns to me in gloomy confusion. Stepping back, I drop to sit on the edge of the coffee table. The floodgates burst again, and I hide my face in my hands, my elbows propped on my knees.

"I'm sorry, Rose," I gasp between breaths. "I really can't."

"At least tell me if I'm right about—"

"Sorry," James says, cutting her off.

He helps me up from my awkward spot on the coffee table, but I don't look at him. I don't move my hands at all. I just lean into his warmth.

"You don't have to take my word for it," he says. "I don't care if you don't trust me, but at least trust Jayde. She's your best friend, right? If you care about her, just drop it. And don't bother with the police. They seriously can't help."

Through the gaps between my fingers, I catch her taking a step closer. "Jayde," she says. "Please tell me. Was it him? Was it Ice?"

Her fingers brush my shoulder—nearly touching the band-aid. *And I break.*

I deflect her hand with my own, pull away from James, and dart up the stairs. They both call after me, but I ignore them. I slam the door as I reach my bedroom. I turn the privacy lock.

The click echoes in my head.

*Like the click of a gun's safety.*

Then, with my back against the cool door, I slide down to the carpet and hug my knees to my chest. My body shakes, wracked by heavy sobs, and my side aches for the first time in days.

*I can't... I just can't deal with this right now.*

Rose seeing the scars and threatening to call the police... She just had to go and guess it had something to do with Ice... *Even if it was obvious, I just...can't...*

*I wish I never told her about him.*

*I wish he never told me about immortals.*

Someone taps the door, the sound low to the floor. James talks to me, his voice soft and low and soothing, but I can't make out the exact words. A hurricane rages in my head, and, between that, the faint throbbing in my side, and my own crying, nothing seems to make it through.

*Now Rose is in danger too.*

*All because I wanted to take my stupid shirt off.*

My phone goes off in my pocket, the vibration grounding me for an instant—a fleeting distraction that eases the worst of the panic. I wipe my eyes with my arm before checking the message.

> **Rose:** I'm sorry, J. I won't tell anyone. I won't call the cops, I swear.

The screen goes dark for a moment. Then a second text arrives.

> **Rose:** If it was Ice, if it wasn't… Whatever. idc honestly. I'm just worried about you.
> **Rose:** (´•‿•`)

I draw a deep breath and drop my phone.

A third text comes through sometime later, but my phone is face-down. I don't care to read whatever else she has to say, anyway. It's enough to know she won't call the police.

Pressing on my temples, I ignore the tingling in my palm and focus on my breathing in an attempt to calm myself further.

*You have nothing to worry about.*

*James is here. He's not going anywhere. And Rose will keep her mouth shut. She won't call the police. She won't find out about immortals.*

*This is fine. Everything is fine.*

*Breathe, Jayde.*

*You're fine. You've dealt with far worse things. This is nothing in comparison. You can handle this. You'll figure something out.*

*Everything will be okay.*

It takes several minutes, but my thoughts eventually slow, and I manage to regain control of my body. Though, as I stop crying, the room falls unnervingly quiet.

James hasn't said anything in a while—that I can recall, anyway. I worry he left, so I turn around, tap a finger to the door, and wait. A few seconds pass. Then I hear a sigh on the other side, and a bit more of my anxiety melts away.

"Are you okay?" he asks. "Do you want me to leave? Or… come in, maybe?"

"No, I'm fine," I say slowly, remembering the text I haven't read yet. "Don't leave. Just give me a minute."

"Okay."

I pick up my phone, but the third text wasn't from Rose.

**Ice Monroe**                                  now
How's it going? Miss me yet?

I stare at the words for a moment—a long, frustrating moment. *He seriously has the worst timing.* With a heavy sigh, I lock my phone and set it on the carpet.

He knows I saw the text. It's not worth replying.

I drag myself off the floor and unlock my bedroom door. When James opens it, I force a smile.

"Sorry," I say. "I'm fine now."

# thirty-nine

I can't face Rose. I can barely bring myself to leave my room for anything other than the bathroom. James brought in everything I've eaten since last night. He's been stuck to me like glue, asking if I need anything every few minutes.

It's so unfair of me. It's selfish. I'm being ridiculous.

But I do appreciate him.

Even if I think he's slightly more terrified of me now.

I adjust the knit band covering my wrist and stare at the strange googly-eyed face on the ceiling from where I lie sprawled on my bed. I keep noticing it, and I feel like it's judging me.

*Speaking of James, though...* I thought he'd be back by now.

I roll onto my side and unlock my phone.

> **Me:** Hey, where'd you go?
>
> **James:** Picking up food
>
> **Me:** You left the house???
>
> **James:** Sorry, driving. Brb

*Ugh.*

I look up from my phone to check the door. The privacy

lock is turned, so I roll onto my back again. And I wait.

My room is quiet, so I hear the commotion downstairs when James returns. But it sounds like he left the house *with* Rose, as I hear both of their voices where I hadn't heard anything before.

I sit up and comb my fingers through my hair. My shoulder doesn't complain at all. My wrist still twinges if I twist it wrong, but it's fine too.

*Maybe I should cut my hair.*

What? No way.

I hear someone coming up the stairs, so I stand from the bed to unlock the door. When I crack it open and peek out, I see James carrying two takeout boxes and drinks.

"Sorry if I worried you," he says with a smile. "Rose convinced me to get takeout."

*I smell…*

"Chinese?" I ask, my voice hushed as I let him inside.

"Yeah. Orange chicken and fried rice."

I close and lock the door after him. "You're forgiven."

He rolls his eyes and hands over one of the takeout boxes. It's still hot, and it smells delicious. I return to the bed and sit cross-legged near my pillow.

"How is Rose? Is she still mad at me?"

"No," he says, joining me on the bed.

I frown. "Just worried?"

"We're both worried, you know?"

"There's no need to worry about me." With a sigh, I open the paper box and stare at the steaming food inside. She must have told him what I like because it's the special order rice without green onion. "I just...need more time to process... everything."

He shrugs before handing me a plastic fork. "You're lucky she doesn't know much about Ice. She swore she won't go to the police, but she'd still like to hunt him down and rip him to shreds."

"Did she tell you that?" *It sounds like her.*

"I mean, more or less, yeah. I talked her down, but I told her, if the idea wasn't absolutely insane, I'd help her."

"Of course you did." I sigh. "What did you tell her, anyway?"

"Not much," he says more mildly. "She knows the obvious, but I told her she'll have to wait until you're ready to tell her exactly what happened. Since I already promised you I wouldn't."

I pick at my food, pushing it around with the fork. "This sucks. I never wanted her to find out like this."

"I know. But she doesn't hate you, Jayde."

"Maybe she should."

"Whether you think she should or not, she doesn't."

I glance at him and force a smile. "Well, thanks for the food. And thanks for talking to Rose for me."

\* \* \* \* \*

The sun went down about an hour ago, and the documentary we were watching is over. I put my laptop to sleep and return it to my desk. When I look back to James, he appears quite thoughtful.

"You don't mind me sleeping in here, do you?"

I blink. "No. It's different, but, to be honest, there's something nice about it. I mean, the other night, I woke up while it was still dark, and seeing you there when I rolled over was…comforting, I guess."

"Comforting, huh?"

He smiles, but his eyes are shadowed over, and he soon frowns. He looks at the floor with his hands clasped in his lap. I cross the room to stand in front of where he sits on the edge of the bed, but he still doesn't look at me.

"Are you okay?" I ask.

He nods.

I glance at my hands. At the scars on my arms. Then I gently place my hands atop his head. His short, messy, orange hair is soft, and my fingers pass through it easily.

*I'm not sure…what I was expecting.*

He looks up with wide, sparkling eyes and a muted, torn expression. Like my touch hurts him somehow.

*Why?*

"Does it bother you?" I ask, letting my hands fall back to my sides. "Sleeping in here, I mean?"

He shakes his head, but his cheeks flush. "It's not like that. It's just— Oh, god, never mind."

*Hm.*

I brush my hair over one shoulder and sit beside him. His eyes track my movement with a curious wariness.

"Are you sure you're not scared of me?"

He flashes a nervous smile. "I am not *scared* of you."

"You can talk to me, you know?" I purse my lips, hoping to come across as approachable. "I want to know how you really feel about all this. And what you think when you look at me."

"When I look at you?"

He glances at his hands. A hint of tension appears in his jaw, and his brows furrow. He takes a deep breath. Then he looks to me again. He raises his hands with some hesitance, and they come to rest on my face, cupping my cheeks. His hands are warm, and his eyes hold an intensity muddled by nervous energy.

"I think…you're beautiful," he says.

My breath catches. A sudden awareness of our proximity. An awareness of his quickened breath and the warmth in his eyes. An awareness of the roughness of his palms and the gentle weight of his fingers brushing my neck.

And I…

*I would* really *like to kiss him.*

My eyes grow wide. My face goes hot. I suck in a sharp breath and avert my gaze. *For some reason…* I raise a hand to hold over his, but I start laughing. My eyes fill with tears and, for some reason, that makes me laugh even harder.

"Is that it?" I ask through laughter.

"What do you mean, *is that it?*" he asks in alarm. "Hey, wait— Are you crying again?"

"No, I'm fine."

His hands fall from my face, and I wipe my eyes. He watches me, confused and uneasy—like he's worried about what I might say now. But it's not like the last time. The tears are gone, and I feel myself grin.

"I guess I wasn't expecting you to say something so normal."

"Normal?" He tips his head, his expression wry but almost

conveying offense. "What the hell did you think I was gonna say?"

"I don't know, but I'm glad." *I'm glad you didn't ask if you should leave again.* "I'm glad I asked you to stay with me."

He looks away with a smile. "I'm glad…you asked me to stay."

Then he sighs heavily and stands from the bed. Glancing over his shoulder, his expression is more mild.

"I'll be right back," he says. "Gotta change into PJs."

I nod. He grabs his backpack and steps out of the room, and I stare at the door without moving. I blink. Then I groan, fall back onto the bed, and glare at the ceiling.

*Somehow, I know…*

If I had kissed him just then, he wouldn't have rejected me. It would've been fine. But I don't think I'm ready to face that yet. I think… Maybe I'm the one who needs more time.

# forty

~ ∞ ~

*"I don't know what to do anymore."*

*"Well, we can't give up, can we?"*

*For a moment, I'm alone in a pitch-black room. I look around in confusion, and, as I do, small lights appear all around me. They float freely in the distant darkness like fireflies. And I recognize the "room" as the place Night called my dreamscape.*

*Of course.*

I'm dreaming.

Nothing feels uncomfortable about the space tonight, which is a nice change, but nothing seems to be happening either. It's just quiet and dark.

More curious than nervous, I start walking.

I walk for several minutes, but my surroundings don't seem to change in the slightest. It's still just as dark, and the tiny lights still flicker softly and drift about. I glance at my strangely illuminated hands. The scar on my palm. Then my feet. For whatever reason, I'm wearing my old Converse. The soles are worn thin, as they are in reality, but the ground doesn't feel hard beneath them.

I look up again, but it's the same as before. A lot of nothing.

*Am I alone?*

Maybe Night is around here somewhere.

I continue walking aimlessly for what feels like an hour, but I don't find anyone or anything. I guess I am alone. Why am I here, then? Night suggested the dreamscape is a place people go when they need to think. What does my subconscious want to tell me?

*Is this a good dream or a nightmare?*

A sudden wind blows through my hair. Nervous, I watch as my surroundings shift, changing from black to a swirled mix of color and shadow until it finally settles and forms a cohesive scene.

I gasp and take a step back, but *this can't be a nightmare.*

The scene is of us—of me and James.

We're outside, talking as we sit on a small patch of sandy earth surrounded by dry grass and scrubby brush. The taste of salt on the cool breeze. It's late, the moment just after sunset when the horizon is still pink as the rest of the sky turns navy.

James smiles with a comfortable warmth that touches his eyes as they glitter in the fading light. The girl sitting beside him returns his smile in a way I can't imagine I could as things are now. Their fingers brush in the space on the sandy stone between them, and they look up at the night sky together.

I look up too.

*Oh.*

We must be miles from Riverview—far from any city. There are no man-made lights in sight, and no faint light pollution in the distance, but the sky is filled with stars. Thousands. Millions.

More than I've seen at once in my entire life, and the color steals my breath. Blue, purple, pink. The stars twinkle in pastel colors, and the silvery Milky Way stretches across the sky above us.

*Amazing...*

I tear my eyes away to look back on my dream self as she watches the stars above. And James...

*They look happy.*

This moment, as the starry sky blankets the world, is so much bigger than either of us. How could we think about anything but the view? Far away from Ice. No thoughts of humans or immortals or the arbitrary differences between them. No fear. No anxiety.

We're just...*together.*

James looks down from the sky to watch the girl sitting beside him. His posture is relaxed and comfortable, and his expression softens while I don't seem to notice—lost in staring at the stars. He smiles without a hint of tired sadness.

Wow. *Rose is right.* He's definitely in love with her.

*Her?* That girl is *me.*

Does he look at me like that now?

Is this the same face Rose saw?

After watching my dream-self stargaze for a moment, he slings an arm over her shoulder and pulls her closer without hesitation. Like it was second nature. The awe never leaves her face even as her attention leaves the sky.

And, as they look at each other, I know exactly how she feels.

~ ∞ ~

# forty-one

"Hey, you awake yet?"

I shift in bed. "Hm? What is it?"

"Are you hungry?"

I open one eye. James is already up and about, dressed in day clothes, his hair damp and messy. I reach for my phone to check the time—it's just after 8:30AM. I sit up to watch him with exaggerated suspicion, but he merely smiles.

"I was having a good dream, you know," I say.

"Was it about me?"

I tug a bit too hard on a tangle in my hair without breaking eye contact, but I can't think of anything to say, so I keep quiet. He laughs, and I sigh.

"Wanna go out and get breakfast?" he asks.

"Like a date?"

"A date sounds nice, right?" He glances over his shoulder and laughs again at whatever puzzled expression I'm making. "But I'll give you time to wake up first."

*This is…extremely weird.* James rarely wakes up this early on his own. *And he's already taken a shower?*

He's definitely up to something. Nothing bad, I'm sure—he

looks to be in a good mood—but he's never offered to take me out for breakfast before.

Is he trying to cheer me up? Or just trying to get me out of the bedroom? *Well, I guess those are basically the same thing at this point.* Maybe he just wants to go on our first date as an official couple?

I'd like to believe it's that simple.

*But why breakfast?*

"I'll be downstairs whenever you're ready," he says, grabbing his keys off the dresser. He grins, his eyes bright, and then steps out of the room.

Whatever he has planned, he sure is confident about it. He didn't look quite the same as the person in my dream, but this is a stark contrast to the nervous glances and empty smiles I'm used to.

\* \* \* \* \*

We're already on the interstate heading north before I think to ask where we're going. For whatever reason, he has to consider the question for a moment. Then he glances at me from the corner of his eye.

"Just a little restaurant downtown."

"Oh?"

"Matt works there," he says. "You still wanted to meet him, right? I know things have been…a little crazy lately, but I figure it can't hurt to introduce you now."

I avert my eyes.

The past few days were *rough*, spent wallowing in self-pity in my bedroom, both to avoid Rose and avoid facing my problems in general. We haven't spoken in person at all yet.

*And I still haven't apologized for freaking out on her.*

But I appreciate the gesture. Getting out of the house, even if only for a couple hours, will be good for me.

He lets out a breath.

"Are you nervous?" I ask with a laugh.

"Maybe a little."

I glance at the scars on my arms. I wore a shirt with three-quarter sleeves and the knit wristband, but the scabs on my forearms are still clearly visible.

"Do you not want us to meet?" I ask.

"No. It's not like that." He laughs, taking a hand off the steering wheel to scratch his arm. "It's just that Matt's my only real friend—"

"Besides me," I interject.

He cracks a smile. "Yeah. Besides you. Anyway, you're my first serious girlfriend in years—or whatever—and I know he's gonna make a big deal out of it."

*Oh?* Maybe he *is* like Rose.

"I'll try to make a good impression," I say.

James pours more focus into his driving as we enter the downtown area, and he eventually parks on the curb. He doesn't pay the parking meter, but I don't mention it as we head down the sidewalk together. *Immortal perks, maybe?* Either that, or this sort of thing is the reason he had a police record before Human-Immortal Affairs scrubbed it.

We walk half a block before I recognize the direction we're heading in. There are a handful of small restaurants further down this street.

When I ask, James confirms the one we're going to as Taquería Parrilla. It's a small Mexican diner owned by one of Matt's uncles, which is pretty cool. Apparently, they rebranded and installed WiFi a few years back at Matt's suggestion, and the restaurant quickly became a popular hangout among the younger immortal crowd.

"He should be here. His shift starts at eleven?"

"Eleven?" I check my phone, but it's just past 10AM. "Why would he show up to work so early?"

"Good question," he agrees as we walk through the door.

A bell dings, announcing our arrival, and I glance around. The restaurant's interior is curiously modern and homey at the same time. Light pours in from the large windows facing the street with red curtains drawn open. The scent of coffee and spice wafts through the air. Several tables are occupied by customers chatting and eating breakfast.

It takes only a second to spot the coppery redhead sitting alone in a window booth at the far end of the restaurant. He's on a laptop, but he glances over his shoulder as the door swings shut behind me. His golden eyes widen for an instant. Then a grin splits his face, and he waves us over.

James and I exchange a passive look before joining him. We sit next to each other on the opposite side of the table from Matt, who closes his laptop and sets it on the booth seat beside him. His hair might be a couple inches longer, but he otherwise looks exactly the same as he did in the photos.

"So, this is the girl you ditched me for," he says.

James flashes a wry smile and scratches the back of his neck. "That's not exactly what happened, you know?"

"Yeah, man, I know."

His voice is warm, casual, and friendly. I'm less nervous than I expected upon meeting another immortal for the first time in weeks, so I hold my hand out toward him.

"I'm Jayde."

"Matthew Barnett," he says, grinning again as he accepts the handshake. "But Matt's fine too."

My eyes land on the raised scar on my palm as the handshake ends. He didn't seem to notice it—or he's at least polite enough to not acknowledge it—and I tuck my hand back underneath the edge of the table.

Matthew glances at James, his eyes bright. "It's great to see you, man. Had me worried for a minute, but you look alright. Better than you did at the party, anyway."

"Yeah, I'm alright," he mumbles. "Sorry about your party, though. I wasn't planning to ditch."

"It's all good. I'm over it. But you gotta be straight with me; this is the same girl Ice was dating back in June, right?"

I cough to mask my dismay. "We were not dating, but, yeah... That's me. I'm the human girl Ice sponsored."

"Right, sorry." He shrugs, still smiling. "Carmen made it sound like you were dating, but that's gossip for ya. I swear that girl only knows what she's talking about half the time."

*Everyone knows Carmen, so everyone knows I was with Ice?*

Somehow, it seems like what happened between us since hasn't gotten out, though. Did James not tell him anything? *For the same reason I didn't tell Carmen when she asked?*

"You know, I thought it was weird that she said you guys were *dating*," he continues flippantly. "Back in high school, Ice was super popular. I mean, you've obviously seen the guy. Girls were crazy about him—a few guys too—but I heard he rejected every single person who had the guts to ask him out. Every single one. I used to imagine he was secretly gay, but I don't think that's true—considering the guys who asked him out were also quite hot."

*Yeah, no.*

Maybe Night was onto something when she suggested Ice is asexual. I mean... No offense to the decent asexuals out there, but I doubt he's capable of seriously romancing anyone.

James rolls his eyes, but he looks uncomfortable—tense and jittery. I won't be able to get away with this line of conversation much longer, but Matthew doesn't seem to mind talking about Ice at all. *Maybe I can...*

"Did you know him very well?" I ask.

"Nah. I saw him around, but we weren't friends or anything. From what I remember, he was kind of an elitist dick, actually." He frowns, pausing to think. "You know, Carmen invited him and Night to my Fourth of July party, hoping you would tag along."

*The party? Wait—*

He laughs. "I'm not surprised you guys didn't show, but I was curious too. This sort of thing doesn't happen often."

"Do we have to talk about this?" James asks with a heavy

sigh. "You know how I feel about Ice, and it's the exact reason why they didn't go to your party."

*I see...*

Ice knew James would be at the party. That's why he wanted to avoid it. But...*Matthew lives in Westbrooke?* I guess that explains why James was in the neighborhood...

"How'd you end up with his girlfriend, though?"

James and I both say I *was not Ice's girlfriend* at the same time. It makes Matthew laugh, and I know for sure he seriously has no idea. James didn't tell him *anything* about what's happened with me, him, or Ice since the Fourth of July. I sure as hell can't bring myself to break the news now—not in a public restaurant, anyway.

"Right," he agrees. "But you never did explain it."

James taps his knuckles on the table. "It's a long story, man. I don't wanna get into it right now."

"Let's just say he's not happy about it," I mutter.

For an instant, I detect a flicker of something in Matthew's eyes. Then his expression mellows.

"Yeah? I guess that makes sense, knowing—" He blinks and glances to James. "Hey, didn't you just run into him—like back in June or something? I feel like you mentioned it."

"Yeah. I don't wanna talk about that either."

The darkness creeping into his voice isn't lost on Matthew, who clears his throat and flags down the waitress—a woman a few years older than us with golden eyes, impeccably sharp eyeliner, and dark hair pulled up in a neat bun.

"Oh, hey, James," she says, flashing a smile. "It's been a

while, huh? Where have you been?"

He glances down at the table. "Ah…"

"Don't ask, prima; he's just been busy with his new girlfriend," Matthew says, snickering. "Anyway, you guys want anything? My treat."

"Your treat?" she asks with a sigh, planting a hand on her hip. "This is coming right out of your paycheck, you know? My dad hates how you give your friends free food all the time."

He shrugs, looking to us with a smile. "Like I said, my treat." *Ah… I haven't even checked the menu.*

"I'll just have chilaquiles," James says without looking at the waitress. "No avocado—or guacamole. And water is fine."

"Bring pan dulce too," Matthew adds.

She sighs again but nods and looks to me with a soft, curious smile as she refills his mug with steaming coffee. "And for you, miss James' girlfriend?"

I scan the menu and settle on churro french toast, much to Matthew's delight—I guess he's the one who suggested his uncle add it to the menu. *It sounds gimmicky, to be honest, but I have a killer sweet tooth right now.*

The waitress confirms our order, takes the menu I was holding, and heads back toward the kitchen. And I watch in amazement as Matthew pours an obscene amount of sugar and creamer into his mug. I look to James, who merely glances away and takes a drink of his ice water.

"Oh, right," Matthew says. "How are things going with your roommate? I heard you guys got into it a few days ago?"

The change in subject seems to relax James, but the new one

is somehow more difficult for me—in part because I don't have any good news to share. *I'd almost rather keep talking about Ice.*

"It's my fault," I mumble. "I still need to make up with her, but I don't know what to say. Since I can't mention…*cats*, you know? And it kinda has everything to do with that."

Matthew nods with some level of understanding. "That's what it's about, huh? Must be rough."

"Oh, it's definitely rough."

I steal a glance at James. His eyes are narrowed in thought as he stares at his hands on the water glass. I wish he told me he kept his friend completely in the dark before we got here. Poor Matthew doesn't even seem to realize how awkward this is for us because he has no idea what he's missing.

"So, what have you guys been up to?" he asks.

"A lot of nothing," James says. "Just watching movies and whatever. Enjoying the air conditioning, I guess. It's better than being stuck at my dad's, anyway."

I stop listening as my phone goes off in my pocket, the soft vibration of a notification distracting me. James and Matthew talk back and forth—something about how nice my house is; something about ways I could apologize to Rose. I check my phone.

*Oh, no…*

**Ice Monroe**                     now
Hey. We need to talk.

*Why now?*

I look up from the message on my lock screen, trying my

damnedest to mask my frustration.

Matthew continues explaining how he once had to apologize to James over something honestly kind of stupid—or at least silly. I smile and nod despite the advice being wholly unhelpful. James looks embarrassed, but he seems in a better mood.

*I can't tell him about the text while we're still here.*

With a sigh, I slip my phone back into my pocket, fold my hands in my lap, and laugh at a joke Matthew just made despite having missed half of it. Both men look at me in surprise.

"In my case, it's a little more complicated," I say, "but I'll keep it in mind when I'm brave enough to talk to her again."

Matthew grins. "If you've been friends for a long time, you'll figure it out. Seriously. James here just ghosted me for a whole month, and look at us. We're good, right?"

"Right," he agrees.

*Uh-huh... You haven't told him what's going on either.*

My phone goes off in my pocket again. I ignore it, determined to keep the mood upbeat and the conversation casual and friendly.

This time, I won't let Ice get to me so easily.

# forty-two

My phone vibrates again.

I feel my eyes narrow, but I don't look away from the laptop screen, determined to get through at least one episode before I crack. *He just won't stop.* I don't want to respond, but this has to be the fifth or sixth message since we left the taquería.

I glance at James. He's lying on his stomach, focused on the show. *I still haven't told him.* I haven't mentioned Ice at all. He was in such a good mood when we left the restaurant. I couldn't bring myself to say anything.

When the episode ends, I stop Netflix from auto-playing the next one and sit up with a sigh.

"Everything alright?" he asks.

I nod. "Aren't you bored, though? You can go downstairs if you're tired of being cooped up in here."

"I don't mind." He watches me carefully, so I try extra hard to play it cool. "This is better than being stuck at Reid Manor, you know? With the air conditioning and internet and all."

"Mm…" I take my phone from my pocket and tap the most recent notification to open the whole conversation.

**Ice:** Hey. We need to talk.

**Ice:** For a moment, if you will.

**Ice:** I know you don't trust me, but I need to speak with you.

**Ice:** We're almost a week into August.

**Ice:** Is James still there? He is, isn't he? His car was parked outside the last time I drove by.

**Ice:** Aren't you tired of him hanging around like an annoying leech? Seeing him for 5 minutes was bad enough. How can you stand it 24/7? Hahaha

**Ice:** Hey, how come you aren't reading these anymore?

**Ice:** Are you ignoring me? ( -_- )

There are more than I thought. *What is his deal?*

I lock the phone and force a smile. "Seriously. I don't mind if you hang out downstairs without me for a while. Rose is probably bored out of her mind too, you know?"

"You can always come with me and apologize to her."

"I'm still not ready to face her yet," I say. It's the truth, but he frowns, and I shake my head. "Just go down without me. Seriously, it's fine. I'll text you if I need anything."

"You sure you're okay?"

"Maybe I need some time to think?"

"Alone?"

"Maybe." *I'm not...really lying.*

I don't care if he says he's cool with spending all day in the bedroom, sitting around and watching Netflix with me. It's not fair. It's sad. He still gets along with Rose despite everything, and I seriously don't want him to feel like he's trapped in here. I don't want him to feel the way I feel.

*I don't want—*

"Okay," he agrees.

He takes a deep breath before leaving the bed. I watch him cross the room. His hand brushes the doorknob, and a chill washes over me.

"James—" I spoke without thinking, surprising myself. When he glances over, I hesitate. "Um… While you're down there, can you make sure the front door is locked?"

His expression shifts, darkening somewhat. He glances at the phone in my hand. My teeth click as I swallow a bit too hard, but I smile again.

"Rose forgets to lock it sometimes, so…"

"Of course," he says as he opens the door. "I can check. Let me know if you need anything else. Please."

"Right."

He leaves.

I take a deep breath and crawl out of bed to sit at my desk instead. I open the blinds and stare through the window. It's a nice day, but my eyes linger on the hedge bordering the cottage next door. It's not flowering anymore, but I can easily picture a white cat sneaking out of it.

There's no cat today, though.

My phone vibrates against the desk.

*Another one.*

**Ice:** Jayde. Answer me.

After rubbing my eyes, I unlock my phone and tap the screen to expand the keyboard. And, unsure what else I can do, I type.

> **Me:** Leave me alone.
>
> **Ice:** Oh, good! You're not ignoring me. Just busy, then?
>
> **Me:** Not really, but I wish you would stop texting me.
>
> **Ice:** Humor me for a moment. Are you willing to talk over the phone?
>
> **Me:** I'd rather not.
>
> **Ice:** In that case, will you meet with me?

*In person?*

> **Me:** No.
>
> **Ice:** I'm willing to meet in public if it makes you more comfortable.
>
> **Me:** It really doesn't. I don't want to talk to you at all.
>
> **Ice:** Work with me here, Jayde.
>
> **Ice:** I was messing with you before. This time, I intend to have a civil conversation.

*A civil conversation? Right.*

But, I wonder… Which time does he feel like what he did was only *messing with* me? When he first pulled a knife on me? When he laughed as he held a gun to my head? When he shot clean through the door I was hiding behind? *Which thing was nothing more than a sick practical joke in his mind?*

*Is that seriously how he feels about what he's been doing?*

I lock my phone, suddenly hyperaware of my bouncing knee and racing heart. With a sigh, I stand from the desk and push the chair in. Then I turn to face my empty bedroom. My laptop set up on the bed. James' stuff lying around.

*This is so weird. But I can't be in here right now.*

Looking to the door, I hesitate. But it should be fine as long as I stay upstairs. They might not even notice I left the room if I'm quiet.

*So...here goes.*

I step out, careful to close the door softly. The second floor is empty, and I hear the TV playing downstairs. *Are they watching Night Hospital?* It sounds like an episode from season one, so I can only assume she started at the beginning for his sake.

I curl up in my beanbag and check my phone again.

> **Ice:** Jayde?
>
> **Me:** You seriously want to meet? Like in person?
>
> **Ice:** Yes. That's the idea.
>
> **Me:** That is not happening.
>
> **Ice:** No? I'm not about to beg.
>
> **Me:** And I'm not about to meet with you.
>
> **Ice:** Oh, you will. My schedule is clear. I can do this all day.

*Ugh!*

"That's crazy," James says downstairs. "You know there's no way that would work in real life, right?"

Rose laughs. "Of course, I know that. I'm a nursing student. But this is a medical drama, my dude. It doesn't have to work in real life. It's called suspension of disbelief."

"Suspension of disbelief only works if the writers don't break the previously established rules of the universe, and this is meant to take place in reality, right?"

There's a pause.

"You watch anime, don't you?" she asks.

"Is that a problem?"

She snickers. "No, but I can't say I'm surprised."

With a sigh, I look back to my phone.

> **Ice:** When are you free to meet?
>
> **Ice:** Any time. Any place.
>
> **Me:** Never. Nowhere. I'm done.

I back out of the conversation before he responds. When he does, I ignore it, flicking the notification banner away, and launch the first idle game on my home screen.

Some time later, the TV goes quiet, and I watch the banister. James and Rose chat about the episode for a moment. He concedes, admitting that the show did *not* break the rules of its own universe in stretching the current possibilities of real medical science. His disbelief was successfully suspended.

I roll my eyes.

*But I understand.* Night Hospital is weirdly engrossing despite the increasingly outlandish scenarios presented in the show.

Footsteps come up the stairs—only one set, so I don't panic —and James steps out onto the second floor. Our eyes meet. He's clearly surprised to see me, but his expression only shifts slightly to the negative as he approaches.

"You sure you're alright?"

*I should tell him about Ice's messages. I really should, but—*

"Yeah, I'm fine," I say, keeping my voice low. "But I hope you don't mind I was eavesdropping a little."

He glances aside with a rather nervous smile. "Nah. It's not like we were talking about anything important. Anyway, I was just coming up to ask if you were hungry."

As I consider it, my phone starts vibrating. *A call.* My heart jumps into my throat. Without looking at the screen, I double-tap the side button to decline the call. Then I shove my phone in my pocket and hop up from the beanbag.

"Yeah. It's about that time, isn't it?"

He nods. "You ready to come down? I'm sure Rose would love to see you."

"Oh, um, not…yet. I'll wait in my room."

We watch each other for a moment. As he searches my face with a soft frown, and I stand unmoving, it seems like there's something more he wants to say. Maybe there is. Maybe he doesn't believe I'm fine. Maybe he knows I'm hiding something.

I lose the smile and tip my head. "If that's okay?"

"Yeah. I just—" He glances over the banister with slightly narrowed eyes. "Never mind. I'll grab us something to eat."

He leaves again, and I dip into the bedroom, where I check my phone to confirm the call I rejected was from Ice. *Not good.*

The texting is bad enough, but I can't have him blowing up my phone with calls too. Someone will definitely find out.

I shut the door and move to sit on the edge of my bed.

> **Me:** Please don't call me again.

The message is marked as read, and, hardly a second later, an incoming call overtakes our text conversation. My cheek catches between my teeth. I tap the screen to decline the call.

> **Me:** I'm serious. Stop.
>
> **Ice:** Or what? LMAO
>
> **Ice:** Perhaps I'll stop when you agree to have an actual conversation with me. (°ᴗ°)
>
> **Me:** I don't want to see you.
>
> **Ice:** Whether you care to see me or not, there are a few things we need to discuss. I'm still your sponsor. You can't avoid me forever.

*God, I wish I could.*

What does he want to talk about so badly, anyway? What is there for us to discuss? I have no idea what he wants, and I'm honestly too scared to ask, especially if it has something to do with his sponsorship.

> **Me:** I don't want to talk to you at all.
>
> **Ice:** Please reconsider.

*Please? Please??*

> **Ice:** Don't forget I know where you live. Hahaha

I groan and fall back onto my bed.

*Maybe he's right.* I can't avoid him forever. Maybe we should talk, but… *Why? How?* Texting is one thing. Even a brief phone call might be…tolerable. But he's insistent on meeting in person now. *How could I possibly agree to meet with him? How could I trust that he won't…*

*How can I be sure of anything?*

\* \* \* \* \*

I roll onto my back and stare at the ceiling for a long moment, my phone on my chest. It's getting late. Will I even be able to fall asleep tonight?

"Hey."

James' voice is soft and kind of sweet. Somehow, he's still in a good mood despite how shady and weird I've been acting all day. When I look at him, his expression matches his voice.

"Wanna go for a walk?" he asks.

Through the open blinds, daylight is fading. This is the perfect time to go for a walk. Without the sun overhead, the heat wouldn't be nearly as uncomfortable. There might even be a cool breeze. *I used to love going out in the evening during summer.*

"Eh…"

"Last I checked, Rose isn't out in the living room. She's not home. I think she went to a party? So you don't have to worry about seeing her."

She's not what I'm worried about, but— *Did she remember*

*to lock the door when she left?*

"Not tonight," I say mildly.

*Ice might be watching the house.*

My phone vibrates. I check the screen.

> **Ice Monroe**                    now
> Work with me here, Jayde. What I have to say
> won't take five minutes.

With a sigh, I unlock my phone.

> **Me:** Why can't you say it over text?

> **Ice:** I hate texting.

*For someone who hates texting, you sure can keep it up.*

"Is everything okay? You've been on your phone all day."

I glance up from the screen. James' voice is level, and he looks more thoughtful than suspicious, but I hesitate, and a soft crease forms between his brows.

"Who are you talking to?" he asks. "Just curious."

I blink. "Ah… My brother, Robbie. He saw that picture of you—the one I shared on FaceSpace—and we haven't talked in a while, so we've been catching up."

"Oh." He rubs his jaw, gaze flicking aside as though trying to remember. "The one who lives in LA, right?"

"Yep. That's the one."

I look to my phone again, and I type more quickly.

> **Me:** Whatever. I'm going to sleep. Please
>        don't keep me up.

I lock my phone and drop it back to my chest.

# forty-three

I set my water bottle aside and glance at James, whose focus is on the laptop screen. He's sitting a bit closer today, and I'm less on edge because I haven't heard from Ice since the meaningless text I woke up to—*but it was sent at 3AM, and I did not respond. No. Today hasn't been so bad.*

I almost feel up to talking to Rose again. Ignoring her feels pointless now, especially if she's half as over what happened as James claims she is.

*I'm not over it, though. It was awful.*

She messaged earlier to ask if I needed anything from the store. I responded—but only to say I don't. Then she asked how I was doing, and I said I'm still working on it. I need more time, yes, but I'm not *really* working on it. I have no idea what I'll say to her when we finally talk again.

I've been…preoccupied.

My phone goes off in my pocket, vibrating. *A phone call.*

I swear *to god*—

"I'll be right back," I say, already leaving the bed with the phone still vibrating in my pocket. "Bathroom."

James frowns and presses the space bar to pause the show, but he doesn't stop me, so I make it to the bathroom before the call goes to voicemail. Of course, Ice's name appears on the screen.

I switch the bathroom fan on, accept the call, and bring the phone to my ear.

"What do you want?" I ask.

"Oh. You answered."

His voice is blanker than I expected. It annoys me, but I repeat my question, and he clears his throat.

"As I said, I'd like to arrange a meeting." Having recovered from his surprise, his voice is more familiar but equally annoying. "In public, perhaps… Unless you don't want to be seen with me."

"I don't want to meet you anywhere," I say, keeping my voice low but not bothering to mask my anger. "Public or not, I don't care. My roommate found out about my injuries a few days ago, you know? I didn't say it was you, obviously, but she's not stupid, and we haven't talked since. I don't know how much more of this I can take. You're seriously ruining my life."

"Your life was ruined the moment you spoke to James, so—"

"That's not funny," I say through my teeth. "Can't you just tell me whatever it is right now? You said it would only take five minutes, right?"

There's a pause. "I'm not sure I can believe anything you say over the phone."

*What?*

I glance at my reflection. At my wide eyes. At the bitterness, confusion, and dread playing about on my face.

"You…think I'd lie to you?"

He laughs. "Why wouldn't you lie? Isn't that what you're

doing to everyone else? Surely, your roommate doesn't know about immortals. Surely, James doesn't know you're on the phone with me now. At least, if we speak face-to-face, I'll know for certain if you lie—because you are awful at it."

*Screw you.*

"So, pick a time and place, and—"

I pull the phone from my ear and hang up.

I stare at my thumb, still pressed to the glass as my home screen replaces Ice's name. I listen to the whirring of the bathroom fan and my own panicked breathing. I will my heart to beat slower, but it doesn't. My chest hurts.

*God...* He is such an asshole.

Does he think I don't know I'm a terrible person? The last thing I need is for *him* to tell me that. But it's his fault I'm like this. I never would have had to lie to anyone if it weren't for him.

My phone vibrates—thankfully just another text—and I click the banner to read it.

**Ice:** Wow. That was rude.

**Me:** Just leave me alone. I'm having a hard enough time rn without dealing with this too.

**Ice:** I'm your sponsor. You did this to yourself.

**Me:** I trusted you. I'm not making that mistake again. I will never meet with you.

**Ice:** You have nothing to lose, Jayde. I'm merely asking for a few minutes of your time, and we may work something out to benefit us both.

*Work something out?*

We text back and forth for a few minutes. He says he won't hurt me if I agree to meet with him—he'll keep his distance—but he won't promise that James will be safe. He can't even guarantee that. *We have to talk before I make any deals*, he says.

This is insane.

> **Me:** Just stop texting me. I don't want to talk about this anymore.

I jab the send button, lock my phone, and slap it face down in the empty soap dish. From now on, I won't reply. *I won't answer another text he sends!*

My hands shake as they grip the rim of the sink. A twinge of pain shoots up my left arm. I glance up from my hands to see my reflection staring at me with glassy eyes, brimming with a wretched mix of anger and sadness. The River Sapphire rests just above the top of the pink scar that pokes out from the neckline of my shirt.

Now, I don't know which bothers me more—the necklace or the scar.

A faint glow reflects off the ceramic soap dish as my phone's screen lights up upon receiving another message, and my teeth grit again. When the light eventually dims, I relax my grip on the edge of the sink and watch my white knuckles regain color.

I meant what I said.

I don't want to talk to him. The mere thought brings a sour taste to my mouth. I think of what he did to me, and the feelings I wasted on him, and it pisses me off. *All of it.* I have nothing else to say to him, and I don't care if he has anything to say to me.

Nothing he says now would change anything.

But my hand reaches for the phone anyway.

**Ice:** Honestly, Jayde? You're being ridiculous.

*Me?*

*I'm* being ridiculous?

My thumbs hover over the on-screen keyboard, but I stop myself from typing. Not even to take James' advice and finally tell Ice to *fuck off*. I'd love to, but responding won't help. It doesn't matter what I say. He won't take no for an answer. I don't know what else I can do, but I do know I can't take this much longer.

*Because I can't bring myself to tell James.*

I look him in the eyes, and I smile and tell him I'm fine. I say nothing is bothering me. There's no real reason I keep checking my phone. I'm just texting Robbie. I'm not worried about anything in particular. The rift between me and Rose is my main concern right now. I just smile and pretend I'm not lying through my teeth.

A tear falls from my eye and lands on the screen.

I never wanted to lie about this too, but everything was looking up before Rose found out about the scars and Ice messaged me. James was finally happy that he decided to stay. He finally stopped acting like he felt it was a mistake. He finally stopped asking to leave.

Even if it's wrong—even if I know this isn't the best way…

I block Ice's number.

# forty-four

"Music@ThePark?" James asks. "It's all local artists, right?"

I nod. "It's fun. I used to go every week during the summer when I was younger, but I've only had the chance to go once this year."

He thinks about it, his eyes locked on my hands as they hold his. He likes supporting independent writers, and he doesn't seem picky when it comes to music, so it's not a stretch to assume he might be interested in supporting local musicians too.

I don't want to be home right now, so I hope he agrees to go. *After blocking Ice, I...*

*No.*

Don't worry about it. The mess with Ice is not the only reason I want to go out with James.

I thought I was sure of my feelings after that dream, but I keep thinking about what Rose and James have said. Maybe they have a point. *How can I really know?* There is no way I could ever feel anything for Ice like what I felt before, but the nasty fallout could have made me desperate for any sort of comfort.

*Desperate to fall in love with someone else.*

And James was right there, more than willing to catch me

with no regard for my motives in staying with him.

Sure, I know I care about him. I'm glad he's in a better place. He's not staying in an abandoned building or carrying a gun around everywhere. He's sleeping at night and reconnecting with friends and taking better care of himself. That's great, and I am so happy for him. But...

*I don't know how to trust anything I feel anymore.*

"I'll go on one condition," he says. "You have to talk to Rose when we get back."

I drop his hands and pout. "Seriously?"

"You guys have been friends since elementary school, right?" He glances away, a hint of tension in his jaw. "She cares about you like a sister—those are her words."

"She said that?"

"Yeah. I mean, she is upset that you lied to her, but she doesn't know how to talk to you about it either. It's a lot, I know, but you can't put it off forever. You can't let this ruin your friendship."

I hope he doesn't think what happened between us is his fault. I was lying to her before I ever met him, and he tried to convince me to tell her about my scars before she got home. It's not his fault I didn't listen.

"Okay, fine. I guess I can talk to her when we get back." I meet his gaze with some hesitation, he gives me a look, and I gasp. "I promise I will!"

He flashes a relieved smile. "Then it's a date."

*Yes!*

We're ready to leave within the hour.

In a brazen attempt to further weasel my way into James' good graces, I offer Rose a small wave and a smile that falters immediately after we make eye contact. She frowns but returns the wave and doesn't glance away until I turn to grab my wallet off the bookcase beside the door.

I step outside after James and stop to lock the door. *Just in case.* My heart is definitely beating faster than it should.

"You good?" he asks.

"Yeah, it's just— We've been in the same house this whole time, but that's the first time I've seen her in three days."

"I know how you feel." His hand brushes my shoulder as he walks past and continues toward his car. "The fixing things part sucks, but it's not so bad once you're talking again."

I skip a step on the landing to catch up. "I believe you."

*She wants to make up too, so I'll try my best for her sake.*

The drive through town is hot and nerve-wracking. We're about to go into *public* public together for the first time since we became a real couple. This is a big event too. A lot of people will see me—see *us*—and I'm suddenly second-guessing my decision to wear a short-sleeve shirt.

*What if we run into someone I know?*

*Or someone James knows?*

*Ugh...*

We make it to Riverside, and James parks in the aging parking lot behind Riverview Community Center, heeding my advice to avoid traffic in the evening. It means we have to walk along the bike path in the killer midday heat for several minutes, but my hip is almost back to normal, and we're both dressed lightly—or *were*, since I cave and pull a flannel on before we leave the car.

We hold hands as we walk. His hands are always warm.

*Maybe I am a bad person for lying, but...*

My feelings for James are different than anything I felt for Ice. I was desperate for Ice's approval and attention, but I was a mess around him. I was so awkward and nervous. With James, my feelings don't seem as intense, but I don't think I've ever been this comfortable around a guy before. Sleeping in the same bed. Cuddling on the couch to watch TV. Walking around and holding hands and feeling like it actually *means* something.

*So why am I still hiding the texts?*

"You're quiet," he says.

I laugh. "Oh. Sorry. I was just thinking…"

"About what?"

"Um—"

My hesitance only succeeds in making him more interested. With a sigh, I tear my eyes from his curiously eager expression and watch my feet as we walk down the sidewalk.

"I was just thinking about how you seem more comfortable around me the past few days," I mumble. "And in general too. I used to worry—you were sad and awkward, you know? But I feel like I don't have to worry as much anymore."

*At least not about some things.*

I look up again, worried he'll take what I said the wrong way, but he tips his head like he doesn't quite understand.

I clear my throat. "I guess what I'm trying to say is that you seem happier and more confident, and I like it."

"Confident?" he asks in surprise. When I nod, he flashes a

sheepish smile, sighs, and glances away. "You kill me sometimes —looking at me like that."

"Looking at you like what?"

"Never mind," he says under his breath, his ears turning red. "You give me weird thoughts, is all."

"Weird thoughts?" I raise a hand to cover my mouth, feigning shock. "Maybe you *are* kind of a creep."

Suddenly, my face is on fire. I stifle laughter, but James does not bother restraining his. He hides his face in his free hand and shakes his head.

"There's seriously something wrong with you," he says.

I grin and look ahead with a new spring in my step.

A couple weeks ago, I almost thought he hated me. I thought he didn't want me around. So this feels unreal. I can't believe that, after everything Ice put us through, we're here—together—having a silly conversation and walking hand-in-hand. The realization fills me with a strange, comforting sense of calm.

*There is no way these feelings aren't real.*

I've been pushing James to be more positive lately. Maybe I should take my own advice.

The popup bandstand clear across the park isn't visible as we near the overflow parking lot, but I already hear the bass drums, twangy guitar, and indistinct vocals in the distance. James looks around, either amazed or intimidated by the vast number of vehicles entering the parking lot and already parked in the dry grass.

"More people will show up as the day goes on," I say. "This is a huge event. Have you seriously never come before?"

He gazes toward the park in the distance with a hint of anxiety. "I have—several times—but it was years ago. I never really… paid attention to how many people there were back then, I guess. Now, I try to avoid stuff like this."

Another story he doesn't want to share? Like the story of how I last came here with Ice? My memories of him haunt me every moment of every day. It's so bad, I still can't seem to convince myself I'm over the person I thought he was.

*Maybe I should explain—*

No. I *know* I should, but…

I just want everything to go well today.

*Just one nice day.*

I'll spend the evening with James. We can eat shaved ice and barbecue sandwiches and dance to music we've never heard before. We can sit by the river and look out over the water. We can laugh about our day and ignore our problems as the sun goes down.

I won't talk about Ice. I won't worry about Rose.

*If I can capture even a fragment of the warmth I saw on my face in that dream…* Well, as long as James is the one I imagine beside me the whole time, I think I'll be fine.

\* \* \* \* \*

*So far, so good.*

I feel like I might melt in the afternoon heat, but we find a nice spot to sit in the shade of a small, red plum tree up the hill from the stage. We listen to the music and chat and vibe for nearly an hour until I mention getting snow cones.

"Are you alright?" James asks. "Is it too hot?"

I shrug. "I'll be fine."

He must have noticed me push the sleeves of my flannel up to my elbows. The heat sucks, yes, but it's not my main concern. I'm pretty sure half the young immortals in Riverview know who I am. *What if I run into someone who recognizes me? What if they see the scars? What will they think?*

"Well, let's get those snow cones," he says, hefting himself up off the ground.

I nod and accept the hand he offers to help me stand. It's not awkward, and he doesn't drop my hand before we start walking. We're halfway to the parking lot where the food trucks are parked when I hear a gasp somewhere behind us.

"YOOOO," a familiar, energetic voice calls. "Do I spy Jayde Palmer and James fucking Reid?"

James freezes beside me like he's about to have a heart attack, and his hand slips out of mine as we turn to look. Carmen's hair is almost fluorescent pink—I saw the new color in a few selfies she shared on FaceSpace since she dyed it. And she is thrilled to see us.

James doesn't move, but I tug my sleeves down as she weaves between people on her way to meet us.

"I knew it!" She grins, her tone accusatory but playful. "I knew you guys were dating. Ever since you shared that photo, I *knew* it."

I laugh, clasping my hands behind my back. "Oh, no. I guess you caught us."

She looks between us, her upbeat amazement fading as a

more muted curiosity flickers across her face. "You guys are kinda cute together... I wasn't expecting it."

"Expecting what?" James asks sharply.

"To think you suit each other," she says with a laugh. "Well, good for you, James. Jayde here is a sweet one."

My face goes hot. "Hey—"

*Also, why does everyone keep saying we suit each other?*

"Oh, right," she says, her expression and tone shifting again as she regards me more seriously. "You still haven't heard anything from Night, have you?"

I shake my head.

"What about Ice?"

I shake my head again as James makes a small sound beside me. "Sorry, I have no idea what either of them are up to."

"No one does," she says with a sigh, though James' discomfort wasn't entirely lost on her. "Oh, well. It was worth a shot, but I should get out of your hair. Have fun, you two."

"See you later," I say.

She slips back into the crowd. The moment she's gone, James releases the breath he was holding and drags his hands down his face.

"Are you okay?"

He nods, though he looks uneasy. "Yeah. Let's just grab the snow cones and get away from the crowd for a while."

"Okay."

I reach for his hand, and we continue on to the parking lot. We buy two snow cones and an order of spiral-cut french fries, and we walk back into the park. I follow James down the hill, past the stage where the band plays, and toward the river.

We leave the main path encircling the park, pass underneath the bridge, and then head into the trees along the riverbank a good quarter mile from the bandstand. Eventually, we reach a secluded stretch of pebbly beach. It's empty, out of the way, and looks like a decent swimming spot—not that I intend to swim.

I balance my snow cone on top of a large, stony outcropping and peel my flannel shirt off.

"How do you know Carmen, anyway?" I ask.

They're friends on FaceSpace, and most everyone seems to know her, but I feel like I'm missing something. He clearly wasn't comfortable around her. Maybe it's just because of our situation—I mean, seeing her surprised me too—but...

When I turn back to look at him, he's watching me carefully.

"She's a friend of a friend," he says.

"One of Matthew's friends?"

He laughs. "One of his exes."

"Oh."

"Eh. They're still good friends." He sits on a smaller boulder a few feet from the water and sets the boat of fries aside. "Anyway, like I said, they're the reason I knew about you. Matt heard of you from her, and he told me Ice sponsored you. He showed me the pictures she shared on FaceSpace. I doubt I would've stopped to talk to you at all if I hadn't recognized you. Isn't that awful?"

*I guess Ice was right about social media, in a way, but—*

"Not really," I say.

"No?"

"You were just curious about me, right?"

He frowns. "I guess…"

"Everyone I've met is curious."

I turn away, step out of my flip-flops, and wade into the water. It's colder than I expected, but the smooth rocks and sandy soil feel nice beneath my feet.

*Mm…*

Maybe I would want to swim if I thought to wear a swimsuit. I wasn't expecting to find a truly private place to hang out during such a crowded event. Though, knowing James, I'm not surprised he knew of one.

"Immortals don't talk openly with humans often—let alone with anyone in the Human Immortal Program—so it makes sense you would be. But you weren't rude or anything, even though you knew I was with Ice, so it's fine."

"I thought I was rude," he mutters, his voice barely audible over the sound of the river and distant music.

"Well, at the very least, you helped me pick up my stuff. And you never asked what it's like to be human. You didn't even mention it."

I look up from a tiny fish swimming in the shallows and turn to find James still sitting on the boulder near the river's bank. He either ignored or missed my joke. He's just picking at his snow cone with a plastic spoon.

"You should come over here."

He glances up. "Maybe I'd rather sit and watch you."

"Why?"

"Uh…" He laughs, but he looks nervous. "I dunno. I'm

having a hard time…processing everything, I guess. Seeing Carmen… The fact anyone knows we're together. Maybe if I watch you a while longer, it won't seem so crazy to think you're here with me."

"Does it bother you that other people know we're together?"

"Maybe a little. Since I know Carmen will tell everyone."

"You want to be with me, though?"

"Of course," he says, just loud enough to make out over the ambient noise. "But I keep waiting for you to realize you're making a mistake."

*I knew it.* I kneel and dip my hands in the cool water. I stare at my fingers, their image distorted by the clear water passing over them, and the thin scabs on my wrist, and I take a deep breath.

*Okay. I can do this.*

I leave the water and stand in front of James. He sets his snow cone down and looks up at me, clearly confused. And I cup his face in my damp hands. His eyes widen, and the warmth of his cheeks crushes the coolness that lingered on my palms.

"I don't think staying with you is a mistake," I say. "I'm not going anywhere, so don't worry about it."

"Why am I so scared to touch you?" he breathes.

"You shouldn't be. I'm not made of glass, James."

He averts his eyes, lip twitching. "I'm sorry."

*Idiot…*

My breath catches, but I don't give myself time to overthink or change my mind. With my hands still on his face, I close the final step between us.

I kiss him.

And he freezes.

He stops breathing as our eyes meet. I realize he wasn't expecting it, and concern stabs at my chest—*a fleeting memory of the Fourth of July*—but he draws a breath against my lips. Then his hands move to my waist. His eyes close, and he melts into the kiss, *into me*, and I have never been so relieved in my life.

I take the tiniest step back and offer a smile. "See? It's fine. I mean, you told Rose we're dating, so you're stuck with me now."

"Jayde, I…"

His hands fall away from my sides, and he averts his gaze, his expression conflicted and hesitant. *I've seen this before.* Suddenly worried, I retract my hands too.

"I'm serious," I say. "I know you like me, and I… Well, I think I feel the same way about you."

"You—"

His eyes dart up, wide with tears pricking the corners. Then a smile splits his face, and he laughs like I embarrassed him terribly. His shoulders shake as he covers his eyes with one hand.

"You can't just kiss me like that," he says, still laughing.

"What? Why not?"

"Do you have any idea how long I've wanted to kiss you?"

"Huh?"

I laugh and take another step back, but he stops me. He pulls me closer, and he uncovers his face, and his smile softens. *A warmth I've never seen.* His fingers run through my hair, and he kisses me again. Softly at first, and then with a sense of urgency like he really has thought of this moment for weeks—like he needs my kiss to live.

*It's strange. But this is it.* This is the feeling I was looking for. This is what I never got to experience while I was with Ice.

"Thank you," he breathes against my lips. "Thank you."

* * * * *

We spend the evening together just like I wanted.

We sit on the riverbank and finish our snow cones and french fries. We laugh and kiss and ignore our problems, and I am *happy* to be there with him.

It feels good. It feels *right*.

We're not fazed when we come across Carmen later in the afternoon. James assures her that he's talking to Matthew again, and he laughs when she asks if she can cut my hair yet.

*Of course, I turn her down.*

We order pulled pork sandwiches from another food truck for dinner and eat in the shade beneath the bridge. We even manage to dance for a few minutes before our mutual embarrassment gets the better of us.

But it never leaves the back of my mind. It's there during the ride home. It's there as I change into pajamas and lie in bed and respond to a message Carmen sent while I was changing.

*It's still there.*

*The Fourth of July. The taste of vodka and lemon. The sting of casual dismissal.*

Even if I never wished I was with anyone but James—let alone Ice—it haunts me that *that* moment was the first thing to cross my mind after I kissed him. I hate it. I hate Ice. I hate... *me.* But I refuse to let Ice or my feelings or *anything else* shatter the happiness I'm desperately clinging to.

"You still have to talk to Rose," James says. "You promised."

I sigh. "It's not my fault she was asleep when we got back."

"Guess I kept you out too late, huh?"

I roll onto my side to better watch him. He stares at me with unrelenting warmth, but his gaze still strikes me as hesitant.

"Did you kiss me today?" he asks.

"What kind of question is that? You were there, weren't you?"

He averts his eyes. "You had a good time, right?"

I sit up and hug my arms to my chest. The slight roughness of the scars bothers me more than usual, but I ignore it.

"Of course, I had a good time. Did you?"

He moves closer to hug me from the side. I feel my eyes grow wide, but he can't see with his face buried in the crook of my neck. I raise a hand to his shoulder. His breath is warm as he kisses my skin.

I don't know why, which makes it all the more frustrating, but tears well in my eyes. I'm not sad. I don't *feel* sad, but I...

"I'm not used to this sort of thing, you know," he breathes. "Feeling okay. Or happy. Or...wanted, I guess. But, uh... You really want me to stay with you?"

*Yep. I'm crying.*

"Didn't I already say that?" I mumble into his short hair. "I practically begged you to stay, didn't I?"

"Did you?"

*Is he—?*

"James?"

"What?"

He lifts his head. His eyes are watering, and we stare at each other, rather puzzled for a moment, as fat, ugly tears roll down both of our cheeks. And then he grins with only a touch of nerves.

"Why are you crying?" he asks, carefully drying my eyes.

"Why are *you*?"

He laughs. "I'm an idiot, remember?"

"Maybe, so am I. A little, anyway."

He kisses me again.

# forty-five

"You're gonna talk to her, right?"

"Yes." I continue brushing my hair. "I already messaged her. She knows we're coming down in a few minutes."

James rests a hand on my head.

A shiver runs down my spine. I ignore it the same way I've been ignoring the mounting sense of unease since I first woke up. I don't want to think about it—or what it means.

I adjust my shirt and force a smile. "Come on, let's go."

We walk downstairs together. Rose is in the kitchen. She looks to be rooting around for food, and she's obviously nervous when she turns to face us.

"How are you?" she asks.

"I'm…better."

"Yeah?"

Avoiding her gaze, I worry my hands at chest level. "Yeah. I am. And…I'm really sorry. The way I acted was—"

She waves her arms about, realizing I'm close to tears.

"I should apologize," she says sharply, stepping closer. "I was confused. And pissed. I still have no clue what's going on, but I should have listened to you. Whatever happened, it was obviously rough, and… Hopefully, it's all under control now?"

*She really knows nothing…*

My arm doesn't itch, but I scratch the edge of the knit sweatband just to give my hand something to do.

"I mean, your guard dog is pretty scary," she says.

"James?" I meet her eyes in surprise. "You're kidding, right?"

She laughs. "For sure. He's a total pushover."

He understandably loses interest in our conversation and walks further into the kitchen. Rose's expression softens as she looks to me again.

"Anyway, seeing you like— Well, I panicked, I guess. I knew you were hiding something. You even admitted it. But…" She smiles, still uncertain. "Anyway, I didn't mean to go off on you like that. Seeing you hurt just set off my maternal instincts or something. I was seriously ready to kick some ass."

"I shouldn't have lied to you," I mumble.

"To be honest, I probably would have kept it a secret too. I get it. I said I'd drive up here in a heartbeat, and I meant it. You just didn't want to worry me while I was out of town."

There's more to it than that, but I nod lamely.

"So, we're cool now, right?" she asks, her tone more relaxed. "You don't hate me for freaking out or accusing James of hurting you or anything?"

I shake my head. "Of course not. I don't hate you. I'm not even mad. I just thought— I don't know. I messed up, and I'm sorry. I've made…a lot of questionable decisions this summer."

"You're still alive, right?"

*Yeah, for now.*

She pats my shoulder, and I glance up in time to catch the bright, reassuring smile that crinkles the corners of her grey eyes. She almost looks like the Rose from before she left for Arizona —from before I went and screwed everything up.

"We used to tell each other everything," she says. "It's okay if you need time to work through…whatever happened, so I won't bring it up again, but I hope you'll trust me enough to tell me the whole story eventually. Maybe I'd be able to do more to help."

*Oh*… I wish that were the case.

"Now then, get something to eat and collect your boyfriend, so we can watch this movie already." She grins. "You know I've been waiting months for it to come out on Netflix."

I nod, vaguely remembering a conversation about the movie back in July. She grabs whatever she decided to eat off the counter where she left it and crosses into the living room.

Then I look to James. "Can you find something for us to eat? I'll be right back. I forgot something upstairs."

"Sure," he agrees with a shrug.

As he pops open the fridge, I turn and head upstairs.

Dread looms over me like a shadow, growing heavier and darker with each step. I shut myself in my bedroom and slip my phone from my pocket. I stare at the notification bubble I've been avoiding since it appeared—the tiny red circle alerting me to new text messages.

After taking a deep breath, I launch the app and tap the conversation to expand it. A series of texts from an unknown number.

> **Unknown:** Did you block me? Hahaha
>
> **Unknown:** Do you think testing my patience is smart, or did you somehow convince yourself I'd go away if you ignore me? It won't work.

Reading the words again, I hear Ice's cold, clear voice like a ghost in the back of my mind. My chest feels so tight, I can barely breathe.

> **Unknown:** Expect a call at 3pm. If you don't answer, you will regret it. Have you forgotten what I said about James? Or your roommate? Her name is Rose MacArthur, right?

I haven't forgotten—trust me.

I just don't want to think about it. *I just*...

If he's seriously not deterred by Rose being here... I would never forgive myself if anything happened to her because I'm too scared to face him.

> **Unknown:** If you do answer, don't worry. I don't want to hurt you. I only want to talk.

Is there a chance we can resolve things over the phone or come to any sort of understanding after what he said before I blocked him? *I doubt it, but it doesn't matter.* Ignoring Ice was a dangerous game from the start. I'm almost surprised it took this long for him to find a new number to text me from.

*I won't respond, but...*

There's still time before he plans to call. I back out of the conversation and unblock his original phone number.

Then I return downstairs.

I snuggle up to James on the couch and eat my sandwich and try to enjoy myself existing in my own house for the first time in days. I watch the movie and chat with Rose, who thinks James and I are adorable. She then complains at length about her need for a new boyfriend who isn't only in it for sex, which leads to an *interesting* tangent that results in James turning the shade of a stop sign.

*Well...* At least one of the men I dated this summer has considered having sex with me—*even if it wasn't until literally just now.*

I pat him on the shoulder, conveying my sympathy, but I'm also far too awkward to discuss sex with Rose while he's around. After another moment of her lighthearted teasing, I end up hiding my face in his shoulder while cackling at my expense.

When the movie ends, Rose puts something else on with the volume turned down to act as background noise before asking what we thought. She watched it in theaters months and months ago, but James and I hadn't seen it before.

All I can bring myself to say is, "I liked it," because it was good, but I don't want to admit I found a few scenes so relatable they made me uncomfortable.

The movie was a bizarre romantic comedy with a supernatural, post-apocalyptic twist. At least, I think it was a romcom—even after watching it, I can't be entirely sure what I was meant to take away from it. There were some horror elements, but it was melodramatic while still being funny and a little sad.

"It reminds me of a book I read a while back," James says.

"Oh?" Rose grins and props her chin in her hand. "What book? This movie was based on a book, you know?"

"It's definitely not the same book, but—"

As they discuss whatever self-published adult dystopian novel James read, I check my phone. No new texts, *but five minutes to three might be cutting it a little close.*

I sit up and announce my intention to go upstairs and take a shower. I wait, expecting Rose to question me for showering in the middle of the afternoon, but she's too engaged in conversation to care.

*Good.* I'm glad they get along.

"I'll be back in a bit," I say.

James kisses the side of my head, and I slink upstairs, where I rush to throw together a random outfit before locking myself in the bathroom.

*Three minutes.*

I turn the shower water on. Then I sit against the wall opposite the door, tear my eyes from my antsy reflection in the full-length mirror, and wait for my phone to ring.

*Two minutes.*

*One minute—*

An incoming call from *Ice Monroe* appears on my screen as the hour turns over. My heart pounds, but I suppress my panic. I take a deep breath, and I accept the call.

"Hello?" I ask, my voice low.

"Good. I'm not in the mood to speak with you over the

phone, so I'll keep this brief." His voice is level, but his words come rather quickly. "Meet me in the trees behind your cottage after midnight. Tonight. I'll arrive unarmed and wait for thirty minutes—from twelve to twelve-thirty. If you don't show within that time frame, a meeting will happen on terms neither of us will enjoy."

*At night? Why? What happened to meeting in public?*

"The talk will cover the terms of my sponsorship," he says.

"Wait, what?"

"I expect to see you then."

"Ice, wait—" The line goes silent before I finish.

He hung up on me.

I stare at my phone for a moment. Then I drag myself off the floor, undress, and step into the shower. I take my time, watching the circular shower drain as sudsy water swirls down it.

I need time to think, anyway. Because I don't understand.

Ice claims he just wants to talk, but how does he expect me to believe he's not up to something? Last time we made plans to meet, he also acted like everything was fine.

*And then he attacked me.*

Why should I trust he'll show up unarmed? Why should I believe he won't hurt me? And what does he mean by *the terms of his sponsorship?*

It doesn't make sense, but I don't have a choice.

I have to meet with him.

As I return downstairs and find James and Rose still chatting in the living room, I wonder *why I refuse to tell him*. He would want to know that Ice has been pestering me like this, but, if he knew, could he do anything to help? Wouldn't it just stress us both out more? Involving James could be more dangerous, anyway. He might do something reckless. *Or leave.*

Besides, I doubt Ice wants to hear from him—let alone have him tag along to our secret midnight meeting in the woods. A fight could break out, and that is the last thing I want to happen, whether Ice is unarmed or not.

*No matter what, I have to protect him.*

# forty-six

James' eyes are closed, and his breathing has the even rhythm of deep, relaxed sleep. I watch him for a while, but I know I'm cutting it close, so I carefully sit up and crawl out of bed.

James doesn't move.

As I get dressed, I catch my eye in the mirror.

*God, I don't want to go.*

What if it is a trap?

What if Ice is waiting for me to leave, so he can sneak in and ambush James? What if he's not unarmed when I get there? Even if it's not a trap, what if I mess up? What if I say something stupid? He may very well have diplomatic intentions going into it, but will the conversation remain peaceful if I accidentally piss him off?

When I check my phone again, it's already after midnight. I don't have time to stand around and worry about *what-ifs*. I have to meet with Ice, and I need to leave now.

With a final look at James—and a whispered apology—I make my way downstairs. I consider grabbing a knife from the kitchen as I pass by, but I don't let myself stop. I take the spare key from the bookcase, unlock the front door, and step out into the mild night. Once I lock the door, I scan the parking lot.

*Where is Ice's car?*

The flashy silver Porsche usually stands out. I thought I would see it, but I don't. Did he walk here? Did he park somewhere else? *Well...* Maybe this is a good sign.

*He can't easily kidnap me if he doesn't have his car, right?*

Careful to remain vigilant, I creep around the side of the house, keeping close to the hedge. I normally find the cool breeze and soft nighttime sounds soothing, but not tonight. Tonight, the forest's looming darkness and everything that comes with it scares the crap out of me.

I take a deep breath, turn my phone's flashlight up to the highest brightness setting, and continue forward. I wish it helped, but I still can't see anything beyond the nearest row of trees.

Okay, I made it behind the cottage.

Okay, I'm inching toward the trees.

*Okay... I really don't want to go in there.*

Swallowing hard, I cross the threshold into the woods.

A low-lying branch brushes my shoulder and sends a shiver down my spine. I jump as a twig snaps beneath my foot. I glance around, shining light on every bush and along the edge of every tree, afraid Ice might pop out of nowhere at any moment.

I wander further in.

As I walk, less light filters from the brightly lit parking lot I left behind. The suffocating darkness creeps closer and closer until the flashlight hardly seems to illuminate the space two feet in front of me.

Having night vision would be nice. At the very least, it

would make this a hell of a lot less nerve-wracking. Ice could be literally anywhere, and he'd have no problem seeing me.

*How far in does he expect me to go?*

Eventually, I step out of the trees and into a small clearing I had no idea existed. Curious and nervous, I walk into the middle of the short grass and glance over my shoulder.

The cottages are at least a hundred yards back. I can't make out the light of the parking lot at all anymore, but I *think* I walked in a straight line. *I hope I walked in a straight line.*

I shine light in all directions to ensure I'm alone before checking the time. It's 12:18—still well within the timeframe Ice set, but I am not venturing a single step deeper into this stupid forest. If I do, *I might not be able to find my way back out.*

A soft rustle from behind spooks me, and I drop my phone.

I turn toward the sound and spot a fluffy cat as it slips through the underbrush on its way into the clearing. The cat stops a few feet away and looks up at me with large, feline eyes, shining in the low light cast by my dropped phone.

"Ice." My voice is hardly a whisper.

"You came," he says. "What a pleasant surprise."

"You just want to talk, right?" I ask, holding my hands close to my chest. "That's all?"

"Yes. That's all."

"I don't want anyone to get hurt."

He tips his head. "Unfortunately, it would be a lie if I said the same."

I prickle. Suddenly wishing I had decided to bring a knife, I take a step back and startle at the crunch beneath my foot.

*Ah. I stepped on my phone.*

I pause to pick it up.

When I look to Ice again, he's already switched to his human form. He carries himself in a passive and nonthreatening manner and honestly seems bored, his hands tucked in the pockets of his unzipped leather jacket. He's not even looking directly at me, but I still feel more uneasy than I did before he morphed.

"What did you want to say?" I stammer.

His gaze flicks in my direction. His expression remains level, but his eyes reflect a greenish hue as the flashlight beam illuminates him, and it lends an air of coldness to his appearance.

"How has James treated you?" he asks.

It's not a question he hasn't asked before, and his tone is light and conversational, but my evening with James at Music@ThePark flashes through my mind, and I hesitate. My heart beats too fast. I tear my eyes from Ice's shadowed face and scan the dark forest floor.

*This time, I don't think I can give an answer he'll accept.*

Night believes this whole mess began because Ice felt like I chose James over him. What would he think if he knew about our relationship? If he learned we're *together*? If he knew I cared for James out of more than just pity or self-preservation?

It's not like I can lie. I'm too nervous, and Ice is too perceptive. *Was coming here a mistake?* Maybe I should have pushed to meet in public, like he originally offered. Getting away from James and Rose might have been a pain, but at least I wouldn't have to deal with *this*.

"Well?" he asks.

*What do I say? I can't say nothing!*

"No complaints," I say finally, meeting his gaze again.

He nods, and I let out the breath I was holding.

"I'm curious, though." His eyes dart away for an instant before refocusing on me. "How on earth did you convince him to stay?"

*What?*

His eyes narrow at my surprise. "You see, Jayde, James agreed to leave your company weeks ago. But he hasn't."

"I—"

He shakes his head, and I shut up. The eerie light his eyes reflect in the dark lends an almost predatory quality to his already cold stare. I can't bring myself to move, speak, or look away.

"Considering the tenuous nature of your current situation, I have to admit I wasn't expecting this," he says, his easy voice carrying little emotion.

As my eyes water, and my hands tremble, something in Ice's expression shifts. The cold malice, if that's even what it was, leaves his eyes, freeing me from the crushing weight of existential dread. He watches wordlessly while I catch my breath, and then sighs.

"Last time we spoke, I was under the impression that your safety was James' main priority, so going back on our agreement doesn't strike me as a sensible move on his part."

*Wait—*

He smiles bitterly. "Perhaps it's my mistake. I placed too much faith in his judgment."

*James agreed to leave?*

No. I don't believe it.

When would they have made such an agreement? Wouldn't he have mentioned something like that?

I open my mouth to argue, but I freeze again. *James doesn't know about the messages either.* He has no idea I agreed to meet Ice tonight *simply because I thought he would be safer if he didn't know. Maybe—*

"I see you weren't aware," he says with a laugh.

I shake my head. "No, I—"

"Never mind that." He sighs. "I'm hardly surprised he didn't tell you, but I am curious as to what happened to change his mind. Did you say something to him?"

I look away.

*Think, Jayde. When did they make this agreement?*

When would they have had enough time to discuss something like that? Has Ice been texting him too, or did they talk some other time? Is he even telling the truth? Is he bluffing?

*Well...*

James finally dropped it, but he asked several times if I wanted him to leave or had anywhere else to go. He never honestly wanted to split up—that much was obvious—but he still asked. Repeatedly. Maybe he held back, unable to commit to leaving until Rose came back. Maybe he thought her arrival would be the perfect excuse to follow through.

Whether or not he could have successfully convinced me in July, he ruined his chance by asserting himself as my boyfriend. It must have been hard to ask again, but he still did, and I demanded he stay.

*How can I tell Ice that? If what Night said is true…*

"I assured your safety should James leave by August," he says. "Why would he put you in danger by staying this long?"

We both knew it was a risk. Even if I had known earlier, I still wouldn't have let him go. Any guarantee that I'll be safe means nothing if James' decision to leave puts him exactly where Ice wants him. *And he wants James dead, so…*

I grit my teeth and glance at my phone. The hand holding it trembles, frustrating me more.

James said he would do anything for me—he would die for me. I was afraid he honestly meant it. He didn't *want* to leave, but what was his plan if I agreed he should? What was Ice's plan if he found out James followed through and was alone?

*Stop worrying about it.*

I ball my free hand into a fist, shift my weight, and look up to meet Ice's careful gaze. He still hasn't moved. His posture remains casual. *He dragged you out here to talk. Just talk!*

"I asked James to stay," I say. "That's why he's still here."

Confusion flashes across his face—a furrowing of his brows, a thinning of his lips—but he quickly smiles again. "Surely, you're bright enough to realize you're better off without that wretched parasite dragging you down? Don't forget he's the reason we're in this mess."

"Do you hear yourself right now? James did nothing wrong!" *What am I saying?* "We're in this mess because you lost your damn mind. This isn't his fault. Or my fault. No. This is all on you, Ice."

He bares his teeth, his eyes wide.

I flinch back, heart racing, fully expecting the worst. I've come to terms with the consequences of my actions, proud enough I managed to speak my mind for once, but he surprises me. Instead of blowing up, he looks away, averting his eyes to glare at nothing while covering the lower half of his face with his fingers.

He's…*brooding?* He's seriously considering what I said?

My muscles relax, but I'm not out of the woods yet—literally and figuratively. Ice is volatile. Unpredictable. *And fast.* This is still terribly dangerous…

"That's harsh," he says vaguely.

"Harsh?" I snap. I struggle to peel my cardigan off without dropping my phone, knowing full well his low-light vision is good enough to see his handiwork. "*This* is harsh. I'm sorry if I hurt your feelings or whatever, but I can't believe you honestly think—"

My accusation threw him off for a second, but he quickly silences me with a passive wave of his hand. I'm still fuming, but my temper cools as he regards me with a more familiar and callous indifference.

"Why is James here?" he asks. "Even if you asked him to stay, why would he listen to you? What did you say to him?"

*Is what I said before not enough?*

Forcing back my rising panic, I remind myself that, despite offending him more than once already, he still hasn't approached me. He's still several paces away, near the edge of the clearing.

He's here to talk. *Just to talk… Breathe…*

"I already told you," I say. "I asked him to stay, so he did."

He blinks. "Just like that? Did he even try to uphold his end of the bargain?"

*Ugh.*

"I think…he did." My voice is quiet and hesitant, weary of the burden I hadn't realized James carried this whole time. "He asked if I wanted him to leave. He tried to convince me to stay with friends or family instead, or…" I sigh. "Anyway, he asked several times, but I always told him to stay."

"Why?" he asks as though the idea is beyond comprehension.

The less he seems to understand, the more apprehensive I become. It's a miracle I ignore the urge to run as he looks from me to his empty hands with wide eyes.

"But James is *nothing*," he says.

"James is better than you!"

His shoulders tense. A flare of anger overtakes his confusion as he glares at me with wild eyes, and his hands ball into fists. The sudden shift in atmosphere leaves me frozen in place and brings the pinprick of tears back to my eyes.

"What did you do?" he asks again, low and dangerous. "What did you *say*?"

"I—"

Something in his voice tells me I won't get another chance to answer, but, at this point, I'm screwed no matter what I say. I take a deep breath, but my heart races, and my courage is quickly waning.

"I think…I love him," I breathe, on the verge of tears.

With a blink, the anger leaves his face, like a slate wiped clean. Now, his narrowed eyes and placid frown betray nothing. *Absolutely nothing.* Then he glances off to the side and tucks his hands back into his jacket pockets.

"I love James, okay? That's why I asked him to stay." When he doesn't respond, I shake my head. "Is that what you wanted to hear? Are you happy now?"

The strength of my voice surprises me, but his outwardly calm demeanor and maintained silence floods me with unease. Whatever it means—whatever he's thinking—it can't be good.

I take another step backward, disturbing the short, dry grass.

He doesn't match my movement. He doesn't even look to see what I'm doing. What would he do if I tried to leave now? If I just took off into the woods?

Would he let me go? Chase after me? *Attack me*?

I wish I knew because every muscle begs me to run. My body knows I'm in danger, and I want to get away—more than anything—but I'm too afraid to try.

Our conversation isn't over quite yet.

*I have to see this through.*

I watch Ice's unmoving figure in silence for what seems like several minutes. My tense legs ache, and the dancing shadows cast behind him by the phone in my trembling hand do nothing to calm my nerves. I just watch him, wide-eyed, for so long.

Then he makes *a sound* that makes me jump.

The sound was short and sharp, like he tried to scoff and clear his throat at the same time. Or, maybe it was some kind of stifled laugh. I don't know. Whatever it was, I did not like it.

"I see," he says coolly.

He turns away, hiding his face completely, but his shoulders remain tense. I hold my breath.

"To be honest, I don't care how you feel—about James or me or anything." His cold, level voice is void of emotion and chills me more than the breeze. "But my patience is wearing thin. If he doesn't stick to the agreement we made, you will both regret it."

*Shit.*

"Just leave us alone." I draw my hands close to my chest again, this time in tight fists. "You have no right to—"

"Oh, trust me, I have every right to do whatever I want." A wry tone slips into his voice as his shoulders shake with silent laughter. "You will regret ever fucking with me, Jayde. James, on the other hand— Well, let's just say he won't have much time for regret."

*James...*

"Goodbye, Jayde."

I turn and race out of the clearing.

He doesn't follow.

* * * * *

I open my eyes, feeling as exhausted as I did when I first laid down. I didn't sleep well.

*How could I, after...?*

I wasn't sure what to expect going into that conversation.

I certainly never thought I'd end up declaring my feelings for James to the *one* person who least needed to know, but denying it would have only prolonged the inevitable. If Ice has been watching the house, he would have figured it out eventually, and it's not like there was anything better I could have said.

*But that final threat…*

At least I know neither of us got what we wanted out of that stupid meeting.

I roll over, accepting the guilt that stabs me as I watch James breathe. He was so relieved after I made up with Rose. As far as he knows, I haven't heard from Ice since the stupid pizza incident.

*But he's been worried this whole time too, right? Since he went back on the deal they made?*

He needs to know.

James deserves the freedom to make his own decision before Ice shows himself with intent to kill one or both of us. But I can't warn him without shattering the illusion of stability I created. I'd have to admit to everything—the texts, the phone calls, last night…

If he knew what Ice said, he would freak out.

*God…*

I hold my hands over my mouth, fighting back tears.

This is the same stupid mess I got myself into with Rose, only so much worse. I never had a good reason to believe Ice would back off if I ignored him. Acting like everything was fine only put us in grave danger. Because of me, James' life is on the line again. *Not to mention Rose…*

Even so, I'm sure James doesn't care. He's hiding things from me too. I don't blame him, so I'm sure he would understand. I'm sure he would forgive me, but…

*How can I tell him now?*

If I confessed to meeting with Ice… If James knew what he

said... *I would lose him.* He would almost certainly choose my safety over his own. He would leave—and he's right; how could I stop him if he set his mind to it? Then Ice could easily catch him alone, *and I cannot let that happen.*

I press my forehead to his warm back.

He shifts slightly, but I don't move. Then he rolls over and looks at me with sleepy eyes. But he kisses me, and I cling to him with my face buried in his chest to hide the budding tears.

"Hm..." His hands move to my back as he pulls me closer. "Everything okay?"

I nod. "Just a nightmare."

He kisses the top of my head. I wish it made me feel better, but it only makes me feel worse.

# forty-seven

It's still there.

The feeling hasn't eased up in the least. A tickle of concern. A hint of unease. The itchy sensation of being watched by some malevolent force hiding just out of sight. *And an overwhelming fear of death.* But I ignore it.

I ignore it, and I move forward with plans to go swimming with Rose, who invited me and James the instant we came downstairs this morning. Most of my scars are out in the open now, and neither my shoulder nor my wrist bother me enough to outweigh my desire *to get the hell out of the house and as far away from it as possible.*

Staring at my reflection in the mirror, I massage the scar on my palm and try to decide which swimsuit to wear. *Guess it doesn't matter what I pick since I'm not taking my shirt off.* I'd hate to ruin the afternoon by exposing the slice on my side too.

I grab the first mismatched bikini top and bottom I see and change. Then I pull on a tank top and a pair of athletic shorts. The knit wristband goes on last, and I look myself over again. The comfortable outfit. The River Sapphire resting below my collarbone.

*Should I take it off?*

*Does everyone have a point? Is it weird to keep wearing it?*

I shake my head. It doesn't matter. Right now, I just need to calm down and hang out with my friends and...*hope for the best.*

Back downstairs, Rose grins at me, looking very much like her usual self, and James' expression is soft and warm, and both things ease my mind as we chat before heading out.

We take Rose's coupe, obviously. It's small, but it has AC and lacks any negative association in my memory. James is in the backseat, reading on his phone between contributing to the conversation Rose carries almost single-handedly.

We're going to the swimming hole her friends took her to last week. She hadn't been there before, but she must have liked it.

"You haven't gone swimming at all yet, have you?" she asks.

"Nope," I say mildly. "Honestly, it never crossed my mind until you mentioned it last week, but it will be nice to get out of town for a few hours."

"Yo, James; you like swimming?"

He glances up from his phone. "Not...really."

"Then why'd you agree to go?" she asks with a laugh.

"Because Jayde wanted to go," he says, flashing a nervous smile. "I mean, I can swim just fine, and I used to love swimming as a kid, but— Well, I guess it's not as fun as I remember."

I sigh. "I think I get what you mean. It's like... I want to go swimming, but something about it makes me nervous."

"Oh—" His expression shifts, and he looks down at his phone. "Yeah, that's basically it."

Rose sighs. "We could have done something else."

"I want to go to the river," I protest—*and not just because I want everyone out of the house.*

The swimming hole is an hour west of Riverview, far enough from town that my anxiety fades almost completely. Far enough, I'm certain we're safe as Rose parks her car on the side of the highway.

I approach the guardrail and look out over the river. The water is deep and slow-moving. Down the steep embankment, I can just make out a small, pebbly beach and several rocks near the riverbank that would be perfect for jumping. I see why Rose liked it. A couple years ago, I would have been all over this too. *But, now...*

"The trail's this way," she says, walking down the shoulder of the road.

Hesitating, I hug my beach towel to my chest. James rests a hand on my shoulder.

"You good?" he asks.

I force a smile. "Yeah. I'm fine. I just feel weird that being out here is such a relief. You know?"

"Yeah." He glances away, and I know he knows exactly what I'm saying, but he quickly looks back and mirrors my smile. "I haven't left town in a while either. It's nice."

"Are you coming or what?" Rose calls, having stopped several yards ahead.

"We're coming!"

I grab James' hand and start down the road toward her.

She shows us the rough trail that winds down the hill to the riverbank. At first glance, I'm a little nervous, but it's not as treacherous as it looks, and we make it down quickly. Most of the beach is still in the sun. Heat soaks into my skin, but being so close to the water keeps it from being uncomfortable.

I lay my towel on the smoothest surface I can find. And I sit. Rose dumps her things next to mine and strips down to her swimsuit. James, standing off to the other side, glances at her. Then he glances at me before looking out over the river.

He did not bring a towel, but he sits close to mine.

"You're not gonna swim at all, are you?" I ask.

He frowns. "I might go in for a minute."

"Jeez." Rose laughs, fluffing up her hair. "You really should have told me you didn't wanna swim before we left. We could have gone hiking instead—or camping, since I don't go back to work until Monday."

*Maybe I should have. Camping doesn't sound bad.*

With a sigh, I stretch my legs and lean back. "Honestly, Rose, I don't mind hanging out here. And it's not like we won't have a good time just because we don't swim."

"Okay," she agrees, narrowing her eyes. "Feel free to change your mind, though. And don't forget to put sunscreen on, you guys. Last time, one of my friends forgot, and the sun fucked her up."

I stifle a laugh. "Will do."

She grins and flashes a thumbs-up before splashing into the calm water. Once it's up to her knees, she dives in. Her head pops above the surface further out, and she gasps.

"Fair warning: It's a little cold!"

"Noted," I call back.

As she swims toward one of the rocks protruding from the water, I turn to James. He looks distracted—lost in thought, I guess.

I tap his shoulder. "You don't like swimming?"

"It's not that I don't like swimming." He sighs and meets my gaze with a mild frown. "I just don't like…taking my shirt off?"

"Oh. Well, me either, you know?"

"Mm…"

I offer a smile. "Maybe I'd feel better about swimming if I still owned a one-piece. But I tossed it before I moved because I never wore it. I mean, I guess I can swim with clothes on, but it's a little awkward, right?"

He nods. His eyes linger on me for a few seconds before he clears his throat and glances away to look out over the river again.

Rose waves at us from atop a rock a good three feet above the water. I wave back, and she jumps, sending a column of glittering water into the air as she cannonballs. Sitting in the sun and watching her swim does make me want to get in.

I dig the sunscreen out of the tote bag she dropped. My chest and shoulders *will* burn if I don't use any.

"I haven't gone swimming in a while," James says quietly. "Only a few times with Matt. Once or twice alone, but…"

"Is there a reason?"

The faintest smile crosses his lips. "Not really."

When I'm done with the sunscreen, I offer the bottle to him. He does not hesitate before accepting it.

"I bet you sunburn bad," I say.

He laughs. "You would be correct."

I watch with pursed lips as he applies the sunscreen to his face, arms, and calves. *Hm... What does he look like without a shirt on?*

Oh.

For the first time in my life, I'm glad direct sunlight turns my cheeks red.

A half-hour later, it's too hot to continue sitting in the sun. I pull my hair into a bun. Then we leave our shoes with my towel and wade into the shallows. The water is cold and sends a crispness up through the rest of my body, but the current is gentle, and it feels good after sunbathing for so long.

I wet my hands and pat my cheeks.

Rose jumps off another rock several feet out, where the river's bottom drops off into deep water. The resulting wave splashes up my thigh, and I shiver.

Then James, standing beside me, asks if I'm wearing a swimsuit. I don't know why it makes me laugh. But it does.

"Of course, but—" I lift the hem of my shirt just enough to reveal the scarring on my side and lower my voice. "I don't want her to know how bad it really was. That's why I wish I had my old one-piece."

He glances away, scratching his shoulder. "One thing at a time, I guess. I'm just glad you guys are talking again."

"Hey, dorks!" Rose calls. Once again perched atop the rock's highest point, she plants her hands on her hips. "You sure you don't wanna jump in? Not even once?"

"I don't know," I call back. "Maybe in a minute."

She jumps into the water. As she goes under, James reaches

for my hand. His skin is rough against the scarring on my palm, but it doesn't hurt, and my fingers no longer tingle with a strange numbness when I close them. I stare at our interlaced hands.

*What is this feeling?*

"Jayde."

I glance up. "What?"

"Dunno." He blinks. "I just wanted to say your name, I guess."

I laugh and splash him with my free hand. "Come on. We came all the way out here, right? If you don't actually hate swimming, we should jump at least once. Rose will nag us forever if we don't. And I kinda want to try."

He hesitates, his eyes a bit wide. Then he smiles and nods. "Okay. Let's do it."

\* \* \* \* \*

I yawn as we walk inside.

It's getting late, the sky growing dark, but we already ate, so I suppose I'm free to relax. I'm pretty sore, though—an unpleasant surprise, considering I didn't do much beyond swimming out to the rock, jumping in twice, and swimming back to the shallows.

"I call the shower first," Rose says as I lock the front door.

She hands her take-home box to me and drops her tote bag on the couch before darting toward the stairs. I wasn't about to stop her, so I'm not sure what the rush is.

*Maybe she just had to pee.*

With a sigh, I continue into the kitchen. I open the fridge and take the second take-home box from James.

"So…" I say, if only to break the silence as I rearrange the top shelf to better accommodate the leftovers. "I know you haven't gone swimming in a while, but you had a good time, right?"

"Yeah. It was fun."

"Good. I'm glad we went."

"Me too."

I push the boxes a bit further in before closing the fridge door and turning around. To my surprise, James, who stands quite close, looks somewhat nervous. Not like…*bad* nervous, but more like… flustered nervous? *Shy? What does that mean?*

I tip my head, and his eyes grow a bit wide.

"Hey," he says. "Would you be upset if I said I find you very attractive."

*Uh—* "No, but I'm sure there's a less weird way to say that."

We stare at each other for a moment, but I'm not sure what I'm looking for in his soft, muted expression. Or how I should feel.

Then he says, "Well, I find you very attractive, and I thought you should know."

"Thanks?" I laugh, but my cheeks feel like they're on fire. "You know, you're not so bad yourself. Um… Actually, you're pretty cute. Especially when you really smile. I mean, your eyes do this thing where they get kind of crinkly and sparkle, and—"

One of those exact smiles sneaks onto his face. His thumb slides up my jaw as his fingers come to rest at the back of my neck. And he kisses me. It's not even the first time we've kissed today, and maybe it's obvious where this was leading, but my breath still catches. I still didn't see it coming. Every time he kisses me or I find the courage to kiss him, it blows my mind to think *we're really together. This is really happening.*

He pulls away, and his hand leaves my face, but I resist the distance between us. An unexpected warmth floods me as I stare into his eyes.

"I think I'm in love with you," I say, the words falling from my lips like water.

He draws a breath. Something about it—the sound or the tiny shift in his expression or *something*—sets off a switch in my brain. Before that train of thought has a chance to finish or James has a chance to respond, I recall what Rose said during the movie yesterday, and my face catches fire.

*Aaaaaaa—*

Bursting into laughter, I cover my face with my hands. He pats my head and chuckles in a way that absolutely does not help.

"You okay?" he asks.

"Yep. I'm fine." I slap my cheeks and look up with a smile. "Just finally having one of those *weird thoughts* I'm sure you're used to. Must have sucked to be you this whole time."

"It, uh— It still sucks," he stammers.

Then his wide eyes dart off to the side, and I find myself laughing again. But I pull myself together and take his hand in mine. He relaxes the moment I touch him.

"Come on. I feel weird standing around in the kitchen."

We head upstairs and into the bedroom. For an instant, I feel like I'm seeing the room clearly for the first time in weeks. A worn throw blanket on my bed. A flat pillow in one of my spare pillowcases.

I glance at James and at my bed again, and I drop his hand before turning to face my reflection instead. Irrationally frustrated, I peel the still-damp sweatband off my wrist, pull my tank top off over my head, and set both on the dresser.

When I catch James watching me in the mirror, my breath comes a bit more quickly.

I glance over my shoulder, and our eyes meet. He looks antsy again, but, even though I know every scar is clearly visible thanks to my bikini top, I offer him a smile.

"So, yeah, this is my swimsuit. Anyway, I think I'll shower in the morning, so I'm just gonna change into pajamas now. If you don't mind."

He blinks, his face taking on some color, and then shakes his head. "Okay, uh… I'll go downstairs and change real fast." He grabs his backpack from the foot of the bed, and his eyes flick up to meet mine. "Be right back."

I wasn't insinuating he should *leave*, but I don't have the guts to stop him from opening the door and stepping out. Though, I do spend an uncomfortably long time staring at the closed door after he does. *Wow.* I don't know much about James, but I'm starting to get some squirrelly virgin vibes myself.

With a sigh, I dig my silk pajamas out of the dresser—the set I haven't worn once since I bought them. I finish changing and check myself out in the mirror.

I might have gained a couple pounds since the end of spring term, *but the injuries are… Hm…* I'm sure they'll heal up decently, like everyone at the hospital said, but they're still annoying, and the scabbed-over gouge on my shoulder is kind of gross.

*Ugh.* If James has had a serious girlfriend before, she was an immortal and certainly way prettier than I am. Probably way less awkward too. But, for whatever reason, he likes me anyway, so…

*I shouldn't worry about it, right?*

I let my hair down from the messy bun and brush it out. I take the River Sapphire off and set it on the end table beside my face-down phone. Then I take some ibuprofen and sit on the edge of the bed.

And I wait.

Eventually, there's a soft knock on the door. James carefully steps through and closes the door behind himself. He did change —now wearing sweatpants and a t-shirt—and he crosses the room to sit beside me. Neither of us say anything. We just sit and watch each other with what feels like passive caution.

Then he clears his throat. "You look good. Ah… I mean, that fabric looks really soft."

"Thanks." I glance down and mess with the hem. The material is incredibly thin and soft. "It's silk. Believe it or not, I bought these the day I bumped into you at the mall."

"Yeah?"

"Yeah."

A sudden gloom washes over me. The weight of how much pain we've both suffered, and the weight of every secret I'm still keeping.

My hands ball in my lap. After a beat of silence, James reaches out to touch my camisole. His hand slides from my stomach to my waist, warmth pricking my skin through the delicate fabric.

"It is soft," he breathes.

A shiver runs down my spine.

My eyes flick up, but it's hard to say what he might be thinking. His expression is murky and curious. His eyes are locked on his hand. And, for some reason, my mind feels completely blank.

"I never thought you'd see me wearing this," I admit with a half-hearted laugh. His eyes meet mine, but I keep talking. "That day at the mall... After you walked off, I couldn't stop wondering what your deal was. You were so weird. And now you're here... Staying at my house... Sleeping in my bed... And I'm in love with you. How is that possible?"

"I don't know..."

*The faintest hint of a scar across the bridge of his nose.*

My smile falters, and my eyes fill with tears. "I'm sorry. I'm sorry I told Ice about you. I'm sorry he hurt you. If I knew how he felt, I—"

He kisses me, pulling me closer as his other hand tangles in my hair. My fingers relax their grip on my shorts, but I'm too nervous to move my hands from my thighs. I feel like...*no matter how much I want this, I don't deserve it.*

"I don't care about that," he says, his voice soft. "I don't care about Ice. I don't care if I get hurt. I don't care about anything but you. If you're worried about something, tell me. I want to help."

*Why didn't you tell me why you were worried? Why did I have to find out from Ice?*

"I'm just tired," I mumble.

*Of all of this.*

# forty-eight

~ ∞ ~

*I'm...standing?*

*For a moment, I hear nothing.*

*Then a crisp, delicate voice cuts through the silence:*

*"Jayde, you're asleep."*

As I open my eyes, I recognize my dreamscape. The void is the same as usual—black and empty, save for hundreds of tiny, white lights that hang in the air like lazy fireflies.

I turn to find Night standing a few paces away, her form brightly illuminated against the vast darkness. As with the last time I saw her, her short, black hair and pale nightdress shift as though disturbed by a light breeze I can't feel.

"I'm so glad I found you," she says, though her brows furrow, and she wrings her hands. "Ice has been acting...strange for some time now, but something was especially off about him today. Of course, he won't tell me anything. I, ah... Well, I don't suppose you have any idea?"

*Ah... I've been trying to forget.*

"I met with him the other night."

"You met with him?" she gasps. "Alone?"

"Yeah, but he didn't do anything," I say. "I mean, he started texting me out of nowhere about a week ago. I blocked him after he wouldn't stop asking to meet up even though I said no a million times, but he messaged me from another number. He threatened Rose. I didn't have a choice."

She frowns, tipping her head. "Why? What was he expecting to get out of meeting with you?"

"I don't know, but I doubt he even got to say what he wanted."

"Well, what did he say?"

"Not much. I only stuck around a few minutes," I mumble, but I hesitate as fragments of a conversation I wish I could forget cycle through my mind. "Wait, no— He asked about James. I guess they made some agreement a while back. James said he would leave, and Ice wanted to know why he never did."

"He wanted James to leave?" Night touches her face and looks away. "Which one of you was he hoping to catch alone, I wonder?"

"I have no idea—not that I want to know."

"And you?" Her eyes dart up to meet mine, careful and uneasy. "What did you tell him? Why did James decide to stay?"

*Of course, she would ask...*

"I told the truth?" I sigh. "I asked James to stay. I didn't know about their stupid deal, but I knew he wouldn't be okay on his own. I guess it wasn't enough, though. He wanted to know exactly what I said, so I told him. I told Ice that I'm in love with James."

"You love him?" she echoes in mild surprise.

"Anyway, he shut me down after that. The conversation was

over, and I took off before anything bad could happen."

She doesn't seem to mind that I didn't answer her question, but her confusion shifts to concern. "Did he say anything else? Anything at all?"

"He said I'd regret it if James doesn't leave, but—"

She nods. "You won't ask him to. I understand."

"But what should I do?" I ask, balling my hands into fists. "You should have seen him. He was seriously out of it."

"I'm aware," she agrees, the dejection clear in her low voice as she glances toward the ground. "I've seen more than enough at home to know he's not doing well. He's been rather agitated the past couple weeks, so I'm hardly surprised he'd react that way after not getting the answer he wanted."

"This isn't my fault," I say dryly.

She sighs. "Sorry. I didn't mean it like that. But I'll try to keep a closer eye on Ice."

"It's not your fault either." I take a breath, but I only feel more anxious. "Thanks for checking in with me, anyway."

My dreamscape falls quiet for a long, tense, awkward moment. I don't know what else to say, and she frowns and looks around as her hair flutters in her strange personal breeze.

Then she meets my gaze. "*Are* you in love with James?"

"I—"

*Sitting in bed, both too scared to actually do anything. James wants to take it slow. Maybe it's because I'm human. Maybe he's more emotionally fragile than I am. Either way, I feel like...*

"Never mind," she says, glancing away again. "I should go. Please take care—both of you."

I want to ask for advice or at least admit that James doesn't know about Ice's threats, and I probably should, but I can't bring myself to. Instead, I assure her that I'll keep the door locked. It doesn't seem to placate her, but she nods, and we exchange small waves. Then her body fades into a fine, silvery mist, vanishing completely as it settles on the inky floor.

Without Night, my dreamscape feels lonely, but the firefly lights continue twinkling and drifting gently through the dark. If I weren't so anxious, I might consider it pretty. It might have been soothing.

*Hiding Ice's texts was a mistake.* I know that. I've accepted that. All I can do now is stay alert and try to avoid a repeat of anything like what went down at Reid Manor last month.

That's all I can do.

~ ∞ ~

# forty-nine

Convincing James and Rose to go out again is easy. After all, it's a beautiful, sunny Saturday morning. Why shouldn't we get out and do something?

I dress reasonably, opting to wear shorts and one of my new shirts with three-quarter length sleeves. I adjust my wristband and put my hair up into a bun that, while still messy, doesn't look as haphazardly thrown together as usual. I even do my makeup for the first time in weeks, even if it is only eyeliner, mascara, and tinted lip balm.

James knocks on the door before letting himself in. My guilt upon seeing him is barely noticeable over the persistent, itchy dread crawling up my spine. *The same paranoia as the Fourth of July. The same crushing darkness I felt before stepping foot in Ice's house for the last time.*

He smiles at me. "Ready to go?"

"Yeah, I—" I take a breath as the worst passes, then I return his smile. "Let's have another good day, alright?"

He nods, and we join Rose downstairs. I immediately feel more comfortable once we're all out of the house, buckled into the air-conditioned car, and on our way to a crowded public location.

First stop: Riverview's Saturday farmer's market.

We buy a few things. Locally grown nectarines, berries, and purple carrots. A loaf of artisanal sourdough that we eat by the handful as we browse the remaining stalls. The bread reminds us that we haven't had lunch, so we head to a food truck and grab something more substantial.

As we slowly make our way back through the market, James points out a flyer posted on a power pole. It's an advertisement for an art festival held at a smaller park near Riverview Community College, clear across town. It's open this weekend only, so we decide to leave the farmer's market to check it out.

"Are you an artist or something?" Rose asks during the drive.

"No way," he says from the back seat. "I'm a consumer only."

"He thought about writing a book, I guess," I say.

"But not writing manga?"

"Hey!" He laughs. "For someone who thinks anime and manga are lame, you sure bring it up a lot. But, no. I suck at drawing, and I've never tried to write manga. I've never even read manga."

"Oh, wow. But you have watched anime. How many?"

"I don't know," he says, sounding a bit defensive. "Who keeps track of that kind of thing?"

I roll my eyes and resist the near-overwhelming urge to tell James that Rose has watched a few anime series on Netflix. *They can work that out for themselves.*

Upon arriving at the art festival, my first impression is that it's the type of event Night would love. There's live music, and several of the vendors are similar to, if not the exact same as, those who attended the solstice festival. Other vendors are selling finer arts and interesting crafts like paintings, handmade quilts, scrap metal lawn ornaments, and delicate glass figurines.

James keeps trying to buy things for me. Every time I show interest in a random piece or bauble, he asks if I want it—like he's itching to buy just about anything. But, thanks to Rose, I own more than enough objectively useless things already. Eventually, he stops asking, though he does buy a pressed leaf bookmark for himself. I don't ask, but I figure it'll join the wooden one hanging from the rear-view mirror in his car.

We spend well over an hour wandering around the art festival, never running into anyone we know or who knows us. I glance at the people walking by our table. Humans. Immortals. None of them seem to notice me at all.

It's strange how…*separated from reality I feel.*

"What's next?" Rose asks. When I look over, she's gazing into her half-empty smoothie cup. "How long do you guys wanna stay out?"

James shrugs. "Doesn't matter to me."

"Maybe we can just hang out around here until dinner," I say. "I mean, it's not too hot out, and the music is nice. Why leave?"

"Sounds good," she agrees.

We find a spot in the shade of a tree away from the main event, where we can still hear the live band, and we hang out as a group. We laugh and talk about a ton of things that don't really matter. Rose's trip to Arizona. Her cousin and the new baby. How she and I first became friends in fourth grade—James' surprise at her more demure past makes me laugh, though I know it's a huge contrast from the stories I told before. We talk about classes we plan to take next term. Things we could do next weekend on her days off.

James does more listening than talking, but he seems invested, and Rose stopped glancing at the scars on my forearms every few minutes.

It's nice. I wish my life could always be like this.

* * * * *

I almost forgot about Ice, but Rose brings up dinner again, and I remember we have to go home.

I do not want to go home, but I can't *say* that. When we left this morning, going home was always an inevitability. Obviously. We live there, so we have to go back.

"What are you guys thinking?" she asks.

When I don't answer, James suggests burgers. She approves, and I have no real opinion, so we leave the park and stop at the In-N-Out halfway between RCC and Oakwood.

I ate here with Rose several times during the school year, but the safe, familiar atmosphere does nothing to combat my rising anxiety. Even so, I do my best to keep calm and have a good time.

We continue chatting and laughing, and James plays a more active role in the conversation than he did at the park. Though, a haunting awareness of danger looms over me, and it only worsens as we pay the check and leave.

Rose parks in front of the cottage, and I stare at the front door at the end of the concrete path. *It's the same. It's the same feeling. The exact same as before… Before I… Before Ice…*

I shake my head to banish the thought and step out of the car.

James and Rose walk through the door and head straight for the kitchen while I hang behind in the living room. They have the cooler bag full of produce, and they're still chatting about whatever we were talking about before we left the car.

I doubt they notice me lock the deadbolt on the front door or peer through the blinds to scan the parking lot. The sun is about to set, but I don't see anything out of the ordinary—*and certainly no silver Porsche*—so I crush my concern down and drop my purse on the couch on my way to the kitchen.

"It's a good thing we ate out," Rose says. She gives the fridge a judgmental once-over while rearranging the contents. "We'll starve if we go on like this much longer."

"We can go shopping tomorrow," I say.

James already has plans to hang out with Matthew in the afternoon, but it will be nice to get Rose out of the house too—even if it's only for an hour or so.

I still don't understand Ice's end goal. He obviously has it out for James, but I keep thinking about what Night said. What's to say he isn't also waiting for another opportunity to catch me on my own when there isn't a promise of nonviolence? Avoiding any situation in which I'm home alone is probably the safest bet.

James, sitting at the table, glances up from his phone with the tiniest frown. "I was gonna ask if you wanted to come with me."

"I'll go next time," I say. "Just have fun with Matt. It's better if I go shopping with Rose, anyway. I know some of what you like, so maybe we'll end up with food everyone will eat."

His eyes narrow, and I flash an unapologetic grin. Rose must have missed both because she doesn't laugh.

She closes the fridge and leans her back against the nearest counter. "Good idea, Jay," she agrees while navigating her phone. "I'll write the list, but I'd hate to embarrass anyone here. Just text me what your picky boyfriend likes."

"I'm not even picky," he protests.

I reach across the table and pat his head. When his expression softens, I turn back to Rose, who seems busy typing up a shopping list between glancing through cabinets.

"You like white or whole wheat bread?" she asks.

James sighs. "Doesn't matter. I'm not picky."

She snickers. "White bread it is."

"One second," I say, crossing the kitchen again. "Gotta grab my phone."

As my foot leaves the linoleum and hits carpet, I hear something from the second floor. *The softest tap.* At first, I justify the sound as the AC kicking on, but a chill runs down my spine, and I freeze.

*Upstairs—*

A white cat perched on the second-floor railing.

The cat's piercing blue eyes meet mine, and it jumps off the banister, morphing in midair. I stumble back to avoid him, but Ice nails the landing and catches me by the wrist before I put enough distance between us. Pain jolts up my arm as he twirls me around and pins it behind me. My shoulder blade presses into his chest as he holds me tight.

My stomach twists, a flare of panicked revulsion. But I'm not alone here. *And, knowing Ice, I'm not the one in most danger.*

*Everyone else—?*

James saw everything. He was at the table facing me the whole time. But all he's managed to do is stand and knock over the chair he was sitting in.

Rose, on the other hand, fell. Her phone skidded a couple feet away. She looks up with wide eyes as she takes in the scene from the floor. She's well beyond Ice's reach, clear across the kitchen and half-crouched against the counter. I can only hope he doesn't have a gun.

"You two just love ignoring me, don't you?" he asks, his voice a low growl. "But I am done being ignored, Jayde."

*This really is my fault, isn't it?*

"How?" James asks sharply.

"How did I get in?" His easy laughter jostles me, but I don't dare move—not only is my left arm pinned, but I feel cool metal at my neck. *The broad side of a knife.* "I copied a key weeks ago, you idiot."

"Who the fuck is that?" Rose asks, her voice both shrill and hushed as she lifts one hand in a way that, at first glance, appears disarming.

Then, slowly, and without taking her eyes off us, she reaches for her dropped phone with her other hand. The movement is subtle and low to the floor, but Ice will certainly notice if I did. She means well, but I already told her she absolutely cannot call the police.

*This changes nothing.*

"Don't move!" Ice and I call simultaneously.

Her hand freezes.

She offers her phone a desperate look before glancing between my face, Ice behind me, and James. He hasn't moved from the table, has both hands raised in submission, and looks like he's about to burst into tears. Upon seeing this, Rose retracts her hand and returns her attention to the *literal hostage situation* playing out before her.

My arm aches, my shoulder twisted at an off angle.

"If you don't know who I am, I won't bother explaining," Ice says. His voice is level, his breathing steady, as though he's having a normal conversation rather than holding me at knife-point. "This girl is better at deception than I thought. I can tell by the dumb look on James' face alone. You never saw this coming. What? Did you think I forgot?"

*Please don't.*

But something in what he said seems to click for James. The wild panic washes from his face, and he frowns. He glances away. Then he lowers his hands, assuming a more defensive posture.

"Let her go," he says. "Your fight's with me, not her."

Rose gasps. "Wait... That's him? *That's* Ice?"

Ice tenses but quickly recovers, and the light pressure held to my neck vanishes. I hear the knife click shut and, from the corner of my eye, watch him slip it into a pocket. Speaking now would be easy, but I can't imagine anything I say would improve the situation.

"*That's him?*" he asks with a laugh. "What is that supposed to mean? What type of person were you expecting?"

I frown bitterly.

He still has my arm pinned, but I am *pissed* and, with the knife out of the way, finally feel up to struggling. He does nothing to stop or acknowledge me—not that my squirming has any effect.

"You did this?" Rose hisses, inching her way up the counter.

*Oh, she is* furious.

Ice ignores her, but I stop trying to pry his hand off my aching wrist and instead wave my free hand frantically in front of my chest, mouthing *"don't move; stay there"* in hopes she'll get the message. She reacts with obvious and angry confusion, but she sinks back down to the linoleum.

*This is so bad.*

Rose is a total wildcard.

At the very least, James knows the stakes and has a fighting chance, but Ice already made it clear that Rose means nothing to him. She's human—worthless and expendable. I have no reason to believe he would think twice before hurting her if she happened to get in his way.

*Please don't think you can stop him.*

"Again, Jayde, I have no real interest in hurting you," he says mildly. "James is right. For once."

He can't be serious. He came here to fight?

*This is worse than I thought.*

Desperate, I look to James. He meets my gaze and swallows hard. His face is pale, petrified, but his jaw sets in determination.

And he looks past me to accept Ice's challenge.

"Wonderful."

*Stop!*

I elbow Ice in the side, solidly contacting ribs, but he doesn't flinch. Instead, he releases his grip on the forearm twisted behind my back. When, on instinct, I draw it to my chest to rub the tender skin with my other hand, he grasps the back of my shirt and tosses me off to one side. I stumble into the fridge, halfway between Rose and Ice.

"Get her out of here," James calls. "Now!"

I don't know whether the words were directed at me or Rose, but it doesn't matter. I'm frozen, stuck to the fridge and desperately wishing I could stop them. But James dodges the first punch and trips Ice up with a dining chair. And all I can do is watch.

I'm too scared to look away.

But watching won't change anything.

Watching is useless.

*I am useless.*

A hand wraps around my wrist. I finally suck in another breath, and my focus leaves the fight as blonde hair and grey eyes streak in front of me.

"Rose," I say, the sound of my voice foreign and distant as she pulls me forward and tears me away from the spot I was glued to.

"Jayde, move!"

*Hey, wait—*

I don't want to leave the kitchen. Anything could happen while I'm not looking. But she doesn't stop. She shoves me through the open washroom door and slams it shut once we're both inside.

The solid *click* of the privacy lock shocks me back to reality.

I look away from the mirror reflecting my blank terror. Rose's expression is dark and animalistic as she stands with her back to the locked door, chest heaving with the effort of having dragged me across the kitchen with little help on my part.

The commotion of a struggle permeates the room's thin walls. I still can't move.

"That's it," she says breathlessly. "I'm calling the police."

*The phone. I didn't realize—*

"Rose, wait—!" I close the distance between us, and my hands reach out to immobilize hers.

For a moment, neither of us speak.

I listen to our heavy breathing and the continued shuffling and muffled insults thrown in the kitchen. I watch her face while she stares at our hands and the phone trapped within them.

We both start as *a body* slams into the wall to my right.

I shake my head to organize my thoughts.

"You can't call anyone," I say, keeping my voice low. "Trust me. I've been through this before. When it comes to Ice, the police can't do anything to help."

*If she calls, he will find a way to twist this around and get us in trouble. It'll be July all over again.*

"But—"

A second crash cuts her off.

The house falls eerily silent.

My breath catches, the warmth draining from my cheeks as a pit settles in my stomach. I drop Rose's hands and stare at the wall from which the final crash came behind, holding my breath to better listen.

*Several seconds pass.*

*It's too quiet.*

"—What?" James asks distantly, his tone indecipherable.

I hear nothing but my racing heart and heavy breathing.

Then the sharp crack of shattering glass in the kitchen spooks me again. A gentler tinkling follows the initial break as pieces fall to the floor. *A familiar sound.*

More silence.

*What...happened?*

I shove Rose out of the way, scramble to unlock the door with shaky hands, and burst out of the washroom.

James isn't in my immediate field of view, but neither is Ice. The window above the kitchen sink is broken. Shards of glass are strewn about both the counter and floor nearby.

Ice must have left through the window.

*But where is—?*

I turn to check the rest of the room, and James stumbles into view. *Limping. Favoring his left side.* As he reaches the counter and places a hand on the edge, he turns to lean his back against it. I assess his condition from a distance. My eyes lock onto his chest immediately, but my mind refuses to process what I see.

"Fucker still fights dirty," he groans.

*No.*

*No way.*

The knife is...*sticking out of his chest.*

# fifty

Behind me, Rose screams. "Oh, god. Oh, fuck. We have to call *someone*."

"Rose." My voice is numb, and I say the opposite of what I'd like to. "Please, don't call anyone. I—"

*What do I do?*

James glances down at the handle of the knife. He was hit in the right side of his chest, a few inches below the collarbone. Bile rises in my throat as his face pales.

He looks up again. "I think I need to sit."

*That does it.*

I glance over my shoulder to make sure Rose isn't on her phone before rushing to help James into the only dining chair that wasn't knocked over during their scuffle. He groans, leaning back to look at me.

"He fuckin' stabbed me."

"Yeah, I see that. Please don't move."

He's dazed as hell, but he reacts with some level of composure and nods agreeably. I drop to a half-kneel to get a better look at what we're dealing with.

Besides the obvious *knife stuck in his chest*, he's favoring his left side—*a broken rib, maybe? Was he hit there? Or kicked? I don't know.* His shirt is torn—*no visible blood*—and a faint bruise is already blooming at his temple. The knife's blade, which is at least three or four inches long, appears completely embedded. All I see is the ivory handle. The wound is barely bleeding, just a small bloom of red around the base.

As far as I can tell, he only has the one serious injury, but who knows what damage the knife might have done internally. There are several vital things within the chest cavity that have no business ever coming in contact with the blade of a knife.

I chew the inside of my cheek.

*The three-hour first aid course I took last fall did nothing to prepare me for this. What did I even learn?*

"What should we do?" Rose whimpers.

"I don't know," I snap. "You're the nursing major here."

She laughs, the short sound dark and shaky. "Alright. Assess his condition— Okay. Fine. He's conscious and responsive, but, um, there's a fucking *knife* sticking out of his chest. Call 911!"

"We can't!"

*Obviously, she's right.*

This injury is well beyond the scope of basic first aid. He needs real medical attention. The hospital. Doctors. Surgeons. Common sense dictates I call 911.

*But I can't.*

James may be defective, but he's still an immortal, and he once mentioned that 911 is reserved for human emergencies. A normal ambulance would take him to Riverview General Hospital, right? For all I know, he could die if he ended up at the wrong hospital. And RDP will definitely show up if I tell a 911 operator that he was *stabbed in my kitchen.*

But who the hell *am* I supposed to call in an immortal-related emergency?

*Okay. Breathe.*

Right now, he seems stable enough. We should have time.

I stand to keep my leg from giving out on me. Rose clutches her phone in a hand held firmly to her chest and stares at me in fearful desperation, but I don't know what to do any more than she does.

*God...* I knew Ice was upset, but I never expected *this.*

As I look around, hoping an idea will come to me, I notice Rose's expression shift. Her cheeks blanch as her attention locks onto something behind me.

"Jayde, he—"

A sound—something clattering to the floor.

I turn to check on James.

While I was distracted, he stood up, toppling the chair in the process. I scan him again, checking for anything I might have missed during my initial assessment. His shirt is torn. No blood. A bruise forming at his temple. His shaky hand reaches toward his chest—toward the knife.

He glances up from his hand to meet my gaze as his fingers close around the handle. My hands fly up to cover my mouth, and I shake my head. But I can't seem to move.

"It's fine," he says.

He tugs once. The blade slides out with a sick, wet sound, and a spray of blood follows it. The impact of warm liquid like someone splashed me with a glass of hot water. Rose screams again. I stare at the red staining my striped shirt, unable to breathe.

Then James drops the knife. As it clatters to the floor, he looks *relieved.*

"What—" I stumble forward and slam my hands over the gushing wound. "Are you insane?!"

I drag him down to his knees before trying to apply more even pressure as we sit on the floor. *How is this happening?* It's such a small wound. It's only the width of a knife's blade, but blood slips through my useless fingers and soaks the front of his pale t-shirt.

"What do we do?" Rose shrieks. "I really should—"

"Do not call 911!"

"Well, who *can* we call?"

"Um…"

James stares at my bloody hands in amazement. Or disbelief. It's hard to say exactly what's going through his mind considering what he just did.

"Hey, look at me," I say.

His wide, amber eyes track slowly upward to meet mine.

*This is very bad.*

"Am I dying?" he asks, his voice blank.

I shake my head and assure him that he *will not die,* but blood spills between my fingers. I can't even tell if my hand's in the right place, as hot liquid flows down my arms and onto my thighs in streams before pooling on the white linoleum between us. It fills the air with a salty, metallic tang and turns my stomach.

There's no end to it. No stopping it.

*It's too much. We don't have time for this.*

"Oh, my god…" Rose paces back and forth near the division between the kitchen and living room. Near hyperventilating, her eyes dart between me and James and the phone in her hand. "We have to do something," she mutters. "He's seriously gonna die. *Ah…* I've never seen anyone die in real life before…"

I shake my head and look to James again.

"Who do we call?" I ask. "There's another emergency number, right? What is it?"

He shakes his head and coughs into one hand. I catch a glimpse of red on his lips and grab his wrist, twisting it to see. *Blood.* A bright, red splatter in his palm.

*Of course, he'd start coughing up blood. Great. Damn it.*

Rose sobs. "Jayde, please do something."

*Ugh!*

"Be quiet! I can't think."

*Goddammit…* He's losing too much blood, growing paler by the second. Rose is right. I have to do something to slow the bleeding—and fast. If I don't, he'll certainly bleed out right here. But what can I do—?

*Wait.*

On Night Hospital, there's an episode where one of the main characters witnessed a drive-by shooting while on her way to work. The guy was bleeding everywhere—at least this badly. While on the phone with 911, she dug a tampon out of her purse and used it to plug the entry wound. Tampons are sterile and absorbent, and they're the perfect size and shape to plug that type of wound.

*A stab wound should be similar, right?*

I don't have time to run upstairs and grab a tampon, but—
*They're just made of cotton fibers, right?*

I press James' hands over the wound and tell him to keep the pressure himself for a moment. Then I grab Ice's knife from the floor and, with its help, tear a reasonably dry strip of fabric from the hem of his t-shirt.

This isn't at all sanitary—nothing like a tampon—and the mere thought makes me want to puke, but it's the only thing I can think to do that has any chance of making a difference.

"Okay," I say slowly. "Move your hands… *Now!*"

His hands fall away. I rip his shirt open where the knife broke through and clear the area of as much blood as possible. It's a pain considering my hands were already slick with it, and the wound continues bleeding heavily, but I need to see what I'm doing.

*Close enough.*

"Sorry if this hurts."

I take a breath, grit my teeth, and pack the strip of cotton t-shirt into the small stab wound.

My stomach twists, bile rising in my throat as he groans and curses, but I can't stop. His nails dig into my side, he leans his head into my shoulder, and I seal my eyes shut. Not looking doesn't make jamming my fingers *into* his chest more tolerable, but it has to be done. Even if packing the wound doesn't stop the bleeding completely, I have to believe it will help.

I pull my hand away as I finish, relieved to see no new gush of blood pulse from the wound. *I'm sure he's still bleeding internally, but this should buy us more time.*

I shake my head to clear my mind. Then I plant my hands on his shoulders and straighten him up to get a better look. His skin is clammy, his eyes dull, and his breath comes in ragged wheezes. He coughs up more blood that dribbles down his chin.

*Shit.*

I fake a smile and cup his cheeks in my bloody hands. "You're gonna be fine, but I really need your help. Who can I call? 911 isn't okay, but, surely…"

Glancing over my shoulder, I find Rose sitting on the floor near the washroom door. She's crying with her head held in her hands.

*Oh, fuck it.*

"James. What's the special emergency number for immortals?"

He returns my gaze with the blankest look I've ever seen in my life. He doesn't seem to understand my question, and I'm not sure he heard what I said at all.

*If this is it…* My hands fall back to his shoulders. I press my forehead against his and stare into his glassy eyes.

*Damn it, Ice. How could you?*

The fog clears from his eyes for a moment, and he frowns. "Jayde? Why are you crying?"

*Am I crying?*

"Who do I call?" I ask, my soft voice breaking.

"Sorry. Ah… Hm."

I close my eyes. Maybe I am crying.

"Just tell me," I breathe. "Let me help you."

Instead of answering, he holds my face in his damp hands, and he kisses me. The taste of blood is overwhelming, but the coolness of his lips is the final straw. I break down into heavy sobs.

"Sorry," he says again.

My vision blurs. "Please, James. Please tell me who to call."

"Love you."

*Stop.*

"I love you too, but—"

He offers me a weak smile, and I shake my head.

As I ask again, his body tenses and seizes. The tremor lasts only a second or two, but his hands fall from my face, and he goes limp. In my surprise, my arms are too useless to stop him from falling to the side and collapsing onto the linoleum.

*I can't...*

*I couldn't...do anything after all...*

"Jayde," Rose calls from across the room. "Is he—?"

"No," I choke.

It's a bit hard to make out with tears obscuring my vision, but he's breathing. *Thank god.* But I still have no idea what to do, and now I don't even have anyone to ask.

I dig my bloody palms into my eye sockets and try to think.

*Should I just call 911? Would an ambulance get here fast enough for it to matter? Would Riverview General be able to help him? Dr. Corel works there, and he's an immortal, so... Maybe...*

Rose gasps, cutting through the static. Her voice is frantic as she speaks quickly, but she never finishes a sentence, and nothing she does say makes any sense. I uncover my eyes, though I don't need to ask what's wrong.

James is gone.

*No.* He's not...*gone.*

A ginger cat took his place in the pool of red blood.

*How?*

I blink, but the image doesn't change. *But how?* I would never believe it was possible if my eyes weren't locked on the cat lying motionless on the floor—if I didn't feel soft fur when I reached out to touch it.

*He...morphed?*

Rose creeps closer, crawling low to the ground, her voice rising as she continues stammering.

"What did—? Is that—?" She tears her attention from the bloody cat to meet my gaze with wild eyes. "Jayde, what the fuck is happening?"

I shake my head. "No, this is...good."

My mind is clear, and I know exactly what I need to do.

I wipe my eyes, and I scoop James' feline form into my arms. His breathing is weak and unsteady, but the strip of cloth is still securely packed into the wound.

As I drag myself to my feet, I turn to Rose with a smile. She stares at me from the floor like I've lost my damn mind. I can't blame her, but there's no time to explain.

"Where's his phone?"

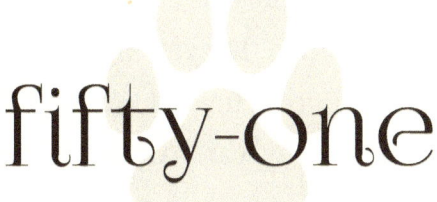

# fifty-one

I call the first familiar name in James' short contact list.

"Hello?"

The answering voice is achingly familiar, and my eyes flood with moisture, but I bite back the emotion. *I don't have time to think about it.*

"Hi, this is, um—" *What am I saying?* "Never mind. James is hurt, and I need to know which hospital to go to. Please, I—"

"Wait, slow down. James is hurt?"

Every word is like a needle to my heart.

"Yes," I gasp. "It's bad. I need to know where to take him, and I didn't know who else to call. It's an emergency."

"Who is this?"

"I'm his girlfriend, but— Just answer my question! I'm human. I know about immortals, but I don't know where to go, and he can't tell me right now."

"Okay, okay," he agrees. "Are you in Riverview?"

"Yes."

"The hospital is, uh…on Centennial Street. Yeah. Centennial. Take him there. I can call ahead for you."

*Centennial. Got it.*

"Thank you." I adjust my grip on James and check on Rose, who has hardly moved. "Can you drive? We need to get to the hospital on Centennial Street. Do you know where it is?"

She nods lamely and drifts toward the front door.

I return the phone to my ear. "Okay, thank you. Will you meet us there?"

"Ah… I'm out of town, so it might be a while, but…" There's a pause. "Is James okay?"

"No. Please call ahead for us."

"Sure thing."

The call ends, I grab my purse, and we head out. Rose climbs into the driver's seat of her car as I pile into the passenger seat with James in my lap. Then the car rumbles to life, and we're off.

She drives like a robot. Silent. Wide eyes locked on the road. Knuckles white from gripping the steering wheel too tight.

*I can't even imagine how she feels right now…*

I'm lucky she's willing to drive us anywhere.

The phone in my free hand lights up with a text, and I glance at the cracked screen.

> **Jesse**           now
> Go straight to ambulance entrance.
> Someone will meet you there.

I repeat the information aloud before slipping the phone into my pocket. Rose mumbles something in return, and I look down to watch James. I stroke his fur as he lay limp in my lap. The area around the wound is matted with blood, but the bleeding has slowed. He's unconscious, his breathing labored and uneven, but he's alive. *As long as he keeps breathing...*

"Is this the right hospital?" Rose asks, her voice trembling.

I glance out the windshield. The darkening sky frames Centennial Memorial Hospital's stark white exterior. It's smaller than I expected—much smaller than Riverview General—but the glowing *EMERGENCY* sign means we must be in the right place.

Her eyes flick in my direction, down at James in my lap, and back at the road before we make the turn into the parking lot. She drives around the building until we find the ambulance entrance, where a few people look to be waiting for us with a stretcher. The car stops abruptly, I open the door, and two of them approach.

A man who might be a doctor asks if I'm here to deliver James Reid. I nod and carefully pass the unmoving cat to him. He frowns as he checks for a pulse. Then he asks what happened.

"He was stabbed," my voice says. "In the chest. There was so much blood. I packed it...with cotton."

The doctor passes James to a nurse. As she hurries back to the others still waiting by the stretcher, he steps away from the car. "We'll take good care of him," he says. "Go ahead and park. Someone will meet you in the waiting room."

"Okay."

Emptiness sets in as the man turns away, but I shut the door. Rose drives forward and parks in one of the nearest visitor parking spaces. Then she drops her forehead to the steering wheel.

"This is a nightmare," she breathes. "Jayde... What the fuck is happening?"

I look down. At myself. At the blood soaking my clothes and slowly drying on my arms and legs. I've seen a lot of blood in the past month, but never this much.

James is in good hands now, but *Rose knows about immortals. She found out because of me.*

"Sorry," I say.

She groans. "Why the hell are *you* apologizing?"

I shake my head. "This is what I've been hiding from you all summer. The whole shapeshifter thing is honestly whatever, but I also hid the fact that I actively have an unhinged stalker who wants James dead. And I—"

"Shapeshifters."

"Yeah. Shapeshifters. Ice told me in June." I sigh and rub my eyes. "I'll probably get in trouble for telling you, but it's a little late to worry about that, isn't it? Since you literally watched James turn into a cat back there."

"Shapeshifters…"

"They're called immortals—but they're not immortal. It's just what they're called for some reason. A…misnomer. They can turn into cats, and they have magic powers. Oh, and this stupid necklace is supposed to let me turn into a cat too."

She sits up. "You?"

"I mean… It hasn't worked yet, but yeah."

She frowns and glances around the car. It's like she has a hard time looking directly at me—because of the blood, I guess.

"So… That was him, huh? Hot Grocery Store Man?"

"Yeah… Ice Monroe."

Her eyes narrow dangerously. "How long, Jayde? How long have you been dealing with this on your own?"

"I—" I glance away as my shoulders deflate. "Things weren't bad until— Well… He found out I talked to James during the rainstorm. I still don't know exactly why, but he's been trying to use me to get to James ever since. I guess this time it finally worked."

"He hurt you?"

"What? You think I got these scars on my own?"

"But… Why didn't you say anything? Like…anything at all? Maybe I could have—"

"What was I supposed to say? I couldn't tell you about immortals, and Ice is…" I shake my head and pop the passenger door open. "There's nothing you could have done. Anyway, I need to go inside. You don't have to come if you don't want, but…"

"No, I'll go with you!"

I glance over my shoulder. Her hands are balled in her lap, and her expression is grave in the low light of the parking lot.

"James was in bad shape," she breathes. "I can't leave you alone here. What if…something…?"

*What if…?*

I frown. "Alright. Thanks…"

We leave the car together, cross the parking lot in silence, and enter the hospital through the main ER doors. A young man wearing grey scrubs stops us, concern furrowing his brow.

"Are you the ones who brought James Reid in?" he asks. When I nod, he examines me more closely. "Are you injured?"

"No. This is his blood."

His eyes narrow suspiciously. Then he shrugs, escorts us to an unpopulated corner of the waiting room, and asks us to sit. We do, and he introduces himself as a medical intern—a student.

"And who might you be?" he asks.

He still strikes me as skeptical or wary, which is reasonable considering I'm absolutely covered in blood. Though, it might also be because we're both human and just drove an immortal in feline form to the hospital.

"My name is Jayde Palmer," I say, careful to keep my voice down. "I'm James' girlfriend. I already know about immortals. I'm registered with Human-Immortal Affairs and everything, so…"

"And your friend?"

"She…" *Well, I can't lie.* "Her name is Rose MacArthur. She's my roommate, but she didn't know about immortals until today—because James morphed when he fell unconscious."

He rubs his eyes. "Okay. We'll contact HIA to let them know, so just sit tight until they show up."

Rose stares at her hands, nervous and guarded, but what he said leaves me strangely relieved. It only makes sense that the hospital has to notify Human-Immortal Affairs, but it doesn't *sound* like I've broken some sacred taboo. Maybe it's fine that she knows.

"Okay, we'll stay here," I agree, "but, um… How is James?"

"Dunno. They took him for triage, but they just sent me down here to make sure everything was kosher with you two. I'm sure they'll send out a nurse with a real update eventually."

Then he looks me over again. "Though, if that's all his blood, he's probably in the OR by now."

"Yeah, thanks," I mutter.

"Also, there's a restroom right down the hall if you want to clean up or anything."

I sigh.

"But, yeah, just make sure your friend doesn't leave until someone from HIA talks to her." When I ask how long that might take, he shrugs. "Anyway, I have to go. That call should be made as soon as possible."

Once he's gone, it's just me and Rose sitting in the corner of the waiting room. A woman in a chair halfway across the room notices me—and the blood—and pales before averting her gaze.

Maybe I should clean myself up. I probably shouldn't look like...*this* when I meet Jesse.

"Are you okay?" I tap Rose on the shoulder, and she looks up with watery eyes. I almost lose my nerve, but I can't put this off. "Will you be alright if I go to the bathroom? I'll try to be quick."

"Sure, but— Am I in trouble?"

I blink. "No? Anyway, I'll be back in a minute. Just stay here."

She nods and drops her head into her hands. I wish I could help her. But there's nothing I can do, so I stand from my chair. I leave the waiting room and find the restroom, where I finally get a good look at myself in the mirror over the sink.

*Oh. That's disgusting.*

It's worse than I thought. There is blood *everywhere*. My

face. My arms. Shirt, shorts, legs. I don't know where to start or how I'm supposed to get it all off.

But I try.

I peel the blood-soaked sports band off my wrist, toss it into the garbage, and wash my hands and forearms in the sink. I take my shirt off and use the clean back to sponge as much of the blood off my legs as possible. Then I wash my face and use damp paper towels to get the rest. My undershirt and shorts are splotched by dark blood, and some remains trapped beneath my fingernails, but I look infinitely better than I did before.

*Okay. Time to wait for Jesse.*

I drop my shirt into the garbage and walk out of the bathroom.

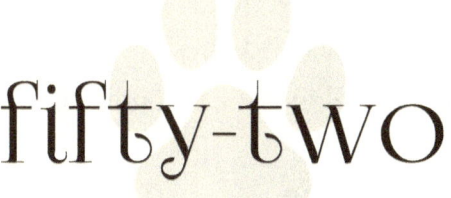

# fifty-two

The instant I sit beside Rose again, it hits me. Like, maybe I hadn't accepted exactly what happened until then. Like something in my mind was blocking the emotional implications—the all-too-real possibilities.

*James is in the OR right now. He was stabbed in the chest.*

*He could die.*

I hold my head in my hands, my eyes locked on the dry blood speckling the white toes of my Converse. I focus on breathing, and I listen to the mindless sounds of the waiting room. The voice over the PA system. The droning chatter of people. Hurried footsteps on tile. The ambulance sirens outside.

*What would I do if he…?*

*What would Ice do…?*

After a while, I hear footsteps approaching more closely. They stop in front of me, and I force myself to look up. I was nervous, but it's just the medical intern.

"You said you're Jayde Palmer?" he asks.

"Yes?"

He glances away with pursed lips. "Okay, that makes sense. Our head of PR called HIA, and a couple agents will be here to talk to your friend in about an hour."

*I want to talk to them too, but—*

"Are there any updates on James?"

"He's in surgery, still in critical condition."

"Will he live?"

"Dr. Edwards is one of the top cardiothoracic surgeons on the west coast. If anyone can help your boyfriend, it's him." A hint of amusement flashes in his bright green eyes, and he offers me a smile—the first one I think I've received all evening. "Besides, it was a single wound, and I hear the blade missed his heart. You're human, so you might not know, but immortals are hardy folks. I'm sure he'll be fine."

"Will he…?"

He shrugs. "I mean, I can't make any promises. He lost a lot of blood, but the odds aren't terrible."

*Gee, thanks.*

"Well, I appreciate the update," I say mildly. "Let me know if anything changes."

"Sure thing. It might be a while, though."

He leaves, and I turn to Rose. She's curled up in the chair next to mine with her knees hugged to her chest and her eyes shut. If it weren't for her periodic sniffling, I might think she fell asleep.

"Hey," I say. When she opens her eyes, I pat her on the shoulder. "You'll be fine. Like he said, the agents just want to talk. Since they're not coming for me, and you found out by accident, I don't think we're in any trouble. They'll probably just have you sign an NDA."

Her frown grows more pronounced. "You had to sign one too?"

"It's why I couldn't tell you anything."

"Oh."

"Yeah. James offered to tell you himself a few times, but… He was never able to turn into a cat before. I wasn't sure you'd believe him without proof, but I didn't really want you to know, anyway. It's been…trouble for me. I wanted to protect you from this."

She doesn't respond and instead glances away, seemingly deep in thought. I can't tell if she understands. I don't blame her if she doesn't. After all, I'm not sure how much of my unwillingness to tell her was for her sake as opposed to my own. Human-Immortal Affairs doesn't care for humans—even ones who are part of the Human Immortal Program—and I was terrified of what they might do if I told her myself. That's not a problem anymore, since she found out because of James and Ice, but there's still the question of how they'll treat her.

So far, I'm not impressed by their services.

I lean my head back and stare at the ceiling.

The medical intern was kind of wishy-washy about it, but he seems to think James will be fine. *How is his surgery going? How much damage was there? How much longer will it take?*

Time passes so slowly here.

I close my eyes and hug my arms to my chest to keep warm. I'm tired, but I'm too stressed to sleep, and I have to wait for both Human-Immortal Affairs and Jesse to show up. I keep my eyes closed, anyway.

It seems like forever before the medical intern returns. This time, he's joined by two smartly dressed individuals—a man and woman both wearing dark uniforms. They don't look happy to see us, but they introduce themselves as agents from Human-Immortal Affairs and ask to speak with Rose.

She stares at them with a flicker of fear in her wide, grey eyes.

"There's no need to look so nervous," the female agent says with a sigh. "We simply need to go over a few things regarding what you've witnessed tonight."

"Okay," she agrees slowly.

I sit up straight, dropping my feet to the floor. "Is there any way I can—?"

The woman sighs again. "Jayde Palmer, right? We understand how this is connected to your unique circumstances, but we only need to speak with your friend tonight."

*Unique circumstances?* I frown pointedly and fold my arms over my chest, but I bite my tongue. Her tone was clear enough. She has zero interest in discussing anything with me, and I doubt I can change her mind.

*Why did I expect anything else?*

"Come on, then," the male agent says before helping Rose out of her chair.

I stand too. "Can I go with her, at least?"

"No."

"Please? I don't want to wait here alone."

"Your friend will be fine," the female agent tells me, frustration leaking into her voice. "I'm sure you'll see each other again in a few hours."

Rose casts a desperate look in my direction, but I don't move to follow them, and she doesn't try to break away. What good would it do? They're in charge, and I don't want to risk making things worse for either of us. So all I can do is watch, eyes watering furiously, as the agents lead my best friend down a hallway and disappear around a corner with her.

The medical intern stayed behind, so I turn on him.

"She will be fine, won't she?" I ask.

He tips his head. "Didn't they *just* say that? What do you think Human-Immortal Affairs does? This is their job. She learned about immortals, so they have to counsel her. Haven't you been through this already?"

"I never spoke with anyone from Human-Immortal Affairs. My sponsor did everything for me. Was I supposed to meet with someone?"

"I'm not sure," he admits, his voice thoughtful as he takes the chair Rose was sitting in before. "It's not uncommon for humans to accidentally learn about immortals. When it happens here, we just call HIA to come in and debrief them. The human signs a Secrecy Agreement, and they're off to continue their normal lives. Maybe it's different for humans with an immortal sponsor? I wouldn't know; I've never sponsored anyone."

"So, this is normal here?"

He shrugs. "Essentially. A human might watch someone morph or use their ability in an emergency, and it is what it is— an honest accident. No harm done in most cases."

"That…actually makes me feel a lot better. Thank you."

"No problem."

He looks like he's ready to leave when a nurse approaches us.

"Oh, hey, Theo," she says. Her voice is mild and soft, and

she looks about as tired as she sounds. "Is this the woman who came in with James Reid earlier?"

With a glance at me, he stands from his chair. "Yeah, this is Jayde Palmer. Jayde, this is Nurse Evelyn. She probably has that update you've been waiting for, but, uh, I gotta get back to work."

Nurse Evelyn's vibrantly blue eyes narrow, and I get the feeling he wasn't meant to hang out here as long as he did, so I just nod. He dips out, and she takes his spot in the chair.

"Is James okay?"

"Surgery is still ongoing," she says. "Our team is working hard to control the bleeding and repair the damage. His blood loss was severe, you know—the blade damaged his lung and a major artery near his heart. Dr. Edwards, the lead surgeon, mentioned that someone performed first aid before he arrived. He didn't say it saved his life, but it certainly helped slow the bleeding. Was that you?"

"I wasn't sure it would help, but I figured it was worth a shot."

"It was." She offers a smile. "Oh. I also heard you were covered in an awful lot of blood when you first arrived. How are you holding up?"

"Better than him, I guess."

Her smile fades, and she takes a breath before slipping something from her pocket. "Here... We found this while prepping him for surgery."

I accept it—a plastic bag with James' name and patient number written on the front. I barely recognize the object inside as the pressed leaf bookmark he bought at the art festival. It doesn't feel like that happened today too.

"Thank you," I mumble.

She pats me on the back and moves to stand. "Hang in there. I'll come back if anything changes."

"Wait—" My fingers close around the bookmark, and I look up through the tears in my eyes. "Do you think he'll make it?"

She frowns. "I honestly can't say one way or the other. Things are dicey right now, but I've seen healthy young men bounce back from worse."

"Okay. Thanks."

She leaves, and I'm alone again.

\* \* \* \* \*

I don't know how much time has passed.

I think I spent some time crying. Perhaps I even began to fall asleep without noticing. I haven't been paying attention to much of anything, so I'm not sure what roused me back to full awareness, but I quickly register the sound of footsteps coming closer.

When I look up, my heart lurches as a man that looks *so much* like James stares at me like I'm a complete stranger—*because, to him, I am one.*

"Hi, um—" My voice trembles. I stand from the chair, smooth the front of my camisole, and clear my throat before starting over, "You're Jesse, right? I'm Jayde. I'm…the one who called you earlier."

"You're his girlfriend, right?"

The similarity of his voice steals my breath, but I nod and

wipe my eyes, hoping no more tears will spring up.

"Yeah, um… I'm sorry for calling you out of nowhere like that, but I didn't know who else to call. So, thanks for telling me where to go."

He frowns. "Don't apologize. You said James was hurt? Is he alright? What happened this time?"

This time? *This…time?*

I shake my head, pushing the myriad of possible meanings to the back of my mind, and drop into my chair again.

"As far as I know, he's still in the OR," I mumble. "He lost a lot of blood. I don't know how it's going, exactly. No one has come by to say anything in a while, so…"

"It's alright." He sighs and takes the seat beside me. "Anyway, thanks for calling. Even if we don't always get along, and even if he is an idiot, he's still my brother."

We sit and wait.

I slip the bookmark into my purse and check my phone for the first time in ages. It's almost midnight. I don't have any important notifications—or messages. I hope Rose is okay, but I can't bring myself to text her.

Jesse doesn't talk much.

Maybe he doesn't know what to say to me. Maybe it's because he and James *apparently haven't spoken in months*. All I know is that this isn't the first time James has ended up in the hospital after being seriously injured—though I can't bring myself to ask for details.

I'm afraid I'd start crying again if I heard anything more.

After a while, Jesse clears his throat. I glance up from my

phone to find him watching me again.

"How long have you known James?" he asks.

"A couple months."

My mind goes blank as he says he knew about me—he knew that James had started dating a human girl. When he admits to recognizing me from pictures he saw on FaceSpace a while back, I force a smile, desperately wishing I knew how to respond.

"You were with Ice Monroe in June, right?"

I freeze. "Um— Yes."

He thinks it over for a moment. His expression is neutral, as was his voice when he asked, but the topic and his interest in it makes me both curious and uneasy. Then he tips his head.

"Does this have anything to do with him?"

"With Ice?" I ask, my mouth dry.

He nods, still oddly unconcerned. And my heart races. But I don't know what to say. *Should I explain?* They haven't spoken in months. Is it my place to say anything?

*Why would he even think to ask if Ice was involved?*

I shake my head and look away. "I didn't see anything. I wasn't in the room. Sorry."

"Oh. Did he do it to himself?"

*What? Why ask...?*

"No." I stare at the floor, my eyes wide and unblinking and locked on the blood on my shoes. "He, um... He was in a fight, and I... I guess he lost. Maybe he can tell you exactly what happened after he wakes up."

*If he wakes up.*

I drop my face into my hands again.

# fifty-three

Eventually, Nurse Evelyn returns with Dr. Edwards.

"Jayde Palmer and— You must be James' twin."

Jesse introduces himself, and I stand from my chair.

"Is James okay?" I ask.

"For now." Dr. Edwards regards me with muted interest. "The operation went well. No complications. We're still monitoring his condition in the ICU, but it shouldn't be long before we move him into recovery. Sound good?"

I nod blankly.

"So, what happened?" Jesse asks.

Dr. Edwards thinks about it for a moment, and then nods. "We should move to a private room to talk."

They lead us through the hospital and into a small room with a table and chairs inside. The floor is carpeted, and the potted plant on a bookshelf lends the room a touch of life, but there aren't any windows, and it bothers me for some reason.

The four of us sit at the table. Neither doctor nor nurse look particularly concerned about whatever they intend to say, but I can't decide whether to be hopeful or nervous.

Dr. Edwards studies his tablet for a moment before glancing

up again. "As a child, James was diagnosed with a congenital mutation—the pediatric specialist who diagnosed him described it as a metabolic disorder preventing him from taking feline form, among other things. However, when he was brought in today, he was in feline form."

Jesse gasps. "You're serious? How is that possible?"

"The blood loss appears to have triggered his body to respond by morphing," the doctor continues. "Blood clots more quickly in feline form, so I imagine morphing was his body's unconscious, last-ditch effort to slow the bleeding. I've seen others morph under similar circumstances, but never someone with the type of condition described in James' medical history."

"It was that bad?"

"There was a lot of blood," I say lamely.

It's still soaked and dried into my clothes and stuck beneath my fingernails. If I'm not careful to remember where I am, it's like I'm still completely drenched in it.

Nurse Evelyn smiles. "It seems James may have not been defective after all. A possible misdiagnosis."

"I'm not confident I would go that far," Dr. Edwards muses. "Until he regains consciousness and heals enough to attempt morphing safely, we can't be sure he'll be able to switch forms at will moving forward, but it is a possibility, as there's certainly no true physical inability to morph in his case."

*That would be great, wouldn't it?*

Jesse considers it for a moment. "The surgery, though—you said it went well?"

"Yes. As I said, he was unconscious and in feline form upon

arrival. We got him into triage. Medically triggered a transition. Once he was in human form, we found a single puncture wound to the chest, which was packed before he arrived—quick thinking on Miss Palmer's part, I've heard. He was anemic and hypoxic, with blood in his airway. We had to open him up to assess the damage, but he was lucky. Truly. The blade missed his heart. It nicked a rib, the pulmonary artery, and punctured his right lung. Took a while to patch everything up, but we managed."

Finally, relief seeps in, and I'm suddenly twice as exhausted as I was before.

"He also cracked three ribs on his left side, and the knuckles on his right hand are bruised—possible hairline fractures. It's nothing to worry about. Though, it seems he was in quite the serious scuffle this evening."

I nod lamely.

"But he'll be fine?" Jesse asks.

"Barring any further complications, your brother should make a full recovery. We'll transfer him into a recovery room in a few hours, and he'll be back on his feet in a few days."

We both let out a breath.

"Thanks for taking care of him."

Dr. Edwards nods. They shake hands over the table, and the four of us file out of the small room. The doctor heads further into the hospital while Nurse Evelyn walks me and Jesse back to the waiting room.

Jesse takes a chair and starts messing with his phone. I linger in front of the chair I sat in before and look to the nurse.

"I'm glad everything worked out," she says. "Do either of

you need anything? Water? A blanket?"

I force a smile. "A...shower?"

"Oh—" She suddenly looks quite sorry for me. "Of course, hun. I can make that happen. Come with me."

*Thank you.*

I tell Jesse I'll be right back, and I follow Nurse Evelyn through a series of hallways. Then we walk behind the OR nurse's station counter—she greets one of her coworkers—and we stop in front of a door.

### Locker Room

### * Employees Only *

She unlocks the door using her keycard and shows me inside. The room looks like a smaller, more intimate, and less damp version of a pool locker room. Two rows of grey lockers, along with a few metal benches and freestanding cabinets.

Nurse Evelyn heads straight for one of the cabinets. She pulls out a towel, a tiny bottle of 3-in-1 soap, and a set of blue scrubs. Then she hands everything to me and points out an adjoined room.

"The bathroom is through there," she says, offering me a smile. "You're technically not supposed to be in here, so try to be quick. I'll wait right outside."

"Alright, thanks so much."

I don't think she saw what I looked like when I first arrived, but it was *not great*. And I'm sure she knows. But who told her?

Dr. Edwards? He's the one who took James from me when we got here, so he absolutely knows how bad it was.

Or maybe it was the medical intern, Theo.

I dip into the bathroom, where I promptly let my hair down, strip out of my clothes, and hop into the shower. After sudsing up and rinsing off, I resist the urge to sit on the floor and feel sorry for myself. *I don't have time*, so I call it good, shut the water off, and change into the scrubs.

With one last glance at my tired self in the mirror, I retrieve my purse and soiled clothing from the edge of the sink. As I turn and head for the door, something falls from the bundle of clothing and clatters on the tile floor.

I look, and I freeze.

Ice's pocketknife, still crusted with dried blood, lies at my feet.

I used it before I packed James' wound, but… *I don't remember putting it in my pocket. Wouldn't I have just dropped it back onto the floor? Why do I have this?*

I glance at the door. Then I shove the knife into my purse and step out to meet Nurse Evelyn.

"Do you feel better?" she asks.

"Yes." *It's at least half-true.* "Thanks again."

She holds out a hand. "If you aren't planning to leave for a while, I can wash your clothes and get them back to you in a few hours."

"Um— The blood…"

"It's fine," she assures me with a smile. "You've been through an ordeal tonight, haven't you? I'll talk with a few nurses, but I figure the least we can do is set you up with clean clothes."

*I feel like I don't deserve this, but…*

I nod and hand over the bloodstained clothing, and she leads me back to the waiting room. When we get there, Jesse is talking on the phone, frustration furrowing his brow.

"—I said I don't know— Well, they said he'll be fine, but— Dude, shut up for a second." He sighs. "If you're that worried, just come down to the hospital and ask for yourself. We're at Centennial Memorial. ...No, I'm about to leave. No, man. He's not even awake yet. I'll come back in the morning."

He hangs up the phone and drags his hands down his face.

I thank Nurse Evelyn a final time. She offers another smile and walks off, and I take my chair again. Jesse looks rather unsettled —but it seems appropriate considering the circumstances.

"Is everything okay?" I ask.

"You know Matt, right? Matthew Barnett?" When I nod, he forces a smile. "Good. He'll be here soon, but I gotta head out. It's late. I drove all the way up from San Francisco to be here."

I nod again, too worn out to argue.

"Let me know if anything changes."

Another nod.

Then Jesse leaves.

I curl up in my chair, take a moment to get as comfortable as possible, and close my eyes.

I expect to be alone for a while again, but it feels like it's only been a couple minutes when hurried footsteps and several startled gasps break the monotony of the droning waiting room ambience. I look up as Matthew approaches with a distressing and relatable panic etched into every facet of his face.

*He smiled so brightly when we first met.* This kind of tragic expression doesn't suit him at all, and it's like another nail driving into my heart.

"Jayde," he says, his voice louder than it should be in a quiet hospital waiting room in the middle of the night. "Jesse said James was in a fight—that he was stabbed or something? What happened? Is he okay?"

I glance around, but no one seems to be paying us any real attention now. "He…lost a lot of blood, but it sounds like he'll be okay."

"Oh."

Blank-eyed, he sinks into the chair beside me. He stares at his hands in his lap for a moment before looking to me again.

"Are you okay?" he asks.

"I—"

*The sharp edge of a knife held against my neck. The warmth of blood splashing my shirt and dripping down my arms. The salty, metallic taste on James' lips.*

I force a smile and shake my head. "I wasn't hurt. I'm fine."

We wait for a while.

Matthew tries talking to me. He's desperate for information —for any explanation as to how and why this happened—but I don't know what to tell him. I don't want to mention Ice, so I don't say much of anything. They can talk about it after James wakes up.

At least two more hours pass before a nurse I don't recognize approaches us.

"Hello," she says. "Are you Jayde?"

I nod. "Is James okay? Can we see him yet?"

"We're just about to move him into recovery. You're welcome

to wait in the room we prepared if you want. I can take you there now."

*Oh, thank god.* I'm sick and tired of this waiting room.

Matthew introduces himself to the nurse while I gather my things. Then she leads us out of the waiting room and into the inner workings of the hospital.

"How serious was it?" he asks as we walk.

"Oh, I wasn't on the surgical team," the nurse says mildly. "I hear he lost quite a lot of blood, but his hemoglobin and oxygen levels are stable now. He should recover."

"Is he awake?"

"No. He's off the ventilator and breathing independently, but he was heavily sedated, so it might be a while before he wakes up."

Matthew glances away, stricken by some complicated emotion. I don't think I made it clear just how serious James' injury was, and I guess Jesse didn't either.

"When will he be moved into the recovery room?" I ask.

"Within a couple hours. A few tests need to come back first. Evelyn told me to take care of you before she went home, and I suppose you've been stuck in the waiting room for ages, so I thought a change of scenery might help. Perhaps you can get some rest there."

*Rest. Ha...*

"Thanks. I really appreciate it."

"Here we are," she says, pushing a door open.

Matthew walks into the empty recovery room while I linger near the door and continue watching the nurse.

"Oh. Right." She holds up a hospital-branded tote bag. "This is something the ER nurses pulled together for you earlier. I hope it helps."

I accept the bag and tell her to thank Nurse Evelyn in case I don't see her again.

"We'll be around soon," she says before excusing herself.

Finally, I step inside the room and close the door. Matthew is still standing, glancing around like he can't believe he's here. Then he looks back to me with an air of hollowness in his expression.

"James will be okay, won't he?"

\* \* \* \* \*

Exhaustion overwhelms me the instant I sit on the padded vinyl bench set into a recess below the room's window. I pull my legs up and lean my head against the wall and listen to the ticking clock and Matthew's footsteps as he paces around the room. But I must have nodded off at some point because one moment I'm wondering how Rose is doing and the next I'm jarred awake by the sound of an opening door.

An unfamiliar doctor and the nurse who lead us here wheel James into the room. He's hooked up to IVs, still receiving supplemental oxygen, and is certainly unconscious, but he's cleaned up, wearing a hospital gown, and covered to the waist with a blanket.

It just looks like he's asleep.

The doctor and nurse arrange his bed and medical equipment

in the room, instruct us to press the nurse call button if there's any problem, and show themselves back out.

Matthew drops himself into a chair at James' bedside.

"Ah, man…" He sighs, deflating slightly. "He got himself real messed up this time, didn't he?"

*Again with the "this time"…*

"Has something like this happened before?" I ask.

"Well…" He looks up with some uncertainty. "It wasn't nearly this bad, and he hasn't landed himself in the hospital in a couple years that I know of, but… Mm… I mean, it's not unheard of for James to get into fights. I guess knives aren't normally involved, though. Do you know who did it?"

I hesitate before saying the same thing I said to Jesse: I wasn't around when it happened. Whoever stabbed him was gone when I got there.

*It's not a lie…exactly.*

James can tell Jesse and Matthew whatever he wants when he wakes up. *If he can even remember what happened.* He apparently fell into a coma due to the amount of blood he lost.

"What time is it?" Matthew asks. We both look to the wall clock near the door—it's almost 4AM—and he groans. "I wish I could stick around until he wakes up, but I work opening. I really can't stay. I have to get some sleep."

"It's okay," I say quietly.

"Do you need a ride home or anything?" he asks, frowning. "I don't have my car, but I could…"

*The house is still… The blood…*

I shake my head. "No. It's fine. I'll just stay here."

I slip my phone from my pocket, but Rose still hasn't called or messaged yet. Surely, she didn't go back to the cottage. Hopefully, she's at her parents' house. Hopefully, she's asleep by now.

"You sure?" he asks.

"Yeah, I…" I look up and force a smile. "I'll be fine here, and I'm sure he'll be awake by the time you're able to come back. I think I'll try to sleep too."

He nods. "Alright, well— I guess I'll see you later, then. I get off at noon, so… I'll probably swing by right after work. Or try to get out early. I dunno."

"Okay. I'll be here."

Matthew heads out, leaving me alone with James' unconscious body and a ticking clock.

# fifty-four

I can't fall asleep.

Instead, I sit in an uncomfortable plastic chair and watch James sleep for a long time. Hours. A nurse pops in to check his vitals a few times, more time passes, and the sun rises, and my mind fills with static as I sit and watch and nothing changes.

A hospital gown doesn't suit James at all, but his expression is peaceful and sedated. Every so often, I mindlessly pick a flake of dried blood out of his hair.

Now, I finally understand.

The lonely misery of sitting in a waiting room for hours. The overwhelming despair trickling in as you watch someone you care about lie motionless in a hospital bed. Did James also watch me sleep and pick blood out of my hair? Or was it too much to handle? Is that why he sat out in his car, waiting for news the whole night?

*Please, wake up.*

I tear my heavy eyes away and look at my hands. The blood is long gone, but I swear I can still feel it slicking my skin. Hot and wet. When I close my eyes, I can picture it perfectly.

*So much blood...*

They praised me for my quick thinking, as though packing the wound may have saved his life, but… No one realizes that James is only here because of me. They fought because of me. Ice stabbed him *because of me*.

No one knows I met with Ice. No one knows about the threats he made. Instead, I chose to hide it from everyone. I don't even know if I genuinely thought it would protect James, or if I was just desperate to keep him from leaving. It doesn't matter either way.

*Either way, it was a mistake.*

James almost died, and Rose learned about immortals in the worst way imaginable. Ice was right when he said I'd regret it.

I rest my head in my arms on the edge of the tall bed. I close my eyes and wonder if I might be able to finally fall asleep, when a sound from behind startles me.

My phone. A loud text tone.

The sound doesn't bother the unconscious James at all.

I check the wall clock—just after 9AM—and leave the chair to find my phone. My heart pounds with nervous energy as I wonder who might have messaged me, and I eventually locate my phone inside the tote bag the nurse left me with.

I sit on the padded bench to check the message. I was hoping it might be news from Rose, but the red notification bubble appears beside Ice's name.

**Ice:** Has James survived?

*Bastard—*

**Me:** Sorry to disappoint you.

**Ice:** Disappoint me? So he is alive?

**Me:** Barely.

**Ice:** Wow. Lucky you! (°ᵕ°)

*Bastard!* He held a knife to my throat. He left that same knife stuck in James' chest and traumatized my best friend. And he still has the nerve to talk to me this way?

> **Ice:** Enough about James, I'd like to arrange
> another chat. Are you willing to humor me
> once more?

*Right. Because that went so well last time.*

My thumb hovers over the keyboard. I loathe the thought of speaking with him at length again, but I might be out of options. I learned my lesson. Ignoring him won't get me anywhere.

Somehow, I need to resolve this matter once and for all. I need to stop being a coward and face my problems directly.

*And, right now, Ice is problem number one.*

> **Me:** What kind of chat?

I glance up from my phone, and my eyes land on the hospital bed in the middle of the room.

If there's any chance Ice is willing to have a real conversation or work something out—anything to get him off James' back—I want to know. At this point, I'd agree to almost anything. But I'm alone, defenseless, and desperate, and he surely knows it.

*Even so...*

> **Ice:** A friendly one, of course. (°ᵕ°)~☆

Does he think emoticons will make me trust him? *Ugh.*

He's up to something, but having ulterior motives doesn't automatically make it a trap, right? He doesn't want *me* dead— just James, though he doesn't seem upset to learn he failed— and the last illicit meeting we had, while terrifying, was more or less civil, so… I wouldn't be in too much danger, right?

*Even if meeting with Ice now means being alone with him for an indeterminate period of time while James is unconscious in the hospital.*

Maybe this is stupid. Maybe I'm crazy for talking to Ice at all after last night—never mind everything that went down before.

*At the very least, I'm a terrible girlfriend.*

**Ice:** Give me a call when you're ready to talk.

I chew my lip.

He'd freak out if he knew what I was thinking—if he knew I even considered meeting with Ice after what he did.

James wants to protect me. I believe that. But, so far, all we've done is keep dangerous secrets from each other. We can talk when he wakes up. I'll come clean about my conversations with Ice.

*I won't let him get hurt because of me again.*

For now, though, it's time I actually do something. I have to stop avoiding Ice. Maybe, if we meet again, I can reason with him. Maybe I can convince him to leave us alone. It's a long shot, but I have nothing else to go on right now. And I certainly don't want to piss him off further. If anything, I should at least call.

*Yeah. I can do that.*

With a sigh, I set my phone aside and dig through the tote bag. My clean camisole and shorts are there, along with a solid red t-shirt with a white Red Cross logo on one sleeve. I also find a bottle of water, a handful of prepackaged snacks that look like they came out of a vending machine, and three cafeteria meal vouchers.

My stomach rumbles, but I ignore it.

I take the clothes into the adjoined bathroom and change. I feel better wearing a normal outfit, but the heart on my wrist itches, and a purple bruise blooms below it where Ice grabbed me.

Back in the recovery room, I dig through my purse. I remove the plastic bag containing the pressed leaf bookmark and James' phone. Then my fingers brush cool metal. I shiver as my hand closes around the pocket knife, but I take it out.

Looking at it reminds me of my own sheer stupidity.

*But it is a weapon.*

I slip the knife into my pocket and find my wallet at the bottom of my purse. With a sigh, I drop my purse in the tote bag, grab a tiny bag of chips before leaving the tote on the bench, and cross back to the hospital bed.

I place James' phone and bookmark on the bedside table.

Biting back tears, my hands ball into fists.

"I'm sorry," I say. He remains asleep and unmoving, and I sigh. "I should be back before you wake up, but, ah… I really hope you don't hate me—whatever happens."

I kiss him on the cheek.

Then I smother my awareness of the dark bruise at his temple and the countless nightmarish possibilities of whatever might happen next, and I leave the recovery room. I walk down the hall with purpose, following the exit signs while desperately trying to look as inconspicuous as possible.

I'm within sight of the hospital's front lobby when I spot Jesse heading my way. *Great. I was* this *close to escaping undetected.* He doesn't notice me immediately, as he's busy reading from a scrap of paper.

I don't *want* to talk to him, and I could probably slip by him if I tried, but I imagine I should tell someone I'm heading out. James will wake up soon, and I'd hate for him to come to alone with absolutely no idea what's happened or where I am. Even if I'm not sure what I'm doing or how long I might be out, I'm glad someone will be here for him.

We make fleeting eye contact, and I detect a flicker of recognition in his eyes before I wave and quicken my pace to meet up with him in the hallway.

I pause, once again taken aback by his presence. They're twins, and Jesse's minor differences—tanned skin, shorter hair, more athletic physique, and lack of under-eye bags or faded scars—do very little to detract from their similarities.

*It hurts, in a way.*

"How's James?" he asks.

"He's okay." I clear my throat and force a smile, careful to keep my bruised arm behind my back. "I mean, he's still asleep, but he was moved into a recovery room earlier this morning."

The news comes as an obvious relief, and I go on to rehash what the doctor told me when they first wheeled him into his room. He should make a full recovery, but he needs to stay in the hospital until he regains his strength.

"I'm just stepping out to get some fresh air," I say, "but you should go see him. I know you guys haven't been talking, but I'm sure he'd be happy to know you're here."

He nods and returns my smile, though he looks fatigued. The expression is achingly familiar... But he's just worried about his brother.

"Thanks again," he says. "For calling last night."

"To be honest, I just called the first name I recognized."

He glances away. "Well, I'm glad it was me. James hates asking for help, so it's a good thing you were there. But I'm sorry we had to meet like that."

*I need to end this conversation before I wuss out or cry. I'm not even sure which would be worse at this point.*

"It's fine," I say. "You should ask James how we met." After a nervous laugh, I hesitate. "But, um... I might be out for a while —I'm not entirely sure—so have him call me if he wakes up."

"Will do," he agrees, flashing a more upbeat smile.

I mirror his smile, though it fades immediately as we go our separate ways. I can only hope that waking up with his brother in the room will lessen the blow when James realizes I'm missing.

*God, I feel awful about this whole thing.*

It's still early, though. If Ice is serious about only wanting to talk, there's a decent chance I'll be back before he wakes up.

As I pass through the hospital's large, glass doors, I suddenly feel even more overwhelmed and exhausted. I got maybe an hour of spotty sleep before they brought James to the recovery room. On top of my struggle with sleeping the past few days, I'm just...

so tired.

*But I have to do this now.* James would never want me to call Ice if he were awake. *For good reason, but still...*

I wander around the side of the building and sit behind a large, manicured shrub with my back against a notch in the wall. The goal is to make myself disappear. Because I know I'm doing something I shouldn't, and I don't want to get caught.

I hold my phone for a moment. This is easily one of the worst ideas I have ever had, but I select Ice's name from my contact list and press *call* anyway.

With a deep breath, I raise the phone to my ear.

It rings once.

Twice.

"That was fast." *Three words, and I already want to throw up.* "I have to say, I was expecting you to take your time."

"You want to talk?" I ask, my voice hushed even though there isn't anyone around to overhear me. "Then talk."

"I'd love to. In person, preferably."

*Of course.* This is the worst-case scenario, but I won't get a chance once James wakes up. I have to do this now and hope he's serious about being civil.

"When do you want to meet?"

He chuckles. "Now is fine, assuming you're free."

"Don't you dare act so casual," I spit into the phone. "You nearly killed my boyfriend."

"He's your *boyfriend* now?" he asks, his voice terribly dry. "Please. I'm going to be sick."

Ugh. *You're* going to be sick?

"Oh, whatever. It's not like I want to talk to you either."

There's a pause. "How is the boyfriend, anyway? Does James know you intend to meet with me?"

"No. He, um… He hasn't woken up yet."

"Amazing." He laughs again. "Though, I suppose I shouldn't be surprised to learn you have a habit of speaking behind the backs of others."

I groan. "Just pick me up, so we can get this over with. I'm at the hospital on Centennial."

"Centennial?" he echoes. "Why, pray tell, is James Reid at Centennial Memorial Hospital?"

"Maybe I'll save that for our *chat*."

I end the call without waiting for a response and jam my phone into my pocket, freezing when it bumps against the switchblade.

*Oh.*

My hand lingers in my pocket, and I stare into the depths of the bush in front of me for a long, quiet moment before I take the knife out. Dark, dry blood is crusted over part of it, but I'm certain this is the same knife Ice used before. I hate to think anything nice about something that's caused so much damage, but *it's pretty*. The steel is smooth and dark with a lighter marbling reminiscent of wood grain, and some type of ivory or bone is set into the handle.

*It's heavier than I expected too.*

After scanning my surroundings to ensure I haven't been spotted, I press the small button on the knife's side. The blade tries to flip out from the handle, but the hinge is jammed. I hesitate before pulling the blade the rest of the way out. It locks into place with a sharp *click*. The metal has the same intricate, swirled pattern as the handle.

*I wonder…*

What went through Ice's mind when he made the conscious decision to use this knife against me? What was he thinking right before he plunged it into James' chest?

*What does he get out of any of this?*

Somehow, though… The knife is almost comfortable in my hand, the handle having quickly warmed to match the temperature of my skin. I've never seen a knife like this before. Knowing Ice, it's probably a custom piece.

*And he probably wants it back.*

With a sigh, I fold the knife and slip it into my other pocket before venturing out from the shelter of the bush. There's a bench not far from the hospital doors, so I head there to wait.

I sit at the empty marble bench with my legs crossed. I eat the small bag of plain potato chips I brought with me, and I feel less nervous than I thought I would.

Several minutes later, I see the flashy, silver sports car enter the parking lot and jump from the bench to stand on the curb.

As the car pulls up in front of me, the tinted passenger window rolls down. Inside, Ice looks wholly unaffected by last night's scuffle. He wears his leather jacket over a fitted t-shirt, and his hair is haphazardly pushed up out of his face. Dark sunglasses hide his eyes, but he flashes a smug grin.

"Hop in," he says.

The fact there doesn't seem to be a scratch on him annoys

the hell out of me, but I comply, and he studies me while I buckle my seatbelt. I don't look at him again. I'd rather not meet his gaze.

"You seem to be holding up well," he says.

I fight the urge to say something dangerous. Instead, I pull my hair over one shoulder, cross my arms, and stare pointedly out the passenger window as we pass a parked ambulance.

"Yeah, I'm fine," I mutter.

The car stops again before we leave the parking lot. When I glance over, one of his hands leaves the steering wheel to push his sunglasses to the top of his head.

"Tell me," he says, his voice matching the hint of tiredness in his eyes. "Why is James at Centennial Memorial Hospital?"

"A hospital is a hospital, isn't it? Besides, this is the immortal hospital, and James is an immortal."

"Truly?" he asks with a short laugh.

I bite the inside of my cheek and massage my scarred palm.

Should I explain what happened after he bailed? Ice clearly doesn't feel bad about what he did, so would him knowing the truth change anything? *Maybe...*

I sigh and meet his probing stare. "James lost a lot of blood. After you left, he...pulled the knife out."

"Moron," he says with a laugh.

"Yeah, I know," I agree, averting my eyes. "Anyway, when he lost too much blood, he, um... He morphed."

"He *what?*"

I ignore the flash of bitterness in his voice and my now-spiking heart rate, and I keep talking, "I guess it was an emergency measure his body took after going into shock and losing consciousness. I'm not sure exactly, but that's how they explained it to me."

He looks away. "Whatever. I suppose it explains why you took him to Centennial."

When he looks at me again, he seems intrigued and somewhat bothered, but no longer hostile. While it doesn't exactly put me at ease, I'm not sure how to feel about it.

"And you're suggesting James would have died had he not morphed?"

*Don't sound so disappointed!*

"I don't know if that's true," I admit, biting back my irritation. "But the surgeon said an immortal's blood clots faster in feline form, so I guess it's possible."

Still mulling it over, he finally pulls the car out of the parking lot, and we're on our way to *somewhere*. I return to watching the world streak by outside the window. A few minutes pass in silence.

"An involuntary reaction to hemorrhagic shock," he whispers as though to himself.

I glance up to find his eyes aren't focused on the road at all. He stares at me with heightened interest while somehow managing to keep us out of an accident.

"What?" I ask, not caring to mask my disgust.

He frowns and returns his attention to the road. "It's nothing. An idle thought, is all."

I'm vaguely curious, but it's Ice, and I do not want to know what sort of idle thoughts might go through his head.

"Where are we going?" I ask. "Your house?"

"I believe so. My house, yes…"

Ice was always a careful, focused driver before, but he seems to be spacing out terribly today. What has him so distracted?

*It's creeping me out.*

With a glance at the scar on my wrist and the bruise beneath it, I cross my arms over my chest again. "I probably won't be there when James wakes up because of you, so this better be worth it."

"You're in luck. This little chat may be more important than I previously thought."

"What do you mean?"

"I'll explain once we're there." He casts me a quick, wry look. "It would be an honest shame if you were to panic and throw yourself from the vehicle."

*What—?*

I grit my teeth, crush the desire to ask a second time, and turn to glare out the window. Neither of us speak. The silence amplifies the awkward atmosphere and nurtures the discomfort that dug deep within my chest when he first asked to meet.

*What is he thinking?*

Maybe I was wrong. Maybe this is a trap.

*It's starting to feel like a trap.*

When we reach the electronic gate leading into Westbrooke, I watch Ice input the code, noting that the PIN hasn't changed since I was last here. Then I stare through the windshield on the drive through the neighborhood. He parks on the curb in front of Night's blue sedan instead of using the garage.

*Does this mean he doesn't plan to keep me here long, or…?*

I glance at the house through the passenger window and hesitate with my hand on the door handle. The Monroe house is the same as any other suburban home—normal and welcoming from the outside—but seeing it again saps my energy and leaves me nervous. I haven't been here since I first discovered Ice isn't who I thought he was.

*The day he pulled a knife on me.*

*The day he sent me to the hospital.*

And, now, I'm here again.

"You're not planning to kill me, are you?" I ask.

"*Christ*, Jayde—" He sighs. "I should hope you don't die."

I turn away from the passenger window to gauge his expression. He looks tired, and he flashes one of the soft smiles he often wore *before*. On the surface, the smile looks the same as the others, but it feels more pensive and offers no reassurance now.

Things have changed drastically since June.

*I've changed.*

Sometimes, I don't know what to think or how to feel about any of this. I used to be desperate for Ice's attention and approval. *How is this the same person I dated back then?*

I guess it doesn't matter. Now, I only want to know what it will take to be rid of him for good.

"Come on," he says before popping his door open. "We can talk inside."

# fifty-five

I hate this.

I hate everything about this. Ice's cool demeanor. The ease with which I agreed to meet with him. His cryptic comments. And the fact I left James at the hospital. But I've come too far to turn back.

*I have to see this through.*

With a nod, I leave the car and follow Ice into the house.

The great room is brightly lit, tidy, and decorated the same as I remember. Exotic trinkets and thick nonfiction books line the shelves, framed artwork and photos dot the sage walls, and the room smells faintly of strawberries.

A wave of heady nostalgia washes over me, leaving me even more conflicted.

I had some good times here, sure, but my last memory of this place is being attacked with the same knife now tucked away in my pocket. I couldn't even walk out on my own. James had to carry me out to his car and drive me to the hospital. *And I'm betraying him by coming here alone and putting myself in danger again.*

"We have a guest," Ice announces as we step into the den.

Night glances up from the paperback novel she was reading. Her attention locks on me, tension creeping into her expression, the book in her hand all but forgotten.

Seeing her is a relief, even more so than seeing her car parked out front was. I haven't seen her outside of a dream in weeks, and I suddenly feel more at ease knowing she's here and okay. Though, I still hide my bruised arm behind my back.

"I can't believe you managed to bring her here," she says.

Her voice is level, but I catch a flicker of concern as she looks between me and Ice, and her frown only grows more pronounced as he grins.

"I don't trust you," she says. "Why is she here?"

He laughs. "Calm down. It's not like I kidnapped her. I only intend to talk, and she agreed to come."

"To talk?" she asks.

My mouth feels dry as my frustration and anxiety build, but I nod. "I did agree to come. And he did say he just wants to talk."

"Do you *want* to talk to him, though?"

"I…" I glance at my hands. "Whether I want to or not, I know we should. So… It's fine, really."

"Are you planning to talk out here?"

"We're going to my room," Ice says. "Alone."

"Alone?" Night's eyes narrow dangerously. "Is that wise?"

"Jayde's fine with it."

"Is she?"

I bite the inside of my cheek. "If you're out here, it should be okay. This won't take long, will it?"

We both look to Ice, who doesn't quite look at either of us, as he seems distracted and thoughtful again. But he shakes his head.

"I can't imagine it will take long."

She frowns. "I suppose I'll allow it since Jayde says it's okay, but I won't hesitate to step in if I hear anything. *Anything*, you hear me?"

He smiles. "Of course. We'll be sure to keep our voices down."

She's hardly impressed, and neither am I, but she appears as placated as she can be.

"Is that all?" she asks, adjusting her grip on her book.

"Yes," he says, his tone curt. "Now, please excuse us."

He continues down the hallway, but I stick around a moment longer when more obvious fear flashes over Night's face. I don't want her to worry. After all, while I was unfairly coerced into meeting Ice, he hasn't threatened me, and I am the one who called him and told him where I was.

"It's nice to see you again," I say.

"*James?*" she mouths.

That's…something I *really* don't have time to explain. I don't know if she has any idea what Ice did last night, but James will be alright, so I opt for a simple and intentionally vague thumbs-up. She lets out a relieved breath and offers a smile.

I return the smile, excuse myself, and meet up with Ice in the hall, where he waits just outside his closed bedroom door. The hallway's cream carpet and muted green walls are unblemished. There isn't a single faint brown splotch, bleach stain, or section of fresh paint that doesn't quite match the rest.

*How? How can it be like nothing ever happened?*

"I should have asked before," he says idly. "You've been at the hospital all night, right? Are you hungry? I could have Night make something for you."

"No thanks," I reply with a taut smile.

Hungry or not, this is a nightmare, and I don't care to drag it out any longer than necessary.

As I drop my smile, his equally artificial smile grows strained. He lets out a short breath and mutters something before opening the door. He then gestures for me to enter ahead of him, but I hesitate and peer through the doorway without moving.

*Even his bedroom is the same.*

I glance toward the den again. At Night. She holds her book in one hand while watching us with an unreadable expression. I trust she'll keep an ear out while I'm alone with Ice, but this still feels like the point of no return.

*We'll be sure to keep our voices down*, he said.

If we do, just about anything could happen once we're shut inside his room. He doesn't seem to harbor any overtly malicious intent, but it's obvious he doesn't want her involved. And I'm not sure what that means.

*Oh, well. Here goes nothing.*

I take one last deep breath and step inside.

Of course, as my eyes dart around the tidy room, the first thing to cross my mind is the Fourth of July. He never mentioned the stupid, drunk kiss after it happened—not even once—but I can't help thinking about it now that I'm stuck here with him again.

He follows me and closes the door behind himself.

I watch him for a moment, but he remains passive and casual, so I steal a glance out the window behind his desk. I stood in this same spot the day he denied having romantic feelings for me. The day he kissed me when I considered leaving.

My cheeks suddenly feel warm.

*I hate it.* I still don't understand what happened in July. I doubt I'll ever know what I meant to him before. It's hard to believe he's the same person...

*Forget about that!*

His feelings don't matter.

I slap a bitter frown on my face and turn away from the desk.

No matter what may or may not have happened between us in the past, Ice seriously tried to kill James last night. This is the same man who spent the entire summer either stringing me along or tormenting me out of what I can only assume is spite. He carved a heart into my wrist. He hurt people I care about over some years-old grudge I have nothing to do with.

But, today, he only wants to talk. He won't hurt me.

Devious curiosity flashes in his eyes as he smiles, looking incredibly...himself, and my courage wanes. I take a step back to keep more distance between us.

*Well, even if he does hurt me, he won't kill me.*

*He doesn't want to kill me.*

*Right?*

He shakes his head and walks past me, laughing breezily. "Are you nervous? Still scared of me?"

*I'm...confused.*

I track his movement, eventually turning all the way around

to my original position facing the window. He tosses his sunglasses onto his desk. Then he sits in his leather chair, adopting a laid-back posture, and gestures for me to take a seat on the bed.

I respectfully decline and remain standing with my arms folded over my chest.

"It's not as though I can hurt you," he says, rolling his eyes. "I left my knife sticking out of your sorry excuse for a boyfriend's chest—or have you already forgotten?"

*You are such an asshole.*

"I know you have a gun," I say through my teeth.

He grimaces. "Yes, well, it turns out I rather dislike guns."

"And? You could easily hurt me without either."

"What kind of man do you take me for, Jayde?" he asks with a laugh. "Besides, if I only wanted to hurt you, I could have easily done so back in the hospital parking lot and saved myself the trip."

*He has a point.*

My hands fall to my hips. "Well, what *do* you hope to get out of this?"

"I haven't decided. I'm still thinking."

*Hm.*

I look around again, and—

A pair of familiar brown leather boots sit on the floor beside the door. The same boots I trashed while walking through the mud to Reid Manor. I assumed they were lost forever, but they're clean and polished. They look as though they were never damaged at all. *And I—*

"Are those my boots?" I ask.

"Oh. Yes. I forgot I had those." His voice is surprisingly blank, so I almost believe it.

"Where'd you get them?"

He thinks about it for a moment. "In July, a Human-Immortal Affairs agent stopped by with a box of…garbage, ultimately— whatever RPD collected on your assault case. He asked if I wanted any of it. The boots are the one thing I kept."

*But…* "Why?"

He shrugs. "They seemed nice, and I thought you might want them back. Was I wrong? I can throw them out if you don't. Or give them to Night."

"No—" I hesitate, embarrassed by how quickly I protested, and lower my voice again. "I like those boots. They were expensive…"

He laughs. "Oh? Have you run into financial trouble relying on James already? Do you need money?"

"No."

I glare at him, but there's something strange about the whole thing. Why decide to keep the boots? Even then, why bother fixing them up? *Was he planning to return them eventually? Did he seriously forget?*

We're both quiet for a moment, and the overt amusement fades from his expression as his eyes flick from my face to my chest.

"You have the River Sapphire."

It's not a question. I'm clearly wearing it.

"And?" I ask.

Without warning, he leaves the chair, but I stand my ground, locking myself into eye contact with him. The eagerness in his expression throws me off—it's an obvious challenge—but I refuse to back down, desperate to maintain my defensive posture.

The knife feels heavy in my pocket.

"Perfect." He grins and clasps his hands together. "I've decided what we should do today."

I bite my cheek, resisting the urge to take a step back.

"I am your sponsor," he continues, his eyes wide. "Like it or not, there's nothing we can do about that fact, and I do hope you reach your full potential. I suppose you could say I'd like to help you reach it however I can."

"My full potential?" I echo.

I raise a hand to touch the River Sapphire. My fingers close around it, and I feel something like a static shock shoot up my arm.

He wants to help me reach my full potential?

*To...see what I'm capable of?*

"How?" I ask sharply.

He cracks a smile. Then he takes another step forward. *Too close!* My hand reaches for my back pocket, and we both freeze.

"Oh?" His bright eyes flick toward the hand hovering above my pocket, and his easy smile widens to a dark grin. "You have my knife."

*Damn it.* I moved without thinking, and it gave me away.

Even if he knows I have the knife, I can't let him walk all over me anymore. *He stabbed James last night. James could have died.* I can't let Ice win. I have to get something out of this meeting.

My hand closes around the knife, still in my pocket.

"What do you mean?" I ask. "How do you plan to help me?"

He watches me carefully for a moment, and then holds out one hand. Empty, palm facing up. "I have an idea," he says. "Hand it over, and I'll consider telling you what I came up with."

*Return the knife first? I don't like this.*

Letting him have the knife seems like a worse idea than agreeing to meet in the first place, and I'm slowly coming to realize that was also a mistake. Once he has the knife, my one bargaining chip is gone. I'll have no leverage. No defense.

*I want to know what he has to say, but...*

I scour his posture, not wanting to miss a single red flag, but his interest strikes me as genuine. With his right hand tucked in his jacket pocket and the other still held out, he waits for me to decide. His expression is neutral—a soft smile and passive eyes.

*His guard is down, and I'm already holding the knife.*

Maybe I don't care what Ice wants to say. Maybe I don't care about the Human Immortal Program or *reaching my full potential* or assuming a feline form. Maybe I don't care about any of that. Maybe I understand why James was so willing to take the fall for what Ice did just because he thought it might keep me safe.

*Maybe...*

Slowly, I remove my hand from my pocket with the switch-blade closed inside it.

He knows I have the knife, but he thinks he's smarter than me. He thinks he has me all figured out. He thinks I'm terrified of him—that I feel powerless in his presence. And, maybe he's right, but that's exactly why he would never expect me to try anything.

Not after what happened last night, when I froze and hid in the washroom.

I glance from the knife to his outstretched hand. He doesn't try to snatch it away. He doesn't move at all. His expression doesn't shift in the slightest, and his focus doesn't leave my eyes. He's just...*waiting*.

*Can I seriously pull this off?*

*We're alone. I have a weapon, and he doesn't, and his guard is down. Will I ever get another chance like this?*

My thumb presses the button on the side of the knife. The blade flicks out from the handle with a sharp, metallic click, and I lunge forward, aiming for his chest.

But the hand that Ice kept so casually tucked in his pocket catches my arm, and the room falls silent.

# fifty-six

I stare at the hand wrapped around my wrist for a long, tense moment before my eyes finally flick up. To my dismay, he regards me with muted amusement rather than the surprise or anger I expected. He doesn't seem the least bit offended or upset that I just tried to stab him.

*He thinks this is funny?*

He releases my arm. My grip on the knife tightens as my hand falls to my side, but he merely shakes his head and laughs, looking away and raking a hand through his hair.

"Nice," he says coolly. "Honestly, that was— Wow. That was certainly something, wasn't it?"

He holds out his right hand.

I have half a mind to give stabbing him another go as hot, bitter tears fill my eyes. But I look from his face to his hand and pause. Through my blurry vision, I notice jagged, pink lines across his palm and in the creases of his fingers.

*Scars? From when? From what?*

Never mind.

I slap the knife, broad side down, into his open hand and turn away. I turn my back on Ice, who now has the knife. *Because*

*I'm crying.* I press the heels of my palms into my eyes and suppress a sob.

*What the hell was I thinking?*

Stabbing him was a stupid idea. It never would have worked. But I still *tried*. What would I have done if I succeeded? How is what I just did any different than what he's been doing all summer?

*What is wrong with me?*

"Oh, get over yourself," he mutters. "Do you want to hear what I have to say or not? You won't get the chance if Night hears you crying and decides to step in."

I nod fervently, still struggling to regain control of myself. I take a deep breath, wipe the last of the wetness from my eyes, and sniffle before facing him again. He flashes a smile that almost passes as sympathetic and glances at the knife in his hand.

I give up and sit on the edge of the soft bed.

"I can't believe you had this." He sounds sincerely impressed as he looks up, though his smile grows wry. "In fact, I'm more surprised you brought it with you than I am surprised that you thought to come at me with it."

I cough.

His smile wavers, and he checks the smartwatch on his wrist. "Excuse me a moment. I'll explain what I have in mind when I return, so… Please, wait here."

I track his path across the room. He leaves, and my attention lingers on the door for a moment. Then my boots. And then…

The closet door used to have a full-length mirror on it, but it's gone now. Well, no… The mirror is still there—or the frame is, anyway—but the glass is missing. Only the pale wood backing and a few silvery shards clinging to the dark, metallic frame remain.

*What happened?*

After thinking on it a moment longer, I realize it doesn't matter. I don't, and shouldn't, care about a stupid broken mirror.

I tear my eyes away, drop my head into my hands, and stare at the carpet near my feet. Specks of dried blood speckle my shoes' rubber toes. My cheeks are still warm from crying.

*This is so weird...*

I can't stand Ice, but I still agreed to come, and I still returned his knife after my pathetically sad attempt at stabbing him with it. He wasn't even fazed. He carried on like nothing happened, and I just went along with it. I gave the knife back. The same knife he sliced me up with. The same knife he nearly killed James with.

After everything I've been through—after everything he did to me—how can we still interact so casually? *Why did I want to thank him for holding on to my boots?* It doesn't make any sense, and I hate it.

James would be so upset if he knew I came here. He never would have agreed to this. *I* shouldn't have agreed to this.

*Ice is right about me.*

This is exactly the same as when I walked out to find James behind his back. Or when I hid my scars from Rose. Or ignored the threat he made during our midnight meeting. It's starting to seem like the only thing I'm good at is betraying the people I care about.

*And none of those decisions turned out well. Why did I think this would be any different?*

I look up at the closed door again.

Of course, I feel bad for coming here. Of course, there's a chance this could end terribly. But Ice's idea has me curious, and I want to work out some kind of compromise. Today, it almost seems that might be possible. He hasn't forced me to do anything or made any direct threats even after I tried to stab him with his own knife.

*Considering that, he's been incredibly reasonable.*

Still… For weeks now, I've desperately wanted to believe Ice couldn't feel anything. I wanted to believe he was an emotionless monster who was playing me the entire time we were together and never felt anything for me. I wanted to believe that because it was easier than…

*Ugh. It was so much easier than this.*

I used to consider Ice a good friend. I wanted to be more than friends. *For a minute, I really thought I loved him.*

That's over.

Anything like what we had in June is impossible now—I could never trust him again—but I still wonder about the real Ice. Is this passive, casual conversation an act? Are all of the soft, thoughtful smiles fake? Was everything remotely good I saw in him imagined or another part of his charming facade?

*How much was real?*

*Does it even matter after what he did?*

The doorknob turns, the bedroom door opens, and I smother my thoughts as Ice steps inside. This is hardly the time to dwell on the past. I came here today hoping I could finally do something to move forward.

I stand, swallowing my nerves.

The knife is missing from his hand, but that doesn't mean he doesn't still have it. He isn't wearing the leather jacket anymore either—now wearing dark jeans and a wine red button-up with the sleeves rolled to his elbows. If he has the knife, it must be in one of his pockets.

I have to stay alert. Watch for any sudden movements.

He meets my gaze and slowly closes the door behind himself. His apparent thoughtfulness makes me even more curious than before. But I'd hate to give him any ideas, so I fold my arms over my chest and feign indifference.

"So, what's your idea?" I ask. "I don't have all day."

He flashes an uneasy smile and scratches his jaw. "I'm trying to work out a way to explain without you accusing me of insanity."

"You *are* insane. Just spit it out."

He averts his gaze. It surprises me, though his hesitance is also intimidating in its own way. *He can't even feign confidence right now?*

"I've been thinking about what you said on the drive here," he says. "James morphed after he went into shock. It was an unconscious emergency measure his defective body took to save his life. Is that not what you told me?"

*I do not like the direction this is heading.*

When he meets my eyes again, I make my discomfort clear on my face. His expression doesn't change in the slightest, so he must have expected that reaction.

"Based on the available information—which, admittedly, is not a lot—I can only assume it was some type of...biological defense mechanism," he continues, his voice level but strangely detached. "I once read that the physical body doesn't want to die regardless of what the mind may have convinced itself, so I wonder if it might be a reflex all immortals have in the event they suffer extreme blood loss."

The surgeon who operated on James said something similar. He'd seen it before in trauma cases with severe bleeding. *But Ice means—*

"So, you think—" I stammer, unable to finish.

He nods, and his subdued frown startles me. I wasn't expecting this. No laughter. No trace of humor. He's not teasing me or messing around.

He's serious. This is a serious idea.

"After everything I—" His eyes dart aside, his jaw set. Then he sighs and reaffirms eye contact. "In any case, I understand if you don't trust me. Perhaps you're wise not to, but I hope you at least believe when I say I am interested in seeing you morph. I didn't opt you into that program for nothing, and I assume you've wanted the River Sapphire to work since I gave it to you. Right?"

"You really mean that? This isn't a trap?"

"It's not a trap, Jayde." The smile he offers is weak at best, and he makes that stupid *cross-my-heart* motion over his chest. "I am not trying to trick you. I swear."

I cover my mouth with one hand and tear my gaze from his face. *If he's suggesting what I think he's suggesting...* Ice's plan is to trigger near-fatal blood loss *in me* because it could *theoretically* force my body to react to the River Sapphire and morph as a last-ditch effort to save my life.

This is stupid. It *is* insane. I am not an immortal—defective or otherwise. I'm human. There's no guarantee it will work even if his theory about immortal biology is correct.

*How could I possibly trust him with my life like that?*

"What do you think?" he asks.

I look at him again. My hands ball into loose fists against my chest upon meeting apprehensive blue eyes that carefully scan my face in return.

*He wants to go through with it here? Now?*

*What should I do?*

Sure, it would be great if he was right, and if it worked, and if I could use the River Sapphire freely after. But what if he's wrong? If this plan failed, I would *die*. I would die, and James would find out that I went behind his back while he was asleep in the hospital and *let Ice kill me.*

"Don't forget that Smoke has healing abilities," he says. "If the wound is small enough, he may be able to save you even if you fail to morph in time."

*This is...wrong...*

His idea is far too dangerous. The alarm bell ringing in my head and the pit in my stomach beg me to decline the offer and ask to leave. Forget the reason I came here. None of that matters if I get myself killed.

I almost refuse, but I hesitate.

"Be honest. Do I have a choice?"

"Of course, you have a choice." He cracks a smile, looking

more like the person I absolutely hate, and gestures toward the door. "My door can't lock. You are more than welcome to walk out on me or scream for Night's help at any moment, but what good would it do? What's to stop me from taking matters into my own hands another day? Wouldn't you rather have the choice now? Wouldn't you rather give yourself the greatest chance of success?"

*There it is.*

I have two options: Willingly follow through with whatever harebrained plan he concocted or leave and continue living in fear, wondering when he'll decide he can't wait to know the answer any longer. One way or another, it'll happen eventually.

*This is certainly the least traumatizing option.*

"Are you sure this will work?"

"No." His admission is blunt, veiled by disappointment, and accented with a shrug. "There's no way to know if something that worked for one defective immortal will work for a human regardless of the River Sapphire's latent potential. It's possible nothing will happen. There is a real chance you will die."

I chew the inside of my cheek, struggling to remain calm in the face of my own death—standing in front of my potential murderer, who watches me cautiously. *I just want to get back to James. Satisfying Ice by doing this might make him ease up on us, so...* I can only hope it works—or, at the very least, hope Ice doesn't let me die.

"Alright, fine," I agree. "On one condition."

His eyes narrow, but he looks more intrigued than suspicious. "What's the condition?"

"You have to return the key you copied."

"The key to your cottage?" he asks. When I nod, the ghost of a smile crosses his face. "Done."

I tense as he reaches for his back pocket, but his hand returns with only a small, brass house key, which he immediately offers to me. I take it and stare at the key for a moment.

*That was...easier than expected.*

"This is the only copy you have, right?"

"Yes."

*That was too easy.*

I shake my head, frowning severely. "You swear you don't have another key? And that you won't make any others?"

"No more keys," he says without hesitation, though his smile widens. "I swear on my life—as little as I'm sure that means to you."

I sigh in exasperation.

"Is that all?" he asks.

I nod. *It's not much, but I don't want to push my luck. This will have to be enough for now.* I tuck the key in my pocket and, steeling myself, step forward to close the distance between us.

"What's your plan?"

"First—" Some of the humor leaves his expression as he holds out his empty left hand. "—I need your arm."

A flicker of familiarity startles me, but I smother the panic and offer him my left hand. His fingers brush over the scarred heart on my wrist, sending a cold chill down my spine. Then he takes ahold of my arm. His grip is surprisingly gentle, and I watch with a sick curiosity while his thumb presses around the inside of my elbow.

After a moment, he taps a spot directly above a dark artery. "Here. This should work."

*Oh, my god...* I tear my eyes away.

"You know what you're doing, right?" I ask.

"More or less."

*Great.*

He looks focused, but I can't concentrate on his face as the knife appears in his other hand. My stomach churns, and my heart races as the now-clean blade flips out of the handle at the press of a button. *Click.*

*What am I still doing here?*

Adrenaline floods my system, and my muscles scream to pull my arm away and make a break for it. To run. To leave the room or call for help. To get Night involved before this can go any further. But I fight my instincts. I ignore the shrill cry in the back of my mind—*I don't have a choic*e—but I can't keep from trembling.

"Look at me," he says.

I check my arm again, eyes passing over the spot he touched before. The knife isn't there yet, so I meet his eyes. He looks calm. Knowing what he's about to do and the risk involved, how can he look at me like that?

This is wrong. *This is so wrong.*

"At least try to relax, would you," he says. "The faster your heart beats, the faster your blood flows, so you'll have more time if you don't panic."

*Try to relax? Don't panic? Are you kidding?*

As I stare into his eyes like he's lost his damn mind, his expression remains level and calculated. His focus shifts from my eyes to my arm. His thumb brushes against my skin again. Cool metal and the gentle pressure of the knife's blade soon replace it.

I don't look.

Someone knocks on the door.

We both freeze.

# fifty-seven

"Ice? Jayde?" *Night.* "Is everything alright in there?"

Ice's expression shifts slightly. His eyes linger on the blade at my arm for a long second before he looks up. I stare back at him. He's still calm. Still serious. But he doesn't speak.

I look past Ice. I look to the door.

"Hello?" she calls, a hint of tension in her voice.

My heart races. My mouth is dry.

*But he's leaving it up to me. What should I do?*

I do not want to go through with this. Obviously. I don't want Ice to cut me again. I don't want to risk death just to see if it *might* activate the River Sapphire. I should be with James right now. I should be there, waiting for him to wake up. *And Ice would have no choice but to back down if I got Night involved now.* He told the truth—the door doesn't have a privacy lock. If I asked for help—if I said *no*—she could walk right in. This could end here, and I could go back to Centennial Memorial.

But I clear my throat, grasp the hem of my shirt with my free hand, and say, "We're fine."

A pause follows, during which my heart seems to pound so loudly I can hear it, and I forget to breathe for a moment.

"Are you sure?" she asks.

"Yeah," I say. "We're just talking."

"Do you need anything?"

*Aah...* "No. Everything is fine."

I look to Ice with the most intentionally vacant and desperate expression I can manage. He takes a breath and offers a hesitant smile.

"We'll be out in a few minutes," he says, his voice more level and convincing than mine.

"Okay," she agrees lamely.

A few quiet, tense seconds pass, and then Night's footsteps make their way back toward the den. And I let out the breath I was holding.

"That was close," he says.

My cheek catches on my teeth. "This isn't funny."

"I never said it was."

His smile fades as his eyes flick down, and he presses the knife to my arm again. I still don't look. Even as the blade breaks skin, I don't look away from his intensely focused expression. The slice is small and quick. Like a needle piercing skin. Or a paper cut. But I know the nasty truth of it.

*This could kill me.*

The immediate sensation of blood bubbling from the wound tempts me to look, but my eyes dart back up at the first suggestion of red.

*Okay, this* might *kill me.*

Ice's eyes widen—in surprise, perhaps—but he soon reasserts eye contact and drops my arm, which falls limp to my side. Warm liquid pours down my arm and drips from my fingertips.

*Already? How is this possible? From such a small wound?*

"What did you do?" My voice is hardly a whisper.

He frowns. "I severed a vital artery in your arm—the brachial artery, if you actually care to know."

*I...want to see. Maybe...one look.*

"Wait—"

Something falls to the floor with a soft thud—*he dropped the knife*—and a hand stops me. The warm, gentle pressure against my cheek leaves me unable to get a proper look at my left side, and the presence of his arm keeps my own just out of sight. All I can make out is a flash of dark red on the carpet.

His other hand moves to my shoulder to hold me steady. I didn't even realize my legs began to wobble. I meet his gaze, confused, but his eyes flick down. The color drains from his cheeks.

"Ha..." When he looks up again, he flashes a smile that looks more like a poorly disguised grimace. "You're making an awful mess of the carpet."

*Ha. Ha.*

It's hard to say whether it's the blood loss or Ice's sick attempt at a joke, but I suddenly feel weak—nauseous and lightheaded.

I try to peek at my arm a second time.

He still won't allow it.

Maybe he's only trying to protect me from a sight troubling enough to make him blanch, but the jaded, bitter part of me that isn't quite ready to die wonders why he'd bother. Does it matter if I look at my arm? What does he care if I see the blood? It can't be any worse than what I dealt with last night.

*What difference does it make to you?*

I raise my bleeding arm instead, but it's numb and heavy. I can only lift it enough to catch a brief glimpse, the skin slick and glistening red, in my periphery.

*Oh, god—*

My arm falls to my side like a lead weight, and I glance down to see the blood pooling on the cream carpet at our feet. I slap my hand over my mouth and tear my eyes from the gore. Not looking changes nothing, and the dizziness only worsens.

*This can't be happening.*

"This is it," I mumble into my hand as my vision blurs. "I'm gonna die here. I just let you kill me."

"Hey—"

He taps my cheek to get my attention, and I reluctantly look over. Narrowed blue eyes betray mild concern as disgust mars his otherwise unaffected expression. *How annoying.*

I drop my hand and press it over the crook of my elbow. Blood pulses beneath my palm and spills between my fingers like hot water from a broken pipe. I can't tell where the wound is— not that it makes a difference. The bleeding is relentless. Easily worse than James' yesterday.

I gasp.

*From that tiny cut?*

"If you don't morph, you're right," he says, his voice low but rough with a new sense of urgency. "You will die here."

*How can I—?*

My vision goes dark, and my legs buckle.

The carpet squishes beneath my knee. That wet sound and the uncomfortable warmth against bare skin set my stomach churning, but I suppress the urge to dry heave and open my eyes, blinking to clear my spotty, blurred vision.

*Ice followed me down.*

He holds my face in his hands, giving me nowhere to look but at him. His expression is murky and unfathomable as he glances at my bleeding arm. His eyes widen for an instant, and he quickly looks up again with a tight, empty smile.

"You know, I would prefer you not die today."

*This is all your fault. I never should have listened to you.*

My left arm no longer responds when I try to move it, but I raise my good arm to hit him. He doesn't stop me. My feeble, trembling fist contacts his chest while he watches with a mild frown.

I hit him again, and he still does nothing.

*Damn it, Ice...*

"I hate you," I gasp, my voice soft and breathless as hot tears fill my eyes. "I hate you...so much."

His expression darkens. He glances away. His hands fall from my face to my shoulders, but he doesn't react even as I raise my fist a third time.

*If I'm going to die here...*

Instead of hitting him, I ball the fabric of his shirt in my hand, press my fist to his chest, and bury my face in his shoulder. His breath hitches, and he tenses at my touch.

But I don't care if it bothers him.

*Why should I?*

I don't care if it's pathetic—if crying is embarrassing. I don't care how he feels about me now or felt about me before all this. I don't care if he's a monster. I don't care if I hate him or not. I don't care about *anything* anymore.

None of it matters.

*I am about to die.*

*I'm seriously gonna bleed out on the floor in Ice's bedroom.*

But he doesn't push me away like I expected. His warm breath tickles my ear, leveling out as he seems to relax.

"You don't have much time," he says.

I sob something along the lines of, "I can't."

"Shh…" He laughs, the sound light. "Night would kill me if she caught us like this, but—"

His hands leave my shoulders and move to my back. As he pulls me closer, his radiant warmth only emphasizes how cold I've become. *God, he is so warm, but…*

*Why now?*

Everything grows fuzzy. Sounds. Physical sensation. Thoughts. I can't feel my left arm, but the blood that must be pulsing from it continues to slick everything. A wet patch spreads across my side and chest as it wicks through my shirt.

*So much…*

"If you die here, you'll never see him again, you know."

*Why?*

My muffled crying falters, and my eyes flutter open, though tears still stream down my cheeks. There's not much to see, but…

*Why mention James now?* You hate him more than anything, right? You hurt me just to hurt him. Wouldn't you enjoy watching him suffer the pain of losing me—especially like this?

*Imagine…the gloating…*

He's right again, though.

If I die here, I *won't* see James again.

I won't get the chance to apologize for lying. I won't be able to tell him how I feel. What would happen to James if I were to die now? Would Ice still want him dead? Would he confront Ice in the name of revenge? *Would someone get hurt?*

My body is numb. Empty. But I think the crying stopped.

I close my eyes again. Ice's hair brushes my cheek as I drop my face to his shoulder. The sharp, metallic tang of blood hangs in the air. But I still smell him over it. Clean and sweet and a bit spicy, like cinnamon and laundry detergent.

*It's the same…as I remember.*

A moment of silence. Just the distant, soft sound of breathing.

"Jayde?" he asks under his breath.

I want to answer, if only to assure him I'm not quite dead yet, but I can't. I don't think I could speak if I tried. A heavy, pervasive sense of cold slowly replaces the sensation of arms holding me. He's so close, I can feel his heartbeat against my chest, but it's not enough to keep me warm anymore.

I feel so cold and so empty and so tired. I should have gotten some sleep before… I should have tried harder. *But now…*

I open my eyes to nothing—a silent and empty void. Like the center of the supermassive black hole from the documentary. Like the impossibly dark horror of the worst of my dreamscape.

I can't move. I can't see. I feel nothing.

*Am I already dead?*

# fifty-eight

~ ∞ ~

*I draw a single breath, deep and shuddering, before all is once again swallowed by heavy silence. I open my eyes, but I'm still there. I'm still trapped inside the black hole's gravity, and I still can't move.*

*No...*

*I can't die here.*

*I can't die like this.*

*Not on the floor in Ice's bedroom.*

*Not before I apologize to James.*

*But I know the black hole—that abyssal avatar of death and eternity—doesn't care what anyone wants. It doesn't care about me. It doesn't care about closure. It doesn't care about feelings. It seeks only finality. The inevitable end to everything.*

*After hours floating in silent darkness, I hear the faintest noise.*

*The faintest electronic pulse.*

*The faintest ticking clock.*

*The faintest...dripping.*

*I take another breath, softer this time as I stir slightly. I'm lying on my side. The ground feels cold against my skin. Then I open my eyes, and...*

How am I supposed to feel?

Does waking up here mean I can't be dead? Or is this just what happens when someone dies? Does everyone end up alone in their dreamscape eventually? Is the universe seriously so cruel it would leave me in this empty void, trapped with nothing but myself and my thoughts for the rest of forever?

I drag myself out of the fetal position and, while still sitting on the cold ground, look at my arms. They're clean and unblemished, marred only by old scars. I'm wearing the clothes I was wearing before Ice cut my arm, Red Cross t-shirt included, but they're also clean, and the River Sapphire is missing.

*What does that mean?*

*What does anything in this place ever mean?*

The lights aren't floating around, but the general atmosphere doesn't feel overtly threatening. The faint sounds from before are gone, though. It's quiet again.

And it's kind of cold.

I stand up and look around, but my dreamscape is empty. No sign of light. No distant noises. Nothing. Just darkness and a slight, uncomfortable chill. I hug my arms to my chest.

*Was this place always so cold?*

"Hello!" I call, my voice echoing for several long seconds.

*Hm...*

I check my pockets. They're empty too. *No, wait—* My hand closes around something small and metallic. I pull it out and open my hand to find a key—the brass copy that Ice made and returned before promptly killing me.

*Ugh.*

I draw my arm back and throw the key as hard as I can. It blinks out of existence in midair, vanishing with a flicker of reflected light. Reflected light from *where*? There are literally no lights here. Where the hell is this light coming from?

*I hate it.*

I open my mouth to curse my dreamscape's very existence, but a soft tap like a footstep on hardwood makes me freeze.

"Aw, that's too bad," a voice says with a hint of amusement. "I rather like this place."

The voice is familiar, but *how?*

I spin around to look, and—

*Me. It's me.*

The second Jayde stands several feet away. We're dressed the same, but her clothes are soaked in blood, and thick red continues leaking from her left arm. It drips from her fingers in broad ribbons and disappears into the black ground as though sucked in.

"Who are you?" I ask.

"I'm you," she says, her tone flat and unimpressed. "Don't you recognize yourself?"

"Sure, but— Why are we here? Am I dead?"

"Dead?" She laughs, flashing a wry smile as she glances at her profusely bleeding arm. "I mean, this looks bad, but why would I know if it killed you or not?"

I shake my head and take a step back. "You're part of my

subconscious, right? Just another part of the dreamscape? I've seen impossible things here before. If you're anything like the rest, you must know something."

"I don't know any more than you do." Her eyes narrow. Then she smiles again, unpleasant and condescending. "But, I am curious… Do you *want* to die? Because, to me, it seems you didn't think this through at all."

"Of course, I don't want to die!"

"You could've fooled me," she says, laughing harder as blood continues pouring from her arm. "You told Night you were fine. You just…*let him cut you*. That is so stupid."

I bite the inside of my cheek. *Do you think I don't know that?*

Her laughter stops abruptly, and she frowns. "I've had enough of this."

The cool intensity in her eyes matches her passive voice, and both remind me of Ice, so I take another step back. She judges me but doesn't follow. Then, with an abrupt shake of her bleeding arm, the blood vanishes, and she's suddenly wearing a hospital gown.

"Do you think he cares?" she asks, her eyes flicking up to meet mine. "Do you think Ice cares if he killed you? Would your death upset him at all? Does he even know how to feel sad?"

*I—*

I drop my head into my hands. "I don't care what he thinks. I just wanted to do something to help. He gave me the key, so the cottage should be safe now. But, after this, I don't know if James will agree to go back. I don't know if he'll forgive me at all."

"You don't even know if you're alive."

"I have to be alive."

"Hm."

I have to be alive.

*I can't be dead.*

*I can't be—*

~ ∞ ~

# fifty-nine

I know I'm in the hospital without opening my eyes. The soft beeping of a heart monitor gives it away, but the hospital gown and crinkly sheets leave me confused.

*When did I become the one in the hospital bed?*

Wasn't James the one hurt? I remember rushing to Centennial Memorial in Rose's car with his unconscious feline form in my lap. I sat in the waiting room for hours as Rose left and Jesse left and Matthew left.

Wasn't I just watching James sleep in inpatient recovery from the plasticky bench in the window? I remember nodding off and moving to the chair at his bedside. The sun rose behind me, and—

*Ice messaged me.* We talked on the phone. I left the hospital to meet him, and he drove me to his house, and...

*We made some kind of deal, didn't we?*

He cut me, and I—

*Blood. Cold. Dark. Hollow, breathless laughter.*

Wait—

I open my eyes, expecting to be blinded, but the overhead lights are dimmed. The room has one, large window, and it's dark outside.

*Oh, no.*

If it's night, James has certainly woken up by now. He's probably been awake for hours. He knows I'm missing, but only Ice, Night, and I know where I went. He's surely worried sick.

*He'll lose his mind when he learns what I did.*

I sit up. *Ahh*— A sharp numbness shoots up my left arm, and it buckles at the elbow. Groaning through the wave of pins and needles, I switch arms—my right can bear the weight but is similarly weak.

*I feel like I was hit by a truck.*

I look at my arm. The garish, hot pink stretch bandage wrapped around my elbow. The wound was so small, and the pink bandage seems more like a patch job I might expect after a routine blood draw rather than the aftermath of a life-threatening injury.

I don't remember leaving Ice's house. I don't even remember leaving the bedroom. I must have lost consciousness before that.

*How much blood did I lose?*

Night knocked on the door. *After that, I can't remember...*

Oh, well. Regardless of what happened, Ice kept his word— not that he promised I wouldn't die, but the brass key is on the metal table beside the bed, along with my wallet and phone.

Looking up again, I assess my situation further. I'm in a private recovery room—not the ICU. I'm still connected to a heart monitor with the volume turned down, and I'm in a bed with crinkly paper sheets, but I must be in the clear. More interesting, the room is fairly large with homey decor, including a dresser, couch, and small two-person dining set. It doesn't look like a normal recovery room—at least not like the ones I stayed in before.

*What hospital is this?*

I glance toward the door and realize *I'm not alone.*

My eyes come to focus on a figure half-slumped in a chair near the door. As much as I wish it were the low light playing tricks on me, I know it's Ice.

*Why is he here?*

I check the time on the wall clock—just after 2AM. Then I look back to Ice. He's wearing green scrubs and appears fast asleep in the small chair.

*This is...weird.*

He picked me up from Centennial Memorial Hospital in the morning, and it couldn't have yet been noon when I agreed to go along with his insane plan. If he brought me here right after— I mean, I imagine he must have if I somehow survived...

*Has he been here all day?*

He's the whole reason I'm here. Why bother?

I scratch near the IV catheter on my wrist and stare at my arm again. The hot pink bandage. The bruise from having my hand pinned behind my back. The heart etched into my skin.

*Ice was behind all of it.*

The person who held a knife to my throat and tried to kill James just the other night is the same man who stuck around in the hospital this long for no apparent reason. I will never understand him, but I'm honestly not sure I want to anymore.

*Ugh...*

My tingling, weak right arm begs me to ease up on it, so I

give in to the urge. I lie down and close my eyes and try to ignore Ice's presence.

But I can't.

Even after several minutes spent lying in bed with my eyes closed while listening to the softly beeping heart monitor and ticking clock and wondering if James is asleep right now, I just can't.

*This is so frustrating.*

Ice is a mystery. I've never been able to guess his motivation —in talking to me or dating me or anything—but if he's sleeping here... *What is he doing? What is he waiting for?*

Falling asleep is obviously a bust.

I sit up again and watch Ice for a moment. There's a full-size couch on the other side of the room. Why is he asleep in a plastic chair next to the door?

*Ugh...*

*Oh! I wonder...*

Did it work? I'm not wearing the River Sapphire, and it's not on the metal table with the rest of my things. Is it possible I turned into a cat after I blacked out? Should I wake him up and ask what happened?

*Should I...?*

"Hey—" My voice is weak and scratchy, so I clear my throat and try again, speaking a bit louder. "Hey, Ice. Are you asleep?"

He tenses in the chair, but soon grimaces and opens one eye that reflects a faint green. "Not anymore."

"I'm alive," I say.

"Yes, I see that," he agrees through a yawn.

"Where am I?"

He stretches his arms above his head. "Riverview General Hospital, of course."

"Why are you here?"

"Good question." He glances at the clock and sighs. "It would appear I fell asleep by mistake. Today was an ordeal, even by my standards."

"Well... Did it work?"

Finally, I detect a flicker of recognition on his part. A hint of a smile, and a hint of familiar arrogance that reminds me who he is.

"Yes, it worked." But he frowns, muddling his expression. "For a moment, I was certain you would die. But my theory proved correct in the end."

I crack a weak smile. "Were you worried about me?"

He hits me with a bleak, tired look before glancing away. It's an honest surprise that even he doesn't think this is an appropriate time for humor.

"Worried...is not the term I would use," he says. "Though, you are fortunate to have separate forms."

*Separate forms?*

"Do they know what happened?" I ask.

He meets my gaze, guarded as though he isn't sure what I'm trying to ask. But I'm not sure exactly what I meant myself. The question was automatic.

*Do they know what happened?*

Do hospital staff know he's the one who nearly killed me? Do the twins know what he did? Did he call Human-Immortal Affairs? Do they know I successfully morphed? Does anyone else know where I am? What's the deal with *separate forms*, anyway?

I could have meant any number of things, and I don't clarify, but he soon takes a deep breath and nods.

"I explained the situation to Dr. Corel," he says mildly, "but it seems he already knew the gist of what's transpired since July. It was…interesting to learn you've been under his care all this time."

*Oh?*

"You know Dr. Corel?" I ask, though his dagger eyes convince me to drop it. "Did you call Human-Immortal Affairs?"

He turns away, lip curling in disgust. "Of course. Corel contacted them the moment I arrived. They swarmed the place. Forced you to morph repeatedly right after surgery. Took a dozen vials of blood—never mind you lost half while bleeding out an hour earlier. When I told them off, they threw a mountain of paperwork in my face and stirred up a variety of menial annoyances to distract me from whatever they were doing. It's no wonder it took you so long to regain consciousness."

*Wow.* They pissed him off, huh?

I guess I can't blame him. If what he says is true, they treated me like a lab rat with little regard for my safety. *Not that Ice has done much better.*

Maybe I should change the subject.

"How do I morph, anyway?"

"The River Sapphire."

*Well, no shit!*

He rolls his eyes, cracking a smile at whatever face I made. "You take feline form if you wear the necklace, and you remain in human form if you don't. The results are consistent and rather unimpressive, to tell you the truth."

*The activation method could be worse, but...*

"Does James know where I am?"

"Of course not," he says bitterly. "I'm your sponsor. There was no need to involve James."

*Of course.* It would have only ended in a fight, anyway.

I sigh. "When can I leave?"

"When a doctor says you can leave."

I frown pointedly, and he flashes a weak smile.

"Look," he says. "I hate being holed up in this godforsaken hospital too, but Human-Immortal Affairs called the shots today. I was advised against contacting outside parties. I kept my mouth shut. I was advised to stay until you woke up. I sat here for hours."

When I say nothing, his expression hardens slightly. "That's it. That's why I'm still here. Understand? And you lost damn near half your blood, so you're staying put until you're discharged."

I understand.

He only stayed because he was obligated to as my sponsor. He didn't want to hang around the hospital for hours or fill out paperwork or listen to Human-Immortal Affairs. Though, I'm almost surprised he'd follow their commands at all. I can't imagine they would have punished him if he just left, considering they certainly didn't punish him for *nearly killing me.* But he stayed anyway.

He absolutely deserves whatever grief they gave him, though. Even if he isn't capable of feeling guilt over what he's done, I hope he feels sorry for himself. I hope this has ruined his life half as much as it screwed up mine.

"Well, I…" *I want to tell him, but I can't.* "For what it's worth, I'm glad you were right."

He smothers the ghost of a smile with his hand. "Yes. I wasn't sure the human body could survive losing so much blood, but the River Sapphire pulled through. Ah… In any case, your feline form is a small, brown tabby."

*A brown tabby…*

The room falls quiet.

Part of me hopes I'm wrong about him and the way he thinks. I desperately want to know if he regrets anything about this summer, but I'm not bold enough to ask. I don't think I'm ready to hear the answer. I doubt I could believe him if he ever said he was sorry.

"Can you leave? Please."

Our eyes meet again, and his betray what I can only describe as *pain*. That look alone almost makes me wish I could take it back even as cool disinterest smooths his features, but it's too late. And I meant what I said when I said it.

"Of course," he says. "You're awake, and you understand your situation. I have no reason to stay, do I?"

He stands from the chair and adjusts his scrub top before pausing to look himself over. He morphs twice in near-immediate succession, returning to human form wearing his leather jacket and dark jeans with the green scrubs folded over one arm.

*Hm.*

His ability has always made me curious, but I hold my tongue.

There's no point in asking. He wouldn't tell me anything—even Night doesn't know much beyond the obvious—and asking would probably only annoy him.

Besides, I need time alone to think. It's better if I let him go.

As he opens the door to leave, he pauses in the doorway. His hand lingers on the doorjamb, but he doesn't turn back to look at me. "You know… As things are, I doubt all three of us will make it out of this alive."

"What?"

"You've realized, right?" His voice is mild, serious and dark and tragically soft, and he still doesn't look back. "It's gone too far. There's no other way. One of us has to die. At least one. But I hope it's not you. I would truly hate to kill you."

"I— That's not—"

What am I even supposed to say to that?

"Oh, before I forget: I left a change of clothes for you. They're in the bag under the chair."

The door closes with a solid click, and I look away to stare at my lap. My trembling fists grip the thin hospital blanket until my arms ache and my knuckles turn white. I don't look away from them even as tears fall to the fabric.

I didn't notice the wet trails on my cheeks until now.

When did I start crying?

*But… Who cares?*

*Ice thinks someone has to die?*

*Why?*

# sixty

Dr. Corel stands beside the bed. He holds my medical chart in one hand, his attention focused on me as we share an uncomfortably long silence. Since we finished going over the basics, and the human nurse stepped out, it's felt like he has no idea what to say to me—not that I blame him, if that's the case.

*I wouldn't know what to say to me either.*

What I did was both insanely risky and insanely stupid. I'm lucky to be alive. Any number of things could have gone wrong. What if Ice was bluffing, and his plan was meant to kill me? What if I hadn't morphed soon enough—or at all? What if he hadn't bothered taking responsibility for his actions and just dumped my bleeding body outside the ER doors instead?

After what seems like forever, Dr. Corel clears his throat, adjusts his glasses, and meets my anxious gaze. His expression isn't unkind, but I suddenly feel very small.

"I'll be honest with you, Jayde," he says. "If you weren't as astronomically lucky as you are to have separate human and feline forms, you would be dead."

Too ashamed to look him in the eyes, I glance toward the River Sapphire, safe in a small, plastic bag on the bedside table.

Dr. Corel set it there when he first came in. Seeing it now doesn't make me feel any better about what I did.

"What were you thinking—to put yourself in such a dangerous situation?"

"I don't know," I mumble.

"You aren't suicidal, are you?" he asks. "Or thinking of hurting yourself at all?"

A voice echoes in the back of my mind: *Do you want to die?*

My breath catches, but I shake my head. I try to remember the details of the conversation in Ice's bedroom. It's all a bit fuzzy, but even after I tried to stab him, he…

"He seemed different," I say slowly. "More sincere than usual, I guess. More like he did…in June. I don't know… It just felt like he meant it when he said he wanted to help me, and it worked. I'm not dead, so…"

*Something else…right before I blacked out.* A heavy sense of cold. Arms holding me tight. A wet warmth soaking into my shirt. The faint scent of cinnamon mingling with rusty blood.

My skin prickles.

*Stop.*

"On an unrelated note, I heard James was recently wounded and admitted at Centennial Memorial."

Guilt pierces my chest.

I hate thinking about James, stuck in the hospital clear across town. I've been too scared to check my phone all morning, but he's surely awake by now—assuming he got any sleep after he regained consciousness and realized I was gone.

"I can only imagine how worried he is, not knowing where

you are," he continues. "James was always careful to keep close during your stays, even if he couldn't bring himself to sit by and watch you in bed."

*Are you trying to make me feel bad?*

I hide my face in my hands. "I know it seems crazy and stupid and selfish to meet with Ice on my own, but I was thinking about James the whole time. I thought that, if I just listened to Ice—if I just did what he wanted once—then, maybe…"

*Maybe it would help James? Ice no longer has a key to my house, and I can morph, but will this really help him?*

"Everything worked itself out," he replies with a sort of cold formality. "Ice saw to it that you morphed, and he relinquished you to the hospital to ensure your survival. As far as Human-Immortal Affairs is concerned, your case is a success. Congratulations."

*Yes, I know. It worked. Thanks.*

Leaving James in the hospital is surely one of the worst things I've ever done, but he never would have let me meet alone with Ice if he were awake. Besides, James' injury is the direct result of me refusing to give in to Ice's demands before.

What was I supposed to do? Tell Night that Ice had a knife to my arm and hope his curiosity didn't get the better of him in the future?

"I'm fine, so James will be fine," I say, *though I'm not entirely confident his forgiveness will come quickly.*

He nods. "I'm sure you believed you were doing the right thing at the time. Agreeing to meet with Ice must have been difficult considering your history."

*Was it, though?*

Either way, I thank him for understanding.

"Moving on," he says with a more pleasant smile, "there are a few things I need to explain regarding your new ability to morph."

"About the separate forms?"

He nods again. "Typically, an immortal's human and feline forms operate like two sides of the same coin—intrinsically linked to each other and sharing relative physiology. However, we don't yet understand the exact science or biological mechanism behind an immortal's ability to morph."

"What does that mean for me?"

"There is woefully little documentation available on immortals with separate forms, and nothing I could find on human immortals. It's rare, occurring in less than zero-point-zero-one percent of the immortal population, so not much is known beyond the obvious. If you consider an immortal's feline and human forms as two sides of the same coin, separate forms are like two different coins linked to the same individual. When you morph, your feline body has no physical relation to the human one."

He pauses, adjusting his glasses before holding his chin in his hand. "Perhaps the inactive form freezes in time, or perhaps it doesn't exist at all unless you're actively using it. You can speculate and theorize all you want, but so little is known, it's impossible to say with any certainty."

I frown, and he offers me a smile.

"All I can tell you is what I observed myself," he says. "Your feline form arrived uninjured. You morphed when the pendant was removed, and the bleeding returned as though no time had passed. There was no sign of clotting, but your human body lost no additional blood while you were in feline form. It saved your life."

"Okay, that's what I thought," I say. "But, um, is it true that the shock of losing so much blood can make someone morph unconsciously—like what happened for me and James?"

"James morphed?"

*Oh.* I guess he didn't know.

He listens as I briefly explain what happened after Ice stabbed James. He pulled the knife out. The blood loss was uncontrollable, and he fell unconscious right before turning into a cat.

He hums, glancing aside for a few seconds before meeting my gaze again. "It isn't unheard of for immortals to morph in response to hypovolemic shock, but I've never heard of... In fact, I've never heard of any immortal diagnosed with a metabolic inability to morph successfully taking feline form after the onset of puberty, but the condition isn't common... It could simply be a biological response to preserve life, but it's also possible that James was misdiagnosed as a child, and his inability to morph was psychosomatic all these years—though, it seems unlikely even considering..."

I cough.

He trails off and laughs with a hint of embarrassment. "I apologize for rambling. It is interesting, however, and I now understand more as to why you believed you could trust Ice's judgment despite the clear risk involved."

*Yeah...*

I wasn't sure it would work, but I didn't have much choice,

and it made some sense to try. Having done something so extreme to satisfy Ice's demands should help moving forward, even if all I got out of it was a key and a promise he wouldn't make any more copies. *And the ability to morph, I guess.*

I sigh. "So, when can I go? It's like you said… James is waiting for me, and I'm sure he's worried. I need to get back as soon as possible."

With a nod, he slips a thin, letter-sized manila envelope from the clipboard containing my medical charts. "Human-Immortal Affairs left this for you," he says. "It's a questionnaire."

He gives it to me, along with a ballpoint pen. A textless version of the Human-Immortal Affairs seal is printed on the back of the envelope. Beneath that, my full name and the last four digits of my Social Security number are sloppily written in permanent marker.

"Feel free to be honest. They already know the details of what happened, and they expect your response to match Ice's account."

"Right," I say dryly.

I move to undo the brass fastener holding the envelope shut, but Dr. Corel stops me.

"Another thing—" When I look up, he offers me a yellow sticky note. "If you need someone to talk to, Gavin is an excellent therapist. He's worked with human immortals before."

*A therapist?*

I accept the sticky note, but my eyes glaze over the phone number and name, *Gavin Schultz*.

"Please consider giving him a call if you get the chance."

"I'll think about it."

I fold the sticky note in half and tuck it into my wallet before returning my attention to the manila envelope. What I remove is a surprise. It really is nothing but a simple, one-page questionnaire and a white return envelope addressed to an office in Seattle.

I set up the hospital bed's fold-out lap table and skim the paper. Excluding the basics—my full name, Social Security number, my sponsor's name, and today's date—it asks three questions:

1. By what method does your Accessory Item activate and allow you to alternate between human and feline form?

2. Describe the events leading up to your first successful feline transformation.

3. Rate your experience with the Human Immortal Program on a scale from 1-5. Circle one.

   1 = Extremely dissatisfied
   2 = Dissatisfied
   3 = Neither satisfied nor dissatisfied
   4 = Satisfied
   5 = Extremely satisfied

*Ugh.*

"And, with that out of the way, you are cleared for discharge," Dr. Corel says. "Complete the paperwork and leave it in the mail drop up front before you go. The postage is prepaid."

I nod, ready for him to leave, but he hesitates as though there's something else he wants to say. When I ask, he sighs heavily and fixes his glasses again.

"This is rather unprofessional of me, and I apologize if the suggestion makes you uncomfortable, but I could arrange a ride for you if you need one."

Unprofessional or not, I jump on the offer immediately.

There may not be many people I trust anymore, but Dr. Corel has never been anything but kind and helpful. I mean, he is a doctor, and one of the few I've met that I genuinely like.

"Ask the receptionist for Taylor when you're ready to leave," he says with a smile. "He's my son, and he can take you to Centennial Memorial."

*His son, huh?*

"Alright," I agree, returning my attention to the questionnaire as he crosses the room toward the door. "Thanks for everything."

I complete the questionnaire to the best of my ability, granting the Human Immortal Program a generous two-out-of-five rating, and seal it inside the envelope. Then I leave the hospital bed. My legs are as unsteady as they were when I got up to walk around a bit earlier, but I power through.

James is at Centennial Memorial Hospital.

He's waiting for me, so I have to go.

* * * * *

I watch my reflection in the large windows as I walk down the hallway toward the front of the hospital.

The clothes Ice left aren't bad.

While the flowy top does little to cover my scars, the cotton shorts are comfortable, and the outfit suits my taste well enough, I guess. It's relatively casual in style, but they're expensive designer brands I would never be able to afford on my own. The tags were still on when I first took them out of the bag. Somehow, they fit perfectly.

I wonder if Ice picked the clothes out or if he sent Night to do it for him. *Eh...* It was probably Night, assuming he seriously wasn't allowed to leave the hospital.

My boots were in the bag too. They're as like-new as I thought when I first saw them in his room. *Did he clean them himself?* Was his decision to stick around so long really nothing more than doing what he was told?

*Whatever.*

My body complains as I walk, but, between the quick shower, new clothes, and my hair up in a messy bun, I look surprisingly decent. Tired, pale, and bitter, but otherwise okay. I don't quite look like I nearly died yesterday.

With a sigh, I slip the sealed envelope with the Human Immortal Program questionnaire into the public mail drop box in the main hospital lobby. Then I approach the reception desk.

A bored woman sits behind it with her chin propped in one hand and her elbow resting on the countertop. She looks up as I approach, revealing violet eyes, and recognition washes over her face. I don't know her, but it seems my arrival caused something of a commotion. She must know exactly who I am, but, if that's true, she doesn't mention it.

"How can I help you?" she asks.

"I'm trying to find Taylor... Taylor Corel, I guess. I was

told to ask for him here."

She nods and presses a button on an interface to her left.

"Taylor Corel to Patient Reception, please. Taylor Corel to Patient Reception." Her voice echoes over the PA system. Then she lifts her finger from the button and turns to me. "Go ahead and take a seat. He'll show up eventually."

*Why do I get a weird feeling about this guy?*

I'm starting to think I'm automatically suspicious of everyone before I even meet them now. It sucks, but I guess it's not the worst thing to come out of what's happened this summer.

While I wait, I hold my phone out of habit. I don't think it's dead, but I'm terrified of powering it on. I can only imagine how James must have spammed my phone after he woke up. *Now that I think about it, that's probably why it was turned off in the first place.*

Facing James in person will be bad enough. I don't think I'd be able to handle a conversation over the phone in advance, even if I could limit it to text.

"Hey, there. Jayde Palmer, right?"

The new voice startles me. I stuff my phone into my pocket and look up to greet the person who addressed me.

*This is Taylor Corel?*

He's a young man, roughly my age, with dark hair and dark clothes and his thumbs tucked in the belt loops of his jeans. As I try to determine exactly what's going on behind his dispassionate expression, I notice his pale blue eyes.

He's not an immortal.

Dr. Corel's son is human.

"Yes, I'm Jayde," I stammer, standing from the chair.

His eyes narrow as he looks me over, but I can't tell whether it's because of my unabashed surprise upon realizing he's human, my injury-riddled body, or my absurdly expensive outfit.

"Taylor?" I ask.

He nods, and my eyes catch the subtle movement of a braided cord that hangs around his neck and disappears beneath the collar of his shirt. *A necklace. A human, adopted by an immortal.*

Is he a human immortal too?

Wait— *Taylor?*

The same Taylor that Night wanted to introduce me to in June? The only other human immortal living in Riverview? *That* Taylor? Carmen and Natalie weren't kidding when they told me he was unfriendly, but I never thought he'd be my doctor's adopted son.

"Come on," he says, glancing toward the exit. "Let's get this over with."

"Okay."

*What else did Night say...?*

Oh. Right.

He hates immortals.

When she first told me, I couldn't understand at all, but my perspective has changed a lot since then. I don't dislike immortals as a whole or anything, but I understand the terrible things that can come out of humans associating with them, and the unfairness of Human-Immortal Affairs. I can only hope his experience was nothing like mine.

He leads me out of the hospital, and I follow him to a very nice black car parked in an employee-only section of the parking lot. Once we're both inside, my curiosity gets the better of me, and I turn my attention on him.

"We're the same, aren't we?" I ask, the question strangely bold and vague at the same time.

He casts a look that easily rivals Ice's dead-eyed jadedness. "If you're asking whether both of our lives were destroyed by cat freaks...? Yes. We have that much in common."

*Wow.*

"That's a bit—" I wave my good arm passively, but I honestly don't know how to respond. "I wouldn't say my life was *destroyed*. Aha..."

He scoffs, rolling his eyes. "No? You don't think so? I know what happened to you."

*You and just about everyone else here, apparently.*

"I read your patient file," he says. "It's disgusting."

"Well, what happened to *you*?" I ask in frustration.

He looks away to stab a key into the car's ignition. As one hand moves to the steering wheel, he lifts the brown cord from beneath his shirt collar with the other. A translucent, lilac gemstone cut into the rough shape of a teardrop is intricately knotted onto the end.

"An immortal saved my life," he says, his voice low. "I was a child, so I didn't get a choice. You made the wrong one, but I still envy you."

*As a child...?*

I take the River Sapphire from my pocket and stare at the rich, blue gemstone set into its silver, diamond-shaped base. I don't...regret accepting the River Sapphire, but...

*He's wrong.*

I didn't choose this life either. I was tricked into it. Ice signed me up for the program without telling me. I didn't know what I got myself into until it was too late.

"Hey," he says wryly. "If you're sick of dealing with it, there's always another way out."

*What is that tone and why do I hate it?*

I watch carefully with my guard up higher than it *ever* was while dealing with Ice yesterday, but Taylor's pale eyes remain cool and unreadable even as he smiles.

"Wanna form a suicide pact?"

I swallow hard, mind blank as my hand closes around the River Sapphire. Then I cross my arms over my chest and turn to glare out the window.

"Just take me to Centennial Memorial Hospital." My voice trembles, but even I can't tell whether it's out of anxiety or anger. "Please."

He chuckles. "I'll take that as a no. It's too bad, though. We could've had fun…for a minute."

*Someone like Taylor—*

*And someone like me…*

What have immortals done to us?

## To be Continued in Afterglow

s.k. kelley

# Content Warning

This list includes potentially sensitive or upsetting topics and themes present, mentioned, or otherwise alluded to in Sidetracked (covering all four parts), so readers can make an informed decision prior to reading. Specific context is not included here, but be aware that this information may still be considered spoilers.

Mental illness (including anxiety, depression, and PTSD)
Suicidal ideation and references to suicide and self-harm
Trauma and abuse (mental, physical, and emotional)
Toxic relationships and toxic behaviors
Injury, blood, and physical violence
Guns and knives (including their use as weapons)
Hospitalization (including references to major surgery)
Prescription drug use (as directed by a physician)
Alcohol use and references to alcoholism
Sexually suggestive content (nothing too spicy)
Swearing and offensive language
Nausea and vomiting

Sidetracked contains **NO** sexual violence

As the author, I acknowledge that characters in Sidetracked display harmful and problematic behaviors. However, Sidetracked is a work of fiction, and is in no way meant to condone, promote, or glorify such problematic and toxic behaviors. My characters are heavily flawed and were not written to be viewed as role models.

www.ingramcontent.com/pod-product-compliance
Lightning Source LLC
Chambersburg PA
CBHW030841030726
47495CB00005B/1316